Oh, Santa!

AN N.L.W ANTHOLOGY

K J ELLIS | BOBBIE-LEA | LIZZIE JAMES |
M. B. FEENEY ELLE M THOMAS |
LYNDA THROSBY | C.L STEWART |
DANIELLE JACKS | R.T. FRITZ | SJ RANSOM

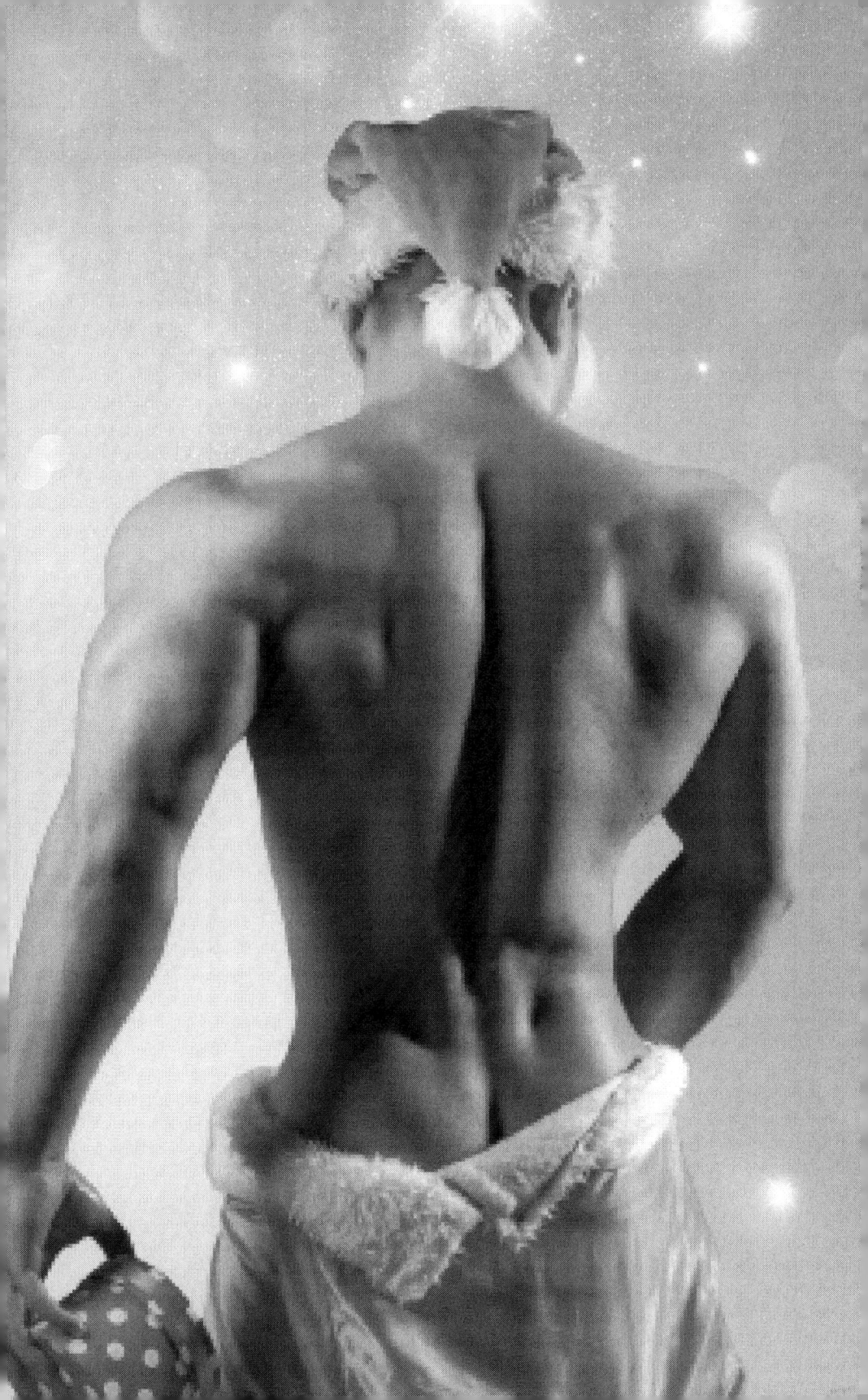

Copyright © 2022

All rights reserved.

Oh, Santa: An N.L.W Anthology

No part of this book may be reproduced in any form or by any electronic or mechanical means, including information storage and retrieval systems, without written permission from the author, except for the use of brief quotations in a book review.

This is a work of fiction. Names, characters, businesses, places, events and incidents are either the products of the authors' imaginations or used in a fictitious manner.
Any resemblance to actual persons, living or dead, or actual events, is purely coincidental.

**Cover designed by Eleanor Lloyd-Jones at Shower of Schmidt Designs
Formatted by Lizzie James at Phoenix Book Designs**

A Stripper for Christmas

by

K J Ellis

A STRIPPER FOR CHRISTMAS
SYNOPSIS

Who knew a knock on my door would change my life.
I made a wish on Christmas Eve, like I do every year. I just wasn't expecting for Santa Claus to be standing on my doorstep looking hot enough to melt the snow.
My friends and I invited him in from out the cold, wondering what the hell is going on.
I soon realized, this Santa Claus was a stripper and had turned up at the wrong address. My address.
What happened after that... was pure Christmas magic and something I'll never forget.

Chapter One

It's my turn to host our mini Christmas Eve party. I say party, but it's more like a small Christmas sleepover for adults. My friends and I take it in turns every year. Lizzie, Emily, Piper, and I get together, drink wine, have some laughs, and catch up with one another. We're all single and have nothing better to do on the night before the big man comes, so why not?

They all arrived a few hours ago and are in deep conversation about something. I'm just out of earshot when they burst out laughing. I'm busy in the kitchen, preparing four Baileys hot chocolates with whipped cream, marshmallows, and chocolate flake sprinkles, so I'm missing out on what has them all laughing like hyenas. I add the finishing touches and pop the drinks on a tray for me to carry through.

I head into the lounge and all heads turn my way.

"What did I do?" I ask nervously when I see them all looking my way.

"We're just asking Santa for our magical Christmas wishes," Lizzie says, chuckling as I place the tray on the coffee table in the middle of the couches.

"I've wished to come into money," Piper says.

I can't help my own chuckle from slipping out. "Sorry, I just don't see that happening. You work in a diner on minimum wage. You'll be saving for an eternity and then be too old to spend it."

"Yeah, maybe you're right." Piper shrugs and picks up her mug of hot chocolate. Seems she's given up on that dream already.

"What did you wish for, Lizzie?" I ask, taking the only empty seat left, which is my cuddle chair.

"What I've always wanted." She beams a huge, cheesy smile.

The rest of us shake our heads and say in unison, "A puppy."

"Yep," Lizzie replies, popping the P.

"And you, Emily? What have you wished for?" I ask.

"She hasn't answered yet," Lizzie tells me before blowing the steam from her mug.

The room goes silent as we wait patiently for her to answer. I spot her chin wobbling, and she's trying to cover up her sadness with one of the cushions from the couch. I don't want to make it known that she's upset in case Lizzie and Piper missed it. From the way they're slurping the Baileys hot chocolate through their straws, I'd say they didn't see it.

She eventually gathers herself. "For my folks to get along again and stop all the fighting. They're driving me crazy." She throws her head back and looks to the ceiling. "They're acting like teenagers."

"Aww, Emily. I'm so sorry." I place my mug down on the table, sit on the armchair, and hug her tight. "I hope your wish comes true. I really do."

She hugs me back. "Thanks, Erin."

Piper breaks the silence, "Make a wish, Erin. You're the last one."

I get comfortable on the chair with Emily. "Oh, jeez. That's a hard one." I think for a second and say the first thing that pops into my head. "To finally find my prince charming, who's just as spontaneous as he is good-looking, and who'll treat me like I'm the only woman on Earth." I start dreaming of said man.

Does he even exist? I hope so. Otherwise, I'll die a very lonely woman.

"Ha, and you thought my wish of having money was stupid." Piper belly laughs, and the others join in with her.

I slap Emily's shoulder playfully for laughing at what Piper said. "Stop laughing. It might happen, and it's more realistic than your wish."

"As much as I'd like you to be happy, I don't think Mr. Noel himself can grant you that wish, Erin," Piper adds.

"Well, it's my wish, and you never know."

Suddenly, there's a thunderous knock on the door. We all pause. Lizzie points at herself then at each of us, counting as she goes. "We're all here."

Piper looks at me, "Are you expecting anyone, Erin?"

I shake my head, just as puzzled as they are. "No. I told my parents I'd see them the day after Christmas, just to show face and exchange a few gifts. Nothing big."

"Are you going to answer it?" Emily asks.

I nod and make my way towards the door. "Obviously."

"Hey, Erin, I wonder if it's your prince charming," Piper shouts, then laughs with Lizzie and Emily.

I turn back to them as I start opening the door. "Yeah, and you're h…" I turn my attention to the person on the other side. "Hot," I blurt.

Holy Mother of Mary.

I meant to say she's *hilarious*, but as I absorbed the attractiveness of the man standing in front of me, my brain had other ideas.

"What did you say, Erin?"

"Who is it?"

They fire questions at me rapidly, but my mind runs blank. I stare at the stranger, trying to recall what the girls shouted at me.

They asked who it was, and well…

"It's… it's Santa Claus."

A very hot Santa Claus.

Chapter Two

I sounded like an absolute idiot telling them Santa Claus was standing in my doorway, but that was the only way I could describe the delicious-looking hottie who's currently checking me out.

Why, I don't know.

Do I have cream on my face from the hot chocolate? I try wiping my face discreetly.

Nope, no cream on my face. So, why is he openly eyeing me up and down?

I'm suddenly self-conscious and start pulling at my silk pajama top. I soon realize I'm showing him more than I thought and end up crossing my arms over my chest instead.

"No, seriously, who is it?" Lizzie comes bouncing around the corner with Piper and Emily hot on her heels.

I swing my head to the commotion behind me, and all three of them have eyes as wide as saucers.

"Well, hello," Piper says.

No one says anything for a couple of seconds. I look at each of the girls in turn as their mouths drop towards their feet.

"Tell me, have you all been naughty or nice?" The sound of the man's voice sends shockwaves through my body, burning me to my very

OH, SANTA!

core, and I can't help but swing my head back in his direction and admire not only his looks but his vocals too.

That is until the girls reply. I'm turning my head left and right so much I'm giving myself whiplash.

"Good!" Emily shouts innocently.

"Both," Piper screams in giddy excitement.

Lizzie can't control herself either, "Naughty. Very, very, naughty." She glances up and down his body, taking in all his good looks.

I don't blame her. The man's a god.

He's wearing a sexy Santa outfit. The red hat, the red coat, the black boots, Santa's sack—everything but a pearly white beard.

Oh, I forgot to mention his torso is completely on show. Every curve and ridge of his sculpted chest ripples with each movement he makes.

I feel my cheeks heating in embarrassment when he finds me checking him out in return.

He leans against the door frame and brings his mouth close to my ear.

"And you?" he whispers softly for no one but me to hear.

I almost forget we aren't alone.

"Me? I'm an angel," I say, trying to act like his presence doesn't affect me. The way my body reacts to him would say otherwise, but he doesn't need to know that.

His eyes penetrate mine as he drinks me in for what feels like an eternity, making me feel self-conscious all over again about what I'm wearing. Or worse, what I'm revealing to him.

I have no idea who he is or what he's doing on my doorstep, but damn, I can't deny how sexy this man is.

Cute like a mama's boy, but handsome and delicious too.

I'm mentally licking him from head to toe, and I know I've been caught when he smirks. A smirk aimed purely at me.

My cheeks heat in embarrassment. What is wrong with me? I'm acting like a kid on Christmas morning and he's the gift I've just unwrapped.

Without asking for permission, he slides past me, purposely making contact, and rubs his chest across mine.

Damn it.

I can't help the weak and pathetic moan that slips from my mouth.

He enters my home, looking around the space. "Where would you like me?" He's looking in my direction, but I've no clue what he's going on about.

I don't miss the girls whispering indecent words in answer to his question.

"Erm, in there?" I lead him through to the lounge.

I'm still unsure what the hell is going on and why he showed up at my door. More importantly, why haven't I asked him to leave yet? My brain is completely fogged by him, and for the life of me, I don't understand why.

I'm shoulder to shoulder with Piper. "What the fuck is going on?" I whisper so only she can hear.

"That, my dear friend, is a stripper." She walks off, chuckling.

I swear my mouth hits the floor.

OMG. Did one of them book a *stripper*? Who even does that for Christmas?

"People actually do that for the holidays?" I whisper again.

Piper nods and carries on laughing at me.

I follow the girls into the lounge and almost crash into the back of Lizzie.

"Shit, sor..." I follow her line of sight and watch as the guy gets ready. I'm only guessing. I've never hired a stripper before, so I don't know what's involved, besides the obvious.

He spins around and witnesses us all openly staring at him.

"I get the feeling none of you knew I was coming." His deep voice vibrates through me. "Which one of you lovely ladies booked me?" His eyes flick from the girls to me.

"It wasn't me!" I spit. "I think there's been a mix-up. We never made any calls for a... a... stripper. Right, girls?"

They all shake their heads in turn, not taking their eyes from the man dressed as Santa Claus.

"This isn't Crosswell Avenue?" he asks, checking his phone.

My eyebrows must be raised as he frowns at me before looking at his phone again. I don't have the heart to tell him he's wrong.

"Sixty-nine Crosswell Avenue?" he asks again.

The laughter echoes around the room, but I find this anything but funny.

"Erm, no. This is *Ninety-six Crosby* Avenue. You're at the wrong address," I tell him.

"Fuck. I'm so sorry. It was dark out and I thought this was the right address. That's what the GPS said, unless I typed in the wrong zip code." I can see the cogs turning as doubt creeps into his mind.

I can't help but feel sorry for him. He must be so embarrassed.

I put the guy out of his misery and try to resolve the situation. "That's okay. Mistakes happen..." I pause. "I'm sorry, I never got your name." I let this guy into my home and I don't even know what I should call him.

"Luke. My name is Luke."

"Luke." His name rolls around my tongue like butter. The name suits him.

He begins to pack his stuff up to leave when my stomach drops in disappointment. Why, though? I wanted him to leave, didn't I?

I can't think about it for long as the decision gets taken out of my hands.

"Wait! Why don't you strip for us?" Piper asks seductively.

"Yeah. The address you're after is an extra hour up the highway," Lizzie adds.

Luke swings his hot gaze my way. "That all right with you?"

My blush deepens. I don't know what to do. The girls are all looking at me, throwing me eager, and might I add, threatening glares.

"Only if that's okay with you?" I ask him slyly.

"Anyone ever told you that you look beautiful when you blush?" He has no shame in announcing this in front of everyone.

You could cut the sexual tension between us with a knife and it still wouldn't calm my racing heart.

"Okay then..." Emily claps her hands, breaking the silence and snapping my focus away from Luke.

"You girls get comfortable and enjoy the show." Luke turns and connects his phone to a docking station he brought with him and starts scrolling through songs.

"Girl, he has it bad for you," Lizzie whispers in my ear as she practically drags me to the couch and pushes me onto it by my shoulders.

"He does not. He strips for a living. He probably tells all the ladies what they want to hear." I try to deflect her attention from me and nod over to Luke, who looks ready.

"Okay, ladies. You ready to rock around the Christmas tree with me?"

Whoops and hollers ring in my ears.

Am I ready?

Part of me is apprehensive about him being in my home, but he can't be that dangerous. He's only a stripper.

Ha. A hottie like Luke, dancing and showing off his magnificent abs is dangerous enough.

Santa, I may have been a good girl, but you sending me this hunk of a man for Christmas will definitely turn me naughty.

Cross me off that nice list. Things are about to get wild.

Chapter Three

The music starts to play and the sultry voice of Usher filters into my ears as he sings his masterpiece version of *Last Christmas*. I was expecting him to dance to something more upbeat or faster, but the moment he begins to roll his hips slowly to the music and runs his hands down the length of the Santa coat, all precise and dreamy, has my own clothes ready to melt off my body.

The way he dances, unhurried and smooth, is like melting butter. The longer you let the heat simmer, the quicker that butter melts, and I'm dissolving in my seat.

His moves mixed with Usher's voice are like silk caressing my body, leaving goosebumps in their wake.

After some long-ass teasing, Luke finally lets the red fur coat slip from his body effortlessly. He saunters over to Lizzie, takes her greedy hands, and runs them up and down his solid, well-defined chest, his movements not wavering once. He grinds to the rhythm of the beat and slowly rotates his hips in front of her. Once he's done with Lizzie, who's practically drooling, he moves on to Piper and Emily, doing the same to them. It has them giggling and blushing like schoolgirls; they're clearly enjoying the show.

I don't blame them. It's one hot, steamy show.

I find myself smiling and shaking my head at their over-the-top eagerness, but the smile soon falls from my face when he turns his heated eyes my way and drinks me in, giving me his undivided attention.

I feel exposed. I feel like I'm being pulled into a different dimension where it's just the two of us.

He prowls towards me with precision and hunger. *Why is he looking at me as if I'm his prey?*

I pinch my thighs together discreetly to ease the ache that's building there. It's no good. I'm ready to combust.

How does he have the ability to affect me like this?

He hasn't even touched me and I'm high on sexual ecstasy.

My heartbeat picks up speed when he comes to stand in front of me. He pauses, looking at me seductively. I hold my breath. He gives me a sexy wink, which excites my body more than it should. Then he drops to his knees and closes the distance between us.

He leans forward, his mouth now touching my ear. "Open your thighs, Erin." My legs open of their own accord. "Tell me, do you taste as sweet as a candy cane?"

My breath hitches, and I can't help but throw my head back in pure delight at what his words alone can do to my body. They affect me more than they should, and he knows it. No one has ever made my body react this way before, and I'm unsure of what to do with myself. He has the ability to make me lose my mind and not care.

I scream when I feel myself being lifted into the air and suddenly flipped upside down. I'm dizzy, and it takes me a moment to realize that my head is by his crotch, but more importantly, his head is near mine as my legs have no other option but to scissor open.

His own excitement is evident.

I don't know how he got me into this position or how he's going to get me out of it, but at this point, I'm past caring. I'm starting to enjoy myself and ignoring the embarrassment that was once there.

Why stop my body from feeling what it needs to?

My enjoyment soon disappears when I feel the material of my silk bottoms tear at the seams from the position I'm in, revealing more than I would have liked to. Thankfully, the girls don't seem to have noticed as they're too busy cheering at his antics.

I'm not wearing any underwear, and I know his face is level with my nakedness. I'm mortified. There isn't a goddamn thing I can do about it from the position I'm in. Even if I let go of his thighs, I wouldn't be able to get my hand between us to cover up my modesty.

I wiggle around, trying my best to loosen his grip so he'll have no other option but to put me down. He could drop me on my head at this point and it would be less embarrassing. At least that way I'd be able to cover myself up and not be on show.

We're suddenly spinning around so his back is facing the girls. I'm out of view to them, but I can make out their feet from my view between his thighs. I was about to thank him, but then I felt his warm, wet tongue run along my clit, causing me to tense in his arms.

What the hell?

I freeze, silently telling myself that I imagined it. It was wishful thinking and nothing more.

Was it secretly what I wanted?

I can't deny my reaction or the fact that it has me wanting more.

I'm dizzy, and it's not from being tipped upside down.

He continues to gyrate his bulge in my face for a few beats before I'm spun back around and placed on my feet again, facing the girls. My balance is off from being upside down, and I stumble a little. His large hands are on my waist, steadying me from face planting the floor.

"Whoa there, darlin'. You falling for me already?" He comes closer to my ear and whispers his next words. "One lick of your pussy has me wanting more."

I hide my face in the only thing I can, which just so happens to be the crook of his arm.

My body wants this. I'm hot and wet for him already and he's hardly done anything to me, but my head is telling me to put a stop to it all.

Which one will win, I have no clue.

Chapter Four

Luke's strip tease was over sooner than I wanted it to be. Time seems to have flown by, and he danced to three songs, ending on the classic, *Pony* by Ginuwine. To say I was turned on would be an understatement. I'm hot, clammy, and have an itch that won't be sated by anyone other than the muscled beast standing before me.

I'm not the only one who's sad to see him go. The disappointment on the girls' faces matches my own as Luke busies himself collecting his discarded clothes——not that there's much.

"You leaving already?" Piper finally asks what we all want to know.

"Yeah, that's kinda what happens when I've finished and get paid."

My eyes almost fall from their sockets when it dawns on me that not one of us thought about payment when we invited him to stay and strip for us. He's done his job, so it's only fair that he should get paid, right?

"How much were you meant to be getting paid for this job?" I ask. He packs his music system in his bag and turns to face me.

"For what I did for you tonight, it's an even six hundred dollars."

My mouth drops to the floor.

I can't afford to pay him that much. I doubt the others could either, even if we put all our money together.

I should have thought of that sooner. Preferably before he started dancing. Scrap that, before he even walked through the door.

I scan the room, looking at the girls. All of them shrug at me, clearly thinking the same as me.

Looks like I'm on my own as none of them seem to know how to help.

"I'm sorry, Luke, but——"

"This one is on me, girls." He winks at me.

"You can't do that. Won't you get in trouble for not charging?"

"I don't have a pimp, Erin. I do this as a side job. So, don't worry. I won't get in trouble." He smiles softly at me.

I stand and try to remember where I left my purse. "At least let me pay you something." This man makes me lose all reasoning. I don't know whether I'm coming or going. No man has ever had this much of an effect on me.

"Call it a holiday gift. It's not your fault I showed up at the wrong address. I'm my own boss. It's all good."

I don't feel right about not giving him a dime, but I can tell by his expression that he wouldn't accept anything from me.

"Are you sure, Luke? I mean, I could give you—" I start counting the notes in my purse.

"I'm sure. I'm all set to go now, so I'll leave you gorgeous ladies to enjoy the rest of your Christmas Eve."

"Wait, do you have to go?" Lizzie blurts out. I narrow my eyes at her when Luke turns to face her and his back is towards me.

"It's the holidays..." Emily begins.

"And late," Lizzie finishes.

"Why don't you stay for a while longer? Surely if there was somewhere you needed to be, you would be there by now," Piper adds.

"Girls, I'm sure Luke has better things to do on Christmas Eve than sit here with us and—"

Luke swings his body back in my direction. "There's nowhere I need to be."

I feel hopeful, but it soon disappears again when I think of him having someone at home, waiting for him.

"Your girlfriend may wonder where you are." I didn't intend to come across as rude, but I think I did.

I'm waiting in anticipation for him to answer and pop my little bubble of hope.

He stares at me intently. "There's no girlfriend."

"So, you'll stay for Baileys and hot chocolate?" Piper chimes in again.

Luke doesn't take his eyes off mine. "Sure. If that's okay with you, Erin?"

I'm mentally cursing Piper and wishing she would keep her mouth shut and let the man leave. The other two girls aren't helping, either.

"Come on, Erin. Luke must be parched after working up a sweat."

I'm gonna murder Lizzie.

I'm unsure of what to say and know I'm looking to some-one——anyone——for guidance.

Emily, she's the level-headed one. She'll know what to do. I cast my eyes from Luke to her as she opens her mouth. "Yeah, you must be thirsty, Luke."

Dammit.

"Like you wouldn't believe."

My gaze snaps back to Luke, and his lip curls as he smirks at me. I don't think the girls have cottoned on to the double meaning behind his words. After all, his back is to them now and he's only got eyes for me.

"It's okay with me." I try my best to act nonchalant.

I'm lying to myself. He only has to look at me and I'm withering on the spot.

The girls jump up and down full of joy and head into the kitchen.

Luke takes the empty seat next to me. "You sure this is what you want? I can leave." His leg touches mine briefly, and it takes everything in me not to moan at the contact. The simplest of touches has me feeling like I'm on fire. It spreads through my body like wildfire. "I don't want to leave. I'd like to get to know you some more."

"Me? Why?" I'm getting hotter by the second.

"Because I'm drawn to you, Erin, and I don't know why."

Chapter Five

I can't answer Luke because, truthfully, I feel the same way about him, and the fact I can't explain why scares the crap out of me.

I'm not a spontaneous person, never have been, but sitting next to him has me wanting to rectify that.

Luke makes me want to try new and exciting things, and I want to do them with him.

How is that even possible? I've just met the guy.

The girls are taking a long time when they only went to make him a drink, and does it really take all three of them for that? What are they doing?

I soon get my answer when I see them all peering around the door, their heads bobbing around the frame. Lizzie and Emily give me the thumbs up, and Piper blows me a kiss before running towards the spare bedroom.

Bitches!

They know I've had a dry spell for a few months now. They think they're clever, but I'll be having words with them tomorrow morning or when Luke decides to leave.

Luke must hear the commotion going on behind us and turns his head to see what has grabbed my attention. To save myself any more embarrassment, I cough and quickly change the subject, letting the sexual tension subside.

"You said before that stripping was a side job. What's your other job?" I asked.

"I have a pretty strait-laced day job. I'm a web designer."

I'm taken aback a little at his admission of what he does for a living. It must show on my face too, as he chuckles.

"Wow. I didn't see that one coming. I mean, I just don't see you as a... a..." I stumble over my words.

"A what?" he asks, full of amusement.

"A computer geek," I whisper, lowering my head to the floor, ashamed that I'm being judgmental.

He gently takes my jaw in his big, manly yet soft hands, and lifts my gaze back to him. "Don't hide from me. You're not the first person to say I don't look like the computer nerd I am."

"Geek. I said geek, not nerd." We both laugh, and it feels good. It feels natural.

"So, I'm a secret geek. Does that make you like me less?" he asks.

"Jury is still out," I tease.

"All right then. While we wait for the verdict to come in, why don't you tell me about you?"

I sigh. I hate talking about myself.

"I'm an artist. I sketch and design illustrations for books. Kids' books, mainly."

"Something similar we have in common, then?"

"It would seem so, yes. My turn." I chuckle and pretend to think long and hard about what I want to ask, but really, I already know the question. "I don't want to pry, but if you're a web designer, why do you strip on the side?" Web designers earn a hefty dollar or two, unless he's a freelancer and needs the extra cash. I'm fully invested in finding out why he does it.

"You've wanted to ask me this since I mentioned that I have another job, haven't you?" He throws me a sideways smirk, and my silk pjs cling to my overheating body. I should really go change as my bottoms are ripped. He can't see anything now that I'm sitting down, but that's not the point.

"I'm that easy to read, huh?"

"Your face can't lie, Erin. In answer to your question..." My mouth has suddenly gone dry, so I grab my mug and take a huge gulp. "It's... for kicks."

I cough and splutter, clamping my hand over my mouth as the hot chocolate threatens to leave my mouth. "Kicks?"

Did he really just say he strips for the rush? I mean, you prank someone for fun, but I've never heard of stripping just for shits and giggles.

"You get your junk out for kicks?" My question comes across as condescending, but I didn't mean it like that. I'm just trying to wrap my head around why he feels the need to do it when he's already got a decent job.

"Yeah. Some people skydive, and some people bungee jump. Stupid people get high to get their thrills. I'm a confident guy who has done the whole adrenaline junkie stuff, so getting my 'junk out' as you put it, isn't an issue for me. It gets the blood pumping in my veins like nothing else." I get that on some level, and he's really good at it too.

"I can see that, though I couldn't imagine seductively stripping for people like you do." I never thought about it before, but just thinking about getting naked in a room full of strangers is enough to bring me out in hives.

"What do you do for fun?"

I think about this long and hard. I can't remember the last time I did something just for fun.

"I hang out with my girls a lot, but my life is pretty busy with work. I used to love the adventures of camping. My pops and I would drive out and pitch a tent by a lake and spend the weekend fishing and exploring. That sort of thing." I think back to the last time I got to do that with him before life got in the way. Now, it's too late, as he's no longer with us.

Luke must see the sadness cross my face. He stands quickly, pulling me up from my seat. His smile is infectious, and I find myself smiling with him, helping me forget my previous thoughts.

I gaze into his eyes, which just so happen to be staring at me intently. Neither of us says a word as the seconds tick by.

It's not an uncomfortable silence; it's more heated than anything. Then Luke breaks it. "Can I kiss you?"

The word leaves my mouth easily. "Yes..." I'm breathless, and anticipation courses through me.

Luke locks his lips with mine the moment the words leave my mouth. It's a gentle kiss that lingers once our lips part, but it's only short-lived as he soon crashes his mouth back on mine. This time, the kiss is hungry and full of determination and eagerness. His hands come up to my face. He cups my jaw in the palm of his hands, deepening the kiss.

I've never been kissed like this before. My toes curl and heat flows through me.

I kiss him back with everything I have. I can't get enough of him.

The feeling of his lips against mine is nothing I've ever felt before and maybe never will again. I decide to make the most out of it, of him, just for tonight, as that's all we've got.

He loosens his grip on my cheek and pulls back, ending the sweet sensation.

Luke's breathless panting matches my own.

I don't want this to end, so I ask for something I haven't asked for in a long time.

I find the courage to put myself out there. "More. I need more," I admit unashamedly, pulling his mouth and body closer to mine.

Luke stands before me, holding out his hand. I take it, expecting him to walk, but I'm lifted into the air and he's wrapping my legs around his waist. I can feel just how excited he is, as his erection is pressed against his pants, hitting me on my sweet spot.

We start moving towards the bedrooms when he stops by his bag and roots inside. He pulls out his Santa hat and grins at me wickedly.

"What's with the hat?" I ask, smiling.

"It's Christmas. Santa never leaves his hat lying around this time of year."

I can't help but chuckle as he guides us towards my room, which I direct him to. "This way, Santa Claus."

I'm about to ride Santa's sleigh, and I know it's going to be the ride of my life that jingles all the right bells.

Chapter Six

I've never done anything like this before. Luke's a stranger, yet I feel a connection with him that I've never felt with anyone before. It's strong, uncontrollable, and I can't deny what my body and heart are telling me.

He places me on my feet.

"Why are you nervous, Erin?" Luke takes my shaking hands in his and rubs his thumbs tenderly over my skin, calming me instantly.

"I don't usually do this sort of thing."

"What, hook up with Santa?" he jokes, lightening the atmosphere.

"Aren't you the joker. I mean… I don't have sex with random guys I've just met, but with you… it feels…" I don't know what to tell him to explain what I'm trying to deal with. I don't want to scare off the first guy to show me this much interest before we've gotten to the good part.

He pulls me in closer, hooking his arm around my back. "Different. Like you've known me all your life. Which is impossible as we only met a few hours ago, right?"

He gets it.

He understands what I'm trying so hard to say. He feels the spark between us, just like I do.

"Yeah, something like that."

His eyes drop to my mouth. I lick my lips in anticipation.

"We share an unexplainable connection, Erin. It's as simple as that." His free hand takes a hold of my chin, gently urging me to look up at him again. "One I wanna explore on a much deeper level."

There's no hesitation in my next words. "Me too, Luke."

He lifts my chin higher and brushes his lips with mine, and just like that, he melts all my worries away, and I bask in the moment.

He kisses me long and hard. I widen my mouth, giving him more, and soon his tongue wraps around mine and we're both hungry for more.

His hands tangle in my hair as mine roam his t-shirt-covered torso.

My feet suddenly lift from the floor when he throws me up in the air again and grabs a hold of my ass.

I wrap my legs around his waist as he walks us blindly over to the edge of my bed. He places a firm hand on my back as he lays me down gently and stands looking down at me.

"So beautiful." He removes his t-shirt in one swift move and begins to remove what little clothing I had on, leaving me spread out on the bed in my birthday suit. I feel exposed, but the way his eyes slowly roam over me, starting at my toes and all the way up my body, causes goosebumps to break out on my hot skin.

I watch in pure fascination as he removes his sweatpants and throws them on the floor where he put his top moments before. "I can't wait to taste you, Erin."

He stands before me in nothing but a pair of boxer briefs and that all-important Santa hat.

"What're you waiting for, sexy Santa?" I want to cringe at how pathetic I sound, but he doesn't seem to notice.

His eyes linger on my exposed body a moment longer before he shuts his eyes and hums in approval. "I'm storing this moment in my memory. Just in case I never get another chance to see you like this."

I sit up on my elbows and watch his every move.

He stalks towards me, leans forward until our noses touch, and with one hand, he leisurely runs a finger from the length of my neck to my hip before he stands to his full height again. Then he drops to his knees and runs his hands along my thighs. Each caress makes me moan in pure bliss. He pulls me to the edge of the bed and buries his face between my legs, licking me delicately. I know I'm already soaking wet. I can feel my excitement dripping down to my ass. He uses his expert tongue and laps up all of my juices. He starts off slow and gentle, then as my impending orgasm builds, he picks up speed and goes to town on my clit, flicking his tongue rapidly until I'm ready to explode.

"Oh, God, please... keep going," I pant.

The tingling sensation becomes too much for me and I writhe around on the bed, gripping the bed sheet for some kind of leverage. I throw my head back and arch my back until I come down from the earth-shattering high.

"You tasted sweeter than I could have ever imagined. No candy cane could ever taste as good."

"Jesus. That was... out of this world," I tell Luke in a daze.

"Have you come back to me yet?" He laughs.

I lift my head from the bed and gaze down at him, his chin glistening from my arousal. "Just about."

"Good, because I'm not done with you. Move up the bed." I do as I'm asked and position myself in the middle of the bed.

He walks around to the bottom and pulls his boxers down.

My mouth forms an 'o' as I bask in the sheer size of him. He's packing down there, that's for sure.

"You're about to make this Santa a jolly man, Erin."

I can't help but giggle and I'm soon forgetting the size and girth of him when he crawls up the bed to me and hovers above me, his arms on either side of my head.

"As it's Christmas, I think we need to bring the festive feel, don't you?" He smirks playfully, and I'm left wondering what festive idea he has in mind.

Before I get to question his motives, he throws my hands above my head and somehow manages to rip the tinsel that was wrapped around my headboard and begins tying my hands together.

"What the..." I'm shocked at how fast he worked. He's definitely done this before. Maybe not with tinsel, but he's for sure tied someone up.

"Do you trust me?"

I find myself nodding confidently.

"I promise I'll undo it if you want me to stop." His eyes let me know he's telling the truth.

"I trust you."

"It's not too tight, is it?" There's concern in his voice.

"No. It's good," I say, reassuring him.

"You ready?" He peers down at me, waiting for my answer.

"I'm ready to ride the sleigh, Luke." The dimples in his cheeks show as he smiles at me. "You like that one?" I ask through my own smile.

"It was a good one, but things are about to get serious. You think you can handle that, baby?" His smile fades, his dimples turn to sharp cheekbones, and his jaw tightens.

"I can handle it," I say breathless and taken aback by how gorgeous this man is.

He lines himself up with my entrance and gently rocks his hips until he's fully sheathed in me.

He doesn't move, thankfully, giving me time to adjust to his length.

"Damn, you're so tight." He drops his head to the side of mine. "I'm struggling with myself here, Erin."

I angle my head so I can see him better. He lifts his head slightly and I can see just how much he's trying to be a gentleman.

"No struggling. I'm ready now, Luke. Please. I need you to start moving," I tell him softly.

"Where have you been all my life?"

"Right here... patiently waiting."

That's all he needs.

He withdraws almost all the way before pushing into me again. We find a delirious rhythm that has both of us in a tizzy. I know he's close, and I'm almost there myself.

I wrap one of my legs around his ass, causing him to go deeper.

"Oh, fuck..." He hits me in the right spot and I'm ready to scream.

"You feel so good wrapped around me. I can feel you pulsing. I'm so close, baby."

"Me too. Keep going," I say between thrusts.

He picks up the pace and pounds into me until we're both a panting mess of tangled limbs.

"Oh, shit, Erin." He bites his lip sharply as he tries to control his wants and needs.

"I'm there. Oh, God, Luke..." I detonate violently like never before.

He thrusts a couple more times until he releases his own orgasm.

"Fuck..."

I'm seeing stars and snowflakes. Fitting considering the time of year.

"Once will never be enough with you, Erin," he whispers into my neck as he gets his breathing under control.

"Who said we can only do it once?" I tease.

"Oh, Erin. You're definitely on Santa's naughty list now. You're a bad girl."

I laugh. "Believe me, I can live with that. It'll be so worth it."

"Tut tut. You know naughty girls don't get a visit from Santa, right?" He looks serious.

"But you forget, I've already received my gift from Santa." I try to keep my face composed.

"You have? What's that?" He arches one of his eyebrows in confusion.

"The best orgasm ever." I can't help it. I laugh out loud. "From Santa himself."

He drops his head, shaking it. "I asked for that, didn't I?" He chuckles.

"Yes, you did." I purse my lips together, causing his eyes to drop to my mouth.

"Might as well make the most out of your gift, then."

With that, he drops his lips to mine and kisses me with so much passion I'm about ready to combust again.

Luke eventually removes the tinsel from my wrists, and we spend the rest of Christmas Eve wrapped up in one another until the early hours, when my body can't take any more and Luke has nothing else to give.

I've never had a man do the things to my body that he had. Parts of my body ache that I never thought were possible. It's most definitely worth it, and if I had to do it all again, just to feel the connection I did with Luke, then I most certainly would.

Chapter Seven

I feel the softness of Luke's lips touching mine in a lingering kiss, which ends far too soon for my liking.

I'm aware it's early and that he's leaving, but I'm thoroughly spent and one hundred percent satisfied to be able to move and acknowledge him saying goodbye.

I must have drifted back off to sleep because, when I woke up, the girls were banging about in the kitchen. Ain't no way any of them rise from the dead before nine unless they're working.

I roll over to the side of the bed that Luke slept on and bury my head in the pillow. It still smells like him. All sandalwood and spice——my new favorite scent.

I recall the events of last night and smile dreamily.

He was so affectionate towards me. I can still feel the tingling trail his fingers delicately traced over every inch of my skin and the way his mouth worked in complete sync with mine. His husky voice that whispered words of endearment was sexy as hell. He made me feel precious and wanted. I've never had that before. The things he did to my body was an experience I've never had before. He was a real gentleman and a damn genius at the same time.

He knew what I wanted without me having to ask for it. It felt like he was made for me and I for him; he was so in tune with my body. I didn't know where he ended or I began. We were one.

I release a happy sigh as I open my eyes and spot a piece of paper lying on the top of his pillow. I throw the covers off me hastily and grab the paper impatiently, excited to see what he said.

I read his manly handwriting, and the butterflies start fluttering around in my stomach. I haven't been this happy in a long time.

> Erin,
>
> I've never felt the way I did with you with anyone else before, especially after one night.
>
> I felt a connection with you from the moment I laid eyes on you. I have a feeling we could be something special.
>
> If you feel the same way, meet me at the big Christmas tree in Central Park underneath the mistletoe at 8 p.m.
>
> P.S
>
> Merry Christmas, beautiful
>
> Luke

Chapter Eight

I jump up and down on my bed like a high schooler, squealing with delight.

I know the girls are running up the stairs by the thunderous pounding of their feet.

I'm still jumping around like a lunatic when they bound into my room.

"Someone got some last night," Piper shouts over my screams.

"I saw the stripper sneaking out of the house around four this morning," Lizzie adds.

"Half-naked and looking just as pleased as you do. Did you get any sleep at all?" Emily asks.

"Did you hear the noise coming from this room last night? Damn, no one got any sleep." Piper smirks.

I chuckle, not in the least bit embarrassed that they heard everything. "I got some, but the bags under my eyes are so worth it." I scuffle to the end of my bed and run at them, hugging each of them. "Don't think I've forgotten the stunt you pulled last night. You left me alone with Luke on purpose. I was so mad at you, but you're all forgiven. Merry Christmas!" We laugh and hug each other again, giving our best wishes to one another.

I start dancing down the stairs and follow the smell of freshly ground coffee coming from the machine as I hum along to *Winter Wonderland*.

"You gonna tell us what happened, or do we have to guess?"

I carry on humming my tune.

"It wouldn't be hard to guess, would it, Lizzie?" Piper says as they all enter the room.

"It was sublime. He cherished me and made me feel so special. And then, this morning, he kissed me, and it was one of those kisses that ended all others, then he left. I thought that would be the last I heard from him, but then I woke up and saw this note he had left on the pillow." I hold up the piece of paper, and it gets snatched from my hands.

"Let's see."

"What does it say?"

I shake my head at the over-the-top eagerness and continue to pour myself a cup of coffee.

I turn and chuckle when I find them all hunched together, trying to read it at the same time.

"OMG!" Lizzie shouts.

"Wow!" Piper adds.

Emily, being the shy, quiet, and reasonable one of us, is the last to finish reading it.

"Are you going to meet him, Erin?"

"Of course she is. Why wouldn't she?" Piper gives Emily a hard stare.

"Well, for starters, she doesn't really know this guy——"

"I think they got pretty acquainted last night." Looks like Lizzie agrees with Piper on this.

"This isn't something I would normally do, but we shared something last night. It was different. I've never met anyone like him before. We had a connection which is hard to explain."

"We get that, hun. Don't we?" Lizzie nods, and Emily drops her head.

"I suppose," she finally whispers.

"You meeting him, then?"

I look at my girlfriends, already knowing my answer. "Yes. If I don't go, I could be missing out on something unreal. And he showed up on my doorstep the second I made my wish. I think this was meant to be."

Chapter Nine

I'm a bundle of nerves as I hesitantly follow the stoned pathway around and head towards the huge Christmas tree standing in the center of Central Park.

It's now dark outside, and the soft, icy snowflakes begin to fall, making the sky look lighter than it should. The park is heaving with people, whether that be out walking dogs, or couples hand in hand, lazily walking from one side of the park to the other, and a lot of tourists taking photos.

I see an opening by the tree and race towards the base of the tall bark. I look up at the twinkling lights, smelling the pine as it breezes past my nose and basking in the magical feeling of Christmas for the first time in a long time.

The snow is falling and blankets the ground in a sheet of white. The lights surrounding the park and on the tree glisten, filling me with nothing but warmth.

I pull the hood of my coat around my head to shield my face from the bitter cold and scan the area. I can't see Luke anywhere.

It's been twelve hours since I saw him. Maybe he changed his mind and decided not to show.

The longer I stand here alone, the more my happiness turns to disappointment.

He's not going to come.

I'm all set to head back home when a tingling sensation creeps up my back and heats me from the inside out.

I spin around and come face to face with gorgeousness.

"Hi," I say breathlessly.

"Hi, Erin. I'm glad you came."

"Me too, Luke."

He brings one of his hands from around his back and lifts it above his head. Following his movement, I spot the mistletoe dangling from his fingertips.

I close the small gap between us, lift onto my tiptoes, and press my mouth to his.

When I open my eyes, his dark blue ones are staring back at me.

"The moment I left you alone in bed this morning, I knew I needed to see you again."

I can't get enough of this man, and everything he's saying hits me deep and hard in the chest.

"Do you believe in love at first sight?" he asks. "I didn't, but then I met you."

"Don't laugh, but I made a wish last night, asking for Mr. Right, then you knocked on my door. You're my Christmas wish, Luke. It came true. So, yes. I believe in it."

"Can I keep you, Erin?" His head is angled to the side as he peppers kisses behind my ear and down my neck.

I place my hands on his forearms to steady my shaking legs and calm my racing heart.

"You're a gift I never knew I needed. Please say I can keep you forever?"

My mind drifts to last night and the time we spent together.

I want that again.

I want that with Luke.

I run my hands nervously up the length of his arms and over his broad chest and shoulders, wrapping them around the back of his neck. "If Mr. Claus promises to make another appearance wearing nothing but that Santa hat for me again, then absolutely. You can keep me," I tell him.

I may have failed at being flirtatious, but I said it anyway.

"You're mine now, Erin. My very own Mrs. Claus. And I'll save my hat for you and you only."

For a holiday I once hated because I was single, it's now my favorite holiday of all.

"I'd love to be your Mrs. Claus one day. Just don't expect me to strip." I laugh.

"Not even for my eyes only?" He winks.

"And have you put me to shame? I don't think so, mister."

"You will," he states with confidence.

It's never gonna happen, but he's more than welcome to treat me to a strip tease every day of the year. That would please me immensely.

"This is the best Christmas I've ever had."

"Me too. I'm glad you showed up at the wrong house on Christmas Eve." I chuckle, and he does the same and shows me his pearly white teeth and dimples.

How did I get so lucky?

"Merry Christmas, Erin."

"Merry Christmas, Luke."

The snow is really starting to fall now, so much that I can't see anything in front of me, but we don't let that stop us.

I lock my mouth with his in an all-consuming kiss that has my toes tingling.

This is the best night of my entire life, and nothing could ever top it.

Who would have thought a chance encounter would have led me to where I'm standing now?

This really is the best Christmas I've ever had, and the best gift I could have wished for.

Christmas miracles really can happen.

The End

FOLLOW KJ

Reader Group | Amazon | Facebook | Goodreads | Instagram

ALSO BY KJ ELLIS

The Counterpunch Series

Isaak

Mr & Mrs Brookes

Owen

Saxon

Jason

Standalones

Worth Lying For: A Stargazing Novel

A Christmas To Remember

by

Bobbie-Lea

A CHRISTMAS TO REMEMBER
SYNOPSIS

Karina
I should be to used my ex-husband letting our son, Charlie down. Never did I ever think that in him doing so would lead to me falling for Santa.

Leo
I have always hated covering for my friend when he needed a day off and couldn't get cover. Imagine my surprise when my teenage crush joins the line with her son and no wedding ring in sight.

Is this our chance?
A Christmas to remember?

Chapter One

Karina

"Charlie, stop nagging me, will you? I have five minutes left of my shift, then we can go straight to the shopping centre," I tell my seven-year-old son.

"But, Mum! I don't wanna miss Santa. It's Christmas Eve tomorrow and he will be busy!"

His father, Lincoln, dropped him off at the American-style diner where I work thirty minutes ago, claiming he'd been called into work. The sorry son-of-a-bitch never needs an excuse to bring his son back early. It's nothing new and another excuse to get out of co-parenting duties. It's a constant battle because he's meant to have Charlie every weekend when, in reality, it's once a month.

"I know, but your dad was meant to be taking you, remember?" I whizz past where he sits on the high stool at the counter, slurping his chocolate milkshake as I deliver my last order to table twenty. On my way back, I ruffle his hair and plant a sloppy smooch on his cheek.

"Hey, Karina, your shift's over. What are you still doing here? Go home," Mac, my lovely boss, shouts from the huge serving hatch. He's so nice to Charlie and me, and very understanding on the occasions my sitter lets me down. Rather than me missing a shift, he lets me bring Charlie with me. I set him up in the closest booth to the counter with his tablet, books, or colouring pens, and he's good to go.

Mac hates my ex with a passion after he cheated on me with the hussy—aka my ex-best friend, Britney. He hates Lincoln even more for the way he treats Charlie. Lincoln spends all his time with his new wife, their two-year-old, and the one that's on the way. Lincoln and Britney seem to have Charlie as little as possible since they found out they were having a second child, but I have an inkling that's more down to her than him. For me, it doesn't matter either way as Charlie and I enjoy spending time together, but that doesn't mean I'm not upset on my son's behalf.

"Come on, champ. Pack up your stuff and put it behind the counter while I go grab my things."

Charlie flashes me the biggest, brightest smile ever.

"Yeah!" he shouts while high-fiving Frank, who is sitting next to him. Frank is one of the regulars at the diner and often chooses to sit with Charlie. He's an older man and often shares his wisdom with him —something my son now looks forward to when he's here

Coming back out from the locker room where we keep our personal belongings, I stop to watch as Frank tucks a couple of pound coins into my boy's coat pocket and zips him up, making sure not to catch his scarf. "Don't tell your mum about that. It's our secret." He tells him the same thing every time, even though he knows I know. Charlie thinks I don't know that he puts it straight into his money box in his room that I placed there just for that reason.

Debbie, one of the girls working today, helps him with his hat and gloves.

Mac spots me staring at the scene unfolding. "You're a loved lady around here, Karina. Both you and Charlie. Here." He shoves an envelope into my hand with my Christmas bonus in it. "This is for you, and the presents over there..." he points to a pile of presents that have appeared on the counter, "...are for the boy. Merry Christmas."

Chapter Two

Leo

"I need you to cover my shift for me today," my best friend and roommate, Bryan, says as he stuffs cereal into his mouth. I gave him the spare room when his landlord kicked him out on his arse and sold up. I felt sorry for him, but to be honest, I like the company. I find living alone to be quite lonely. It's not forever, though. I know he has been looking for a forever home to share with his girlfriend.

"What? No way. It's the day before Christmas Eve. It's gonna be hectic in there today. Get Freddie to do it." Bryan has a regular yearly gig at Greenwood Pines Shopping Centre as their resident Santa. I've covered for him a couple of times when he's been desperate, and I hate it. I love kids, but their parents get all pushy and annoyed when their kid freaks out at being handed to a bearded man in a red suit.

"He can't do it. I've already texted him. Please, Leo. It's cash in your pocket." He knows I don't need the money, but he uses that reason every time.

"Fine. Why can't you do the shift?"

"I promised Beth I would take her Christmas shopping last week, but I was too hungover from the night before. She got pissed off with me and made me promise to take her on her next day off, which is today, and there's no one to cover for me. I already asked Gruff." Gruff is his boss. He got the nickname because when he shouts, his voice gets gravelly and rough.

"Ha, you should know better. She doesn't let you get away with anything."

He once faked a sickness bug because he didn't want to go to her parents' house for dinner. When she came round with chicken soup after her parents' dinner, he was playing a computer game with Freddie and me. We had no clue about any of it. She was really mad, and she made sure he paid for it.

"Let's just say I've learned my lesson. Your shift starts in an hour. I'll ring Gruff and let him know. Thanks again, Leo."

"I'd better get going, then."

My walk to the shopping centre was refreshing in the crisp white snow and the bitter cold air that turns your cheeks pink and your nose red. The streets were busy with people scrambling about for their last-minute bits and bobs. I love everything about Christmas. To me, it's magical and the most wonderful time of the year.

I only wish I had a special someone to share it with.

"Hey, Gruff. How's it going?" I ask as he walks into the small closet-like room where I'll transform into Santa.

"Hey, Leo. Thanks for stepping in. The queue is already backed up to Jackie's Juice Bar and it isn't even nine-thirty yet." I laugh as I continue getting into costume. "Okay, I'll leave you to it. See you out there."

❄

The whole day has flown by and my time as Santa is almost over. I call the next kid over and realise there are only two left, but that's not what has me overjoyed. Standing behind a young boy is a beautiful angel.

I'm captivated and can't stop staring at her.

The little girl around the age of three or four sitting on my knee demands my attention, bringing me back to the present. "Be a good girl," I tell her, "and I'll see what I can do." Her mum nods her thanks before ushering her away.

The next child is easy to handle because his mum and dad just wanted a photo of him sitting on my knee.

Then it's the angel's time... I mean, her son's turn. She has no clue who I am thanks to the beard—not that it bothers me. It meant I could watch her from afar.

"Ho! Ho! Ho! Merry Christmas," I sing merrily. "Now then..." I look up to his mum, who mouths his name at me. "Charlie, have you been good this year?"

"Yes, sir I have. Ask Mummy."

I smile at the cute very well-mannered kid. "And remind me, what did you ask for in your letter to me?"

"I'd like an Xbox, some games, and some toy cars too."

"Anything else?"

"I really wanted a puppy, but Mummy said not until I'm older."

It breaks my heart to see him unhappy at this time of year.

"What's the matter, Charlie?"

His facial expressions change the moment his eyes land on his mother. He takes his time before answering. "I changed my mind. All I want for Christmas is a new daddy. One that will love me and Mum and stop her feeling lonely."

My jaw hits the floor. This kid has broken me. There's no way he's aware of what he's just declared.

Charlie jumps down from my knee, clearly finished. Just as he's about to wander back to his mum, I have a thought and pull him back.

"Hey, Charlie, what do you say we get your mum to come and sit on Santa's knee? She can make a Christmas wish for herself!" His face lights up brighter than Rudolph's nose.

"Hey, Mum! Come here." He beckons her over and she smiles as she wanders towards us. "Mummy, sit on Santa's knee. It's your turn." He goes to stand in the spot where his mum was waiting only moments ago.

"Ho! Ho! Ho! Merry Christmas, Karina." The fact I know her name shocks her. "Charlie and I think you've been a good girl and should ask Santa for something extra special this year." A quick look over at the little boy tells me how happy he is. Karina's cheeks flush.

"Well, there isn't really anything I want."

I lean in closer to her ear so only she can hear.

"Karina, it's me, Leo Anders, from high school. Do me a favour and meet me in ten minutes. I wanna talk to you but not when I'm dressed like Santa."

A small smile graces her face. She does remember me.

Karina is gorgeous, but she always was. In high school, I had the biggest crush on her. She was the popular girl going out with the star striker. I was just a defender. I was fast and built, so I was good at it, but I was no striker like Lincoln was in the popularity stakes.

"Oh my gosh, Leo. I can't believe it."

"Shh, I'm Santa Claus, remember?" I joke.

"Right, got it."

"Thanks, so…"

"I'm taking Charlie down to the food court for dinner if you wanna meet us there?"

Christmas miracles do exist.

I can barely hide my happiness.

"See you both there."

Chapter Three

Karina

Leo Anders.
 I can't believe it's really him, and he's smoking hot too. I mean, he was hot back in the day, but now... I can just make out the muscles in his arms through the Christmas sweater he's wearing. My mouth waters and my thighs clench. The temperature in the dining court suddenly shoots up.

He looks around for me, but it's busy. I stand and wave, so he can see me.

"Hey, Leo. Over here."

He waves back and picks up his pace.

I sit down again before nerves sweep my legs from under me.

"Who's that, Mummy?" Charlie asks.

"An old school friend that I haven't seen in a long time. He was on the football team with your dad. Is it okay if he joins us for dinner?" It was just meant to be the two of us. His dad has already neglected him today for 'work'. I don't want him to think I would do the same.

"Okay, Mummy. He can stay." I thank my lucky stars that I have a child who isn't rude or turns people away.

45

"Hey, Karina." I stand once again as he holds out his arms. I step into his embrace as he kisses my cheek. The scent of his cologne wafts up my nose. It's a hint of vanilla and sandalwood, and it suits him.

He releases me, and I find myself saddened that I'm no longer in his embrace. It confuses me as I'm overwhelmed by my sudden feelings toward this...I guess very handsome man Then he reaches out his hand to my little boy, who's watching the exchange with a grin on his face. I don't know what the hell is up with him.

"You must be Charlie. Nice to meet you."

Charlie shakes his hand but says nothing and continues to grin.

"Sweetie, this is my old friend, Leo. He went to school with your daddy and me." His smile drops at the mention of his dad.

"Speaking of Lincoln, how is the star striker? I haven't seen either of you in years."

"He's at work again," Charlie says grumpily. It breaks my heart to see him like this. He takes each rejection that little bit harder.

"He got called into work while Charlie was at his place, so he dropped him off at the diner I work in."

"I see. So you're no longer together?"

"That would be a hell no."

"What happened?

"Lincoln was meant to be bringing Charlie to the mall today to see Santa, but I'm doing it instead. Charlie, why don't you choose what you want to eat?" I huff out an annoyed sigh, wondering how Lincoln could do that to the wonderful son he has.

"Well, I for one, am glad he bailed today because I get the pleasure of your company." He looks me dead in the eyes, holding me captive.

"Can I have a big cheeseburger, chips, and some fizzy pop, please?" Charlie asks.

"That sounds yummy. I'll have the same," Leo tells Charlie, and his face lights up like the fireworks on bonfire night. Lincoln would pull a face at the thought of eating a burger and chips, preferring to eat healthy foods in order to keep up his stamina for the football field. He always said greasy foods made him sluggish. He carried it on into adulthood and would never let Charlie eat them either. I, on the other hand, let him have what he wants. He's full of energy and burns it off quickly.

"Three big cheeseburgers with chips and side salads coming up." I go to stand, but a large hand stops me in my tracks.

"This is my treat. What drinks do you both want?"

"Lemonade, please," Charlie pipes up.

"Same, please."

With a swift nod, Leo heads to the counter to place our order.

"Mummy, after dinner, can I go into the play pit before we go home?" He gave me his cheeky, butter-wouldn't-melt smile.

Damn, this kid knows how to get what he wants. Especially with me.

"Sure, but only for a little while. I don't want to be here all night."

"Yes!" Charlie exclaims, fist-pumping the air and making me giggle.

"Someone's happy. Did Father Christmas come early or something?" Leo is back with our drinks.

"No, but Mummy said after dinner I can go to the play pit. Do you wanna come too?" I frown. He's never asked me to go in with him. Why would he want Leo to?

"Thanks for the invite, buddy, but how about I stay and keep your mum company while you play instead?"

Charlie seems happy enough with that.

"Okay." He picks up his drink and slurps through the straw, saying no more on the subject.

Our food arrives quickly, and we all tuck in between bouts of small talk. Charlie seems to get on well with Leo as they talk animatedly about Christmas.

Before long, we're heading inside the play pit where Leo and I sit with our drinks. Charlie runs off to the slides with a friend who's already in there playing.

"Now I have you alone, what happened with you and Lincoln?"

I think about what to tell him, settling on the whole truth. There's no point in sugar-coating what he did.

"He cheated on me with Britney."

"Your best friend?"

"Yeah, the very one."

"Wow..."

"I caught them in bed together a couple of years ago, so I kicked him out. He didn't try to make amends and ran straight into her arms, her bed, and her home. He's been there ever since."

"What a loser."

"They married as soon as our divorce was finalised."

"I'm so sorry." I glance up and spot the sincerity in his eyes.

"He has a toddler with her now, but what really gets me is that I was the one who supported her through the pregnancy."

"And you didn't know?"

"I had no idea the kid was his, and now he has another one on the way. In Lincoln's eyes, that means he has less time for his son."

"He didn't know a good thing when he had it."

"Agreed, and he's meant to have Charlie every weekend."

"He changes his mind regularly, I take it?"

"Most of the time he drops him off early or doesn't have him at all because he either gets called into work or Britney is having a hard time with her pregnancy."

"That shouldn't affect you."

He's right, it shouldn't. Yet, I allow it to. I've tried so hard to be civil with Lincoln, purely for Charlie's sake. Everything Lincoln chooses to do affects our son, and it seems I'm the only one who cares. Sometimes, I wonder whether it's best to cut all ties with him, then we wouldn't have these problems. But then I imagine the look on Charlie's face. I don't want to be the one that puts a permanent sad look on my son's face, so I choose not to do anything. But is carrying on like this really what's best for Charlie? I just don't know.

"I just can't win with him at the minute. It's not fair on either of us." I realise I'm telling a man I haven't seen in years my life story. There seems to be a calm and welcoming aura around Leo, and that's why I find it easy to talk to him.

"Wow. I never thought he would cheat on you, much less with her."

"Imagine my surprise."

"He hated her in school."

"Yeah, I know. But he seems to have gotten over it."

"Remember the rumour that went around about her getting it on with half the hockey team *and* the teacher?" I nod as I remember. "Well, it was Lincoln who made that up." He smirks

"You're kidding me?"

"Not at all. He would brag about all this shit in the locker room."

I'm stunned into silence. I never knew that. Not that I care now.

"It's none of my business what they get up to now. I almost scratched her eyes out when I first found them together, and I haven't spoken to her since, nor do I want to. Charlie calls her the wicked stepmum, and I don't stop him. As for Lincoln, I'm civil for Charlie's sake, but I hate him for wrecking my life."

I feel the tell-tale sting of tears but blink them away. I've cried too many times over him. Well, no more. It's onwards and upwards from now on and time I moved on with my life. Seems I have the perfect way to start.

"What're you doing tomorrow?" I ask out of the blue.

"Whatever you want me to be doing."

"You sure you don't have to be somewhere? It is Christmas Eve tomorrow, after all."

"Nope, my flatmate is at his girlfriend's, and my parents are no longer around."

"Oh, I'm so sorry, Leo. What happened to them?" I feel awful for bringing it up.

"Freak car accident. It was a few years ago."

"Come spend tomorrow with me and Charlie, then. We will cook up some lunch." It was more a statement than a question and I left no room for argument.

Chapter Four

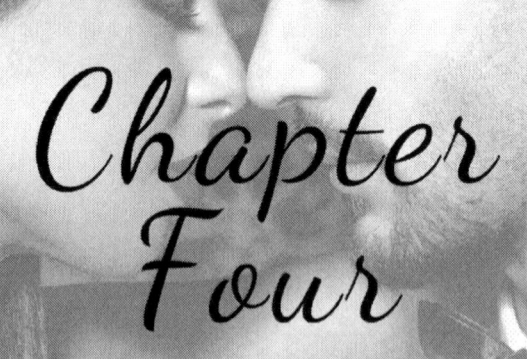

Leo

Last night, I was so close to telling Karina how I felt about her. How I've always felt about her. In high school, I couldn't get her out of my head, but she only had eyes for Lincoln. But that was then, and this is now.

As soon as I realised it was her in the queue, all those forgotten feelings came rushing back. I had to speak to her and find out what her story was. I knew she and Lincoln got married, but she wasn't wearing a wedding ring, and that intrigued me. Then, before we parted ways again, she invited me around to her place today, and I wasn't about to pass that up.

While Charlie was playing yesterday, I mentioned to Karina that he had asked Santa for a few things. By the look of confusion on her face, I guessed she didn't have a clue about half the things he wanted. She told me that he hadn't even mentioned a games console before, but even if he had, she couldn't afford one on her diner wage. An idea started to form in my head. I couldn't give Charlie a father like he asked for, as he'll only ever have one dad, but I could get him the Xbox he asked for.

After Karina and Charlie left for home, I stayed at the shopping centre and went hunting for a gaming store. For once, I was able to use the money I had sitting in the bank for some good. To make someone happy. Why sit and watch Karina struggle to find the cash for one when I can do it? If one thing is clear from seeing her with Charlie it's that she will do anything to make that boy happy. I picked up the console and a handful of games. Once I was done there, I looked around for some other bits for him, but also for Karina too. I spent the night wrapping them up before climbing into bed.

❄

I woke this morning excited that its Christmas Eve for the first time in years. I haven't felt this way about a woman in a long time. Now I'm sitting in my vehicle outside of her house. I'm a bag of nerves, and I don't know where they've come from. I find my big boy pants and get out of the car, choosing to leave the gifts in the boot for now, only taking out the huge food and drink hamper I bought last night. My mother always told me a gentleman never turns up empty-handed. I think she meant flowers or chocolates—possibly wine—but as it's Christmas, I thought this would be a suitable choice.

Ringing her doorbell, I'm nervous, even though I saw her only last night. The door swings open and I'm almost knocked off balance when she comes into view. She's wearing tight black jeans that make my mouth water, with a festive red top. Her dark brown hair is down, framing her beautiful face.

"Wow. You look stunning. I mean... gorgeous. Well, stunningly gorgeous." I stumble over my words. We stand staring at each other for what feels like forever, both of us blushing. Me for being a babbling moron, and Karina because I complimented her, I'm guessing.

"Thanks. Wanna come in?"

I nod frantically, then hear Charlie shouting.

"Mum, is that Leo?"

I can't stop myself from smiling.

"Yeah, it is." She steps aside just in time for Charlie to come barrelling toward me. I manage to place the hamper on a nearby side table in the hall just before he jumps up at me. Seems I made a good impression on at least one person last night.

The jury is still out on the other.

"Hey, buddy. What's this for?" I ask, putting him back down on his feet.

"Just glad you're here." He pointed to the basket of food I placed down moments ago. "What's that?"

"Ah, that's a gift for you and your mum. Wanna help me take it through?" He nods and tries to pick it up. Cute little grunting noises come from his tiny frame, but it's just too heavy for him. He lets go and huffs.

"How about you lead the way and I take it for you?" He marches in front of me, and Karina just looks on, grinning like the Cheshire Cat.

"He's taken to you, Leo."

A smile forms on my face again, "So I see."

"He isn't one to take to strangers as quickly as he has you. Have you cast a spell over us... I mean... him?" she stammers. It's good to know I have her under my spell too. I need to play it cool because I don't want to push her too fast and scare her off.

A phone rings from somewhere in the house and she jumps as she begins to look around for it. I place the hamper on the kitchen worktop. The ringing stops and Charlie reappears with the phone in hand.

He passes it to his mum. "It's Dad, for you." His bored tone is sad to hear.

Karina frowns as she takes the phone from him and leaves the room.

"Hey, buddy, Wanna help me put this stuff away?" I try to cheer him up by keeping him busy with the food items I pass to him. I watch as he inspects every can, bottle, or packet, wondering what it is. He turns his nose up at the Christmas pudding, but his eyes light up when he sees the chocolate fudge cake I put in there in case they didn't like the pudding.

Karina comes back into the room looking as forlorn as Charlie did when he gave her the phone.

"What's up? Bad news?"

Her expression could paint a thousand words.

"That was Lincoln." Her gaze shifts to Charlie. "He won't be coming tomorrow. Instead, he's stopping by to see you today. After lunch."

His face drops, and it's like a punch to the gut. I want to make this kid happy. It's a shame his own father doesn't want to do the same. Karina sees his disappointment and goes over to hug him.

"Does Daddy not love me anymore?"

"What on earth makes you think that?" Karina asks.

"He never wants to see me. He's always with his other family."

I saw the tear roll down Karina's cheek, even though she tried to wipe it away before it was seen.

Lincoln has a lot to answer for.

"Oh, of course he does, Charlie. He loves all his children the same. He's just so busy with work and... well, he doesn't live with us anymore, so he can't be with you all the time."

He seems to ponder this for a minute. His shoulders relax as he continues to take items from the counter and put them away.

Karina looks at me, for what I'm not sure, but I put my arm around her shoulder and pull her into me.

"What time is he coming? I'll make myself scarce."

"No way. This is my house and I want you to stay. If you want to, that is. I mean, you don't have to. Shit, I'm making a mess of this, aren't I?"

Karina steps out of my embrace, embarrassed as she tries to hide her face in the fridge. She finds a place for the wine to chill and places other food items away where there's space, trying to take as long as possible. She eventually finds some courage to face me again.

"Let's make a start on lunch, shall we," she states more than questions, but I'm not gonna argue with her.

Chapter Five

Karina

Lunch was quiet, the mood sombre, and poor Leo wasn't sure what to do with himself after the bomb that Lincoln's call let off. My mobile pings, letting me know I have an incoming message.

Linc: Just left, be there in 10.

"Was that Lincoln?" Leo asks. He isn't happy about Lincoln ditching his son on Christmas Day at all. Neither am I.

"Yeah, he's on his way. He'll be here shortly."

Charlie is currently engrossed in *Jack Frost*. It's a shame to interrupt his movie when he's only just calmed down. My ex-husband has a lot to answer for.

"Hey, sweetie, your dad will be here in a minute. Why don't we pause this and watch it after?"

Charlie rolls his eyes, huffs, and gets up from the floor.

The doorbell echoes through the house, announcing Lincoln's arrival. I go to let him in while Leo stays with Charlie in the living room.

"Hi," I say as I open the door, letting him in. I know I don't sound particularly happy right now, and it probably comes across as rude, but he upset our son on Christmas Eve.

"Hi. Where is he?" Lincoln seems eager to see Charlie. He hands over a couple of small, gift-wrapped boxes. *Is that it?* For Christmas, he gets his firstborn two small gifts. I open the closet and place them in there. I should be thankful he bothered at all, really.

"Listen, before you go in and see him, you should know he isn't too happy with you. And quite frankly, neither am I. He was looking forward to you coming on Christmas Day, and on top of that, I'm getting questions from Charlie now."

"About what?"

"Whether you love him."

"That's ridiculous."

"He doesn't understand why you don't see him anymore, and when you finally do take him, he comes back early because you've conveniently been called into work or that bitch Britney doesn't want him there."

"It's not like that."

"Whatever. At some point, you're going to have to put him first for a change." I didn't mean to rant, but seeing my boy so cut up over this, it spills out. Anyway, why should he get an easy life? He needs to take responsibility or walk away.

"Britney's not a bitch, Karina."

"We'll agree to disagr—"

He cuts me off. "Britney is my wife and it'll serve you well to remember that."

"I couldn't give a rat's arse who she is. What I do care about is our son. You remember him, right? His name is Charlie, seven years old, about yay high." I indicate with my hand against my hip. I'm on a roll now, and I can see he's trying to hide his annoyance at me.

"Look, we need to talk, and clearly, I need to square things with Charlie, but this reaction from you isn't helping matters, Karina."

My mouth opens and closes in shock. He's finally agreed with me. We do need to talk. I have been saying this for months, but yet again, he was busy with work, or his wife.

"Just go and see him. He's in the living room waiting for you." I follow him through and find a crying Charlie sitting with Leo comforting him.

"What the hell is going on? Charlie, are you okay?" Lincoln asks. "Come here, son." Lincoln holds his arm out for him, but Charlie is hesitant. He eventually gets up when he sees Lincoln getting annoyed.

"Hi, Linc. How's it going?" Leo stands, having let Charlie go, hand out to shake Lincoln's. It's clear that Lincoln has no clue who he is.

"Who the hell are you?"

"Leo Anders from Pinewood High. We were on the football team together," Leo tries, and I watch as recognition registers on Lincoln's face.

They shake hands, but Lincoln is looking at me with questioning eyes. I know what he's thinking, but I'm not going to confirm or deny it.

"It's been a while, Leo. What have you been doing all this time?" Lincoln asks, though it's only a show of trying to be polite.

"Ah, you know, just making my millions," Leo jokes. I get the feeling this might turn into a pissing contest any minute the way these two are sizing each other up.

"Leo, let's go in the kitchen and leave Lincoln and Charlie alone." I take hold of Leo's hand and lead him into the kitchen away from whatever the fuck that was.

"Wow, I knew he was a dick for having left the best two people in his life for the school bike, but I heard you both in the hall, and so did Charlie. I can't believe he got so upset over you calling her a bitch but not over how Charlie is feeling." I realise I'm still holding his hand when I feel his grip tighten as he speaks.

"Don't worry about it. It's done now. It's not like I want him back. I just want him to be in Charlie's life. It's Christmas, so no more sadness," I say more cheerfully than I feel.

"Oh, I almost forgot. There is a boatload of gifts for you and Charlie in the car. I didn't want to bring them in, in case he saw them. We can sneak out now and get them while he's occupied with his dad."

I can't believe my ears. Leo bought us a huge hamper full to the brim of luxury food and drink. Now he tells me he has gifts too. It's all too much, and not at all necessary.

"Oh, Leo, you really shouldn't have. I don't have anything for you," I say, feeling awkward.

"That's okay. Your company has been enough. I would've spent all of Christmas alone had I not come here today, so it was my pleasure."

He's alone for the holidays? That's not right. I can't have that.

"All of it?"

"Yeah, my flatmate, Bryan, spends all of the holidays with his girlfriend. He won't be back until Boxing Day evening."

"Then you'll spend the whole day here with us, and the same goes for tomorrow. I won't have you alone on Christmas Day." I have more than enough food. I always do too much, so having another mouth to feed makes no difference to me.

"Really? You want me to come for the day? Are you sure?" I can see he wants to say yes.

"Of course. Come on, let's empty the car."

I look in the boot with shock. He didn't just get one or two gifts. He was right when he said 'boatload'.

"What the heck did you buy him?"

"I kinda went back and bought him the Xbox he asked for. I know I probably should have asked you first, but it was what he asked for and you had mentioned that you didn't have the means to get one for him. It wasn't until after we parted that I had the idea and, well, I just wanted to give a little gesture to repay you for the invite."

"That's so sweet of you, but it's too much money for you to spend on a gift for him."

"Money is no object. Please, I wanted to do it. Don't worry about it now."

I agree to let it be. It was a lovely thing for him to do.

We've just hidden the last of the gifts in the coat closet when Lincoln strolls into the kitchen.

"Karina, can we talk for a second?"

"Sure, what's up?" I ask.

"I'll leave you to chat and go sit with Charlie." Leo goes to step away, but I stop him, linking my arm with his.

"There's no need to leave."

In truth, the look in Lincoln's eyes tells me it's bad news and I'm gonna need to have Leo here to hold on to. Leo gives me a nod and places his hand on mine in the crook of his arm.

"I have news that I didn't want to tell you today, especially with what you told me when I first got here."

"Just get on with it, Linc." I feel my heart sink. Is he sick or something?

"I have a new job with better money and a chance to own the company one day." He looks sheepish, but I don't know why. This is good news for him.

"That's great. Congrats." Leo beams.

"Yeah, that's amazing news. So, why aren't you happy?" I ask.

"Because... it's in Spain,"

Wait, did he just say Spain?

"Huh?"

"I'll be working in the family business."

"What family business is this?"

"Brit's parents are over there, as you know, and they are getting ready to pass the business over. With Brit being an only child, it goes to her, but she isn't interested in it full time with the baby coming, so I'm taking over. It would be stupid not to, and Brit will have her parents too. It's a win-win."

I feel the fire inside me burning through my veins. "Excuse me?" I shout. "A win-win? She'll have her family? What about yours, Linc? You have a son here, or did you conveniently forget about that once again?"

Leo's grip on me tightens as I get more heated.

"No, I didn't just forget about him. Jeez, Karina. I'm not a monster. I love my son and he'll always have a place to visit in the holidays."

I want to hit him right now. He hardly sees his son as it is. What does he think moving to another country is going to do to their already strained relationship?

"You're leaving me?" A tiny voice comes from the doorway.

"Shit," Lincoln mumbles.

Charlie runs up the stairs to his room with tears in his eyes.

OH, SANTA!

I start to chase after him with Lincoln hot on my heels. I spin to face him and stop abruptly.

"Don't you dare. Just go, Lincoln. Don't you think you've hurt him enough?"

"I want to explain it to him."

"Go live your happy little life with your new family in Spain, and do us a favour. Don't come back. Charlie will be so much happier without you in his life, messing him around, wondering if he'll see you this week or next." I turn away, ready to resume pursuit of my upset child, but Lincoln takes hold of my wrist.

"We have to talk about this, Karina. I leave January tenth."

"Go now for all I care."

"Look, I didn't want to upset anyone. Not now. Not at Christmas time, but when else was I meant to tell you?"

The nerve of this guy.

"Just go. I have your mess to clean up once again."

"For what it's worth, I'm sorry."

"For what exactly? Upsetting him or leaving him? Or for spoiling his Christmas?"

"I love my son."

"You've always been a selfish bastard, Lincoln Fox. But I never for one second thought you would ever hurt him the way you have since you cheated on us and left. Now, get the fuck out of my house." I stand my ground while he stands there with his mouth hanging open in shock that I stood up to him.

Leo, who had stood back giving us space, steps up behind Lincoln. "I'll see you out."

I finally leave the kitchen to comfort my sobbing son.

Chapter Six

Leo

I wait until I see Karina vanish up the stairs.

Lincoln spins on his heels, and before I know what's happening, my fist connects with his face. He bends at the waist, holding his nose, which is now seeping with blood.

"What the fuck? Are you kidding me? Shit!"

I shake my hand out as pain erupts from my knuckles. It's been a long time since I hit a person, but damn, that felt good. He hurt that little boy and his mum so many times. He chose Britney over them, and now he chooses her and her family over his own child. Karina was right. Charlie will be better off without him in his life.

"That's the last time you hurt them, Lincoln. Now, I believe she asked you to leave."

He has the nerve to smirk as he stands to his full height, trying to intimidate me. That might have worked back in high school, but he isn't the star player anymore. He's nothing now.

"You think you have your feet under the table here?"

"That's none of your business."

"She isn't interested in you. She wasn't back then, and she won't be now."

"You know nothing."

"I always knew you had a thing for my girl. We may not be together, but she has my kid, and she'll always be my girl because of it."

"Save it, dickhead."

"You have nothing to offer her. The last I heard, you didn't even have a job."

I have to laugh at his audacity. "No, you're right. I don't have *a* job. I own the damn company and hire people so I don't have to work every day. I told you before, I've been making my millions." His face drops. "So, I have plenty to offer her and Charlie." I force him back towards the front door.

"You've got money, so what?"

I don't normally like rubbing it in people's faces that I have money, but he's rubbing me up the wrong way, and after his trying to put me down, he needs to be put in his place. I reach around him for the doorknob and pull the door open. "Bye." I push him gently over the threshold and onto the porch.

"She'll never love you, Leo."

"Is that so? Shame you won't be around to find out. You'll be living la Vida loca in Spain, right?" I smirk and slam the door in his face, then flick the lock shut. I hear movement behind me.

"Has he gone?" Karina asks as I turn towards her.

"Yeah, he just left. How's Charlie?" It's the only thing that's important right now.

"He's upset and scared he'll never see his dad again."

"I'm sure that won't be the case."

"I didn't correct him because if I get my way, he won't see Charlie ever again."

"You're angry right now—"

"I won't give Lincoln the opportunity to hurt my son again." Tears roll down her face.

I throw my arms around her to comfort her.

She wraps herself around me, drawing all the warmth she can from me, and it feels so right, me holding her like this. Like she was meant to have been there all the time.

"So, I was gonna just order a Christmas Eve takeaway for dinner tonight, but what if I order all three of us some instead? My treat," I say into her hair.

Karina pulls away from me and smiles as she begins drying her eyes on her sleeve.

"Can I have pizza, please?" Charlie appears at the top of the stairs. He's red-faced with swollen eyes, and it tears my heart apart.

"Of course you can, buddy. I mean, if your mum says it's okay for me to stay for dinner." We both glance at Karina, awaiting her answer.

"I feel ganged up on here," she jokes. "But I don't see why not." Charlie bounds down the stairs and high-fives me with a small smile.

"So, pizza for Charlie, and what about you? Do you want pizza, or do you want Thai, Chinese, Italian... you name it, you got it." I watch as her face lights up.

"I'm good with pizza. I have some menus in the kitchen drawer."

We ended up with two different pizzas, fried chicken, fries, chicken bites, and burgers, with cans of fizzy drinks to go with it. Charlie had changed his mind back and forth when he was looking at the menu, so I just ordered a bit of everything. It was worth it to see his smiling face when it all arrived. Needless to say, we're all stuffed, and the leftovers have gone into the fridge. Charlie must have eaten himself into a food coma because he passed out in the middle of me and Karina on the couch while we finished watching *Jack Frost*. I carry him up to bed with Karina leading the way. He didn't stir once. Finding out his dad was moving thousands of miles away has wiped him out.

We head back downstairs, where Karina makes us both a hot chocolate, and we get comfy back on the couch.

We talk about anything and everything. What we've both been up to over the years, where I'm living, and what our interests are. She tells me how she and Lincoln had decided that she would be a stay-at-home mum, while he worked, until he committed adultery. That's how she came to work in the diner she's currently employed at. I tell her about the tech business I own. How it started out as just me, a lone wolf, which is how the company got its name, Lone Wolf Technologies.

"How are you single?" she asks. "I mean, you're the perfect catch for some lucky lady."

Is this my shot? After everything today has thrown at her, is now the right time? I decide that it's now or never. I lean in closer to her. Her breath hitches, and I pause.

"Can you be my lucky lady?" I whisper. This time, she leans into me, taking control as our lips crash together. My hands find their way into her hair, allowing me to take control. I gently kiss her lips, savouring her touch. She murmurs out a moan, which makes my dick hard. I hold onto her hips and lift her without breaking our connection and place her on my lap so she's straddling me. She gasps and pulls away. I know she felt something; I felt it too. A connection. I also felt her briefly rub against me. She wants this.

"I'm not sure I remember how to do this." She blushes, and I frown in confusion. Surely she's had sex since the break-up.

"I don't think it's something you forget how to do," I reassure her.

Her eyes drop. "No, you don't understand. It's been two years since I last did... this." Karina motions her hands between us. "I don't just bring men into our lives, Leo. I have Charlie to think of and won't bring any random guy into his life who will not stick around."

I lift her chin so I can look into her eyes. "He thinks we're just friends, right? As much as I hate to lie to him, I'm happy to let him believe that until we know where we're at with whatever this is. We've only just met again, so I know how important it is to take it slow." I tentatively kiss her again, only softer this time, showing her that we're in no hurry.

She shuffles forward and grinds herself on my dick.

I growl into her mouth, then take her lip between my teeth and tug softly.

"The bedroom is upstairs," Karina says.

There's no need to tell me twice. My cock is solid. Without a backwards glance, I stand, picking her up by her arse. I kiss along her jaw, blindly walking towards the stairs.

I can hardly believe my luck.

Chapter Seven

Karina

I can't believe I'm being so bold with him. I never throw caution to the wind like this, and whilst it feels right, it's nothing short of reckless, yet I still want it. I still want him.

He puts me down at the top of the stairs, so we can tiptoe to my room down the hall past Charlie's room. I've never been so thankful that our rooms are on the opposite side of the house and not next to each other.

Once inside my room with the door closed, I lean my back against it and relax a little. It's short-lived because Leo is on me in an instant. His whole body presses against mine as he smothers my neck in open-mouthed kisses. His hands trace every inch of my body. The only thing wrong is there's too much material blocking us from really feeling each other. I take the lead and strip off my top, exposing my impulse buy yesterday at the shops. It was worth every penny just to see the look on Leo's face as he takes in the red satin balcony bra with white fluff along the cups. It was my present to myself this year.

"Please tell me you're wearing matching knickers?" I drag my bottom lip between my teeth, giving him my best seductive eyes and nodding.

He growls again as he slips his shirt off. "Get on the bed. I want to unwrap my present early."

I do as he says, leaving my jeans on. He's taken his own jeans off and stands at the foot of the bed in just his boxer shorts, hunger in his eyes. Looking at his tented erection, he has nothing to be ashamed of.

Leo climbs onto the bed and nestles himself between my legs, reaches for the button on my jeans, and undoes them. He pulls them over my hips so my knickers come into view. My jeans are off seconds later.

"I want to take my sweet time with you, worship you like you should be worshipped, but if I don't feel you on my dick soon..."

She cuts me off by placing her index finger on my lips. "Leo, just shut up and fuck me."

I'm speechless. This woman is incredible.

"Yes, ma'am," he replies as he pulls my underwear off. He stands to remove his own.

Standing proudly in front of him is the biggest cock I've ever seen. Not that I have much to compare it to, because I've only ever been with Lincoln. I lick my lips as my mouth waters in anticipation.

I slip out of my bra and throw it to the ground.

"You're gonna be the death of me." He pounces onto the bed and hovers over me. "Are you sure about this? It's not too late to back out." He waits for my reaction.

I wrap my legs around his waist and my arms around his neck and pull him in so close I feel his dick rub against my pussy. Arousal seeps from me. I can't wait any longer, so I tighten my legs a little more and he slips right in on a low growl. Burying my face in his neck, I muffle my own groans of pleasure, aware I need to be quiet.

Oh my God. I feel so full in the most delicious of ways. I'm just about to tell him he needs to start moving when he rears his hips back and slides into me again, slowly at first, but he soon begins to pick up the pace. He moves at a punishing rhythm, making my arms fall from his neck. I hold onto the spindles of the headboard as he thrusts into me. My head thrashes about as the feeling gets more intense, and I quietly moan out my pleasure. I'm right on the cusp of my orgasm. My cries turn to hums as he crushes his mouth to mine in a bruising kiss. We swallow each other's groans as we come together in a spectacular fashion. He rolls by my side as we both lie there panting, trying to catch our breaths. It was messy, it was fast, and it was perfect.

Leo holds his arm out and pulls me into his side, where I place my head on his chest. We lie like this for a long while, me listening to the rhythm of his heart as it slows down to a steady beat. I'm tired and can feel myself drifting off.

"Did you know I had the biggest crush on you at school?" Leo's sleepy voice says in a sexy, husky tone that makes me squeeze my thighs together.

Down, girl. You just got your fill. *Yeah, but you have two years to make up for*, I argue with myself.

I think back to high school when I only had eyes for Lincoln. He was my world back then. The team was always there around him, and my besties were always around me. Naturally, that meant Leo was always in the background. I recall he was always nice to me.

"I didn't back then, but thinking about it now, you were always hanging around with us since you were on the team. You always asked me if I was okay and stuff. I figured you were just being friendly. I guess I read that wrong."

"I thought I loved you back then, but now I know I did." He chuckles lazily as he drifts off to sleep.

I'm dumbstruck. Surely he didn't mean to say that. I lie still on his chest as soft snores fill my ears, lulling me into sleep.

❄

It's Christmas morning, and I lie awake with the most exquisite ache where I was ravaged more than once last night. The man has some stamina, that's for sure.

I hum to myself with sated glee at the thought of last night and what we shared.

He woke me at stupid o'clock in the early hours of this morning, kissing my neck and making me moan. It wasn't long before he had his head between my legs and I was screaming into my pillow. Afterwards, we went downstairs and laid out all the presents ready for Charlie before he took me back to bed and ravished me some more, then we both drifted back off to sleep.

I begin to wonder if I'll disturb him if I get up to relieve myself, but I feel him roll over and slide up behind me and wrap his arm around me, his arms holding me tightly to his front. I can feel his morning wood nestled in the groove of my arse cheeks as we spoon. I daren't open my eyes in case it's a dream and he isn't really there.

I open one eye to find Charlie's little face looking at me, confused.

"Oh, shit. Charlie." I sit up quickly, grabbing hold of the sheets as I go. I disturb Leo in the process, but I don't care. Charlie comes first every time. He sits up, wondering what's going on until he sees Charlie. Mumbles of curse words come from his direction.

Chapter Eight

Leo

"Hey, Charlie, look. I..." I try to take hold of the situation, but I'm not sure what I'm meant to say here. I look to Karina for guidance, but she looks just as dumbfounded as I am.

Then, just when I thought it was gonna be the beginning of the end for us, he runs to the end of the bed, climbs up the middle, and starts to bounce happily.

"Leo! I didn't know we were having a sleepover. You could have shared my bed."

And there it is, from the mouth of an innocent child.

Karina beams proudly behind him like only a mother can.

"Thanks, Charlie, but I kinda liked spending time with your mum. Would you mind if I hung around with you guys sometimes?" I ask him, hoping he will say yes.

"Did Santa send you? I asked him for a new daddy."

The look on Karina's face is priceless. I never told her the things he asked for.

"Has Santa been?" she asks him, trying to change the subject.

"Yeah, Mummy. He came already. Can we go down and open my

presents now?" He bounces some more before he jumps and lands on his arse. He crawls off the bed and starts dancing around like he has ants in his pants.

"Go wash and brush your teeth first, then we can go down," she tells him, but he's out the door before she can finish the sentence. "Quick, get dressed," she whispers.

I do as I'm told because I don't want him running in here while I have my junk out.

"Well, that went better than expected."

Karina looks mortified by the situation now Charlie's out of the room. Once dressed, she looks me square in the eyes. "Is that what this is all about? He asked you for a new daddy, and you think you can fill that role? Did you think by getting in my pants that I would think you're now daddy material?"

"Honestly, I didn't even think too much about what he asked me for. I wasn't even meant to be there that day. I was filling in for a friend. But I saw you in the queue about twenty minutes before Charlie's turn."

"Is this some sort of game?"

"No! As soon as I saw you, I knew I wanted to talk to you. Then, when Charlie asked for a new dad, I knew you were single. It felt like fate had finally fallen into my lap."

"Charlie can't take any more loss, Leo."

"It won't happen."

"How can I be sure?"

"The girl I had a crush on all those years ago walked back into my life and was single, and even after all that time, you can still make my heart beat faster."

"I don't know what to believe."

"The past twenty-four hours have been the best of my life..." *Sure beats making my first million any day.*

"I've loved having you here, Leo."

I blow out a sigh as I stalk around the bed to get closer to her. I need to show her how it feels to be close again. Taking hold of her hip in one hand and losing my other in her hair, I pull her towards me and kiss her passionately.

We pull away from one another when a small arm wraps around my thigh, and when I look down, Charlie's free arm is wrapped around Karina's. He looks up. "I'm done, Mummy. Can I open my presents now?" He grins wide to show off his freshly brushed pearly white teeth.

"You sure can. Let's go."

At the bottom of the stairs, I tell them to go on ahead and start opening presents without me. "I'm going to make us all something to drink."

God knows I could use a coffee. Besides, I think Karina needs a minute away from me. As the coffee machine finishes pouring out our drinks, I head to the fridge and grab some orange juice for Charlie. I pop them on a tray and make my way to the living room, where Charlie is excitedly ripping into a gift. Handing out the beverages, I take a seat next to Karina and place my hand on her knee. I feel her tense under my touch, but she makes no attempt to move. I get that it's gonna take some time to get used to a man being around again, but now he knows, I see no point in hiding my affections.

"Are you not opening your presents?" I ask her.

"Yeah, Mum. Open this one. Santa doesn't usually bring Mummy presents. Does this mean you have been good this year but you were a naughty girl the other times?"

I almost spit my coffee out as the memory of round two comes to mind. Karina was riding me hard last night and I called her my naughty girl.

"No. It means I asked him to give any gift that was meant for me to someone else who needs them more." This woman is the most selfless person I have ever known. I have to make her mine.

"Wow, look, Mum! I got an Xbox."

"Aren't you a lucky boy," Karina says, giving me the side-eye. "That wasn't in your letter to Santa." She flicks her gaze back to him as he opens the remote control car I bought him. The excitement on his face is more than I could've asked for.

"No, I asked Santa for them, and he got them."

I watch him as he opens a few more gifts, and then as Karina opens the gift Charlie handed to her. There's shock on her face when she lifts the lid on the box. Light shining from the diamonds reflect onto her beautiful face. She picks the bracelet out of its protective case and the shimmer casts rainbows over the walls.

"Oh, my, Leo. This is too much. I can't accept it," she whispers so Charlie doesn't hear her say it's from me and not Santa.

"Yes, you can. You deserve it. Something special for *someone* special." I know it's cheesy, but it's true. She was always someone special and that hasn't changed.

"Thank you," she mouths, and I can't help it. I smile so much my cheeks hurt.

"You keep opening gifts. I'll go make us all some breakfast." I leave the room feeling like the king of the world.

I rub my hand over my front left pocket and feel the flat bag still there.

I'm whisking up the mix for pancakes when Karina comes in. She rounds the counter and heads towards me. When she's close enough, I wrap my arms around her waist and our lips meet. The kiss is deep and passionate. I want the kiss to tell her how much I want her.

Too soon, she pulls away, her cheeks flushed. "Did you mean it?" she asks.

"Mean what, sweetheart?" I'm not sure what she wants to know, but I do know that every word I've ever spoken to her was true.

"Last night, you said that back in the day you thought you loved me but now you *know* you do. What does that mean?"

I pull her tighter to me. "Back then, I told myself that I couldn't love you because I didn't know what love was. I convinced myself that it wasn't possible to love you. Then, the other day in the shopping centre, you were like this amazing beacon of light that lit up a dark room and all the feelings I had for you came flooding back. It was like love at first sight all over again. I wanted to tell you but didn't want to scare you away."

She fists my shirt in her hands as tears roll down her face. "You still love me?" Her gorgeous features contort in a mixture of shock, happiness, and fear.

"Yes, I love you. I think I always have, and I know I always will. Do you think you could love me eventually? I want us to work, and I would love Charlie like he's my own."

"I felt it too. Love at first sight. That's because I love you too."

As soon as those words leave her mouth, I lift her and swing her around in a circle. Placing her down on the kitchen island, I stand between her open thighs and take her face in my hands, looking deep into her soul through her expressive eyes. I know I will spend the rest of my life loving this woman.

Epilogue

It's been a whole year since Karina came back into my life. I have never been so grateful to Bryan for needing me to cover his shift for him that day. Bryan and Beth found their dream home and planned on seeking a mortgage. Bryan had proposed on Christmas Day, so they figured a mortgage was right for them. I couldn't let them start married life already in debt. I brought them their home as a wedding gift. After all, he is my best friend, and I owed him, I guess.

Lincoln and his family moved to Spain in the new year, which devastated Charlie.

He gained a sister, not that he has got to meet her yet. Karina was right. He finds every reason to not have Charlie. This time, it's because he needs to settle into the job before he starts taking time off. I even offered to fly all three of us out to Spain so he could meet his new sibling and see his father while not taking up to much of his time. Heck, he didn't even have to pay for it. Karina was fuming with him for upsetting Charlie again.

We soon made him happy again as, on Father's Day, Karina announced she was pregnant. She is due to give birth to our son at the end of January. I sold my flat and moved in with Karina and Charlie soon after.

She insisted on working in the diner for as long as she could. Mac reluctantly agreed as long as she stayed behind the counter and sat on a stool towards the end and just took orders, rang them through, and made drinks. That all ended last week when she thought she had gone into labour. Both Mac and I agreed enough was enough and told her that her maternity leave had officially started. She chose wisely not to argue with us.

Now, it's Christmas morning, and I'm up before anyone else. I hardly slept a wink last night, nerves getting the better of me.

"You're up early. Everything okay?"

"Yeah, of course. Want me to make you a cup of tea?"

"Urgh, you read my mind." She sits on the stool at the breakfast bar, looking shattered.

I place her tea in front of her and kiss her forehead.

"I wanted to ask you something before Charlie gets up. I wouldn't want to get his hopes up if you said no."

"Jeez, should I be worried?"

"No, but I need to get this out. I knew how I felt as soon as I saw you. You and Charlie have come to mean the world to me, and now we have a new little one on the way. I couldn't be happier, except for one thing. I've kept this in my pocket for a while now, but I think maybe now is the right time to give it to you." I pull out the velvet bag from my pocket. "I'm suddenly extremely nervous." I chuckle, and she smiles back at me, calming me instantly. "Karina, this, us, it feels right, and I hope you agree." I get down on one knee and pull the ring out of the bag. I hold it up to her as she jumps off the stool and joins me on the floor.

"Are you being serious right now?" she asks me in disbelief.

"As a heart attack, baby. Will you do me the honour of becoming my wife?"

She throws her arms around me with force, our baby bump almost knocking us off balance as she begins kissing me all over my face.

"Is that a yes?"

"That's a million times yes." I place my ring on her finger and kiss her with all that I have. "Wow, it's beautiful, Leo."

"Baby, the ring is perfect, just like you." I take hold of her hand, which the ring now proudly sits on, and kiss it. "I promise to love and care for you and Charlie until my dying day."

"I didn't think I could love you any more than I already do, but the fact you've included Charlie in all of this means the world to me. Leo, you came into my life when I needed it most. Not just for me, but for my son too. I'll forever be eternally grateful to you. I never imagined a Christmas like this. Thank you."

Our lips meet again, sealing the deal that will change all of our lives for the better.

I pull away enough to whisper, "Merry Christmas, Karina." I hold onto her, and though I want to kiss her again, having her in my arms is enough.

All of my dreams have come true. I feel like the luckiest guy alive. The one present I wanted and never expected to get, and she's in my arms.

I feel like a kid on this Christmas morning; one who finally got the present he'd been asking for.

This time last year, the most important thing in my life was my company. Now, I've gained a family, and one I'll treasure every day of my life.

I thought getting the girl last Christmas was something I wouldn't forget, but this one really is a Christmas to remember.

The End

Mistletoe Kisses

by

Lizzie James

Chapter One

Faith

"Hello?!" Emma waved her hand in my face, clicking her fingers impatiently at me trying to grab my attention. "You're not even listening to me, are you?" She rolled her eyes at me.

"I'm sorry. I was just thinking . . ." I turned my gaze to face her, instead of on the very good-looking barman at the bar who was pulling pints that currently had my focus.

"Thinking. Right," she said in a sarcastic tone. "Perving, you mean." She turned in her seat to look at where I was pointing. "What is your obsession with him?" She cocked her head to the side before she turned back to face me. "I just don't get it."

"I'm not obsessed," I quickly defended myself. "He interests me."

"How?" She stirred the straw in her daiquiri cocktail before she looked back up at me. "You do know that he's a manwhore, don't you?" She cocked an elegant eyebrow at me before she went off on another tangent. Her watch beeped a reminder at her, alerting her attention down to her wrist. "Oh, I have to go but I left your outfit on the end of your bed for you. We didn't have many spots left open but I really appreciate it." She stood up and grabbed her handbag before leaning down and kissing my cheek. "See you later! Be there by 6:00 p.m."

I stared after her, watching her run out of the bar and into a busy snow-dusted street. I really didn't like the way she said, 'not many spots left open'. I knew that I was going to regret this.

Each year, Emma helped out in our local community by hosting Christmas activities. Last year she helped to run the Christmas markets; the year before she directed the children's play in the local community hall. This year she had upgraded and was running a 'Meet Santa' event in the middle of town. It was also operating as a base to take in donated presents for children in local cancer hospitals. It was a lot of pressure but I knew that Emma would do a fantastic job. She never buckled under pressure.

Turning back to finish my sandwich, I jumped in surprise when I saw that I was no longer alone. Sitting in her seat was now the barman that I had been gawking at: Jack. He was a manwhore, just like Emma had said but he was always nice to me. He and I had gone to school together and I had always classed him as a friend. Not a close friend but still, just a friend. He was a year older than me and a few inches taller. He always had a slight stubble on his cheeks and had dark brown hair— the same shade as mine—that was long on the sides. He always had it brushed back from his face and always found a way to make me blush without even trying.

"Where did she go running off to?" He reached over and stole a fry off my plate, dipping it in some tomato sauce before popping it into his mouth.

"Off to save the world somewhere." We both laughed at my words, knowing I was probably right.

Emma always had to be doing something. She worked over at the children's hospital and I know how bad it must affect her to see all of those sick children each shift she worked but she never let it show. She always had a smile on her face and usually had a project she would be focusing on. She had been dating Jack's friend, Paul, for a few months and they seemed to really click.

I never thought that they would last; especially as they are complete opposites. He's a science teacher and loved a good crime book and she is

. . . Well, she's Emma. She's basically the adult version of Tinkerbell. Feisty, cheeky, and always seemed high on pixie dust.

Paul was usually a quiet person but he was an interesting guy. He loved science programs, especially documentaries about the stars and the galaxy. If we ever had a quiz, I usually made sure Paul was on my team so at least it stopped everyone looking at me to give an answer that I'd probably not have a clue about.

"So, are you going to be hanging out with us and Santa later?" Jack asked.

I giggled, imagining him being around so many children. I think that it would be his idea of hell.

"Yeah, right." He reached over for another fry. "I'm not as gullible as the rest of you."

"What do you mean by that?" I asked.

"Come on." He laughed loudly. "You and Paul can never say no to that woman."

"True." I admitted, smiling widely at him. "I had best be going." I stood up and grabbed my handbag from under my chair before dropping some cash from my purse on the table for him. "Keep the tip and maybe I'll see you later." I gave him a small wave and walked to the door, forcing myself to keep my eyes looking forward and not to look back.

If I looked back, it would just show how desperate I fucking was and obviously obsessed with the man I was therefore proving Emma right all along.

After walking home, I was equal parts regretting telling Emma that I would help her out with the 'Meet Santa' event and nervous at the thought of whatever godforsaken outfit she had left for me.

Unlocking the door, I chuckled when I saw that she had left cupcakes on the table for me. She could be a real sweetheart sometimes but I knew that they were just part of the bribery to keep me on side. It also told me that whatever outfit she had left for me was going to be bad.

Dropping my bag at the table, I walked further into the apartment and headed toward my bedroom door. Flicking the light on, my eyes went straight to the bed where my outfit was lying there.

Just fucking kill me now.

No! Actually, I was going to kill her. She was so fucking dead when I got my hands on her.

I grabbed my phone out of the pocket of my jeans and dialed her number. Unsurprisingly, it went straight to voicemail.

"You are so dead!" I mock-threatened her. I turned back to look at the outfit, cringing at the green curved shoes with a bell on each end. "So dead. Next time warn me before you make me an elf!" I giggled before saying goodbye in our normal style. "Love you, bitch."

I tossed the phone on the bed, glaring at the outfit with way too many fucking bells on one last time before I stripped out of my clothes and grabbed my towel. After waiting for the temperature to warm up, I climbed under the hot spray and began soaping my body up.

I hated that my thoughts wandered to Jack. He was so out of my fucking league and it was pathetic how much of a crush I had on him. I still stupidly hoped that he'd come by and see us later on, even if it would be to take the piss out of us.

Shaking my head, I washed my hair and after rinsing the suds off my body, I climbed out of the shower. I wrapped a towel around myself and squeezed the excess water out of my hair before disappearing back to my bedroom.

After plaiting my hair and adding a light coating of foundation, I begrudgingly changed into my elf costume and placed the hat on my head, chuckling as the bells jingled away. Green definitely wasn't my color.

I stood up and checked my reflection in the full-length mirror on the back of my bedroom door, cringing at the sight that greeted me. I had on green boots that were curved upwards at the toes with a large bell on each of them that jingled with every step that I took. Red and white striped stockings covered my legs that led to a green dress that came to just above my knees. The petticoat of the dress was red and hung a couple of centimeters past the hem of the dress with a black belt fitted at the waist. The top part of the dress was fitted with three large green buttons that led to a red collar.

I cocked my head to the side, chuckling when the large bell jingled on the red and green elf's hat that was on top of my head.

I really hoped that Jack didn't come by now. I was never going to live this down.

Chapter Two

Jack

Sliding the key into the lock of my apartment door, I was looking forward to a night of doing absolutely fuck all. Pulling drinks in a bar all day and serving tables weren't as glamorous as it was made out to be.

Walking in, I frowned when I saw that Paul was still here. I had expected him to be gone already.

"Hey, man!" I called out into the apartment before taking my jacket off and tossing it on the back of the sofa. "I thought you'd be long gone by now."

"I'm just going." He said as he walked into the lounge with a backpack thrown over his shoulder. "I'm going to change there."

"Why?" I frowned at him before my eyes trailed to the backpack. "Is the outfit that bad?" I grinned at him, trying to imagine whatever torture Emma had planned for him.

"No!" he quickly defended. "Maybe . . ." He chuckled before he grabbed his coat from the back of the chair by the door. "You going to be here when I finish?" he questioned, looking over at me. "Or are you going out with one of your fan club tonight?"

OH, SANTA!

I chuckled at his wording. "Nah. Quiet night in for me tonight, man. Tell Emma I said hey, though."

"Will do, man," he replied, giving me a two-fingered salute before he opened the door. "Save me some take-out if you decide to get one!" he shouted at me as the door swung shut behind him. I knew that whatever outfit was waiting for him in that bag would be torture.

"Poor fucker," I muttered to myself.

I walked to my bedroom and after quickly stripping, I climbed into the shower, groaning as the heat from the warm spray hit my body. I could feel the tension slowly begin to ease from my body and as I soaped myself up, my mind went to where it normally did whenever I took a shower.

I closed my eyes, imagining Faith on her knees. The image of her kneeling on the floor of the shower cubicle, sucking me off as the water droplets trailed down over her naked skin was making me hard as fuck. I groaned and took my cock in my hand, squeezing hard before pumping myself. I rested my other hand on the tiled wall, dropping my head as I continued imagining how wet and warm her mouth would feel and how soft her hands would be as she fondled my balls.

Before I could stop myself, I felt my balls began to tighten and seconds later, my orgasm hit me and I was squirting my cum against the tiled wall.

"Ah, fuck." I dropped my head back against my shoulders, letting the water run down over my chest and wash the evidence away. I was so screwed when it came to that woman and she didn't even have a fucking clue.

I finished washing up and rinsed my body before climbing out of the shower and wrapped a towel around my waist. I reached up and wiped the condensation off the mirror before grabbing my toothbrush. Looking at my reflection as I brushed my teeth, I realised that I'd need a shave soon. I usually had a scruff but it would slowly turn into a beard in a couple of weeks.

Washing my mouth out, I popped the toothbrush back into the holder next to Paul's and walked back into my bedroom. I grabbed my phone and took a look at my notifications, cringing when I saw that I had a couple of missed calls from some of the girls I had stored on my phone. I stared at them for a moment before my thoughts trailed back to my shower fantasy.

Going to my contacts, I moved down to Faith's number. I had gotten it when Paul had not so subtly slipped it on a piece of paper for me. He had been goading me since to grow a pair and ask her out. I hesitated over pressing the button, nervous to call her but also not wanting to make the first move. Every time that I saw her, I would always attempt to ask her out but each time, my nerves won out and it never happened.

She knew that I was a player and that I only kept girls around to be a fuck buddy; I didn't have time for relationships. They always looked like such fucking hard work and being tied down to one woman was never something that I was really interested in.

With Faith, though...

Fuck, I would be interested in a bit of effort with Faith, though. I'd put in the fucking effort.

She was fucking beautiful. She had long brown hair, pouty lips, pale skin and a body I just want to crush against my own whenever I saw her.

She had no fucking clue how tightly she had me wound up and it made me frustrated as fucking hell. She'd drop into the bar every day to pick up her lunch or to meet Emma for a cocktail and she'd always be wearing her sexy fucking office outfits. She had no idea how many times she had starred in my one-handed fantasies.

I think that I had probably fantasized about her in every fucking position that I could imagine and I'd experienced many.

Before I could decide, my phone began ringing and Sylvia's name flashed across the screen.

I shook my head and tossed the phone aside on to the mattress, not in the mood for any female drama tonight. I walked into the kitchen and uncapped a bottle of Budweiser, thinking about what food to order tonight. I hadn't joined the boys in an Xbox gaming session in a while and I think tonight having the place to myself while Paul is out doing fuck knows what at Emma's little event would be a good time to get one in.

Taking a swig, I placed the bottle on top of my chest of drawers before my phone started ringing from where it was on the bed. Picking it up, I grinned when I saw Paul's name displayed on the screen.

"What's up?" I asked. "She killed you yet?" I joked, not giving him a chance to respond.

"Dude. Don't even start," he threatened. "You coming by?"

"Why?" I asked. When the fuck did I ever go to one of these community events? I hated kids so there wasn't much of a chance I'd go to one knowing full well it'd be overcrowded with kiddies and their parents.

"Because I know you'll not want to admit this but . . ." He paused for a moment before continuing. "Faith is here and she's looking very . . ."

"Why the fuck are you looking at Faith when you're supposed to be in a relationship with Emma?" I snapped.

He laughed at my outburst. "Don't get defensive! Just thought you might want to come down and check her out in her very sexy stockings."

Before I could say anything, he put the phone down, hanging up on me.

I stared down at the phone, not quite sure whether he was pulling my leg or whether my wet dream was actually in a pair of stockings at whatever event they were at together. I shook my head before grabbing a clean black t-shirt and jumper, slipping them over my head before I grabbed my jacket.

The fucker knew that there was no way I'd be staying home alone when he dangled Faith in stockings in front of me.

Chapter Three

Faith

"Is murder always a crime?" I muttered to myself as I looked at the number of children that were waiting outside to sit on Santa's knee.

"Not always," Paul replied from behind me. I heard the bells on his shoes jingle before he stopped behind me. "Depends on who it is, I guess."

I laughed at him before turning around to face him.

"If I didn't love her like a sister, she'd already have an ax in her back."

"Wow!" Emma said from the doorway. "I'm really feeling the love in this room." She rolled her eyes at me before she walked toward us. She stopped to kiss Paul before she turned to face me. "Okay, first . . ." She placed her hands on my shoulders and turned me around to face her. "You are an elf." A cheeky grin appeared on her face. "So, let's try and look happy." She walked past me and tapped Paul on his ass.

"Okay, elf, let's go!" She grabbed her clipboard off the table and pasted a beaming smile on her face.

We all turned to the doorway of Santa's bunker and waited for Santa to join us. As we all waited for our jolly fat man to join us, I looked at Emma, wondering where the hell he was. I looked back to the doorway, relieved when Santa finally decided to join us.

Moments later, he came through the door, fixing his beard into place.

"I'm here! I'm here!" He grinned over at us. "So, these are my naughty elves!"

"Some of the time," Emma muttered. "Paul, Faith; this is Nick. Nick, this is Paul and Faith."

"Hi." I smiled at him and reached forward to shake his hand, stepping back for Paul to do the same. "So, have you ever been a Santa before, Nick."

Nick. You couldn't write this stuff. He was literally our very own St. Nick.

"Only three years." He rolled his eyes toward Emma. "Can't ever escape this one."

"Ah, I see." Paul grinned. "Did she get you to sign your contract in blood or ink?" He put his arm around Emma's shoulders and pulled her into his side.

"I am *not that bad.*" She mock punched him in the arm before she held the clipboard against her chest. "Is it my fault if you can't say no to me?"

I rolled my eyes at the lovesick pair before I clapped my hands together, eager to move this along.

"Okay, then. Let's get this party started. Where do you want us?"

"Okay, so the presents are over here." She led Paul and me across the room, pointing out the ton of chocolate Christmas themed selection boxes that were wrapped. "The red ones with the white bow are girly themed and the blue with the white bow is for the boys." She turned to face us. "I figure you guys can alternate. One of you takes the entrance and lead the little darlings to Santa while the other monitors the exit and hands a present to the parent and child when they leave." She turned to face us, looking too much like a drill sergeant for my liking. "How does that sound?"

"Exciting," we both muttered at the same time before laughing at our timing.

"Okay, then. I figure Faith can take the first hour on child duty and then you can both swap. Oh, I almost forgot. Whoever is on child duty needs to take a picture of the kid and Santa. How does that sound?" She walked away, going back to Santa, not bothering to wait on a response from either of us. She was most likely going to instruct Nick next on what she wanted him to be doing. Besides sitting on his ass talking to the little angels waiting outside.

Just fucking kill me now.

I walked over to the entrance, taking a small peek outside. I reached behind me and smoothed my skirt down, not really wanting to flash Santa or any of the children when I bent down to greet the little ones. I looked across at Paul and chuckled when I saw he was on his phone talking to someone.

He looked across at me, catching me staring at him. He gave me a cheeky wink before I could look away and hung up the phone.

"You might be getting a visitor later." He grinned over at me before he nodded his head from side to side, making the bell on his hat jingle.

I giggled at his actions before I watched Santa fix his hat in the right position.

"Ready?" I asked, kind of cringing at the evening ahead.

"Ready." Santa Nick nodded his head at me, grinning as I pasted a cheery smile on my face and turned with Emma to greet the first child in the line.

"Just try and enjoy yourself," Emma muttered beneath her breath.

"This is going to be hell," I replied back.

As we opened the door and saw just how many children and parents were waiting to meet Santa, I knew without a doubt that this was going to be the last event I would ever be helping her out on. Friend or not.

❋

After taking way too many photos on the camera, the end of the day had finally come and the time where I could remove this stupid outfit when I got home. Every time I moved; it was followed by the sound of jingling bells. It was enough to make me detest the idea of Christmas and never want to see another child again.

OH, SANTA!

"I hate your girlfriend," I muttered to Paul as we watched her wave at Santa Nick. "I mean, I love her, but I hate her too."

"Guys!" She squealed and came skipping back over to us. "That was so much fun." She wrapped an arm around each of us and squeezed us tightly before letting us go. "I knew you wouldn't let me down."

We both looked down at her with a 'are you fucking kidding me' expression on our faces. Like we had a choice in helping.

"Seriously, I owe you." Some people were immune to dirty looks and Emma was obviously one of them.

"I'm going home," I muttered. "I'm tired, my feet hurt, I'm hungry, and I just want my bed."

"So dramatic," she muttered behind me. "We'll see you tomorrow. Paul and I are going to stay and tidy up so we don't have to do it tomorrow."

I couldn't contain the giggle when I saw Paul's face drop in disappointment at her words.

He narrowed his eyes at me in warning, obviously having heard my giggle. A smirk appeared on his face before he nodded his head at the doorway.

"Have fun walking home." He took Emma's hand and pulled her over to where some leaflets were littered on the floor.

I frowned, wondering what he meant before I shook my head and left them to it, too tired to wonder what he meant. I walked outside, cringing when I felt the cold wind blow against me.

Why didn't I bring a damn coat?

I began walking down the path, regretting my decision to come in only my outfit when I saw someone standing at the end of the path.

Great, last thing I needed was some weirdo hanging around outside a children's and parent's event after hours. This is why I should have a car. Less chance of bumping into random strangers.

Before I could look away, the stranger turned around, surprising me when I saw who it was.

"Hey, sugar." Jack grinned at me, staring at my striped legs before making a slow path up my body. He stopped at my chest before he looked up to my face. "You make one sexy elf."

I laughed, feeling embarrassed as a sudden warmth began to travel up my neck to my face. The last thing I needed was to become a bright red beetroot and match the red stripes on the damn leggings as I touched my cheek in response, cowering at the thought. Fuck he was so damn sexy.

What the hell do I say in response to that?!

Chapter Four

Jack

Staring at Faith, I grinned when she ducked her head, hiding her blushing face from me.

Whenever I imagined being with Faith—just me and her—I never imagined she'd be a blusher. I loved it. I couldn't lie. It made me wonder if she blushed all over. I looked down at her chest, wondering how far down I could make that blush travel if she would let me.

"Stop staring at me like that!" she snapped suddenly, surprising the hell out of me before she stormed past me.

"Like what?" I grinned, loving how much sexier she looked when she was having a tantrum. "I'm just saying you make a sexy elf." I looked down at her legs, wondering how far up those stockings went. Were they knee-highs? Thigh-highs? Gulp! I didn't honestly care but I knew they'd look fantastic wrapped around my waist as I pinned her against a wall.

She blushed at my comment before she spoke.

"I'm sorry," she muttered. She wrapped her arms around herself and I knew she was probably a little chilly wearing only that outfit. "I'm just tired. My bitchy side comes out when I'm tired."

"It's cool." I shrugged my arms out of my coat and slipped it over her shoulders.

Her eyes moved down to my chest before a small smile appeared on her face.

"Thank you," she whispered. She slipped her arms into the sleeves, chuckling when they hung down past her hands. "What about you?" she asked. "That jumper doesn't look very warm."

"I'm fine." I shrugged my shoulders, not liking the idea of her worrying about me like that. No one had worried about me like that for a long time and I wasn't really sure how I felt about it. "I'm not very cold." I slipped my hands into my jean pockets, loving the way that her eyes followed the actions.

I was enjoying having her eyes on me. More than I thought I'd like.

We walked the rest of the block in silence. She looked lost in her thoughts and I was eager to know what they were. That surprised me a lot because I never gave a fuck what a woman was thinking about when I was with her. When I was with a girl, it was just sex. Plain and simple. With her, though . . .

With her, I wanted to know what she was thinking.

"Well, this is me." She came to a stop and pointed at her building. "Thank you for walking me home, Jack." She slipped the coat off and held it out to me. "Thank you for lending me your jacket."

I reached out and grabbed it, freezing when our fingers touched. I loved the spark that shot through me at the action and as I looked at her, I let myself believe that she may have felt it as well.

"Fancy a drink one night?" I smiled down at her, not wanting to laugh at how out of place she looked. Not just in the outfit but with that ridiculous hat on her head.

"Jack." She sighed before pulling the hat off her head. She must have unconsciously agreed about the hat. "I don't think we should do that." She shook her head at me and I hated that she looked so miserable when she said that.

"Why not?" I asked. I grasped my jacket tighter in my hand and let my arm drop to my side.

I don't think that I had ever had a woman turn me down before.

"Because." She reached up and tucked a loose strand of hair that had fallen free of her plaits back behind her ear. "I'm not some fuck buddy, Jack."

I wasn't prepared for the shot of anger that travelled through me when I imagined her being someone's fuck buddy. I didn't like it. She wasn't going to be anybody's fuck buddy if I had anything to say about it.

"I know," I agreed.

She nodded at me and I hated that a shadow of hurt traveled across her face. She turned away from me but before she could get too far, I grabbed her wrist, stopping her from getting too far away from me.

"Come out for a drink with me," I said, repeating my words. "One date. One chance. I promise I won't screw it up." I stared into her eyes, trying to be as honest as I could with her.

She was right when she mentioned fuck buddies. That's all I knew. I had never been in a relationship before and had never been committed to anything longer than a couple of weeks with another woman.

I don't know why I was thinking about anything long-term with her. It was likely we'd have nothing in common and would only cause heartbreak for the other but all I knew was that I couldn't continue having a one-handed relationship with the shower fantasy version of her.

I wanted more and I wanted it with her.

She stared back at me for a moment before she slowly nodded her head.

"Okay," she whispered. "One chance." She stepped away before she trailed her fingers across my palm. "It should be interesting." She turned to the door and took a step closer to it.

"Interesting how?" I asked, confused by her choice of words.

"I'm not like those other girls you've dated before, Jack." She raised her hand and gave me a small wave before she disappeared inside.

I turned away, giving myself a mental fist pump before my phone vibrated in my pocket with a text message from Paul.

Won't be home tonight. Staying at Emma's. How did it go with your elf? – P

He was such a nosey fucker. Emma and him made a good pair.

Knowing him he'd probably drop a hint in front of her when the two of them got back to Emma and Faith's apartment and try and embarrass her.

Got myself a date. Don't embarrass her.

I placed my phone back in my pocket and shrugged my jacket on before I walked the rest of the way home in silence. I could feel my phone vibrating with incoming calls but I didn't bother checking it. I had a feeling it'd be a female and after tonight with Faith . . . No way was I going to do anything to fuck it up.

I heard her clearly. One date. One chance.

Entering my building, I ran up the stairs, concerned I'd get busted in the hallway by the nympho in the apartment at the top of the corridor. She made me look like a saint. She was a cougar and I think that she had a different man with her nearly every time that I saw her.

Ducking in through my doorway, I frowned when I saw the answering machine flashing.

"Fucking hell," I muttered, looking down at the flashing number. Nine fucking messages.

I shook my head, pressing the delete button, not in the mood to go through them. It made me an asshole but I didn't care. The only girl I was interested in was Faith and I was determined not to screw it up.

Chapter Five

Faith

"Morning," I muttered as I walked out of my bedroom. I lifted my hand in a wave at Paul sitting at our worktop, still dressed in his t-shirt and pajama bottoms, eating a bowl of cereal. I looked down at my pajamas—strappy top and pink and white spotted bottoms—and took a seat next to him.

"How long have you been up?" I asked him.

"Not long." He shook his head at me before he reached for an empty bowl in the middle of the worktop and poured some crunchy cereal before drowning it in milk. "Here you go." He slid the bowl in front of me before offering me a spoon.

"Thanks." I took it off him and spooned some into my mouth. "I love that you know I need lots of milk in my bowl."

He laughed at my wording before he shrugged his shoulders dismissively.

"Well, we've done this a few times. I should have figured it out by now." He grinned down at me before he spooned some more flakes into his mouth.

"Good morning sunshines!" Emma greeted us as she came out of her bedroom already dressed for the day. She was in what I referred to as her 'business suit dress'. Her hair was curled and she had a full face of makeup on. "You're looking so happy today, Faith," she said in a dry tone. "Morning, sweetie." She bent down and kissed Paul before she ruffled my hair as she walked past me. "Did you have fun last night?"

"Tons," I muttered.

"So." She took the stool next to Paul, leaning her elbow on the worktop and holding her chin. She gave me a sickly-sweet smile before she asked the question she'd probably been dying to ask me since she and Paul came home last night. "I hear that someone has a date."

I glared at Paul, cocking my head at him. "Really?" I muttered.

"What?" He laughed at me, holding his hands up. "I only mentioned it."

"Right." I spooned the last bit of cereal into my mouth before I stood and dropped my bowl and spoon in the sink. "I'm going to take a shower."

"Will we see you at the workshop this evening?" Emma called after me.

"Like I have a choice," I muttered quietly.

"I heard that!" she yelled. "5:00 p.m. We start at half-past."

"Yeah, yeah." I closed my door, cringing at the day ahead of me.

I had a long day of working in the local council's estates office manning the phone and doing boring data entry work before I'd be back in my jingling outfit. I think I must have been a total bitch in my past life because karma really had it in for me.

❋

It was hours later and I was locked in the ladies' toilets at Santa's workshop, fixing the stupid green hat on my head. These next two weeks leading up to Christmas Eve couldn't come fucking fast enough if you asked me.

I jumped in surprise when a loud banging noise came from the door.

"Faith, I need you!" Emma shouted through the door.

OH, SANTA!

"What is it?" I called, unlocking the door and yanking it open. "What is it?"

She looked freaked out and was pacing outside the door.

"What's the matter?" I asked. I pulled her into a hug and rubbed my hand up and down her back, trying to calm her. "What's wrong?"

She pulled back from me.

"My Santa has just put his resignation in."

"What?" I shrieked. "Why?" I looked past her, seeing Paul standing at the doorway. "Do you have another Santa?" I didn't give her a chance to respond. I walked past her, going straight past Paul to find out what the hell was going on.

Nick was standing in the middle of the workshop dressed in normal clothes.

"What's going on?" I asked him.

"I'm sorry, Faith." He slid his coat on before dropping his hands at his side in a defeated gesture. "I have to travel out of town. My mother has taken a nasty fall and I need to go and see her."

"Oh." My shoulders dropped and I knew that there was no way that I could say anything.

I had come in here with the idea of asking him what the hell he was playing at but as I looked at him, I could see that he really didn't have much of an option. It was his mother. Of course, he had to go.

"I'm really sorry, Nick." I stepped forward and hugged him, tapping him on the shoulder before pulling back. "If there's anything that we can do."

"Thank you." He looked past me and I knew that Emma and Paul had joined us in the room. "I'm really sorry to let you down, Emma."

"Don't be silly." She walked toward us and pulled him down into a hug. "You get going and let us know how she's doing, okay?" She pasted a brave smile on her face. "We'll be okay. Honestly." She smiled as Paul stopped at her side before he shook Nick's hand and wrapped his arm around her shoulders.

We waited for Nick to go before I turned to face her.

"This is easy to fix," I muttered. "Just promote Paul to the Santa position and..."

"No," she said, shaking her head and cutting me off. "I chose Paul as an elf because he's so friendly and he loves kids and . . ." she paused to look up at him before she grabbed my hand and pulled me over to the other side of the worktop. "He will kill me if I make him Santa. Plus, with all the hours that he works . . ."

I looked past her, freezing when I saw that he was talking on his phone to someone.

"I think I have an idea," I said.

I walked past her, holding my hand out for the phone in his hand.

"Is that Jack?" I asked.

"Uh . . ." he held the phone out to me before he raised his hands in a 'backing off' gesture and walked over to Emma.

"This is Faith," I said into the speaker. "I have a huge favor to ask of you. How quickly can you be at the workshop?"

Chapter Six

Jack

Standing outside the back door to the workshop, I was waiting to see why the hell I had been summoned to my version of hell. When Faith's sweet voice came on to the line, I was intrigued. She knew how I really wasn't fond of this place so the fact that she wanted me here had my thoughts going in two different directions.

"You're here!" She opened the door and quickly closed it before pressing her elf-dressed body up against it. "I have a humungous favor that I need to ask of you and I need you to say yes."

"Not sure I like the sound of that." I chuckled when she ducked her head to the floor. "Yeah, I'm *really* not going to like this, am I?" I stared at her waiting for a response. "Ask and I'll see," I added, trying to make her comfortable enough to just say whatever she had brought me here to say.

"Okay." She nodded at herself before she looked up at me. "I need you to fill in temporarily as Santa at our workshop."

I stared at her for a moment before a loud laugh escaped me.

She rolled her eyes at me before she crossed her arms and cocked her hip to the side waiting patiently for me to stop laughing.

"I'm sorry." I chuckled again before giving her a serious look. "I'm just trying to think of all the ways I can say no."

"Please!" She clasped her hands together and rested them beneath her chin, begging me to change my mind. "I need you to do this. There's no way that I can let her down."

"The way I see it, if there's no Santa you win." I waved my hand toward her, indicating her outfit. "You get out of elf duty and can go back to your normal routine."

She blew out a breath before she pushed back off the door and walked toward me.

"Jack, I can't let her down." She stopped in front of me and looked up at me, her beautiful eyes shining up at me. "She needs this. I have known Emma for seven years and I have never let her down. I don't want to start now." She reached down for my hand and gently grasped my fingers. "Please . . . Say you'll do it."

I groaned, leaning my head back against my shoulders before looking back down at her.

"I fucking hate kids, Faith," I muttered. "And Christmas. And to be honest, people in general."

She giggled at my ramblings before she entwined our hands together and squeezed gently.

"So, is that a yes then?" she asked, grinning up at me.

I stared down at her, hating the way that she had me wound around her little finger. I usually prided myself on being an unsociable bastard but when she looked up at me like that—like she trusted me—it made me agree to anything that she was asking.

"This is going to cost more than one fucking date."

I said it as a threat but when she gave me a sexy smile and took a step closer to me, all thoughts of threats went out of my head.

She let go of my hand and slid both of her hands up my chest before entwining them around my shoulders. The action brought her upper body closer to mine and as I looked down at her dressed in the most fucking ridiculous Christmas costume ever, all I could think about was peeling those stockings down her legs.

"Well," she whispered. "I was hoping for a lot more than one promised date."

OH, SANTA!

I wrapped my arms around her waist and rested my hands just above her ass.

"And what were you hoping for?" I asked, eager to know what the hell was going on inside that head of hers. If it was half as filthy as the thoughts that were going on inside of mine, then I definitely wanted her to continue talking.

"Well, you know how Santa has a naughty and nice list?" she asked.

I nodded my head, wondering where she was going with that question.

"Well." She leaned up and kissed the corner of my mouth, surprising me a little with her actions. "I can be a very nice elf." She smiled at me before taking a step back, trailing her hands down over my chest. "But I can also be a very naughty elf for Santa."

Fucking minx.

I had been with my fair share of women and none of them had ever made me want to fuck them as badly as I wanted to fuck Faith.

I stepped toward her, loving it when she took a step back. With every step that I took, she backed further up until she was back against the door. I placed my hands on either side of her, grinning down at her. I knew that I was making her nervous but she had me wound so fucking tightly with her flirtatious looks and teasing touches that I was almost ready to burst.

"I'm going to kiss you." I trailed my hand down her side, resting it against her hip. "If you're not going to stop me . . ."

"Kiss me," she whispered. She slid her hand up over my shoulder before she tangled her hand into the back of my hair. "Kiss me now and I might let you unwrap me later."

"Fuck," I muttered before I bent my head and pressed my lips to hers.

She gasped against my lips, parting her own and allowing my tongue entry. She tugged me closer, pulling my body against hers as she collapsed her weight back against the door. She tightened her fingers into my hair before she placed her other hand on my shoulder, crushing our upper bodies closer together.

I trailed my hand down her side and grasped her thigh. Before I could move this more in the direction that I wanted, we were interrupted by a way too fucking cheery voice coming from behind the door I currently had Faith pressed up against.

"Did he say yes?" she yelled through the doorway.

Faith giggled against my lips before she moved her hands down and rested them over my chest. She gave me a gentle push and slowly pushed me backwards.

"You have my full permission to offer yourself in sexual favors, if you need to!" Emma shouted through the door.

"Fucking hell," Faith muttered. She pushed me back a little more and turned around. She squared her shoulders back before she opened the door. "Really?" she asked in a monotone voice.

"Well?" Emma asked.

We both turned to look at Jack and he rolled his eyes before speaking.

"With what Faith has just offered me, how can I say no?" He grinned. "I still hate kids, mind you."

Emma giggled before she reached for Faith's hand and tugged her toward her.

"You are a lifesaver." She leaned her head against Faith's shoulder. "Thank you, Faithy."

Faith wrapped her arm around Emma's shoulder and squeezed.

Chapter Seven

Faith

I looked back over my shoulder at Jack and smiled when I saw that he was watching me and Emma walk away from him. I never expected him to ever agree to it but I was very happy that he did. Using my body to trap him in a corner was my idea but when he stared down at me, I knew that this wasn't completely one-sided.

He stared down at me like he wanted to kiss me but until he pressed me up against the door, I had fooled myself into thinking that we were just flirting. When he kissed me, I don't think I had ever felt that spark before and I wanted more. With his hands on my body, I could see myself being another of his girls and I really didn't care anymore.

"Well . . ." Emma giggled before she continued, "I can see that my sexy elf has been encouraging Santa."

"Emma!" I tapped her on the arm, embarrassed. "This is bad enough without you making comments like that."

"Did you kiss him?" she asked.

I looked over her shoulder, grinning when I saw Jack staring over at us. Paul was standing near him talking but judging by the dirty smirk on his face, I don't think that he was listening.

"You totally kissed him!" She stared at me with a look of shock. "You dirty elf!"

"Shut it." I rolled my eyes at her dramatics. "You've got a bunch of kids waiting to see Santa. Shouldn't you be over there training your new Santa?" I waved my hand toward him before my eyes drifted back over. "Your very sexy and fuckable Santa, I might add."

She huffed at me before she turned around and walked over to him.

I walked over to the back of the room, groaning when I saw my reflection in the mirror. My belt was twisted a little and my hat was cocked to the side. After a quick fix, I looked presentable for the little darlings. Making out with Jack was obviously not good for my fashion choice.

"Okay, guys. Let's get this show on the road." She clapped her hands enthusiastically before she walked toward the door. "Santa, don't let me down!"

I turned to face him and froze when I saw him taking a seat in the big chair. I never thought I'd ever find Santa Claus sexy but watching him sitting there, I suddenly wished I was allowed to sit on his knee.

He turned his head and caught me staring at him. He pulled the beard down while his eyes trailed down over my body.

"Maybe later, elf," he said, giving me a sexy wink before he fixed the beard back into place.

"I am so fucking screwed," I muttered to myself, trying my best to ignore the stares from Paul and Emma. "So fucking screwed."

❄

Jack's first shift as Santa went a lot better than I expected. Considering that he hated children—or so he said—I had expected him to panic or stumble or something. He didn't, though. He just got on with it. He chatted with the kids, asking them if they had been good, what they wanted and if it was super crazy, he'd usually say he'd work on it.

When it came to the last child of the night, I was surprised by the feelings that went through me as I watched him with her. She was so little and had the cutest blonde curls. She was currently telling him about school and how there was this little boy that was always pushing her.

"Maybe he likes you."

She giggled at his words before she exaggeratedly shook her head.

"Maybe he does." He tapped his finger on the end of her nose. "Try talking to him next time you see him. See what happens." He grinned at her before he picked her up and helped her off his lap.

I held the small, wrapped selection box out to her and gave her a little wave before she walked out the door with her daddy. I closed the door after them and smiled over at Emma when I saw her talking to Jack.

She looked so happy right then and I knew that she was just as surprised with Jack tonight as I was. She nodded at him before she walked over to me.

"Thank you, Faith." She squeezed my hand before she placed the keys in my hand. "Lock up when you're done?"

I nodded at her, watching as she grabbed her coat and left with Paul. They looked strange together; mostly because he was dressed as an elf and jingling with every step he took and she looked like she had just stepped off a top runway show.

Turning around, I was surprised that Jack was still here. He was back in his normal clothing and was removing the red coat before folding it and placing it on the chair. His beard was also there but he still had the hat on his head. He walked over to me with his cocky swagger and placed his hands on my hips.

"What are you grinning about?" he asked, looking down at me.

"You." I reached up and took the hat off his head before tossing it behind him onto the chair where the rest of his uniform was. "You did really well tonight."

"Yeah?" He leaned down and gave me a quick kiss on my lips before he pulled back. "Better than you thought?"

"Loads better." I reached up and placed my arms around his shoulders. "So, when are you taking me on this date of ours?"

He looked nervous when I asked him that and I secretly loved that I could make him nervous. He had been with his fair share of women and

I don't think he ever got nervous with them normally. He was a manwhore for a reason.

"Well, as we are both shackled to Christmas duty now," he started. "I was thinking we could go out for a drink or two after work tomorrow?" He stared down at me, waiting for my response.

"We could." I grinned up at him, prolonging the torture a little for him. "I could ask Emma if we could finish an hour early. If you wanted to."

"Think she would mind?" His hands tensed on my hips and I knew that this moving slow with a girl was probably completely different from his usual speed.

"I think she would be fine with it if I asked nicely." I looked into his eyes, loving the way they gazed down into mine. "You saved her ass today so I'm pretty sure she won't mind." I trailed my hand up to his neck, stroking my fingers through the curls at the back of his head. "Maybe we can go dancing as well?"

I giggled when he grinned at me and I knew that he wasn't expecting it.

"I think I can arrange that." His eyes flicked down to my lips before he stepped away. "Can I walk my little elf home?" he asked in a low tone, making the butterflies in my stomach take flight once again.

"Yeah." I nodded my head before grabbing my coat and slipping it on, smiling when he did the same. "I'd like that." I quickly locked the workshop up and took his hand in mine and allowed him to pull me into his side.

Chapter Eight

Jack

"What the hell is taking so long?" I muttered to myself. I looked at my watch, groaning when I saw that Faith had been in that bathroom with Emma for way too fucking long. I looked up when the door opened and Emma walked out, followed by Faith.

Fucking hell.

"Do I look okay?" she asked, smoothing down the skirt of her dress. She was wearing a cream dress that came to her mid-thigh and it had shiny gemstones glittered all over it. Her legs were bare but were looking shiny as fuck and she was standing there in a pair of cream heels.

"Beautiful," I choked out.

She gave me a beaming smile when I said that and I loved that I could make her look at me like that.

"You look really beautiful." I uttered coyly as I slid my hands into my jean pockets, unable to stop staring at her. "Are you ready to go?" I asked.

"Yeah." She nodded her head before taking her coat from Emma.

She quickly slipped it on and grabbed her clutch purse before she walked over toward me and held her hand out for mine. "I'm ready."

"See you later, guys." I gave Emma and Paul a two-fingered salute before I led her out the door and down the block.

"So, where are you taking me?" she asked. She swung our arms from side to side and she looked so relaxed.

"Not far." I looked down at her shoes as we walked further toward our destination. "I'm afraid to take you too far. Especially in those ridiculous heels."

She laughed. "I can probably walk further in these heels than a pair of sneakers," she bragged.

"Uh . . ." I looked down at her disbelievingly. "You think so?" I asked.

"I know so." She giggled at me and she looked so confident in her assessment. "I spend enough of my day in heels at work."

"True." I nodded my head up ahead to indicate where we were going. The Mocka Lounge was just up ahead. It was primarily a cocktail bar but it also had a small dancefloor. I couldn't see her being able to dance in those heels but I guess we'd see.

I led her into the bar and grabbed a table for us. I smiled when she immediately removed her coat and reached for my hand across the table.

"This is nice," she complimented.

It was a little quiet in here tonight, which I was happy about. On the weekend, this place was usually overcrowded but during the week, it made sense that it quieted down. Tables were lit up with a candle on each table and soft jazz music played out from the speakers.

A waitress arrived at our table and we quickly ordered drinks; a pint of cider for me and a strawberry daiquiri for the beautiful lady. They soon came and it was just us again.

"I'm a little surprised that you brought me somewhere so . . ." She paused and it looked like she was searching for the right word. A wicked smile came on her face before she continued. "So romantic, I guess." She played with the stem of her glass and it made me think of her hands someplace else. "I didn't realize that manwhores knew there was such a thing as romance." She was mocking me now.

I rolled my eyes at her before I reached for my pint and took a gulp.

"I can be romantic," I bragged.

She raised her eyebrows at me and I knew that she thought I was trying to pull one over on her. In other words, she thought that I was lying.

"No, really." I shook my head at her before continuing. "I can be romantic. I just . . ." I shrugged my shoulders, not seeing our date go down such a serious path. "I have just never been with anyone that I found it worth the effort to be romantic with."

"Wow. That sounded really romantic." Her words sounded cold but she grinned at me to show that she was joking. "So, am I different, Jack? Am I worth your effort?"

"I've had a crush on you since high school." I grinned at her, secretly loving the way her gaze was on me. "Every time that I saw you, I'd try and build up the courage to ask you out but I . . ." I stopped talking, not really sure how to word it.

"But you what?" she asked. She stroked her fingers across the back of my hand.

"You're beautiful," I whispered. I could tell that my words had confused her by the look of confusion on her face. "You've *always* been beautiful, Faith. Now. Back then. I was just some geeky teenage boy and you were . . ." I blew out a breath. "You were the beautiful girl that I would *never* get a chance with."

"That was so long ago," she muttered. She stared at me for a moment before a short laugh escaped her. "Whenever you would come near me, I would get so nervous." A beautiful blush stained her cheeks and I was desperate to know what had embarrassed her.

"Nervous?" I asked, stupidly repeating her words back to her. "About what?"

What the hell did she have to be nervous about?

"Because . . ." She looked up at me from beneath her eyelashes and the action made her look so damn fucking sexy. "Because I *wanted* you to ask me out."

We both laughed at her admission.

I turned my hand over and gently clasped her hand in mine before I pulled it up to my lips and gently pressed a kiss on the warm skin.

"Well, I guess it's a good thing we are no longer teenagers."

I looked toward the dancefloor behind her, smiling when I saw there were a few groups of people on there dancing. I stood up and held my hand down to her.

"Do you want to dance with me, Faith?" I asked.

She stared up at me for a moment before she slowly nodded her head.

"I'd like that," she whispered. She held her hand up and slipped it into mine before standing and following me to the dancefloor.

I took her body in my hands and began gently swaying us to the slow beat.

"What is it?" I asked.

She was looking up at me funny and I knew that whatever was going to come out of her mouth would be interesting.

"It's nothing," she said, shaking her head.

"Tell me." I gently dig my fingers into her ribs, grinning when a loud laugh escaped her.

"I just wish," she said, "that we could have done this sooner."

Fuck, so did I.

I tilted my head down to hers and pressed my lips to hers. I was starting to become addicted to her kisses.

Chapter Nine

Faith

Walking home with a guy at the end of the date had always been awkward. It's coming to the part of the night where you're thinking about the kiss. Should I kiss him? Do I wait for him to kiss me? Will he ask me out? Did he like me enough to ask me out again?

With Jack though, walking home with his hand in mine, I didn't have any of those questions. Maybe it was because we had known each other since high school but there weren't any of those nagging worries of liking each other enough. Or maybe because technically, we had already had that first kiss. It was comfortable between us. Familiar, I guess.

"I'll walk you up," he said, tightening his hand on mine.

We slowly ascended the staircase with him leading me up.

I didn't want tonight to end. It was so perfect. I don't know what I had expected but I was surprised at him tonight. I had naively expected him to be flirtatious or—I don't know—to just treat me like he probably treated the rest of the women that he had been with but he didn't.

He was open. Easy to talk with. He was funny as well and whenever his hands were on me, I felt beautiful. Sexy, even. I never felt beautiful but when he was touching me, I felt wanted.

"This is me," I said, pulling him to a stop.

He looked at the door behind me before he took a step closer to me. He backed me up against it and I hoped that he didn't want this night to end either. He placed his hands on either side of me, caging me in.

"This is where I leave you then." He stared down into my eyes and I knew from the smirk on his face that he could no doubt see the lust that I had for him in my own eyes.

"Do you want to come in?" I asked. "Emma is staying at yours tonight."

A moment of silence passed between us before he slowly nodded his head and took a step back.

I turned around and took my keys out of my clutch purse. I slid the key into the lock, cringing when my hand shook before I turned it and opened the door. I flicked the lights on and gave him a small smile as he walked past me over the threshold. I tried not to think too hard on what the hell I was doing. It had been a few months since I had been with a man.

I shut the door and froze when I felt him press his body up against my back.

He dipped his head and trailed his lips up the column of my neck before I felt his lips kiss against the arch of my shoulder.

"You taste delicious," he whispered into my ear before I felt him suck my earlobe into his mouth.

"Do you, uh . . . Fuck." I was stammering now but when I felt his tongue peek out and lick up my throat I was done for. "Do you want anything to drink?"

His hands wrapped around my waist before he stepped forward and pressed me harder against the door. He reached up and grasped my breasts and roughly kneaded them, paying particular attention to my nipples that had become peaked and tight against the material that was at the moment in the way of his warm bare skin.

"Does it feel like I want a drink?" he asked. He rocked his hardness into me from behind and I knew that I was so fucking screwed with this man.

If he could make me feel like this fully clothed, I knew that one night with him was nowhere close to ever being enough.

He leaned his hand up and grasped my chin before turning my face to meet his.

"If you don't stop me now, I'm going to take you into your bedroom and worship this body that's been plaguing me for too damn fucking long."

Fuck me. Straight to the point. My body throbbed with need.

"I want you," I whispered.

I gasped when he grabbed me by my upper arms and spun me roughly around to face him before he slammed me back against the door and placed his lips down on mine.

He thrust his tongue into my mouth before I felt him reach down and grasp my thighs. He roughly parted my legs before I felt him lift me up by my hips.

I grabbed hold of his shoulders and wrapped my legs around his hips. I moaned when I felt him rock against me, feeling him so much more in this position. I grabbed the collar of his jacket and pushed it back, smiling against his lips when I felt him shrug his shoulders to pull it off. He threw it to the floor before I felt him grasp the bottom of my jacket against the door.

I quickly did the same with my own jacket, relieved when he grabbed it and tugged it down over my arms. I grabbed it from him and threw it over his shoulder, giggling when he wiggled his eyebrows at me.

"Where's your bedroom?" he asked. "Unless you want me to . . ." He gestured his head to the door before giving me one of his sexy grins.

"First door on the left," I whispered before I bent my head and kissed behind his ear.

He stepped back, wobbling when I tugged on his earlobe with my teeth.

"Ah, shit," he gritted out before I felt him tighten his arm around my waist. He walked straight to my door, stopping at it to reach down and grasp the handle. He huffed after a moment when he couldn't grab it.

"Do you need help finding the knob?" I giggled against his neck, unable to resist from taunting him.

"I got it." Seconds later, he pushed the door open before he marched us through the doorway and stopped at the bottom of the bed. He lowered me down to the floor, chuckling when my heels fell off before my feet could touch the carpet.

I placed my hands on his shoulders and slowly turned us before giving him a gentle shove until he was sitting on the end of my bed. I smiled when he placed his hands on my hips and pulled me closer to him. He parted his legs and pulled me closer until I was standing between his legs.

Looking down at him, I knew that he had been with many women and I knew that there was a chance that I would never measure up to them. They were beautiful, glamorous, and way more experienced than I was sexually. As I looked down at him, loving the way he looked up at me, I knew that right here, right now, they no longer existed for him. He looked at me like I was the only one for him and I loved the way that made me feel.

I reached down and grasped the hem of my dress before I slowly peeled it up my body.

Every inch of skin was now exposed and it felt like his eyes were burning into me and it was a burn that I think I was more than happy to blaze in.

Chapter Ten

Jack

Watching her pull that sinful as fuck dress up her long body was making me hard as hell. This woman had been making me sexually frustrated daily for a while now but as she revealed her body to me—the body that I had been obsessing over in my shower fantasies—I knew that one night of her was never going to be anywhere fucking close to enough.

She had burned me and it was a burn that I knew I was never going to soothe if we weren't together.

She pulled the dress over her head, her hair falling down her back as she tossed it aside on the floor.

I looked down and grasped her hips, loving the sight of her in her lace lingerie. She was lit up in the light from the doorway and it was enough to ruin any fantasy I may have had of her. The real deal was more fucking sexier than anything I could have ever predicted. She was wearing the sexiest fucking white bra and matching boy shorts. It had lace trim around the cups that led to the sexiest fucking cleavage I'd ever seen.

I had always been a thong man but seeing her in these shorts that cupped her ass cheeks. Fuck me, she looked like my own wet dream come to life. I pulled her closer to me and kissed her stomach over her belly button.

"That tickles." She trailed her hand through the top of my hair before resting it at the back.

I grabbed the back of my t-shirt and quickly pulled it up, revealing my upper body to her. I loved the way that her eyes travelled over my chest before moving to the tattoos on my arms.

"Come here," I whispered. I placed my hands on the back of her thighs, the tips of my fingers gently touching the curves of her delectable ass cheeks and pulled her closer.

She quickly took the hint and placed her knee to the side of me, climbing astride me.

"Like that?" she asked. The action brought her cleavage level with my face. She settled her ass down in the gap between my parted legs before placing her hands on either side of my neck. "Don't drop me," she whispered. "I don't want to fall."

I stared up at her, getting the sense that she was talking about something else. Was she trying to tell me that she didn't want to fall? That this was just a one-time thing and that falling wasn't even an option?

"I think I'd like to fall with you," I whispered.

Being honest with a woman was never something that I usually did but I had wanted this woman for far too long. I'm not saying I wanted forever but I was happy to take a little longer than just one night.

"I don't believe in Prince Charming, Jack." She shook her head and it made me want to kick my own fucking ass at how defeated she looked. "I never took you as a forever guy." She brought her face closer to mine. "Don't change for me, okay?" She stared into my eyes, waiting for me.

"Okay," I whispered. I really didn't know how to fucking reply to that. I didn't expect her to fall at my feet but I also didn't expect her to say *that*.

She pressed her lips to mine before pushing me back, making me lose all thought and reason. When she was on top of me like this, my body took complete control.

I grabbed her around the waist and rolled us over before crawling up the bed, chuckling when she clung to me, her arms and legs wrapping around me, bringing her body flush against mine. I collapsed down against her, chuckling when her hands immediately went down to my belt buckle.

"Eager, are we?" I asked.

"Yes." She quickly undoes my belt buckle and pops open the button on my jeans. "Off. Now," she ordered.

"You're sexy when you order me around." I climbed off the bed, kicking my shoes off before standing up and undoing the zip. I groaned when she slipped her fingers beneath the elastic of her underwear and began sliding them down her sexy as silk legs. "Ah, fuck." I quickly grabbed a condom out of my pocket and shoved my jeans down my legs before kicking them off to the side.

She kneeled up on the bed, unclasped her bra and tossed it at me with a wicked smile on her face.

"I never knew you were so dominating in the bedroom." I loved teasing her as that beautiful blush appeared that never failed to disappoint me.

"What can I say? I'm a naughty elf." She reached out and pulled me toward her before collapsing back down on the mattress. I tossed the condom next to us, loving the sight of her beneath me.

"Maybe you and Santa need to have a performance review." I wiggled my eyebrows at her again, loving the laugh that escaped her.

"I think that could be beneficial," she whispered in a sexy tone. "I am sure there's a lot that Santa could teach me about where I'm going wrong." As she said this, she moved her hand down between us and grasped my cock, giving me a few pumps.

"I think my naughty elf is teaching me a few things," I gritted out. I moved my hand down and pushed two fingers into her, fucking loving how wet and warm she felt.

She moaned when I thrust my fingers inside of her, arching her back. This brought my attention to her tits that were begging for my mouth.

I dipped my head and sucked one of her nipples into my mouth, chuckling when she rocked her hips against my hand. Her hand dug into the back of my hair, holding me against her breast, obviously loving my mouth on her.

I could feel her begin to tighten around my fingers, so I quickly pulled them out and leaned back, kneeling in between her legs.

"Where are you going?" She had a sexy pout on her face and I knew that she had well and truly screwed my entire fucking world up. "I was almost..."

"I know." I grabbed the condom next to her head and quickly tore it open before sheathing it over my cock. "I want to be inside of you when you come."

"Do you only have one...?" She looked down at the condom in my hand, obviously disappointed at the idea.

"Only one with me." I pumped my cock a few times before I grasped myself and lined my cock up with her entrance. "One time with you is nowhere near enough, Faith."

She looked up at me surprised.

"Is the manwhore actually committing to something?" she joked.

"I already told you," I whispered before leaning down and kissing her lips. I pushed my cock inside of her heat before pulling back and thrusting back in. "I'd like to fall with you."

I thrust my hips forward, groaning as her muscles tightened around mine.

She moaned at the action before she parted her lips and pulled my mouth down to hers.

"Enough talking," she whispered against my lips before she wrapped her legs around my waist and rocked up against me.

Chapter Eleven

Faith

Lying in bed the next morning, I chuckled when I saw Emma walking past the open bedroom door. We hadn't closed it after our night together and Emma had no tact. Seconds later, she proved it by walking straight into my bedroom and plonking herself down on the bottom of my bed.

The action woke up Jack and I could have smacked her for it. I was enjoying my uninterrupted staring at him.

"What's going on?" he gritted out. His arm tightened around me before he leaned down and kissed the top of my head where I was laying it on his chest.

"Aw, you guys!" She let out a loud squeal before she continued, "You two are so damn cute together."

"Emma!" I snapped. "Don't you have somewhere to be?" I glared at her, waiting for her to get the hint.

She rolled her eyes at me before she got up off the bed.

"Obviously, I'm intruding," she needlessly declared. "I'll see you both at the workshop later," she called before she closed the door.

"Sorry about that." I lay back into the crook of his arm, smiling up at him.

"What are you smiling about?" he asked. He grinned down at me before I felt his hand begin tangling in the strands of my hair.

"You," I admitted. "Just surprised that you're still here." I shrugged my shoulders, not really knowing how to explain my thoughts without them coming across as bitchy.

"Surprised," he muttered, repeating the word. "Because I'm a manwhore." He didn't use his fingers to indicate quotation marks but his voice did.

Did he really not see himself as a manwhore?

"Jack . . ." I started. I held the blanket to my chest, not wanting to start an argument naked but he seemed content to want to have this conversation now. I wrapped the blanket around me and scooted to the edge of the bed.

I froze when I felt the mattress dip and seconds later, Jack came around the bed, wearing only his boxers.

"Don't run away from me yet," he said before he knelt down in front of me, stopping me from escaping. "Why am I getting the impression that last night was just . . .?" He stared at me for a moment before he reached up and tucked a loose strand behind my ear. "Was last night just a one-night stand?"

"I don't know what you want me to say," I whispered. "If I say it was just one night, I'm lying to you and if I say it was more than a one-night stand, I'm kidding myself." I placed my hand on his. "Either way I lose."

He stared up at me and I knew what he must have been thinking. He was probably thinking that I was being such a girl about it.

"Okay." He nodded his head before he spoke again. "Last night was amazing."

He gave me one of those boyish smiles of his that I loved so much.

"It was," I whispered.

"And it's something that I definitely want to do again." He leaned up and kissed me, swallowing my moan as he did. "So, I'll say what I said to you before. Give me one chance. One chance to do this and let's see what happens."

"What about all of those other girls?" I asked.

"They don't mean anything to me," he gritted out. "I want you. Just you." He looked so honest and truthful when he said that.

I wanted so desperately to accept what he was offering me but I was afraid to. I had never had anything long-term or serious with a guy but if he wanted to give this a go, I was willing to try if he was.

"Okay," I whispered. "One chance. No other girls."

"None." He beamed at me, giving me a breath-taking smile before he leaned up and sat next to me on the bed. "One chance," he vowed, repeating my words back to me. "One chance and only one girl." He gave me a sexy wink before he leaned down and kissed my lips before pushing me down on the bed.

❋

The weeks had slowly passed by and it was now Christmas Eve.

Emma and Paul had decided to go and visit her parents so it would just be me and Jack. Neither of us had family that we still spoke to, so we had decided to spend Christmas together.

I was excited about it. Jack had always been unattainable to me; the guy that I thought I could never get and would never have a chance in hell with. Now, he was my person. He had become the one that I was excited to see each day and whenever I had something new to share, he was the one I was excited to tell.

Considering I hadn't been the easiest one in this partnership to be open with him, he hadn't made me regret it. He'd changed his number and our nights together just kept getting more perfect. If you had told me that I could have something like this with Jack, I would have told you that you were crazy.

"Are you ready yet?" he asked, coming in through the open bedroom door. "We're going to be late for the little—"

I looked up, wondering why he had stopped talking. "What's the matter?" I pulled my stripy tights up my leg, giggling at the way that he was gawking at me.

"Fuck," he muttered. He shook his head before he asked his next question. "What happened to your stockings?" he asked.

"What stockings?" I asked.

"That first night I turned up at the workshop," he explained. "Paul said that you were wearing stockings."

I laughed loudly at him when he said that.

"No stockings, I'm sorry." I stood up and pulled the tights up beneath my dress before letting the skirt drop, covering my upper thighs from his gawking. "Would you like to see me in a pair of stockings?" I walked over to him, swaying my hips more to tease him.

"You know I fucking would." He grasped my ass cheeks beneath the skirt and pulled me against him. "I'd also love to peel those fuckers off you."

I giggled at him, knowing exactly how much he would love that.

"I hope we have an amazing Christmas together," I whispered. I reached up and wrapped my arms around his shoulders before leaning forward and pressing my lips to his.

"Merry Christmas, baby," he whispered.

ALSO BY LIZZIE JAMES

Kindred Series

Missing Piece

Perfect Fit

Rough Love

Tangled Series

Tangled Web

Tangled Lies

Tangled Truths: A Tangled/Kindred Crossover

Tangled Pieces

Winter's Rose Duet

Safe With You

Live For Me

Standalones

Gravity Happens

Shared World Novels

Confessions of a Troubled Rebel: A FratHouse Confessions Novel

Devastated by Fire: A Firehouse 13 Novel

Lost in Between Series
(Co-written with C.N. Marie)

The Lies of Gravity

The Sins of Silence

The Ink of Denial

The Christmas Stand In

by

M. B. Feeney

Chapter One

Ever since we'd met at college, myself and my best friend Morgan had a regular Saturday Netflix night. Not only would we watch a movie with a pretty lead boy, but we'd make gin cocktails and get giggly over our lack of a love life. We both worked long hours – me at a family run law firm, her as a realtor.

Having been friends for almost ten years, Morgan eventually found her person in Alec. The two of them were in the process of planning their wedding and had recently managed to buy themselves an apartment, which left me living alone in the studio we'd shared up until then.

"Hey, I finally figured out a solution to your 'Christmas problem'." Morgan announced as she entered my kitchen where I was mixing up our drinks for the evening and slapped a piece of paper face down on the counter.

"What 'Christmas problem'?"

"You know, the fact you have to take a plus one to your company meal and Ronan broke things off with you six months ago." I rolled my eyes.

"Oh, *that* problem."

Ronan had been my college sweetheart from our sophomore year, up until he'd decided he'd needed to 'find himself' and went traveling. Since then, his Instagram feed – which I most certainly did not stalk on a regular basis – had been full of bikini clad beauties on Thai beaches.

"Yes, *that* problem."

"Well, it's not much of one. I can just take you. You get on well with the people I work with, and we always have fun. I'm sure Alec won't mind me borrowing you for the day before Christmas."

"One; yes, he would as we're setting off that day to drive to his parent's place. And two, your firm would never accept it."

Again, she was right. Working for a family run business certainly had its perks, but the downside was their values. All company gatherings were compulsory attendance, and a plus one was always expected. They wanted their staff to be happy and in stable relationships as it shone a positive beacon on the company as a whole. As I was over thirty, my recently single status had caused somewhat of an uproar, both at work and with my mother who had been planning for grandkids since I was about twelve. I loved my job, adored the company, but the slightly old-fashioned aspect got to me at times. For ninety-five percent of the time, I was able to shrug it off; the holidays were tougher to deal with. Especially after the disaster of Ronan.

"Urgh. How am I going to find a date who doesn't have Christmas plans already, and can pretend to stomach me for a day?"

Using an extended finger, Morgan slid the piece of paper over to me with a smile on her face. Confused, I turned it over.

Rent-A-Date
Christmas Packages

SILVER: - $75 (+ a plate)
Two hours at dinner
Matching outfits
Tell a few jokes
GOLD - $150 (+ a plate)
Three hours at dinner
Cute backstory about how we met
Details about what I do for a living
Be extra nice to your parents/hosts

PLATINUM - $350 (+ a plate and a doggie bag)
-All day
- Kiss your mom/female host on the cheek
- Help clean up after dinner
- Tell you I love you in front of everyone
Email for booking: rentahunter@mail.com

"Are you joking? You expect me to pay someone to be my date for Christmas? Not even I'm desperate enough to 'rent a Hunter'."

"Look, bitch." I laughed at her nickname for me, as always. "There's two weeks until the holiday. You're always working, which is great, and as mentioned before, every available guy already has plans. It's your only option." I hated that she was right.

"I'll think about it." I poured out two large glasses of cocktails and handed her one.

"Don't think too long or this Hunter guy will be booked up." She took a sip, wincing at the strong gin and bitterness of the lime juice. "Olivia, I love you like a sister, and I am envious of your statuesque curves, but my God. You need to not be in control so much. Let go of the grip you have on life and have fun."

❄

After three hours of drinking, I was buzzed to hell and Morgan was dancing around my lounge to some godawful girl band I'd never heard of.

"Come on, Liv. You need to let loose. Dance with me." She held her hand out in the hopes I would stand up and dance with her. Shaking my head, I got to my feet, wobbled a little, and went into the kitchen where the remnants of our pizza delivery had been scattered across the counter tops.

I spotted the piece of paper Morgan had brought with her and read it again. What would be the harm in paying someone to be my date for a day? It worked for Emma Roberts in *Holidate*. Admittedly, that was a little different, but potato, potahto. Sticking my head around the doorway, I checked Morgan was still distracted as I grabbed my phone and opened my email app to my personal account. Struggling to see the screen clearly and hoping my autocorrect didn't make me look like an illiterate idiot, I began to type.

|*TO: RENTAHUNTER@MAIL.COM*
|*FROM: LAWYERBARBIE@MAIL.COM*
|*SUBJECT: CHRISTMAS DATE.*
To whom it may concern (I assume your name is Hunter),
I would like to book the Platinum Package with yourself for a company Christmas meal five days before the actual big day – which leaves you free to book some more jobs if needed. No declarations of love are required, but a cute backstory would be appreciated.
I look forward to hearing from you.

I signed my name before I could completely chicken out and slid my phone back onto the worktop, I rejoined Morgan for more drinks and danced with her until the two of us passed out on the couch.

Chapter Two

"Rise and shine you pair of reprobates." Alec's voice was far too loud and cheery as Morgan and I woke with a groan, our bodies stiff from spending the entire night sharing my couch.

"I hate you. The wedding's off," she almost growled at him, making him grin.

"You adore me and can't wait to be my wife." He bent over to kiss her, his face screwing up at the smell of her alcohol morning breath. "Did you ladies have a good night?"

Squinting, I watched as he walked into my kitchen. From the banging, I knew he was cleaning up after us before cooking us some breakfast – the same as he did every Saturday morning. I adored him like a brother, and he looked after Morgan and me as we didn't make the best life choices when it came to alcohol.

"Who's renting a date?" he called out, confusing the hell out of me. I looked at Morgan who looked none the wiser. Alec walked out of the kitchen holding a piece of paper.

"Oh, shit." I jumped out of my seat and, on unsteady legs, ran into the kitchen to grab my phone. "Oh shit, oh shit, oh shit." I muttered to myself as I opened the email app.

|TO: LAWYERBARBIE@MAIL.COM

|*From: rentahunter@mail.com*
|*Subject: RE: Christmas Date.*
Hello,
Yes, my name is indeed Hunter. Great assumption 😉
I have checked my diary, and I am indeed available that day for your company meal and can book you in for the Platinum package.
Please respond to this email to confirm and we can discuss payment.
Yours sincerely, Hunter.

"What did I do?" I sank back onto the couch, internally cursing drunk me for sending the email. I started to swipe across the screen to delete it, but Morgan stopped me.

"Don't you dare delete that email. Reply and confirm."

"Morgan, I love you, but I am *not* paying for a Christmas date. I'll go solo and the partners will just have to put up with it." My voice was far more confident than I felt.

"Why not?" Alec asked, now he was no longer grinning. "No hassle, no commitments, and best of all, you don't need to see the guy again after."

"Not you too!" I whined as Morgan nodded her head before wincing at the movement. I took a perverse pleasure in her pain.

"What could go wrong?" she asked, looking at her fiancé. Easy for her to say, she had someone who wanted to spend time with her, by choice. The lucky bitch.

"Er, oh, I don't know. People could find out and I'd be ridiculed and become a laughingstock at work. I'll forever be known as the woman who had to pay someone to date her." My hands flailed of their own accord, something I only ever did when I was close to having a meltdown.

"Why would anyone find out? This guy's probably an actor so, for the money he's earning, would put on the performance of a lifetime."

"Great. I'm only worth spending time with for $350." I placed my head in my hands, groaning. How did I even manage to get myself into this situation? Oh, that's right, my best friend. Turning my head, I glared at her.

"Honey, you're an amazing person. Anyone would be honored to spend time with you. You're just a little...desperate right now." Morgan wrapped her arms around me. "And besides, who says something won't develop between you and this Hunter guy?"

"Babe, don't get ahead of yourself." Alec chided her. "Look, just book the date and make the most of it."

Morgan handed me my phone, open to Hunter's email.

"If you don't, I will." Knowing she was deadly serious, I looked down at the email and began tapping on the screen.

|TO: RENTAHUNTER@MAIL.COM
|FROM: LAWYERBARBIE@MAIL.COM
|SUBJECT: RE: RE: CHRISTMAS DATE.
Dear Hunter,
Thank you for the prompt response. Please book me in for five days before Christmas, the Platinum package.
Send me payment details asap, and I'll get squared up.
Many thanks
Olivia Bond.

I hit send and leaned my head against the back of the couch.

"So, what now?" I asked no one in particular.

❄

After paying out $350 for a fake date, I waited for another email from Hunter to confirm the booking. Although I was insanely busy at work, I was constantly refreshing my personal email, wondering how I was going to explain losing out on that kind of money on a fake date that never happened.

"So, what are you gonna do if he doesn't hold up his end of the deal?" Morgan asked as I left the office to grab lunch at my favorite deli.

"I have no fucking idea, Morgan, probably blame you." I didn't mean to snap, but she'd been questioning me for almost three days about this Hunter guy and I was already frustrated as hell. "I'm sorry. It's not your fault. I'll raise a claim with PayPal, go to this meal alone, and then hibernate over Christmas."

"Honey, you're a lawyer. You could sue him."

"I'm not chasing after a guy I paid to be a fake date. I need to just forget all about it once I get my money back."

"Fair enough. I'm sorry."

"Morgan, you don't need to apologize, sweetie. I shouldn't have emailed him when I'd had one cocktail too many."

"You do you. I gotta go but keep me up to date." After promising her I would, she ended the call. Immediately, I opened my email.

|TO: LAWYERBARBIE@MAIL.COM
|FROM: RENTAHUNTER@MAIL.COM
|SUBJECT: RE: re: re: CHRISTMAS DATE.
Hi Olivia,
Apologies for the delay in getting back to you. Things have been crazy. I just wanted to let you know I received your payment and have got our 'date' booked in my diary. We need to discuss the 'cute backstory' part of the agreement and I usually prefer to do this in person as it gives clients an idea if they want to go ahead with the date.
I'm not gonna lie, I online stalked you a little and see we're in the same city, so if you're willing, we could meet for coffee and work out the details.
Let me know if this is okay with you. If not, we can always discuss it over the phone.
Yours, Hunter.

The first thing I felt was relief at not being ripped off, the second was nerves. Was I really going to meet up with a strange guy – who could end up being absolutely anyone – to plan out a lie to tell the people I worked with we were dating?

Absolutely.

I replied, sending him my cell phone number so we could arrange a place and a time to meet up. Then, I sent Morgan a text to update her as I waited for my lunch order before going back to the office.

It was strange. I'd stood up to some of the hardest judges and prosecution lawyers you could possibly face in court, but meeting a guy was the thing that sent me into a state of panic. But I knew what I was doing in my job; when it came to meeting guys, I had little to no idea – I hadn't needed to as I was with Ronan for so long.

As I walked into her office, letting my assistant Riley know to hold my calls for at least another hour, my phone buzzed in my hand.

Do you work weekends? If not, do you know the coffee shop on Regan and South? Hunter.

Replying that I did, we set a time to meet, and that was that.

Chapter Three

Fighting yet again with a hangover on a Saturday, I found myself walking from my apartment to the coffee shop Hunter had chosen. I hadn't told him, but it was my local place, and I was glad I didn't have to travel across town for this meeting. I needed coffee and a pastry to soak up the extra strong gin cocktails Morgan and I had put away the previous evening while she had come up with theories about Hunter.

I think, around one a.m., she'd decided he was going to be older than me, slightly overweight, with a bad combover. It had made me laugh at the time, but in the harsh light of day, I really hoped he wasn't. Although, it would be just my luck.

"Hello, my darling. Your regular hangover cure?" the barista called out as I approached the counter.

"Zac, I think you might be the love of my life." I grinned at him as I pulled some money out of my purse to pay for the large, black coffee and an apple danish.

"So, what brings you in so early on a Saturday after cocktail night?"

"I'm actually meeting someone."

Zac's eyes lit up at my words.

"Is he pretty?" he asked, making me chuckle as he looked around the shop.

"I don't know and please keep your voice down." I picked up my order and began to walk away to find a table. Zac followed me under the pretense of clearing tables.

"Wait, what? You don't know? A girl as gorgeous as you needs to have a pretty boy on her arm." He tilted his head to the side, like a cute puppy. "With your Mediterranean coloring, you need someone dark to complement you."

"Nope. It's a... business thing." It wasn't exactly a lie.

"Oh, boring." He finished clearing discarded cups and plates before disappearing back behind the counter. As I sat down, the door opened, and two men walked in. The first was the physical embodiment of Homer Simpson. I ducked my head and hoped he wasn't Hunter. As I scrolled through my Instagram feed, I sensed someone approaching my table.

"Olivia?" A soft, male voice said my name. Taking a deep breath, I locked my phone and looked up. It wasn't Homer. This guy was the complete opposite and for a moment I couldn't quite work out how to form words. "You *are* Olivia, aren't you?" His light grey eyes sparkled from what I could only assume to be amusement at my reaction to him. Maybe this was why he did a face-to-face meeting; did he get a kick out of women's reactions to him?

"Sorry, yes. Yes, I am." My legal training took over and I stood up to shake his hand. I couldn't help but notice that if I was wearing my usual heels, I would tower over Hunter who was the same height as me as I stood opposite him in my converse.

"Cool. Let me just grab a drink and I'll join you. Do you need a refresh?"

"No, I'm good. Thanks."

As he walked away, I couldn't help but openly admire him. He was slender from what I could see under his long jacket and his long hair was tied up in a messy man bun type top knot. Making sure he was busy, I unlocked my phone and sent Morgan a quick text.

Shit! Rent a date is HOT!

As Hunter made his way back over to me, I silenced my phone and shoved it into my purse, ignoring the dramatic thumbs up Zac was shooting me from behind the counter.

As Hunter removed his jacket, I couldn't help but notice the flex of his biceps under his tee which was pulled tight across his chest. Feeling a lump in my throat, I forced my eyes to his face which was angular in all the right ways. His jawline was sharp and covered with unfairly attractive stubble and his lips were ridiculously and pleasantly plump as they pulled into a wide smile. By the time I met his eyes, I knew he'd caught me checking him out, but I refused to be embarrassed about it. This was a business meeting as far as I was concerned, and I needed to assess what I was paying for.

"Hi, I'm Hunter." He introduced himself unnecessarily, making me laugh. It was a good icebreaker and made me feel instantly at ease in his company.

"Hi. So, I really need to know… what's with the whole renting yourself out thing?" It was something that had been on my mind since I'd first seen the flyer.

"It started as a joke with me and my friends back in college. One of them was struggling to find a date, so I said they could hire me for a couple hours. He didn't as he met his now fiancée, but the idea stayed in the back of my mind. I only ever do it when I'm low on cash, and it's usually fun."

"Doesn't it feel a bit… like you're prostituting yourself out?"

"No, because it's all platonic and never evolves into more than a business agreement. I make that clear from day one." He didn't seem offended by my blunt question, thankfully.

"Has anyone ever offered you more money to ignore that rule?" I had to ask. I needed to know what his morals were.

"A couple times, but a firm yet gentle refusal is always my answer. It's supposed to be a bit of fun, and I make some easy money at the same time. All completely innocent." I couldn't help but scrutinize him, wondering where the catch was. He was a great looking guy but was charging people to date him. Something must have shown on my face because he chuckled softly before speaking again. "It's no different than asking a friend to be a plus one. The money and the details mean that nothing untoward will happen."

"I can appreciate that. I deal with contracts and details all day, so I get it." Taking another sip of my drink, I wondered how to word my next question. Eventually, I asked, straight out. "How does your girlfriend cope with it all?"

"I don't have a girlfriend. So, that's not an issue. But if I were to meet someone who had a legitimate issue with what I was doing, I'd have a conversation with her before making the decision whether I stopped or not."

"That's fair."

Out of the corner of my eye, I could see Zac watching us and I tried to ignore him, but it was hard with the way he was bouncing around like an excitable puppy. When I looked back at Hunter, he'd pulled a small notebook out of his jacket pocket.

"So, let's hammer out these details." He grinned at me, his smile wide and lighting up his entire face.

❋

It was the final week of work before the holidays and I had been spending almost all of my time in my office, making sure everything I needed to do was complete before we closed our doors for a few days.

One of the partners stuck his head around the door. "Hey. I forgot to ask. I need your plus one's name for the seating plan for Christmas dinner." His wife was the one who organized all our company meals to perfection.

"Sure, his name is Hunter Drake." At my words, a slight look of shock passed over his face, but he managed to control it quickly. He clearly hadn't expected for me to actually bring someone.

"Oh, okay. I'll pass it along." He left my office. I began to count under my breath; as I reached five, his head reappeared.

"So... Hunter? New boyfriend?"

"It's fairly new." I hedged, not wanting to give myself away.

"New and he's coming to Christmas dinner? That's pretty... quick." I'd expected this question. It was one of the smaller details Hunter and I had planned out during our meeting.

"He's Canadian, and he can't get home for the holidays as his family are overseas visiting his sister who's studying in England. He was at a bit of a loose end, so I thought I'd invite him along." He laughed at my words, gave me the thumbs up, and left my office again. I knew that by the end of the day everyone at the firm would know about Hunter. Our coffee meeting had prepared me for any questions that would be thrown at me, at both of us.

Finally, once it was dark outside, I shut my computer down, and made sure my mail that needed to go out first thing was on Riley's desk. Then, after a quick check I hadn't forgotten anything, I pulled my jacket on and left the office. The cool evening air was a blessed relief from the stuffiness of being inside all day, and I decided to walk home rather than hail a cab. It was only about ten blocks, but the weather was clear.

As I walked, I heard my phone chime in my bag. Pulling it out, I saw a text alert from Hunter. Since our meeting in the coffee shop, we'd texted a few times, just to confirm details and make sure we had our story down. Morgan, naturally read way too much into our having contact before Christmas.

I know it's not part of your package, but how do you feel about matching outfits?

If you have an all black outfit, go ahead.

You treat this as if it's my first time being a fake date

Silly me. See you on the big day.

I slid my phone back in my bag smiling to myself. All I needed to do was to get through this one day, then I could breathe a sigh of relief. I'd already told the partners I was heading home for Christmas and wouldn't be able to spend time with them, so I didn't need to find a fake date for that. As for New Year's, I was spending it with Morgan and Alec at their party, so again. No date needed.

As I let myself into my building, my phone began to ring. This time it was Morgan.

"Hey, what's up?" I asked, waving at the concierge behind the desk.

"What are you wearing on Thursday?" she asked. I couldn't help but roll my eyes. My best friend was determined to make Hunter fall for me, regardless of how many times I told her it was just a business deal.

"Just a black dress."

"Which one? You have about thirty in here."

"In here—wait. Are you in my closet?" Ending the call, I jabbed the call button for the elevator and waited impatiently for it to arrive. Finally, at my floor, I let myself into my apartment, where I found Morgan throwing clothes all over my bed. "What the hell are you doing?"

"Finding you the perfect outfit to knock Hunter's socks off and get him to fall in love with you," she responds as if it's the only answer she could possibly have.

"Honey, I love you. But this needs to stop. This whole thing is a one off. Once Christmas is over, I'll never see him again. And that's how it should be."

Morgan's head is deep in my closet, so I'm not completely sure she's heard me until she withdraws, a shoebox in her hands.

"Look, I know he told you this is just a way of making spare cash, but maybe that's a line. Maybe it's his way of finding someone to settle down with, weeding out women who are only looking for some arm candy to show off; by charging people, he could be analyzing how much they appreciate what he does for them."

"You've thought way too much about this." I glanced at the box in her hand. "No, I'm not wearing those."

"Honey, they're *Manolos*. Why are you hiding them in the back of your closet?" She'd withdrawn one of the black pumps out of the box and was stroking it lovingly.

"Ronan bought me those last Christmas. I wore them to his company's New Year's party, then things between us went to shit. I couldn't bring myself to throw them out, but swore I'd never wear them again."

"T-t-throw them out? Are you insane, woman? These are like the Holy Grail of shoes." She hugged the box to her chest as if she expected me to rip it from her grasp and put it in the trash.

"You can have them if you want. Wear them with pride." Morgan stared at me as if I'd sprouted another head and I couldn't help but laugh. "I'm serious. Keep them."

With a squeal she pulled the second pump from the box and slid both onto her feet. Ever since college we'd shared clothes and shoes – grateful we were the same size and build – so this was nothing new, not really. It was merely the price tag attached to the shoes that changed things.

"I love you, have I told you that recently?" She managed to clamber over the pile of clothing on and around my bed to wrap her arms around me.

"You tell me every Friday evening, under the influence of gin, but it's always appreciated. Enjoy the pumps, I'll find some others to wear."

My phone chimed from my purse that had been abandoned in the lounge on my way to hunt down my best friend. As I unlocked the screen, I couldn't help but smile at the message from Hunter. A photo of himself reflected in a full-length mirror, and dressed all in black with the caption 'will I do?'

"Oh, is that him?" Morgan snatched my phone out of my hand and pinched at the screen to zoom in Hunter's face. His hair was loose, the dark curls framing his face in a way that I couldn't resist staring at.

"Yes, that's him." I tried to get my phone back, but she danced away, still scrutinizing the photo much in the way I had done with the man himself.

"Honey, he's beautiful, and it's not very often I say that about a guy. I can't wait to meet him." I stared at her.

"You're not going to. One-time thing, remember?"

"With a face like that, I suspect you'll see more of him. You're a sucker for a pretty face and he won't be able to resist you when I'm done with you." She gathered my long dark curls into her hand, trying to twist them into an intricate up do while I stared down at the picture of Hunter.

Oh, shit.

Chapter Four

As arranged, Hunter picked me up from home at just after one p.m. Rather than buzz him into the building, I told him I'd be right down through the intercom. I gathered a jacket, my purse, and the bottle of wine I'd bought to take and left my apartment. As I waited for the elevator to arrive, I tugged at my dress, hoping to make it appear longer than it was. Morgan had insisted on this particular one because of the slash of red under the bust that she swore gave me a figure to die for. Also, it matched my favorite Louboutin pumps perfectly.

When I exited my building, Hunter was waiting and if I was honest with myself, he took my breath away. Not that I would ever admit that to Morgan if she asked, or anyone else.

"Hey, you look amazing." His eyes raked my body up and down, lingering on my legs and the shoes for longer than was absolutely necessary. When he finally lifted them to my face, he didn't even bother looking embarrassed.

"Hi. You look pretty good yourself." Copying him, I looked at his dress shoes, tailored pants, fitted black shirt – with the red tie Morgan suggested he wear so we matched – and his hair hanging loose around his shoulders. As I took in the dark brown curls, my fingers itched to run through the locks to see if they were as soft as they looked.

Slowly, I met his eyes, matching his smirk with one of my own. "What?"

"Nothing. Shall we get going?" He opened the passenger door for me before walking around to slide himself in behind the wheel. He'd already told me he would limit himself to one glass of wine with dinner in case either of us needed to make a quick escape, which I appreciated.

"Nervous?" he asked as he pulled out into the light traffic.

"Petrified," I admitted. His light chuckle made me smile. "How do you do this so well and with confidence?"

"I was a drama major at college."

"You know, that explains so much." I couldn't hide the sarcasm in my voice and hoped I wouldn't offend him.

"What's that supposed to mean?" He looked at me, a smile playing at the corner of his mouth.

"Only an actor would be insane enough to charge to be someone's fake date for special occasions."

"Like I said, I get short of cash now and then. It's tough trying to catch a break, so I do what I can to pay my rent and eat."

"Oh, no judgement from me, the paying customer." I laughed as I looked away and out of the window. Soon, the city dissolved into the suburbs as Hunter followed the sat nav to the address I'd given him. The radio played softly in the background, and I could hear him singing under his breath. "You're one of those annoyingly talented people who's good at everything, aren't you?" I couldn't help teasing.

"I wouldn't say annoyingly, but I've worked hard at my craft."

At the soft assertiveness in his voice, I turned in my seat to face him better, tugging at the hem to stop my dress riding up any further than it already had simply by getting in the car.

"Believe me, I know all about hard work. What acting work have you done?" I was genuinely interested in knowing more about him.

"Mostly commercials and I've been in a couple music videos. Still not caught that big break yet though."

"I'm surprised you aren't in Hollywood. Surely it would be better for you there?" Luckily for me he wasn't. Otherwise, I'd be making this journey alone.

"I lived there for about five years and hated every minute. I only go if I need to for an audition or a meeting with my agents. I like it here. It's where I first lived after moving down from Canada."

"Yeah, about that. Where in Canada are you from? We kinda never got round to discussing that."

The rest of our journey was spent listening to Hunter tell me about his hometown in New Brunswick, his family, and how it felt leaving them to chase his dreams. He asked me endless questions about my upbringing and family, telling me about his tattoos, one abstract art piece for each member of his family, until we arrived.

❄

I sat in the car staring at the house belonging to the managing partner seriously debating asking Hunter to turn around and drive me home. I would write off his fee and tell the firm I had a migraine or something. I was just about to turn to him and ask him to take me home when the managing partner himself knocked on my window, making me jump.

"Great, you're here." He pulled open my door to help me out and to my feet. "And this must be Hunter, how lovely to meet you. We've all been so intrigued as this one here hasn't told us *anything* about you." He held out his hand as Hunter joined us. The two of them shook hands as Hunter wrapped an arm around my waist which didn't go unnoticed.

"Lovely to meet you, sir."

"Oh no. No sirs here. Call me Philip." He led the way into the house. Hunter let go of my waist and took hold of my hand instead, giving it a squeeze of what I hoped was reassurance.

"Oh, don't you look beautiful." Irene, Philip's wife, was waiting at the door to greet us and gave me a hug. "And who is this handsome young man?"

"Irene, this is Hunter, my...."

"I'm her relatively new boyfriend. We're still in the categorizing stage." He took over, charming the older woman with a kiss on the cheek as he handed her the bottle of wine and a bunch of mini orange roses I hadn't noticed he was holding. "From both of us, to thank you for inviting us into your beautiful home for the holidays."

"Oh, I like you." Irene giggled before grasping hold of Hunter's hand and pulling the two of us into the lounge where the rest of the guests were mingling. We'd only just been able to rid ourselves of our jackets when Irene began to introduce Hunter to a bunch of people whose names he had no chance of remembering – not that he would need to after the day was over. I grabbed myself a large glass of wine and followed to make sure everything went smoothly as my nerves shot into overdrive.

Hunter never let go of my hand once as he made pleasant conversation with my colleagues – Irene had banned 'shop talk' at any of these get togethers – and held his own despite not knowing anyone in the room, not even me if we were being honest. I was impressed and relieved.

Everyone seemed to want to speak to him, grill him about me and he dealt with it amazingly, only having to defer to me when he was asked something about my working environment I hadn't considered. I had wondered if we would need to escape for a while to go over everything we had discussed over coffee, but Hunter was clearly a pro.

❄

As we were called into the huge dining room at the back of the enormous house, I managed to escape to the bathroom. I grabbed my phone from my jacket pocket on my way through the house to check for messages. There was a bunch from Morgan, so I decided to give her a quick call.

"Oh my God. I've been messaging you for over an hour. I thought Hunter might have kidnapped you. Alec's been trying to stop me from calling the police." I rolled my eyes at her dramatics.

"You do realize this was all your idea? Anyway, I'm fine. He's been the perfect gentleman and is keeping his end of the deal." I spoke quietly in case anyone happened to overhear me.

"That's great. Now, stop talking to me and go get him."

"Morgan, stop. It's not gonna happen."

"Never say never, my love." With those parting words, she hung up on me. Taking a deep breath, I rinsed my hands under some cool water and exited the bathroom. I slid my phone back into the pocket of my jacket and made my way into the dining room. Due to the amount of chatter going on, the only person to look up at me as I sat back on my seat was Hunter. The smile on his face was bright and fond – he really was an excellent actor – as he squeezed my hand before returning to the conversation he was having with Philip.

"Someone's pretty smitten." Riley, my assistant, commented as she passed me a huge bowl of mashed potatoes. When I looked at her face, she used her eyes to indicate Hunter.

"Oh, I don't know about that. Things are still new." I was starting to flounder, and I'd been seated for less than a minute.

"How did the two of you meet, anyway? You never mentioned him before the other week." Her brown eyes were inquisitive as I struggled to remember the agreed upon story we had concocted.

"We met because I clearly can't multitask." Hunter had finished his conversation with Philip and had turned to join in with the one Riley and I were having. "I kinda spilled coffee all over her while I was checking my email on my cell."

If I hadn't known it was a lie, I would have believed every word. His face, when I glanced at it, was open and his voice was clear as he spoke.

"Ouch." Riley commented with a small giggle. She *never* giggled; she was too much of a hard ass. So much so, there was a long running joke in the office that Donna from *Suits* was based upon her. Nothing fazed her, nothing but a pretty Canadian actor it would seem. Maybe once this was all over with, I could set the two of them up. The idea was a good one, but it left a bit of a sour taste in my mouth that I needed to rinse away with a sip of wine.

I passed her the potatoes as Philip stood up to begin carving the enormous turkey Irene had just placed on the table in front of him.

"Happy Christmas everyone," he called out before attacking the bird expertly.

❄

Once our plates were loaded, Philip and Irene insisted everyone around the table expressed a wish for the coming year. It was something they did every year, so I'd been prepared. I just had to wait as I was going to be the last to speak.

As I waited my turn, I couldn't help but notice how close Hunter and I were sitting and how his hand had once again covered mine. Irene kept darting glances at us with a soft smile on her face. Many of the guests were hopeful for positive changes for their families, friends, and home lives. A couple joked about the 'no work chat' ban continuing which made Irene grin.

"And Hunter, what are you hopeful for next year?" she asked when it was his turn.

"Apart from the usual for my family, friends, and myself remaining happy and healthy, I'm hopeful I remain a clumsy oaf. Without that, I wouldn't have met this wonderful woman or be here with amazing company and delicious food." I was sure I heard all the women in the room swoon at his words, myself being one of them as he leaned over and placed a soft kiss on my cheek.

"Things may be new, but you hooked him good," Riley murmured into my ear low enough so I was the only one to hear her as Philip called on me.

"Obviously happiness for my friends and family is at the top of my list, but I'm hoping to retain my good health and continue being given coffee." I winked at Hunter who chuckled low as everyone began to tuck into their food. Despite our first meeting happening over coffee, he didn't know many people in the office refused to speak to me until I'd had my morning double espresso.

As we all ate, the conversation flowed around me as I watched Hunter from the corner of my eye. He'd seamlessly fitted in with these people who didn't know him or about our deal, and I felt a sense of undeserved pride about it. His conversations with the people I'd worked with for a while and who I knew well were lighthearted and he didn't look or sound out of place at all.

Riley continued whispering in my ear about him, but I was able to tune her out as I ate and complimented Irene on yet another wonderful meal and get together. I knew that as soon as I walked into the office after the holidays, she would be accosting me and firing questions at me as if she were the state prosecutor. Maybe I could call in sick...

Chapter Five

"Please, Hunter. Go and sit back down and enjoy the conversation. I can manage." Irene patted his cheek as she took a pile of plates from his hands. He'd been trying to help her clear up for almost twenty minutes, but she'd thwarted his attempts. Every time he'd picked something up, she would glance at me before turning him down and try to get him to sit back down next to me. He was persistent though, and it was all because of the contract we had, regardless of how endearing it made him. I noticed he had tied his long hair up in a messy top knot and the sight of it caused a slight fluttering in my stomach that I would never admit to, ever. His hair when loose was gorgeous, but this look... it was something else with the way it showed off the lines and angles of his face.

"So. You and Hunter, huh?" My favorite associate, Rebekah, sat in Hunter's seat with a full glass of red wine.

"What about us?" I turned my gaze to her face. Her blue eyes sparkled as she waited for me to elaborate. I didn't.

"You're cute together." I managed to keep my eye roll internal.

"Rebekah, I'm too old to be considered 'cute' when paired with a guy." I was in my mid-thirties. There was nothing 'cute' about me anymore.

"Not when the guy looks like that, you're not." She nodded her head. Turning, I saw Hunter and Philip across the room, chatting with some of the paralegals. They were all smiling and laughing, and I noticed Hunter had stuck to his word and held a cup of coffee rather than any alcohol. As if he sensed me watching him, he turned and flashed me a smile and a wink before returning his attention to the men around him.

"You two have it bad," she continued.

"What? No, we don't." I could feel my face heating up. "We barely know one another. It's all very new."

"Sure. But the way you two look at one another... there's more to it than you're letting on." The look on her face was shrewd, but I was spared from answering by Hunter placing his hand on my shoulder. The smile on my face was natural as I looked up at him.

"Didn't you want to be heading back soon?" he asked. I looked at the slim watch on my wrist, shocked at how late it was. I did want to get back home, but I was also loathed to end the day. I'd enjoyed having someone with me who paid me attention, even when speaking with someone else. The way he'd held my hand or rested his arm along the back of my chair and played with my hair had felt so natural.

"Yeah, can I finish this first?" I held up my almost full glass of wine.

"Of course." He leaned over and placed a soft kiss against my cheek.

"So, Hunter. What do you do when you're not spilling coffee on unassuming women in coffee shops?" Rebekah asked him as he slid into an empty chair next to me, laughing.

"Well, when I'm not a full-time bartender or a part-time actor, I like hiking and camping."

"Well, I hope you get this one out into some fresh air, she spends far too much time in her office."

"Maybe I will." He winked at me. "What do you say to a nice hike one weekend?"

"The words 'nice' and 'hike' do not belong together in my vocabulary. "What's wrong with a lazy stroll?"

"Strolling is great too, but hiking is so much better."

"Sounds like you have your work cut out there, Hunter. Good luck. I'll catch you lovebirds later before you leave." Rebekah stood and walked across the room to join her fiancée.

"Lovebirds, huh? I guess we're better at this than we thought." Hunter's voice was low to prevent us from being overheard.

"Well, you're clearly a professional who is very good at his job." I took a sip of wine to hide the way my face wanted to screw up at the mention of this being a job for him. I'd almost forgotten as we'd interacted with my work family. Almost.

"You've made it very easy." I couldn't help but look into his eyes, their hazel color transfixing me.

"Hey... were you wearing contacts the first time we met, because I swear your eyes were grey." I blurted the question out without thinking, making him throw his head back as he full on belly laughed at me. I sipped at my drink, crossing one leg over the other as I waited for him to calm down. I could feel people looking at us, but I didn't care.

"Sorry, I didn't mean to laugh, but I wasn't expecting the question."

"I'm glad I'm able to amuse you." Feeling a smile twitch at the corner of my mouth, I looked down at the glass in my hands. I'd drunk faster than I'd realized, and it was almost empty now, which meant we would be leaving soon. The idea was appealing to me less and less.

"Please accept my apology, but to answer your question, my eyes change color all the time. I never know what color they are until someone points it out."

I didn't know how to respond, so I drained the last of my wine and placed the glass on the table to the side of me.

"I need to run to the bathroom, then we can get going. I'm sure you've got things you need to be getting back to this evening." Uncrossing my legs, I stood up and smoothed my dress against my thighs. When I looked down at Hunter, his eyes were locked onto my legs. With a smirk, I cleared my throat.

"Uh, yeah. Sure. I'll get our jackets while I wait."

❄

Standing hand in hand with Hunter as we said goodbye to Philip and Irene in their grand foyer didn't feel as weird as it should have, and I could be forgiven for forgetting the entire day was a business arrangement as his long fingers threaded themselves through my own.

"It was lovely to meet you both. Thank you again for welcoming me into your beautiful home." Hunter placed a kiss on Irene's cheek and shook Philip's hand.

"You were most welcome. I only hope we get to see you again." Irene smiled at the both of us as she pulled me in for a quick hug after handing Hunter a goody bag of leftovers.

"That would be lovely." Slowly, we began to walk toward the front door. With a final goodbye, we exited the house and made our way to Hunter's car.

As he opened the door to let me in, my phone began to ring in my jacket pocket. Pulling it out, I saw Morgan's name flashing on the screen.

"Hey, how's it all going?" she asked when I answered. Sliding into the passenger seat, I watched through the windshield as Hunter jogged around to get in beside me.

"It's been good. We're actually just leaving to head back into the city."

"Oh wow, that's early."

"It's a long drive, and I'm sure Hunter has other places he needs to be." Out of the corner of my eye, I saw a twitch in his jaw as he started the engine and pulled away, beginning the drive back.

"I'm sure he doesn't. Hey, put me on loudspeaker a minute." Doing as I was told, Morgan's voice soon filled the car. "Hey, Hunter. Have you got any plans this evening?"

"No." There was a hesitancy to his voice.

"Well, let the beautiful woman direct you to my home address and come and join in the impromptu party myself and my fiancé are hosting."

"Wait, you're supposed to be out of town," I cut in.

"Yeah, that kind of got sidetracked. Al's parents decided to go on a cruise for the holiday, and my parents are down visiting my sister, so we're stuck at home getting very drunk." Hunter chuckled at the way Morgan was slurring her words slightly. "So, come and join in the festivities."

"You don't have to," I told him. "You can drop me off and go on your merry way." The words almost stuck in my throat as I realized I didn't want that to happen. "This isn't part of the agreement we have."

"It sounds like fun." He smiled at me, looking away from the road for a moment. "We'll be there in an hour," he called out to Morgan who squealed until I cut her off.

As he drove, I watched him out of the corner of my eye, trying not to be too obvious about it. I already knew he was good looking, but seeing him with his tie off, his shirt collar undone, and his sleeves rolled up as he handled his car with ease and confidence, I could finally admit to myself I was ridiculously attracted to him. Groaning internally, I looked away and out of the window. Trust me to ruin a business arrangement this way.

I wanted to broach the subject of our day, but I was a bit too scared to. Nothing about his demeanor told me it had been an unmitigated disaster, but I guess I wanted to impress him. Hunter was obviously very comfortable in his skin, and I'd had to pay someone to be my date. If that wasn't a complete contrast, I didn't know what was. So, I kept quiet, enjoying the soft music and the masculine scent of a relaxed Hunter sitting next to me.

Chapter Six

Letting the two of us into the apartment, I was assaulted by the sound of loud music and laughter. I led Hunter through into the lounge where Morgan, Alec, and a few of our other friends were sat around drinking and chatting.

"You can relax now, you're off the clock." I told him as I took his jacket off him and hung it with mine on the back of a chair.

"I'll do my best." He grinned at me as Morgan and Alec approached us. My best friend had a sly smile on her face as she pulled me in for a hug,

"You must be Hunter. I've heard a lot about you." I rolled my eyes as she took her time in scrutinizing him. Eventually, Alec took over, introduced himself with a handshake, and rescued Hunter by taking him into the kitchen to get a drink. The moment they were out of sight, Morgan whirled around to face me. "He is gorgeous. And the two of you look great together."

"Morgan, stop. Our date is officially over. Just let the guy relax and have a few drinks." The two men rejoined us, Hunter handing me a large glass of wine. I was touched he'd remembered I preferred white over red, something Morgan noticed too judging by the look in her eye.

"Come on, I'll introduce you to everyone." To escape my best friend, I led him across the room and began to make introductions. Even though we didn't tell the complete truth about how we met, it was nice to not have to keep up a pretense.

As Morgan and I stood in the kitchen pouring ourselves more wine a few hours later, I could see through into the lounge where Hunter was laughing with Alec and his brother. As he spoke, his hands waved around, making me laugh.

"You have a crush on rent boy," she stated.

"Please, don't ever call him that again, especially not where he can hear you," I scolded, my words beginning to slur slightly.

"But you didn't deny it."

"I've known the man for like five minutes. Yeah, he's a nice guy, but that's it."

"Honey, you forget how long I've known you for. You like him, and if the way he looks at you is anything to go by, he likes you back." At her words, my eyes instinctively found Hunter who had his head thrown back in laughter, some of his hair coming loose from his man bun. It was a very different look to the one he'd worn during dinner with my work colleagues. "Oh yeah, you've got it bad. I can't ever remember you looking at Ronan like that." Morgan nudged me with her elbow before leaving me alone.

Alone for the first time in what felt like days, I stood, leaning against the countertop, sipping at a glass of water. Morgan wasn't completely wrong; I *was* attracted to Hunter. Not only was he extremely good looking, but he was a genuinely nice guy. Admittedly, most of the time we'd spent together, he'd been acting, but more than a couple of times, what appeared to be his true personality seemed to shine through the mask he wore.

"Hey, you okay?" The man himself appeared in the kitchen to grab another bottle of beer. Once he opened it, he stood next to me.

"Yeah, I'm good. You?"

"I'm great. It's nice to be able to have a few beers, but I'm guessing I'll be calling an Uber rather than driving home." He chuckled. As he took a long pull on his drink, I couldn't help but watch the way his throat constricted.

"That's Morgan and Alec for you. It's not a party if there isn't a bathtub full of ice and beers. No one leaves sober."

"Sounds like a great night."

"It usually is."

Silence fell over us as I looked down at my feet. I had abandoned my shoes at some point. I loved my heels, but there was nothing better than being barefoot. As I looked up, I caught Hunter's eyes roaming over my face. A fizz of excitement flowed through me as we locked gazes.

"Er... thanks for inviting me tonight. I mean, neither of us had much choice, but thanks anyway." His voice had dropped low, rumbling deep in chest.

"Well, it's the least I could do to thank you for today."

"You kinda already did by paying me." I couldn't help but laugh. "But this, tonight, this is different. I usually drop a date home and then head back to my apartment to hang out with my roommate."

"That sounds... fun. I haven't had a roommate since those two crazy kids out there met."

"I love him like a brother, but sometimes I need my own space. I think that's why I like hiking so much. I can just be on my own, with my own thoughts."

"Sounds nice, but the word 'hike' still makes me feel ill."

"Have you ever been hiking?" he asked, an amused smile on his face.

"I can't say that I have."

"Then you'll have to try it. There are some great, easy trails just outside the city."

"Are you asking me to go hiking with you?" The wine had loosened my tongue and I blurted out the question. I thought I saw a hint of panic flash across his eyes before he locked them onto mine.

"And what if I am?"

"Will there be a charge?" We were flirting, and I was enjoying every moment.

"I'm sure I could waive it, just this once." My heart fluttered as he turned and took a step closer to me. I could feel the heat radiating off him as he placed his hands on the worktop either side of me. "I mean, I don't do that for just anyone I'll have you know."

"Oh, really? I should feel honored." I couldn't help but lick my lip at his proximity, the small movement attracting his gaze. When he looked back up at me, his hazel eyes were darker than they had been earlier.

"Yes, you should."

What was happening here? As much as I was enjoying it, I was confused. I wanted him to kiss me, but I didn't want him to think of it as part of his 'job' as my date for the day.

"I'll consider it then." I smiled at him.

"Please do. I think... I think I want to see you again. But not as a client." His honesty both shocked and thrilled me.

"I'd like that too." My voice dropped to not much more than a whisper as his gaze fell to my lips again before flickering back up to my face.

Fuck it. I gathered his shirt in my fists and pulled him toward me, our lips finally meeting. As I gripped his shirt tightly, Hunter's hands drifted up and down my sides before coming to a rest on my hips. What started out as a light touch soon turned into him clutching me tightly as our kiss deepened and intensified.

The taste of beer and salty snacks was on his tongue; it swept around my mouth, creating a fire deep inside me. I let go of his shirt and lifted my hands until my fingers were entwined in his dark curls. Holding the soft strands tightly, I tried to get us closer.

Hunter's hands moved from my hips, moving up my side until his thumb brushed the underside of my breast, setting my skin on fire through the thin material of my dress. It made me moan out loud which in turn caused Hunter to chuckle deeply against my mouth.

All too soon, he pulled away, his chest heaving and his eyes bright. I could feel my own breath catching in my throat as he caressed the side of my breast with his thumb.

As he opened his mouth to say something, Morgan entered the room, moving around pouring herself a fresh drink, seemingly oblivious to what was happening. Or so I thought until she winked at me before returning to the party.

"As much as I'd like to take this further, someone else's kitchen isn't the ideal spot." Hunter's voice was huskier than I'd heard it all day, and I couldn't help but feel a little smug about being the cause – at least I hoped I was.

"Shall we join them?" I asked, hoping he'd say no.

"Maybe just to say our goodbyes... I'll order us an Uber."

Placing a quick kiss against his plump lips, I practically skipped out of the room to let everyone know we were leaving.

ABOUT THE AUTHOR

M. B. Feeney is an army brat who finally settled in Birmingham, UK with her other half, two kids, and a mini-zoo. She often procrastinates by listening to music of all genres as she tried to get just one more paragraph written on whichever WIP is open at the time. She is also a doodler and a serious chocoholic. Writing has been her one true love ever since she could spell and self publishing is the culmination of all her hard work and ambition.

Her publishing career began with two novellas, and she always has multiple projects under way, in the hopes that her portfolio of what have been described as "everyday love stories for everyday people" will continue to grow. Always having something on the go can often lead to block which eventually gets dissolved by good music and an even better book.

Her main reason for writing is to not only give her readers enjoyment, but also to create a story and characters that stay with readers long after the book is finished, and possibly make someone stop and think "what if..."

To keep up to date with her work and to see exclusive teasers of upcoming works, join her Facebook Group or follow her on Instagram for an insight into her working life, and living with her family and mini zoo.

You can also sign up to her newsletter.

ALSO BY BY M. B. FEENEY

The Rare Breed Series
The Busker and the Barista
The Bassist and the Best Friend
The Senior and the Surfer

Standalones
A Rookie Romance
Girls and Boys
Her Best Friend's Brother
Honour
It Started in Texas
Just Like in the Movies
Looking Back from L.A.
Masquerade
Mile High
Right Click, Love
The Exchange Series
The Neighbour
The One That Got Away
There She Goes
Where There's a Will...
While You Were Asleep

Christmas Wishes

by

Elle M Thomas

CHRISTMAS WISHES SYNOPSIS

They say you never forget your first, and that's certainly the case for Gemma Anderson. Brad Newman was her first crush and first love, not that he ever paid attention to her, or so she thought.

One Christmas at a friend's party, Brad shows her that the attraction is mutual and before Santa makes his way down the chimney, she has given him the ultimate gift, her virginity.

Every Christmas she remembers that magical experience until fate steps in and both of their Christmas Wishes might be about to come true.

Prologue

EIGHT YEARS BEFORE

The sound of Mariah Carey's *All I Want For Christmas* sounded out as I entered Chelsea Morgan's front door with a group of school friends. Her parents were the most liberal of all of ours and had agreed to her throwing a Christmas party in their home. We usually had a school disco, but after a flood it got cancelled, as did the last week of term, although we were all given work to complete at home.

As soon as I entered the main part of the house, my eyes landed on Brad Newman and his best friend Jacob Glaister. They were stood next to a huge Christmas tree that twinkled with hundreds of fairy lights. The smell of pine gave me a sense of comfort and familiarity making me think of my grandma who always insisted on a real tree. Brad was the best looking boy at our school and I had a huge crush on him. We'd known each other all of our lives really, everyone knew everyone where we lived but over the last year or so, my crush had grown to epic proportions. Brad and I were in some of the same classes at school and we'd worked together in paired and group tasks before but I usually ended up making myself look stupid when in his presence. He didn't give me a second glance, not really.

I continued to ponder just how attractive I found him. He was tall, his deep brown hair was bouncy, dark and permanently messy in a good way. His eyes were dark, but blue rather than brown and thoughts of kissing his crooked mouth often filled my dreams. He wasn't exactly muscular, but he looked as though he'd be firm to the touch. I blushed as I imagined touching him, and if the twinkling Christmas lights didn't have the audacity to illuminate him at that very second making him look even more attractive.

Brad looked serious when Jacob whispered something to him and then he looked up and his eyes landed on the group of girls I was with. Momentarily I thought he was looking at me, but he wouldn't be, would he?

It turned out that Brad hadn't been looking at me, I knew this because he had spent most of the night chatting to one of the other girls, chatting, making eyes and occasionally placing an arm around her middle. If jealousy really was green I must have resembled *The Incredible Hulk*, and yet I was powerless to look away as their performance continued, only interrupted by Brad drinking something that made him wince as if in pain.

Making my way into the kitchen to the sound of East 17's *Stay Another Day*, quite possibly the least Christmassy song ever, I found some punch made from cheap booze. Singing along to the song I wondered what it would be like for Brad to stay another day with me, not that he'd ever left me because he wasn't mine. After my fourth or fifth glass of punch, and still wincing at the foul after taste, I decided I had seen enough of Brad, drunk enough alcohol and craved someone who wasn't and would never be mine for long enough. I was going home.

Leaving via the back door, I was startled to hear someone's footsteps following me, and when I ignored them, my name was called. "Gemma, Gem."

At that point, I knew exactly who it was.

"Where are you going?"

"Home," I called behind me, swaying slightly courtesy of the combination of cold air and the alcohol in my system.

"Are you drunk?" Brad had caught up with me and was blocking my path at the side of Chelsea's house that was in darkness.

"No more than you."

He giggled and if that didn't make him look more gorgeous than usual. I giggled too.

"Let me walk you home."

"Why?" It was a genuine question. He hadn't given me the time of day all night, which wasn't unusual, not really, and now he was offering to walk me home. It made no sense.

His response came in the form of pushing me back against the wall and then his face moved closer until his lips were almost touching mine.

"Because I want to walk you home and to kiss you."

I was literally speechless.

He perceived my silence as me having no objections to what he'd suggested and all thoughts of no longer craving him were gone. Then his lips covered mine. We kissed for long, beautiful seconds before he pulled away and grinned down at me. He took my hand in his and led me towards the street, not stopping until we reached his house.

"Do you want to have a party of our own. My parents keep wine in the summerhouse, and it's still early."

I had no objection to that plan if it meant I got to spend more time with Brad. He led me down the path that took us to the back of his house and then we ran to the summerhouse that sat at the bottom of the garden. He stepped on the porch and opened the door before hitting a couple of switches that saw it light up with the fairy lights on the outside and some lamps inside as well as a Christmas tree in the corner.

As he had said, there was wine and we both drank a couple of glasses, albeit straight from the bottle between bouts of kissing and touching each other. Perhaps it was Dutch courage because the kissing and touching quickly led to more kissing, more touching and the shedding of clothes.

Naked and drunk we lay together and savoured every second before we made love, or at least that's what I told myself it was. I had never done anything beyond kissing a boy before and the reality of sex surpassed every idea I'd ever had, or maybe that was just sex with Brad.

That night was the best night of my life and when Brad walked me home, I swear I walked a foot taller. I was happier than I had ever known myself to be and was sure just one look at me would tell the world what had happened. It had been amazing and special, for us both, of that I was certain, however, the following day when Brad couldn't even look me in the eye, never mind speak to me, I realised how wrong I had been.

The previous night, whilst it had meant everything to me had obviously meant nothing to him and like that, Brad Newman, my crush, the boy I had loved from afar and the one I had given my virginity to had broken my heart.

I hated him.

Chapter One

This night was a bad idea, the worst. Agreeing to come to the Christmas party already felt like a mistake and there was only one reason for that, Brad Newman. I still hated him, and it was totally warranted, not to mention, reciprocated. Not only was he my ex . . . was he my ex? Is that how he would have described me? Definitely not, so maybe he wasn't my ex, but I knew the exact title to give him now. My boss.

At school together we'd not really had much to do with each other beyond the occasional paired or group work, a nod in the corridor or a smile across the classroom if someone was being a dick or we had a useless supply teacher. His mum worked at the same department store as my mum and as such we'd ended up at the parties our parents occasionally threw and as the store threw a huge Christmas party for employee's children, we had been forced together even before high school, albeit once a year.

Then after that fateful night, eight years before when he'd shown me I was nothing to him, I had vowed to not think about it. *It* or him. That plan had been going swimmingly, until, after graduating with a business degree and having honed my skills in junior marketing and PR companies, I was appointed as a team leader for a new company that had literally taken the social media world by storm and almost immediately began to expand into every market area you could think of.

Following several interviews and aptitude sessions, I was offered the job and quickly moved to the city to begin my career. I had been newly single and thought this might be the fresh start I needed. Then, I turned up for my first day at work and discovered who my new boss was. He was actually *the boss* and owned the whole company, although had used various personas of a consortium in order to maintain a distance from the business when it had really taken off, only allowing his true identity to be revealed on his terms. I had begrudgingly thought that was quite a savvy thing to do, but never told him that and never would.

Anyway, we were introduced because he's very hands on, in the office every day so liked to meet each new member of staff, and always remembered their name. *He never forgets anyone!* I rolled my eyes when I was told this after I'd been introduced as the new girl, however, that was based on the fact that he had forgotten that I was alive after that night eight years previously. So, presumably he never forgot anyone at work, however, the girl he shagged in his parent's summerhouse, that's who he forgot. Me. Strangely, I thought he was going to forget me for a second time, but he didn't. He acknowledged me, explained we had attended the same school, but left it at that. If I was honest, he had never pretended to have forgotten me as a person, just that we'd had sex. I had avoided him after that night for the few months until I went to college and although our paths crossed via mutual hangouts and people, he never approached me or acknowledged me beyond a nod before scurrying away.

❄

I got out of the taxi, having refused the option of public transport when dressed as I was. Tonight was the final working day of the year and the night of the company Christmas party. It was all expenses paid at a very popular night club that Brad had hired out for the night. There was free booze and food provided so it was unlikely even the most un-Christmassy employee wouldn't be in attendance.

Standing at the roadside, I glanced down at my very short and sexy

Santa's helper outfit that was essentially a green elf costume that clung to me and finished just past my thighs. I had put on red and green stripey tights, and heeled, black ankle boots as it was bloody freezing. For some reason, I had put my long, dark hair into plaited pigtails and added a hair band that had an elf's had, complete with a bell at a jaunty angle.

Making my way indoors, I suddenly felt nervous. What if I'd misunderstood and it wasn't a fancy dress thing? Or worse still that the other staff hated me and had waited the four months I'd been working with them to get the chance to trick me into dressing up like the dickhead I would appear as the only one in fancy dress. Security on the door didn't bat an eyelid at my appearance so I assumed I mustn't stand out like a sore thumb. That was reassuring. I followed their directions and found myself in the midst of a dancefloor of bodies, all of them in fancy dress, a jazzed up instrumental version of a dance track playing, and the aroma of perfume, alcohol and pine coming from the huge Christmas tree that filled one corner wafted around until it assaulted my senses. I noticed the volume of wrapped boxes beneath the tree and liked the attention to detail that made the aesthetic authentic.

One of my closest colleagues and someone I had come to consider to be a friend, Gene, was the first to approach me. Seeing him dressed as Freddie Mercury made me realise that not everyone had gone with Christmas fancy dress. In fact, very few had gone with that particular theme, although we did have a lot of women dressed as Mrs Claus.

"Look at you, gorgeous." Gene pulled me in for hug and a kiss to the cheek. "You look amazing. Loving the hair," he told me giving my pigtails a tug.

"Never mind me, look at you."

"Derek is a huge fan, so I figured I might just get myself a little early Christmas gift tonight, if you get my drift."

I totally got his drift. "Well, spare me the details in the new year, but good luck with your plan."

"I don't need luck, but you, you need all the luck in the world to find a little something under the mistletoe this year."

"Oh, please, I am happy as I am."

Gene looked horrified at my claim. "Poppycock!"

"It's true. You have met your soulmate, the one, and Derek is a hot, sexy chef, if a little mature for me."

"And gay, darling, oh, and all mine."

"Yes he is, and I am happy as I am. I may have mentioned that."

"Hmmm." Gene wasn't convinced. "We'll see, so, for now, let's drink and dance."

❄

The night was going great. The music was pumping, a variety of tunes to get people dancing and Christmas songs, although I expected as the night went on the Christmas classics would become more prominent. Drink was flowing and everyone was having the best time. Brad himself was a no show, and as much as I wanted to deny it, I was disappointed. Not that I had any expectations of him if he did turn up to the party. It's not like we were friends. Beyond professional interactions, we didn't engage. That was fine. It had to be. He seemed to go out of his way not to engage with me. It wasn't that he wasn't friendly or wouldn't share a joke with staff, he would and he did, just not with me, and again, that was fine – or at least that's what I told myself.

"Penny for your thoughts, Gemma?" Gene came to sit alongside me on a bench just off the dancefloor where we watched on as one of the guys from security dressed as a snowman approach one of the reception team who was dressed as a gift and began to undo her bow!

We both laughed, wondering if the tie detail around her very skimpy outfit really did hold her costume together.

Gene nudged me, giving me a reminder that he had asked me a question.

"Nothing, I was miles away." I gazed around the room, and that is when I spotted him. "Shit!"

Gene followed my gaze and laughed. "Now I wouldn't mind finding him coming down my chimney or anywhere he wanted."

"Ha! So much for you planning a tryst with Derek tonight, plus, I think our boss, or as he appears tonight, Santa, is all about the ladies."

"Sad but true!"

"You know if dating was listed on IMDB he would have a top rating with performance after performance and they'd all keep coming back for more, supermodels, actresses, socialites, just really beautiful women and not a single negative review. He'd have accolade after accolade and not shitty ones that nobody takes seriously, but Oscars, Tonys, Emmys, Grammys..." I was getting side-tracked and if I was honest with myself a little jealous.

"You know Grammys are music awards, right?" Gene seemed to ignore my overzealous fixation and rambling.

"He probably has them singing like bloody songbirds too!"

Gene laughed. "You might have a point. He has the world at his feet and he is certainly enjoying it to the max right now. I mean, look at him..."

I struggled to do anything that didn't involve looking at Brad when the opportunity arose, and tonight was no exception, although, if he ever looked in my direction mid-ogle, I quickly dropped my gaze or grabbed my phone and pretended to talk. I had zoned Gene out and only tuned back in when his words caught my attention.

"Plus beautiful Brad has his hands full, literally."

I couldn't take my eyes off the scene before me. Women surrounded Brad, like bees around honey, or a similar, less pleasant analogy. Some of the women were from our company, others were from the club's staff. He held his audience captive, each of them hanging on his every word, or his arm. One had moved so close to him that her boobs were touching him and as he moved his hand to talk, he appeared to cup a breast. Their eyes were fixed on his animated movements as he regaled and charmed them, just as he had done me all those years before. Regret and sadness washed over me. The way he had them eating out of his hand really was something else, all of them thinking they were the one he was focused on when I wasn't sure any of them were.

"And a Pride of Britain award," I seemed to announce to a startled looking Gene. "He'd get one of those too, for charitable acts to the desperate and grateful." I sounded bitchy and bitter now and that clearly didn't escape my friend.

"Gemma, what's going on with you, you and the boss? I can see you fancy him, which is fine, we all do, but is there something else? Am I missing something?"

I considered my next words carefully. I liked Gene and he was my friend, but I didn't know him well enough to tell him who had popped my cherry, the circumstances of it, especially not as our boss was the *who*. Before I could say anything, or precisely avoid saying anything, Gene spoke again.

"Have you got a crush? Again, it's fine, we all do. Was he the school hunk?" He barely took a breath. "Or is it more? He doesn't have the reputation for shagging the workforce and to the best of my knowledge, he never has here, but . . ." He looked awkward.

"More?" I howled, forcing laughter I didn't feel. "Okay, guilty as charged, I have a full-on, big and embarrassing schoolgirl crush, always have." Loud and raucous laughter left me now as I attempted to mask the truth with a half-truth I supposed. The laughter gained the attention of the people around us, including Brad who was now staring, his eyes trained on me as if he was seeing me for the first time, and if I didn't blush like the schoolgirl I'd told Gene I was.

"Looks like you've gained your crush's full attention now."

Gene was right, but at that precise second I was unsure if that was a good thing, a bad thing, or all my Christmas wishes being granted.

Chapter Two

Having become the proverbial rabbit caught in headlights, the headlights being Brad's eyes that held my own, I froze, clueless as to what I should do. I didn't need to do anything because as I watched him striding towards me the decision had been made. I became aware of Gene elbowing me, meaning he hadn't missed our boss's movements either. His muttering in my ear confirmed that.

"Gemma."

He stood before me now, in all of his beauty. If Santa really did look like this we should bring him out more than once a year. My mouth had gone dry, my eyes were out on stalks and apparently I had lost the power of speech.

"I wanted to say hi, you know, because, well, it's been a while." He seemed to be stammering a little but at least he wasn't making small talk.

"Didn't you see me in the meeting this afternoon? You know, the one where I was discussing the actual percentage of sell through following social media exposure."

He grinned and if my heart didn't skip a beat while my stomach flipped as the scent of something fresh and musky assaulted my senses.

"Touché. You look well."

"As an elf?"

He laughed now. "As an elf or anything else."

I actually bloody blushed at his compliment if that's what it was.

A loud cough reminded us both that Gene was still there.

"Hey, Gene, how's Derek?"

"Brad." He smiled in acknowledgement and winked at me.

Arsehole.

"Derek's good thanks. He was hoping to make it tonight, but the restaurant is so busy."

Brad nodded. "Yeah, I know. I've been trying to get a table for the last three months!"

Derek was amazing and his food was to die for so a three-month wait was nothing. I hadn't been to the restaurant, but Gene regularly brought food into the office and shared with me.

"I'll let him know you're struggling to book. I'm sure I can pull a few strings. Maybe we could make a night of it."

I stared, my mouth gaping as I considered that Gene may have just made a pass at our boss while I watched on. I quickly dismissed that idea. If he was looking for a side piece, Brad was unlikely to be it as I believed he was straight and surely you wouldn't take a prospective side piece to your boyfriend's restaurant. Gene howled as he heard how his words may have sounded, either that or at the horrified look on mine or Brad's face.

"Bless you. Both of you," he said with a wave of his hand between us all. "I meant, you, me and Gemma, and maybe Derek can join us if it's a quieter night."

"Ah," Brad and I said in stereo.

Before anyone could say anything, Gene began to wave across the room, not that I could see anyone waving back or even looking in his direction, and then with a token, **gotta go**, he was gone, but not before he gave me another wink.

"Just the two of us, then?"

I was hot and my breathing felt compromised. Brad was too close and like this, in his immediate presence and under his undivided attention, I was sixteen again. Sixteen, awkward and unsure what to do with my crush's attention firmly focused on me. Shit! Brad Newman was still my crush. I thought I was well over him, as he had been over me from the second we'd touched after that party. Bitterness and hurt were rising to the surface now, both things I thought I no longer felt. Apparently, I hadn't so much got over them as suppressed them, and the hatred I always told myself I felt? That was nowhere to be found and begrudgingly, I acknowledged it never had been.

"Looks like it, but I am sure there are dozens if not hundreds of females who'd be only too happy to let you join them."

A tiny frown passed over his face, but all too briefly before it was gone and he laughed. "And why would I want to join them when I made a point of joining you?"

I had nothing.

"Exactly. How are you? I could not believe that the Gemma Anderson that was recruited to my team was you."

"Why? Didn't think I'd amount to much?" I was getting annoyed and whilst I could tell myself it was because Brad was insinuating that I had exceeded his low expectations of me, I knew it was anything but that. I was pissed because he had shagged me and cast me aside when I had considered him to be all my Christmases wrapped up with a bow on top that night.

"Gem, what the fuck is the matter with you?"

My heart sank and then soared hearing him call me Gem, something only he had done.

"I just meant it was a shock, surprise, a good one to discover that the person with the same name as you was in fact, the same person as you."

"Oh." That was all I had.

"And for the record, I never, ever thought you were or would be anything but amazing. You were always going to amount something great in everything you set your mind to."

"Oh," I repeated and flushed a deeper shade of crimson. Not through embarrassment but with pride and pleasure that he held those opinions of me.

"You want to address the real elephant in the room?"

I stared at him, heard his words and then looked around us. Why would there be an elephant?

Brad's laugh made me refocus and reconsider his words.

"Ah, that elephant."

"Yeah."

"Do we need to?" I wasn't sure we did. I wasn't sure I did because what I didn't need to hear was how much of a juvenile and foolish mistake me and my virginity had been to him.

"We do. Come on." He reached for me, and taking my hand, prepared to lead me away.

"Now! You want to discuss this now?"

"Certainly looks that way." He was already pulling me away from the party.

The sound of Mariah Carey's *All I Want For Christmas* sounded around us causing Brad to stop and stare down at me.

"Looks like they're playing our song."

I was agog. Since when did we have a song?

"I remember seeing you at Chelsea's party and this song was playing."

I couldn't believe he'd remembered that detail.

With no more words we were moving again, down a corridor until we found ourselves in a dark hallway and then a storeroom.

Chapter Three

Finding myself in a dimly lit storeroom containing cleaning supplies and spare admin items was not how I had anticipated the evening going.

"Brad, you . . . we, do not need to do this."

"You may not need to. I do." His face contorted and I was unsure if he was angry or hurt. "That night . . ." He ran a hand through his hair and took a step back from me, as if he couldn't bear to be so close to me.

"For fuck's sake, Brad! I got the message loud and clear eight years ago; we went to a party, got a little tipsy on punch that probably contained paint stripper and God knows what else, we kissed and fooled around before ending up in your parent's summerhouse where we had, erm . . ." I wasn't opposed to uttering the word sex, and yet, here I was struggling to string those three letters together. "Sex! And it was so hideous that you could barely look me in the eye never mind speak to me and now that's all out in the open, let's move on. You own the company I work for making you the boss of me and all of my bosses and that's it. We do not ever need to discuss the fact that you popped my cherry and cast me aside, breaking my heart."

I was already regretting saying most of that, possibly all of it, but Brad, he looked completely and utterly horrified. However, I was unsure if his horrification was due to the incident itself or me reminding him of it. I reminded myself that he had been the one who was desperate to rehash this so presumably it was the incident itself.

"It wasn't fucking hideous!" he told me, angrily. "It was the furthest thing from hideous I had ever known."

Before those words had time to resonate, he was rushing me, pressing my body between the wall behind me and his hard body. It was like leaving Chelsea's party all over again. His hands pushed through my hair allowing him to tilt and move my head into the perfect position for his lips that had already found mine. He kissed me like he owned me and it felt like the most natural thing in the world. First kisses were hard, although this wasn't technically our first kiss, however, this should have been a little awkward, maybe more awkward than the first time, but it wasn't. It was anything but. It was as though my lips and his were made to fit together, move together, draw gasps and pleasure from each other because that is exactly what they were doing.

Brad began to move his mouth along my jaw to my ear while his hands began to trace the outline of my body, skimming down my length until his hands came to rest on my hips.

"How could you think it was hideous?" he asked but didn't appear to need a response. "I have never forgotten you, Gem, never."

I wasn't sure this wasn't a line he was spinning me, but I wanted to believe it.

"I have imagined this moment more times than it's probably healthy to admit. The chance to speak to you, to explain."

My arms were already around his back and shoulders but hearing his words and the conviction I perceived to be in them had me pulling him closer, encouraging him to continue, physically if not with his words. He took my cue perfectly, a hand coming to rest on the back of my thigh, lifting my leg that wrapped around his hip, allowing him to step in closer, pressing himself against me as his head lifted allowing his eyes to burn through to my very soul. The feel of his obvious arousal pressing against my core had me moaning a long, deep mewl that caused a grin to spread across his face.

"I never expected you to walk into my office the way you did," he told me as he rocked his hips, moving his length against me, arousing me, my nails beginning to flex into the flesh of his shoulders and back. "I thought we might run into each other, casually in a club or a bar, maybe even the local back home, but we never did. I even considered suggesting a school reunion, but there are very few people I'd want to be reunited with from back then."

"Very few?" I managed to eke out as his hips continued to push his hardness against my softening and wet core that must have been obvious to him by now.

His grin broadened. "You need me to spell it out?"

I nodded. I may not have needed it, but I certainly wanted it.

"O-k-ay," he drawled, his eyes darkening. "You know that Glaister and I have remained friends."

I nodded again. Jacob Glaister was Brad's best friend from school and he too worked for Brad's company in the I.T. department.

"Shit!" I cried as Brad managed to stroke across my clit.

He chuckled and if he didn't make the same move again causing me to hit my head off the wall behind me as it rolled back.

"Oh, yeah, school reunion. So, the only reason for a school reunion would be you. I may have overexaggerated when I said a few because I should have said just one person."

"Me?"

"Yes, fucking, you! Now are we done talking?"

Before I could reply, the head of his erection was pressing against my clit.

"Definitely no more talking."

The feel of my dress being raised was followed by the sound of my stripy elf tights being torn, and then a finger slid beneath my knickers.

"Fuck, you're so wet."

His finger ran through my arousal, his eyes closing as if in ecstasy as his thick digit entered me, quickly followed by a second. I was already so close to finding my release. I couldn't quite believe it. I knew it had been a while since I had been with anyone but all we'd done was kiss, albeit amazing kisses, and Brad had obviously touched me, however, being ready to come all over his fingers within seconds of them moving inside me was crazy.

Reaching down, I fumbled with the waist of his Santa suit trousers and reached inside to find his erection that I immediately began to palm.

It was liberating and further excited me to hear his groans of pleasure and desire at my touch that elicited his excitement.

"Fuck! If you keep doing that, I'm going to come."

I giggled. "Isn't that the plan?"

He joined in with my laughter. "Yeah, not quite so soon for me, though."

I squeezed him harder as my hand moved back and forth along his length.

"You want to play dirty?"

My uncertainty as to what he meant by that question was short-lived when his thumb joined the party and circled my clit.

"Brad, I'm going to come."

"Isn't that the plan?" Because of course that comment was going to come back and bite me.

My whole body began to prepare for release. I tightened around his fingers, my breathing hitched and if I didn't ride his bloody hand.

"Fuck, Gem, come on, baby, come for me."

Losing track of what my hand was doing, I was surprised that as my own climax hit the first stream of Brad's cum streaked across my hand. Cries, pants, screams and breathless mutterings surrounded us as we each realised what had happened. What we'd done.

"I didn't mean for that to happen," Brad began.

Was he kidding me? He had approached me, brought me into a fucking storeroom and although I had been more than willing, he'd fucked me, again, well, fucked me with his hand, but close enough, only to tell me it was a mistake, again. I say again for telling me it was a mistake, but the reality was that last time this had happened he hadn't told me it was a mistake; he'd simply treated me like one.

"Un-fucking-believable, Brad. Fool me once shame on you, fool me twice, more fool me for not doing this last time . . ." With a swift jerk of my knee in the direction of his groin, he doubled over, barely able to breathe never mind speak, and after pulling my skirt down, I strutted to the door, opened it and couldn't help but laugh as I heard George Michael uttering the words to *Last Christmas* talking about having your heart given away — relatable. With those words still ringing in my ears I walked away and vowed never to make this mistake again.

Chapter Four

Waking a few days later in my childhood bedroom felt surreal. It was Christmas Eve and I was home for the holiday season but since being in that storeroom with Brad a couple of nights before, I felt out of sorts. Being back here I felt more out of sorts, almost like the teenage version of myself. I wasn't as emotionally devastated at being such a disappointment to Brad this time round, however, I did feel more stupid the second time. The implications of seeing him around as a kid had been awkward, but it had been temporary as we had both eventually left our parent's homes and moved on with our lives. This time it was going to be harder because I would have to see him every day at work and even if he ignored me I would still be faced with him on a daily basis. I wasn't in a position to up and leave my job, and even if I was, why should I?

The gentle rap at my door stopped my thoughts and as my mum came into sight with a cup of tea, I forgot about Brad, sort of. She sat on the edge of my bed and we chatted about everything and nothing. I didn't think I could ever move back in with my parents on a permanent basis, but I missed this closeness.

She was still chatting about Christmas plans, from her last minute food shopping to wrapping final presents when she sprang one particular plan on me that included me. "The Newmans can't wait to see you later."

"The Newmans? See me? Later?"

She frowned as if my words that were her own repeated made no sense.

"Yes, the Newmans. They're having a party."

"I can't go." The words flew from my mouth a little garbled.

"Why?" My mother knew I had no plans, so her question was reasonable and I had no answer beyond the silence that followed. "That's settled then. It's a shame Brad won't be there, but I'm sure you'll know some other people."

"Brad won't be there?" The reason why I couldn't go that she was unaware of was Brad, and now it appeared that reason wouldn't be there.

"No. Shame for his parents, but he's very successful now and is away for Christmas and New Year."

"Away?"

"Gemma, are you okay? You keep repeating what I say but in a bit of a weird way."

I could hardly tell my mother that I had been bitten by Brad Newman twice and that the second time was days ago and that I didn't know how I was ever going to face him again. I also couldn't tell her that I was hurt by him, twice and that I still liked him. That last bit I wasn't really ready to acknowledge myself, so telling my mum was a step too far.

"Sorry, tired and Brad's my boss now."

"Gosh, of course, and you and he had that teenage crush thing." She smiled a little coyly while I flushed crimson.

"Hardly!" I huffed but it wasn't a convincing sound.

"Gemma, it's a natural part of growing up, a crush."

I needed her to stop because I had crushed on Brad, but if she thought it was mutual she was. My mind wandered and only stopped when I realised that my first and last orgasm had been courtesy of Brad.

"Anyway, Brad is off on some exotic island with one of his girlfriends."

Well if that wasn't like being dowsed in icy cold water. *One of his girlfriends*. I didn't know if that made me feel worse or better. Definitely worse... jealous to be precise. It was for the best that he wouldn't be there I told myself and at the same time I reminded myself that Brad didn't have girlfriends as far as I knew or if any of the office rumours were to be believed. That made it worse. He had taken off somewhere exotic with one of the many willing casual flings he was known for. I ignored my own correction that he wasn't known to publicly shag around either, but then this little jolly he'd embarked on wasn't public, was it? It had come from his parents to mine.

"Breakfast will be ready in ten minutes, so, get your lazy bones out of bed," my mum said before bouncing up and landing a kiss to the top of my head and heading for the door allowing the sound of *It's the Most Wonderful Time of the Year*.

Some divine entity really did have a warped sense of humour with the current soundtrack my life was being subjected to.

❄

Arriving at the Newman's house was strange, familiar and welcoming, but also a little daunting. They were lovely people and during any interactions had always treated me kindly with something akin to fondness, but I couldn't forget that the summerhouse at the end of their back garden had been the scene of my lost virginity.

Mr and Mrs Newman greeted me with genuine affection and congratulated me on my recent recruitment to Brad's company. They told me how proud they were of him and Mr Newman joked about their son not being too awful a boss. I found myself telling them he was a wonderful boss because it was the truth. They ushered me towards the expanse of food and drink that was available and as I grabbed a glass of something sparkly and a sausage roll, I felt someone stop next to me. Glaister, Brad's friend and my colleague.

"Jacob, hi."
"Hey, Gemma. You okay?"
"Yeah, you?"
"Yeah. It's weird being back here as adults, isn't it?"

I laughed and nodded. "And yet Brad escaped it even if we're standing in his parent's home."

Jacob rolled his eyes. "Jammy git!"

We chatted for a while, about old times, work, life in general but when a few people Jacob knew from school came over, I exited.

I wandered around a little, pausing to stand with my parents as they chatted with friends, allowing them to boast about my degree of which they were incredibly proud. With an excuse of recognising someone on the other side of the room, I moved on and mingled fleetingly as I took in the room. It was beautiful, the whole house was, but where I stood was essentially Christmas in one room.

In the far corner from where I stood was the Christmas tree, looking as though it had been transported from the front of a Christmas card. It was perfect with symmetrical branches and baubles, clear lights evenly distributed, flickering and flashing as if in tune with the music that played. The music wasn't like a disco or a nightclub DJ but a string quartet that stood to my side near the French windows that led to the garden. I remembered that Mr Newman had been a member of a local orchestra as well as teaching stringed instruments so presumably they were contacts of his. They were playing a combination of modern and what my dad would call timeless classics. I wouldn't have thought a string quartet was my thing, but I liked it. It was sophisticated and provided background noise, ambience rather than in your face, won't be ignored, blaring from speakers style music. As I prepared to go outside, I saw a few couples including my parents and the Newmans taking to the middle of the room to dance, holding each other as they moved across the floor.

Once on the terrace that overlooked the garden, I felt nostalgic, even more so when I saw the summerhouse illuminated at the bottom of the garden. With a glass of wine in my hand, I made my way down the garden, cursing my heels as they sunk into the grass. Bending, I pulled my shoes off and carried them, not wanting to damage Mr Newman's well-tended lawn.

The grin on my face proved unmoveable as I got closer to the summerhouse, the memories it held were bittersweet, but right now, I couldn't regret them. As I'd got ready to come here tonight, I had given myself a talking to. Brad and I had been sixteen that night and he had been my first. We were young and I had been lucky enough to have my first time with someone I knew and trusted, someone who had been my crush for years. I had heard so many friends over the years talk about the horror, awkwardness and dissatisfying experiences of their first time and I had never been able to relate. My first time had been sweet and almost romantic. It had hurt physically at the time, but Brad had taken such care of me, and it had brought the most intense pleasure, pleasure I had never experienced before. I pushed aside the voice telling me that the pleasure I had known since then had only been surpassed a few nights before in a storeroom.

Stopping, I looked around from my position on the deck. This place looked identical to that night, right down to the flickering fairy lights that sat around the edge of the roof and twirled around the long posts on each side of the entrance to the porch. Through the windows I could see lanterns and lamps shimmering subdued lighting, shadows and shapes being cast around the interior where a long sofa sat loaded with throws and cushions. I was sure that couldn't be the same one as the last time, first time I was here, but if it wasn't, it looked almost identical. Then there was the Christmas tree in the corner.

"Déjà vu."

Standing at the door, I decided that a little trip inside, just for old time's sake couldn't hurt. In fact, maybe this is what I needed to do to put the whole Brad Newman thing to bed, so to speak, once and for all. I needed to grow up and get over my crush. Even after our little tryst at the office party and Brad's behaviour, which incidentally had still been dickheadish in my opinion, I needed to accept that sex with us was great for me, but possibly not as good for him or he wouldn't have regretted it, twice.

I turned the door handle and the sense of familiarity and nostalgia almost overwhelmed me, and then my senses were hit with something else, something fresh and musky. I didn't need to look around or wait for him to speak, I knew he was there.

Chapter Five

"Gem." Just the sound of his voice calling me that did weird and sexy, clenching things to me.

I closed the door. So much for growing up and getting over my crush. I knew I was likely to end up sprawled out beneath Brad calling to deities minus underwear before I left here.

"Why are you here?" Turning, I was greeted by the sight of him standing in the far corner, bathed in light, looking delectable.

"It's my parent's home and their Christmas party," he replied dryly.

"And you're supposed to be on an island somewhere with your latest fuck buddy!" I spat the last two words out venomously and he smirked.

"Jealous?"

"Hardly." I was. Very.

"Will you sit down, so we can talk?"

I dropped into the far corner of the sofa like a petulant teenager with my arms crossed tightly across my chest. "Talk. Just talk."

"Whatever you want, Gem."

This would have been so much easier if he stopped calling me Gem. Nobody called me Gem. I really liked that it was something unique to him.

"You look amazing." His eyes were full of desire as he took in my appearance in a fairly typical and predictable little black dress with a sequined body that came just past my thighs and sheer, ballooned sleeves. As I had only planned on walking from the house to the taxi and then to the Newman's front door, I had opted for bare legs. My feet were bare too as my shoes were currently next to the door where I'd dropped them.

With a roll of my eyes, I pushed aside my annoyance at myself for being so pleased to see the heat in Brad's gaze. "Talk then!" I snapped, attempting to repel my attraction to him.

"The other night—"

I cut him off. "When you used me and then dropped me, is that when you're referring to?"

He looked annoyed. The tightly knitted frown marring his brow and the way he tapped his fingers against his knee were tells that he wasn't happy with my words. "I was more thinking when you overreacted, refused to listen, jumped to conclusions and all but rendered me incapable of walking. That is when I am referring to!"

Yes, he was angry and it was rolling off him in waves, and damn if pissed off Brad wasn't turning me on as much as smooth, charming Brad did.

"So, you're telling me you didn't use me then drop me?"

"Correct." He sounded sincere and when I risked another glance at his face, he looked it too.

"You can't really blame me. You have form."

"What the fuck does that mean?"

"Here, in this very location, the scene of the crime was the first time you used me and dropped me."

"Not true!"

"So, you didn't use me and drop me either time we, you know?"

"I didn't."

I stared at him in total disbelief. Did he have amnesia or selective memory or was he just a complete and utter dick who was trying to manipulate me into thinking this was all in my head and somehow I was in the wrong here?

"The other night when I said I hadn't meant it to happen. I hadn't, but not because I didn't want it to."

I watched as his hands moved to cup his groin in a protective manner. My lips quirked into a small smile.

"If you'd let me continue, you'd have heard me explain that I'd wanted to talk to you, and apologise for sixteen-year-old me, for how I behaved after we'd had sex. Then to explain that I'd wanted a conversation, not to end up with us both coming in a cupboard, but to talk and to ask you out on a date."

"A date?"

"Yes. A date. Dinner, drinks, talking, laughing, maybe some dancing and hopefully a kiss goodnight. However, as soon as I got you alone, all I could think about was kissing and touching you. Why do you think I've kept my distance all these months that you've been in my offices?"

"I thought you regretted me, what happened here." I twirled a finger above my head to indicate this place.

"No, but I get why you might have got that feeling. It was the opposite of that for me. I was overwhelmed by how it was between us, how it made me feel. How you made me feel."

I wasn't sure whether I was going to laugh or cry. He'd felt it, like I had. It had been special and something momentous.

"You were my first and I didn't know if that was normal, or even a good thing. It scared the shit out of me. Obviously, the boys at school, we'd talked. The ones who'd already had sex described how it felt and then there was us."

"Us?" I hadn't been sure I was his first because he seemed to know what he was doing in a way I didn't.

"Yes. It wasn't how they said it would be . . . I mean physically it was kind of how they said, but none of them had spoken about the feelings during and afterwards. You knocked me on my arse, Gem."

"I'm not entirely sure I ever got back up, Brad."

He nodded. "Relatable."

I laughed.

"It wasn't a joke. Seriously, that night changed me. I wanted to see you the next day and talk about it, make you my girlfriend." He smirked. "I sound like a pussy, don't I?"

I shrugged. "Maybe, maybe not." I offered him a smile. "So why didn't you?"

"When I saw you the next day, I thought I was dying; my heart raced, I was sweating until I was clammy and my chest tightened. I couldn't do it to myself because if I felt like that after one night, one time, what the fuck would it feel like to do it again?"

"That doesn't entirely make sense."

"I know, but it did at the time. It took me years to figure it out, to experience life."

"You mean sex when you say life?"

"I suppose, but not just that. However, sex was never like it had been with you. I could never replicate it and I tried."

I wasn't sure how I should feel at that revelation and was conflicted with jealousy that he had tried to replace me with a string of women and pleasure that he had never managed to.

"Well, not until that storeroom the other night, and we didn't actually have sex."

"Everything you said about that night in here . . . it was the same for me. I was as overwhelmed as you . I had no idea anything could feel that way, that good or intense. You took my breath away."

"I'm sorry," he said and I could feel the panic rising that even with his heartfelt confession he was about to bail again.

"You're sorry?"

"Yeah, I didn't want to take your breath away. I should have stayed."

"Why?" I didn't care if I sounded needy or pathetic now. I needed to hear what he had to say.

"To make you breathe deeper than you'd ever breathed before."

I wasn't even sure what he meant by that, not really, but at the same time I did. He wanted me to breathe like never before, for those breaths to spur me on to greater things, to spur us both on to experience more of those feelings neither of us had ever felt before or since. Those were the most romantic words I had ever heard never mind been on the receiving end of. Sniffing back tears and a tsunami of emotions, I found myself up on my knees and crawling towards him.

"Brad." I never got another word out before he reached for me, pulling my face to his where he kissed me.

❄

Time ceased to exist as did the world beyond the four wooden walls that surrounded us. There was simply *us*. Nothing and nobody else. We were an entanglement of limbs and sensation as clothes were lost and skin found the heat and comfort of skin to press against. I was incoherent, just sounds, gasps, murmurs and moans as my whole being came to life. This wasn't just a physical act. My mind and emotions were all in attendance at this celestial happening.

"Fuck, Gem." Brad moaned as he released my mouth that was sore and probably swollen courtesy of the kisses it had been subjected to. A glorious and sweet subjugation and one I might never recover from.

I had committed my last time in this place with Brad to memory. Every detail was etched on my brain and carved into my heart, but when it ended it had left a sweet ache. Brad being my first wasn't something I ever regretted no matter how much it hurt afterwards. At the office party, in that storeroom, I had gotten a snippet of Brad with eight years' experience, and whilst I didn't want to dwell on who or how he had developed his skills, right now, I was reaping the rewards of it.

His kisses traced lower, settling in my breasts, one nipple being teased and pinched between a finger and thumb, while the other had been captured in the wet heat of his mouth. My back was arching off the sofa but that only served to arouse me further since Brad was positioned between my open legs so that every time I arched, my sex was literally rubbing against his hard length. With my fingers lacing and knotting in his hair and gasps of desperation echoing around me, I was desperate for more.

"Brad, please."

His eyes shot up until his gaze held mine and then a small smile moved across his lips as they continued to hold and suck my nipple and I was sure he was going to ignore my plea.

My nipple was released with a loud pop. "What do you want, baby?"

"You, inside me, now."

To my relief, he covered my body, his lips delivering a series a gentle, delicate kisses along my jaw before moving to my lips. As his arousal found the heat and moisture of my sex that was already softening further in preparation for him, he withdrew his lips so he could gaze down at me, his eyes holding mine. Gently, he nudged his way in to begin with and then with a little more force pushed his length inside until we were joined. My whole body reacted to the sweet invasion, but my internal muscles that squeezed and tightened around him were going into overdrive.

"Shit! I think you may have grown since last time we did this." I hadn't planned on saying those words to flatter him or stroke his ego, it was the truth.

Brad's reaction was to laugh. "Thanks. I should say that whenever I imagined doing this again, I hoped it might last longer than the first time, but if you keep doing that squeezing and pulsing thing, I fear it won't."

"You imagined us having sex again?"

"Oh, yes, many, many times and in case you were wondering, my imagination didn't do it justice."

I was momentarily stunned.

"You okay if I move now?"

"Yes."

Slowly, and with what felt like precision, Brad's movements began. Every thrust and stroke was timed to perfection, stimulating and pushing me ever closer to the pleasure I craved and dreaded at the same time. I needed this. I needed Brad like I needed my next breath but I was scared that he might run again once this was done. His speed increased, driving us both closer to the edge of release. With his arms stretched straight at either side of my head, his face was above mine, his eyes fixed on mine, watching my pleasure build. Instinctively, as I felt my tummy tighten and coil in preparation, my hips began to work with his and my hands stroked up his arms until they clung to his biceps.

"Brad."

"Gem, come with me, baby."

I had no choice in coming, but it did coincide with Brad finding his own release.

Chapter Six

Straightening the skirt of my dress, I risked a glance in Brad's direction. We had lay together on the sofa, spooning and basking in the afterglow of the mind-blowing sex we'd shared. This experience had blown the first time out of the water and I knew it was something I would never forget, although, if Brad dumped me on my ass again, I might wish I could.

Brad was fastening his boot as I risked another glance in his direction.

This time, his eyes met mine. "Gem."

Shit! He was going to do it to me again. When would I learn? I was about to make it three for three. Tears were already burning and I didn't know that I'd be strong enough to stop them from falling.

"Gem," he repeated, cupping my shoulder to spin me to face him. "Hey, what's wrong?"

The first of my tears had already escaped and was rolling down my cheek. I shook my head, unable to put my fears into words.

"No!" Brad cried, brushing my tears away. "I was going to say, tomorrow, we should have breakfast together."

"Really?" I managed to squeak out.

"Yes, really. I know I got it wrong before and I get why you thought I was doing the same at the party, but I wasn't and I am definitely not casting you aside now. It's taken me too long to get a second chance so I'll be damned if I am going to blow it. Ever since that first time, you've been my only Christmas wish."

"Really?"

"Really."

I could feel another wave of emotion and possibly fresh tears coming over me. "Every Christmas party I've been to since made me think of you."

My admission made him smile. "So, breakfast?"

"Yes." The grin threatened to split my face.

"Good. And the day after that, and the next one and every one thereafter."

I laughed, assuming Brad was being dramatic, romantic even.

He stared down at me. "Never been more serious."

"Yes," I whispered, tempted to pinch myself to prove this was real because this was better than any fantasy I had ever dreamed.

"Sorted." Brad leaned down and landed a single, delicate kiss to my lips. "Let's go."

With my hand safely tucked in his, we headed for the door and once it opened we could hear the muffled sounds of music coming from the house. The closer we got, the clearer the music became, the string quartet having been replaced by the original versions from a laptop. When Brad opened the door we were greeted with the words about not wanting a lot for Christmas – Mariah Carey *All I want For Christmas.*

"Our song."

Hearing him call it that would never get old.

"Fate," said Brad causing my heart to lurch once more before grabbing my hand and leading me into the middle of the dancefloor.

We laughed and kissed as he twirled me around, both of us singing along until the music got cut off abruptly. The sound of chimes signalled it was midnight. Christmas. Taking me in his arms again, Brad pulled me in close and kissed me. Like properly kissed me, surprising the people around us before a series of calls and hollers were heard, the latter coming from Jacob who followed it up with muttering of *about bloody time.* When we broke our kiss, I noticed my parents looking on and smiling with Brad's parents just behind them, none of them looking surprised to find Brad in attendance or us together. It seemed we had the parental seal of approval as well as Jacob's. My eyes quickly returned to Brad who wore a slightly crooked and very sexy smile.

Mariah Carey was suddenly back and playing from the beginning.

"It's taken eight years, Mariah," Brad began looking up as he addressed the woman singing. "But I finally got all I wanted for Christmas."

Brad was back to saying things that made me get all sappy and soppy.

"Me?" I asked, probably sounding as sappy as him and also a little needy.

"You," he confirmed before *I Wish It Could Be Christmas Everyday* interrupted. "I think it might be from now on," he said and then made a vomiting gesture that made me laugh before I reached up, pulled his face to mine and prepared to kiss him again.

"Merry Christmas, Brad."

"Merry Christmas, Gem."

FOLLOW ELLE

Twitter | Facebook |
Reader Group | Instagram |
Amazon | Goodreads

ALSO BY ELLE M THOMAS

Standalones

Disaster in Waiting

Revealing His Prize

Falling Series

New Beginnings

Still Falling

Old Endings

Love in Vegas Series

Lucky Seven

Pushing His Luck

Lucking Out

Valentine's Vows

Winter Wishes

Revelation Series

Days of Discovery

Events of Endeavour

The Carrington Siblings

One Night or Forever

Family Affair

The Illusive Lovers Series

Swipe Right For a Knight

The Nanny Chronicles
Single Dad
Pinky Promise

Christmases Lost

by

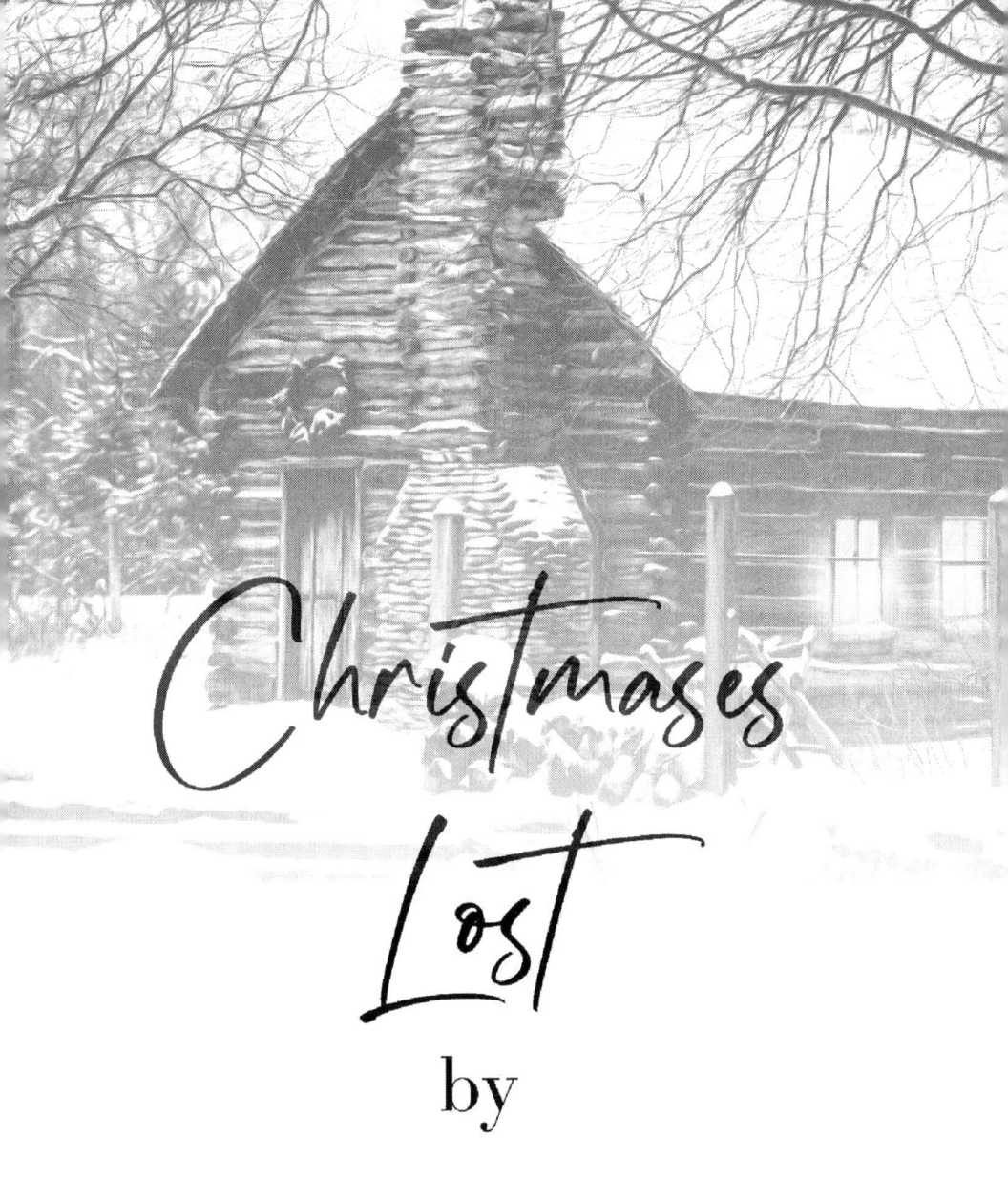

Lynda Throsby

A Short Story

"Taxi!"

Oh, crap. That's the seventh taxi that's ignored me. Checking the time on my phone for the millionth time, I realise I'm going to be late. Why the hell didn't I pre-book a taxi to take me? Typical of me. I leave everything until the last minute. I don't know if this huge old case can take much more of me dragging it behind on these pavements, not to mention it's killing me. Normally, I would have brought a smaller case, but I have gifts for the family inside.

I see the next taxi approach. He's not getting away from me; it's now or never. I jump out in front of it with my arm raised. I screw my eyes shut as I hear the screech of his tyres as he brakes just before the long blast of his horn. I open one eye slowly and see the face of the driver. He's glaring at me and mouthing what I can only presume are profanities whilst waving his hands around. I shrug and try to give him my million-kilowatt smile.

"Are you free?" I mouth, still smiling.

He's an older man, and my charm isn't working on him. I move slowly to the door, hoping he doesn't pull away before I get it open. Shoving my heavy-ass case and shoulder bag in first, I climb in.

"I'm going to Heathrow airport, please. Sorry for jumping out at you. So many taxis have passed and ignored me. I have a flight to catch and I'm running late." I glance at my phone yet again. "Very late. Oh, no. I may miss my flight and I know it's the last one out with it being Christmas Eve. Why the hell didn't I leave yesterday as planned? Oh, that's right. I work too bloody much." I'm muttering away to myself when I realise we're in motion, as I'm thrown sideways. I put my belt on quickly and look up just as I see the rear of a car inches away from the front of the taxi. My head jolts to the side as my driver swerves to miss it.

Bloody hell. He's going to kill me before I even make it to the airport.

There is so much traffic. How he dodges it is beyond me, but I hear horns blaring as we pass. I shouldn't complain; I do need to get to the airport.

My phone buzzes in my pocket, and I reach for it to see who it is. Work. No, I will not answer it. I promised once I finished and shut my workshop door, that would be it.

The vibration continues in my hand.

No. I will not answer it.

"Hello, Borbon Bespoke Jewellery. How may I help?" Shit. "I'm sorry, I'm out of the office until after the holidays. Could you please e-mail me your details and I will get back to you on my return? Oh, I'm sorry, sir. It takes a couple of weeks from design to finish, depending on the piece. Sir, please don't be rude. Well, maybe if you had thought about it a couple of weeks ago instead of leaving it until Christmas Eve, we would have had time to make one. No. I'm sorry, it would take me at least two weeks, like I said. No, there is no way I could do it tonight and get it ready. It's Christmas Eve. I may be good at my job, but I'm not a miracle worker. I'm sorry you feel like that, sir, but there is nothing I can do. Happy Christmas to you too, and goodbye."

The cheek of it, calling me useless and incompetent whilst shouting at me. How the hell does he expect me to make a unique bracelet at this hour?

By a miracle and a disgruntled taxi driver just wanting rid of the crazy woman, we arrive at the airport. He manages to find a space, tells me it's thirty quid, then proceeds to glare at me when I don't offer a tip. Not likely. He ripped me off. It only usually costs me fifteen pounds. I don't bother arguing. I'm just so grateful I'm here and still have time.

I walk through the airport, and there are people everywhere, sprawled out in every available space. I look at the boards and see lots of flights have been cancelled. That explains it. Luckily, my flight is just showing an hour's delay. Typical. I almost get killed in the taxi to get here to then find it's going to be late. I was rushing when leaving home and didn't check on the flight status. The lead-up to Christmas is my busiest time, for obvious reasons. I work non-stop from late September to Christmas Eve. Work this year just seems to have exploded. There haven't been enough hours in the day. I'm getting great recognition, though, and it helped that a couple of my pieces have been on the red carpet at premieres this year.

I knew booking a flight for today would be tough, but I haven't been away for so long. Since losing Toby, my work has been my life. I never stop and have a break, and I don't celebrate Christmas anymore. It's a sad time for me.

❄

After a three-hour delay, I'm finally boarding. I head towards the back of the plane where my seat is located. Economy for me. I don't throw away my money if I can help it. Some might say I'm quite stingy; I just say I'm cautious. I put my carry-on in the overhead bin, grab my blanket from the seat, then, just as I'm about to sit down, I notice the seatbelt is fastened with a DO NOT USE sticker attached to it.

Great. What now?

I sit for a few minutes and wait before trying to move. It's busy with people trying to get to their seats. I head to one of the air stewardesses.

"Excuse me. My seatbelt is fastened and says do not use." She looks at me with disgust for interrupting her talking to one of her colleagues.

"What seat are you in?"

"Forty-five C."

"Yes, we know that seat is broken. If you just sit back down for a few minutes whilst people board, I will check with my manager where we can re-seat you." She turns and walks away, and I trundle back to my broken seat and wait.

People around me are quite giddy. I don't blame them. I was like that once and I should be now, I just can't get there. I'm beginning to regret this. I have butterflies in my tummy just thinking about what's going to greet me in Toronto. I haven't seen Sylvia or Charlie since the funeral. I know I should have visited sooner; I just couldn't bring myself to go back without Toby. The only times I ever went to Toronto were with or for Toby.

I watch as the air stewardess walks towards me.

"I have spoken to my manager, and unfortunately, there are no more available seats in economy. As the seat is broken, it's illegal to have a passenger use it. The plane is at capacity as you can imagine with it being Christmas Eve."

Wait, what is she telling me? My mind goes ten to the dozen. I've built myself up for this trip over the last few months. As much as I would like to get off and just go home, I know I have to do this.

"What does that mean for me?"

She looks hesitant. I know she doesn't want me to start anything.

"There's only one seat available on the plane. It's in first class. Unfortunately, if you want that seat. there is an additional charge to pay."

I hold up my hand. "Wait, what? Hold up. The seat I booked is broken, which means it's your responsibility to find me an alternative seat. I've paid for this seat. If the only seat you have available is in first class, then that is not my problem and there is no way I'm paying anything additional when it's not my fault. Now, if you can't fix this, please get me someone who can."

I dismiss her. I don't know who I am right now. I'm never confrontational. Maybe the man on the phone in the taxi riled me up more than I realised by being so rude to me. The taxi driver was just as rude too. I think I've had enough.

Five minutes later, a different lady walks up the aisle towards me. I know everyone around me is watching this play out. I shuffle in my seat, my palms starting to sweat. I'm preparing myself for the confrontation I don't want to have.

"Hello, Ms Borbon. I'm Nancy, the manager on board today. I understand your seat is broken and the only available seat on the flight is in first class. Unfortunately, it's against company policy to upgrade anyone complimentarily. We can either move you to first class for a fee, or you will need to vacate the plane and speak to the ground staff for the next available flight. Regrettably, there is nothing more we can do as we are at full capacity. I'm sorry. We also need to move you now as the plane is ready to leave. If you decide to leave the plane, it will delay the flight further to retrieve your hold luggage."

I'm stunned. What the hell? This is not my fault, but I'm being made to feel like it is, and I'm now going to delay the plane.

With everyone watching me, I don't want to make a scene. I get up and retrieve my carry-on bag from the bin above, move to the front of the plane and stand in the galley. I turn on Nancy.

"Look, Nancy, I understand the plane is full, but I also understand this is not my fault. I have paid for the economy seat, and it's broken, which is not my issue. I'm not paying to upgrade into first class. I can't afford to upgrade. If I could, don't you think I would be in there anyway?" I point to the cabin just ahead of us.

I'm really trying to stay calm, but my voice is quivering as I raise it. The last thing I want is for them to call the police to have me removed. I've seen articles about that on the internet. I hang my head. I need to get to Toronto. It's Christmas Day tomorrow.

"I really am sorry, Ms Borbon. I spoke to my superior and they said you can have the seat in first class at half the upgrade price. You do, however, need to decide now as we have a slot we would like to keep before we're delayed any longer. Could you excuse me for one minute?" I hear a bell ring and she heads into first class. It's only moments before she returns. "Okay, it's all set. You're good to move into first class."

I look at her, bewildered. "I haven't said I'll pay yet."

"It's okay, it's all sorted for you. Please can you take your seat so we can prepare the plane for departure? Thank you, Ms Borbon, and I am so sorry for the inconvenience." She shows me to my seat.

I place my bag in the overhead bin and take my seat, fastening my belt. Just as I do this, another steward crouches in front of me. He hands me a menu to take my lunch order. *Wow, this is something else.* He then quickly comes back with a prosecco before taking his seat for take-off.

As soon as we level out, there's a hive of activity. The crew rushes around, preparing the food. One comes around to each of us and pulls our table tray out and sets it with a cloth and cutlery. Not plastic ones. These are proper metal ones. They bring out our food individually, as it's been cooked fresh. I have champagne with my lunch of medium-rare steak, dauphinoise potatoes, and greens. It's like being in a five-star restaurant. Well, almost.

I finish my lunch and am waiting for someone to come and sort out my tray table. I have no idea how it works, and I want to get my phone and headphones out of my bag above me. I must look impatient as a man suddenly appears that I hadn't noticed. He takes my empty dishes away and places them on what must be his seat opposite me. How could I not have noticed this god of a man before?

"Here, let me help you with these and I will show you how the tray table works."

His voice is smooth like velvet, with a strong Canadian accent, and I feel myself blush. He shows me the table is worked electronically, and he presses the buttons. I watch as it slides away.

"Thank you," I croak.

He starts to lean in towards me. I'm trying to retreat deeper into my seat to get away from him. He's getting into my personal space, and all the while he's maintaining eye contact with me. I can't tear myself away from those beautiful light blue eyes of his. They are framed by the longest dark lashes I've ever seen on a man. He reaches for my seatbelt and unbuckles it for me.

"Can I help you with your bag?" He stands up, smiling.

He knows full well the effect he's having on me. I just nod. He reaches up and takes my bag down and passes it to me. I grab it from him. He somehow manages to stroke my fingers with his. I gasp at the electricity coursing through me from his touch and feel my face burning.

"Thank you," I whisper.

He smiles. "Would you like to get a drink at the bar?" He nods his head behind me. I sit up and look to where he's nodding.

Holy cow, there's a bar there. I look at him. Do I want to have a drink with this man? Hell, yes, I do, but then Toby pops into my head.

It's been five years tomorrow since I lost him. Christmas Day. It was the worst and best day of my life, and it's why I don't celebrate Christmas. I sit back and sigh. I don't look at him. I can't do it, as much as I want to.

"Hey, it's okay. I was just being friendly. You looked lost sitting here. I'm going to go have a drink. I prefer it to sitting in my little space for seven plus hours. If you feel like joining me, that would be great. Gives me someone to talk to." He smiles, winks, then turns and heads to the bar.

I sit contemplating, wondering what in hell just happened, clutching my bag to my chest. What must I look like?

I glance behind me and see him sitting at the small bar. He's got his back to me, and it looks like he's talking to the air steward. He's in a white button-up shirt. I noticed when he was in front of me that he had the top few buttons open. Looking at his back, I can see the strain on the material as he leans on the bar. He has extremely broad shoulders, and he's tall.

Nancy appears and asks if I want a drink. I hesitate.

"May I take mine at the bar, please?" I ask as she pours me a Coke.

She smiles and nods. Instead of giving me the drink, she walks to the bar. I watch as she puts my Coke on the counter. It's right next to the guy, but then the bar is so small, it would be. He looks at Nancy, who blushes as he says something to her. I'm glad it's not just me he has this effect on. I can see she's telling him the drink is for me, and he turns and smiles. I have no choice now but to go and have my drink with him.

I slowly lower myself onto the stool next to him. He turns to me with that captivating smile of his.

"Hi," I squeak.

What is wrong with me? Again, Toby comes barrelling into my head, followed by the guilt over speaking to another man. I pick up my Coke and gulp it down for a distraction. That was the wrong thing to do. I start to choke as it goes down the wrong way. I stand up, trying to catch my breath. The guy is out of his seat and rubbing my back as I'm bent over, gasping. Oh, no. He must think I'm the biggest idiot going. I stop choking and finally catch my breath.

"Thank you. I'm sorry about that."

"It's okay. It happens to the best of us. Are you okay now?"

I nod and sit back on the stool. He stays standing, making sure I'm good. I look back at him. His smile is to die for, and his hair is blonde and messy; I like it. He takes his seat and grabs his glass; it looks like it's a whiskey or a scotch.

"I'm Mark. Pleased to meet you ...?" He places his glass on the counter and holds out his hand to greet me. I just look at it. "Erm, that's how we say hello where I'm from." He laughs. He puts me into a kind of trance with that smooth, deep voice. He lowers his head to look me straight in the eyes. I take his outstretched hand and shake it. "I'm Mark," he says again, smiling at me, waiting for me to tell him my name, but the touch from his hand has all these sensations coursing through my body again, and I just can't compute anything. He's still holding my hand, not wanting to let it go. "Hello?" he says, and I look up into his eyes

"I'm sorry. I'm Heather. Nice to meet you too, Mark." I pull my hand away and grab my glass as an excuse to get out of his hold and stop the shocks coursing through me. "So, do you come here often?" I say, trying to break the ice and not look like the awkward, simple girl I'm appearing to be.

He smiles again and nods, sipping his amber liquid. "I do. I frequently travel back and forth from London to Toronto. Home is Toronto with my family, and I work a lot in London. How about you?"

He has a family. I look at his ring finger to see if he's married, then shake my head.

"No. I've been to Toronto a lot, but it's been a few years since I was last there."

He raises his eyebrow in a questioning way as he watches my face. I look down at my glass, moving it from side to side.

"Are you okay, Heather? You look a little sad." His eyes look worried, and his brow dips slightly as he watches me. I give him a little nod, and his lips slightly turn up in a small smile.

"It's hard for me to go back. I've dreaded this day for a few years." I don't elaborate and he doesn't push me. "Have you and your family always lived in Toronto?"

"I was born in Toronto. My mom and sisters are there. My papa was a New Yorker and left when I was four. I don't know where he is. I don't remember him. I travelled with my grandfather to London a lot from when I was a teenager. He was a successful businessman. He was in retail and dabbled with property. He taught me everything I know, and he was more like a papa to me. I took over his business when he passed away. It's been a few years now, and I still miss him."

"I'm sorry for your loss."

His shoulders rise in a shrug. "Enough of the sad talk. What's your story, Heather? Why are you off to Toronto? Why's it been so long since you've been back?"

Oh, no. I don't want to go into all that. Think. Think.

"I've just been so busy with work. I have a small business and it's really taken off lately, so I don't have much time for anything else at the moment."

"So, why are you dreading going back?"

"Oh, just the fact I haven't been there for so long. I have relatives I haven't seen, and I just get nervous going back, that's all."

We sit and talk about all sorts. I don't elaborate on Toronto and why I dread going, nor do I tell him more about my business. I find him easy to talk to, which is unusual for me. I'm always awkward and reserved, talking to strangers.

The time seems to fly by—no pun intended—and it doesn't seem long before Nancy comes and asks us to be seated for landing.

I look at my watch. "I can't believe we've been sitting here talking for all this time. Thank you, Mark, for making the flight an easy one for me. I really appreciate the distraction. I hate flying."

"No, thank you, Heather. It's been a pleasure talking to you. If you don't mind, could I give you my number? Here, pass me your phone and I can put it in for you. If you want to meet up whilst you're in town, I would love to take you out for dinner. If you have time, of course. I know what it's like catching up with family and friends, and with it being Christmas as well." He looks a little sheepish as he says this. He's been nothing but confident all this time. He must have a lot of women coming onto him or sat at home, waiting for his call.

I take it he doesn't have a wife or girlfriend if he's asking me to dinner. Maybe he just likes to talk and it's nothing more.

"Earth to Heather." I look at him and see he's holding his hand out for my phone. I pass it to him after unlocking it. He types away, then, as he passes it back to me, he somehow manages to stroke my fingers again, sending those shocks through my body. "What do you say?"

"Yes. Okay, Mark. That would be lovely."

But I know I will never phone him.

※

I collect my luggage, and rather than rush out to the meeting area, I take my time. I'm quietly hoping customs will stop me for a search, just to prolong it. No such luck. I head through the exit doors, keeping my head down, pretending to look at something in my hand.

"Heather! Heather, oh my goodness." I hear her before I see her.

I lift my head just as Thea comes barrelling into me. Thea is Toby's little sister. He has an older sister too, Fiona, but she lives in New York.

I just about manage to catch Thea before she knocks me over. "Heather, oh how I've missed you. Why didn't you come see me before now? Why didn't you call me? I missed you so much."

Guilt washes over me. I know I should have come back sooner, but I wasn't in the right mindset to do so. I'm still not sure I'm there yet. Everywhere I go will bring back all my memories of Toby and me. I stand, hugging Thea to me, and tears slip down my cheeks. I look up just as Sylvia and Charlie approach. Tears run down Sylvia's face, and that sets me off even more. She hugs me as I hug Thea. We're all a blubbering mess.

Charlie coughs. I look at him, then gently move out of Sylvia's hold and hug him. Toby was the image of Charlie, and this hurts more than I thought it would.

"Come on, love. Let's get you home. You must be shattered after that long flight. I kept watching the flight and saw it getting delayed. I was worried it was going to get cancelled. Good job it didn't, hey, love." He hugs me to his side.

In the car to their house, Charlie natters away. I love Charlie; he's a real Yorkshire man. He moved to Toronto for work. I remember it like it was yesterday because it broke my heart the day Toby told me they were leaving the UK. I cried for days. We were fourteen and in love. Everyone asked how we knew. They said we were too young, but it never fizzled out. Even after they left, we kept in touch and spoke to each other almost every day. Toby wanted me to go and live there as soon as I turned sixteen, but I lived with my gran and there was no way I could leave her. I lost my parents when I was seven, in a car accident. That was one of the reasons Toby's death was so hard. What are the chances my parents and my husband would die the same way?

Toby came to the UK to visit a few times, and he proposed to me on my seventeenth birthday. Of course, I said yes. I loved him. Everyone said we were too young. Even his parents were against it at first. Who knew I would be widowed at twenty-one?

Christmas Day was his favourite, and I wanted a white winter wedding, so we decided Christmas Day would be our special day forever and got married the first Christmas after Gran passed away. I decided to move to Toronto to live with Toby once I lost Gran. We got married not far from where he lived; it was an intimate dream wedding with just his family. As the wedding meal finished and we were just relaxing and talking, Toby got up, saying he had to nip home for something, and that he would only be about twenty minutes. It was cold and snowy out, and I didn't want him to go on his own. I wanted to go with him, but he insisted I stay where I was in the warmth of the hotel bar. He kissed me and told me he loved me and that he was missing his wife already.

I never saw him again.

Some old man jumped a red light and smashed into Toby, sending his car rolling down a verge where it came to a stop against a tree. I was told he died on impact. I later found out he had only gone to Sylvia's house to pick up my wedding present. It was a beautiful husky dog. By some miracle, the dog survived the impact. I clung to the dog when the police brought him to me and didn't let go for days. He was my comfort. It was the last piece of Toby I had. Dusky, my dog, lives with Sylvia, Charlie, and Thea. I decided to go back home to the UK. I couldn't stand the thought of living in Canada without Toby, and I couldn't take Dusky back with me. It broke my heart to leave him, but I wasn't in the right frame of mind to look after him. I could barely look after myself.

Charlie is still nattering away; he's telling me about the changes that have been going on. Thea is sitting beside me, holding my hand tight.

"How's Dusky doing, Thea? I bet he's big now, isn't he?" She smiles and then goes into a full-blown account of how he's been doing. I can't wait to see him. He won't remember me; he was just eight weeks old at the time.

As we pull up outside their house. Memories come flooding back. I can picture Toby grabbing my hand as we sat in the car the day I moved to be with him, He was so excited, full of plans for our future. We lived in the annex at the back, and I was going to build up my jewellery business with his help. He had some amazing ideas.

I stare at the house wiping away the tears flowing down my cheeks. I'm not sure I can do this; it was a bad idea. My heart is breaking all over again.

Sylvia opens my door and takes my hand. She leads me to the house, pulling me into her side as we enter. I'm shaking with the anxiety and anticipation of how I'm going to feel when we get inside. I stop and hold my breath at the threshold, my eyes scanning, half expecting Toby to appear. I screw them shut then slowly open them again, taking a deep breath. They've re-decorated, which I'm both pleased and sad about. I also notice there is nothing Christmassy around the place. They don't have a tree up, pretty much like me. I stand still, looking around, remembering everything. It all plays out in my head. The very first time Toby brought me here, he was so giddy about it. The time we made out on the couch when everyone was out. Him coming through this very door with the biggest bunch of flowers after an argument. I can't help the tears coursing down my cheeks. I wipe them away, then turn and smile as the three of them stand watching me.

"I'm sorry. It's just hard. I knew it would be. I'm sorry for not being in touch. I've struggled so much, but I'm okay now. I laugh at the amazing times we had and I'm grateful I had Toby's love."

Charlie takes my cases up the stairs to my room. Sylvia rushes to the kitchen; I saw the tears on her cheeks. She's finding this as hard as I am. Thea comes at me again, only this time, I fall backwards onto the couch.

Just then, a huge ball of fluff pounces onto the couch next to me. Thea laughs as Dusky starts to climb on her. He reaches me and licks my face in excitement. I laugh and grab him to me to give him a hug. I nuzzle his neck, thinking of Toby. Maybe Dusky does remember me, unless he's just this friendly to everyone.

He's gorgeous. He has brown, black, white, and tan fur. I pull back to look at his face, and he has the bluest of eyes. Mark flashes into my head. He had almost the same colour eyes. Guilt washes over me yet again, thinking of Mark whilst in Toby's family home, hugging my wedding present from him.

❄

I'm trying to sleep. I know I should be fast asleep by now with the time difference, but I'm wide awake. This place holds so many memories. I feel sadness and loss, but I also feel so much joy and love. Now I'm here, I realise this is what I needed to help me move on with my life. I will never forget Toby, but I think it's time, and Toby would want me to move on.

Just then, my phone buzzes. I grab it off the side and see it's from Mark Plane. I have to think for a second. I don't know a *Mark Plane*, then my heart does a flip as I remember those eyes and lips. I laugh out loud. I thought Plane was his surname. He just meant Mark from the plane. That's cute. He must have sent himself a text from my phone when he put his number in mine.

Hey, Heather. Sorry, you're probably fast asleep. I just wanted to check in with you and see how you're settling in after worrying about coming back. I hope it's better than you imagined. Hope you don't mind me texting you. Love to catch up with you soon if you have any free time. Mark

I'm both surprised and flustered, but if I'm completely honest, my tummy is in knots and my heart is racing. I'm not going to reply to him. Not right now, anyway.

❄

OH, SANTA!

I wake with a start and bolt upright. Dusky somehow managed to get into my room and pounced on the bed, scaring the life out of me. He looks at me, wagging his tail. I open my arms, he jumps on my chest, and I hug him to me, burying my face into his neck. I suddenly remember it's Christmas Day. For the past four Christmases, I've stayed in bed doing nothing except watching documentaries all day. I buried myself until the day was over. I couldn't stand all the hype and Christmas films on the TV.

It's also my wedding anniversary, but we were only married for three hours. Three fucking hours. I get so angry even now. All it took was three seconds to take him from me. The one thing I am grateful for is that the old man who ran the red light also died that day. I still feel bitter towards him and his family, and I know I shouldn't. I know they suffered losing him on Christmas Day, but it was all his fault I lost my husband. We had our whole lives ahead of us.

It's very sombre in the kitchen as I approach. I don't think any of them know what to say to me. In all honesty, I don't know what to say to them either. I sit down as Sylvia pours me a cup of tea.

"Do you want some toast, love?" I nod and smile. We can't go on like this every year. We all have to get past this, and now is the time to do it. I think it's up to me to start.

"Do you all go to church still? I think I would like to go to church. I've not been for so long. We also need to see if we can get a turkey and make a good old Christmas dinner." The room seems to freeze as everyone looks at me. "Look, I love Toby with all my heart. I always have and I always will. It's been five years and I think now is the time for us to celebrate his life. We need to make Christmas the celebration of Toby from now on, not the sad day I've always made it. We need to start enjoying things again. Toby would hate the way we are. It's being here with you all that has given me the courage to say this. What do you think?"

Charlie looks at Sylvia, and they nod. I think I see relief in their faces, and Charlie's shoulders loosen a little.

"Well, love, I think you're right. We have never celebrated Christmas since that day. It's also your wedding anniversary, and I think that should also be celebrated. From now on, Christmas Day shall be celebrated as Toby Day. He loved Christmas so much." He reaches over for my hand and squeezes it.

I nod at him as a tear falls onto my cheek. Sylvia grabs my other hand and squeezes it, nodding her approval at me. Thea gets up from her seat and stands behind me, wrapping her arms around my neck and hugging me. Just then, the door opens, and I hear a toddler crying. I turn and see Fiona walking through the door with a young boy in her arms and bags over her shoulder. I get up to help her as she's struggling. Sylvia also gets up and takes the little boy. Another man walks in behind with two suitcases. Once Fiona is free of the boy and bags, she hugs me to her. She's always been like a big sister to me, and I've missed her so much. She's two years older than me and Toby.

"Oh, Hev. I've missed you so much. I couldn't believe it when Mum told me you were coming. We flew in yesterday, but it was so late we stayed at a hotel." She's hugging me as Sylvia is trying to shush the little boy. I turn to look at him and I'm struck by the resemblance to Toby. "This little monster is Joshua Toby. We call him JT. He's just turned two, and don't we know it? Here, JT. Come and say high to your Aunty Hev." She takes JT from Sylvia and places him in my arms. He immediately stops crying. "Well, if you have that effect on him, you can stick around." She laughs.

I'm just so struck on the resemblance; I would swear it was Toby as a toddler in my arms. I mean, I've seen all his baby pictures, and JT is the spitting image of him.

He looks at me and starts to play with strands of my long brown hair that I forgot to tie up. Toby used to do that; twist it around his fingers, only he didn't suck his thumb at the same time like JT.

"Wow, Fiona. He's just like Toby. I can't get over the resemblance. I didn't even know you had a little one."

"Two, actually." She smiles and turns to the man who twists around and lifts something up. I see it's a car seat with a sleeping baby inside. "You have two nephews. I couldn't wait for you to meet them. This little sleeping cherub is Thomas Junior, named after his daddy. Hev, meet my husband, Thomas. Thomas, this is my sister-in-law, Heather." We shake hands and greet each other.

OH, SANTA!

❋

We had an amazing remember Toby Day. Sylvia and Charlie already had everything for a Christmas dinner, so we all cooked it together. It was the best day I had had for so long, and I felt like a big weight had lifted from my shoulders. I got another text from Mark Plane on Christmas Day, wishing me a Happy Christmas, which was nice of him.

Boxing Day was an enjoyable day. We played games, then went out for a meal. I can honestly say it's been the best couple of days I've had in for what feels like forever. Today, though, most of the family is back at work.

I go into Toronto City to do some shopping. It's been so long since I was here. The last time, I was picking my wedding dress up. I smile at the thought. I forget how cold it gets here. Thank goodness for the underground walkways they have.

I enter Randolf department store. I used to love coming to this store with Toby. It's like our version of Harrod's.

I want to get something for JT and Thomas, as well as something for Thea and Dusky. I'm walking around with my arms full of stuff when I suddenly turn and bump into someone and drop everything. I bend to pick it up just as the other person bends to help me, and we bump heads.

"Ow," I shout, falling back on my bum and rubbing my head. I don't look at the other person. Not yet, anyway. It's probably some old lady who's going to start on me at any minute. I open my eyes and I'm shocked to see Mark Plane crouching down in front of me.

"Well, fancy bumping into you here." He smiles and offers me his hand to help me up. My heart skips a beat or two at his deep, rich, velvety voice. My eyes must be the size of saucers. I mean, how could it be him I literally bumped into?

I hold out my hand. Big mistake. The shocks course through my body again, and I let go, falling back on my bum.

He laughs and stands up. "Come on, Heather. Let's get you up. You don't have the best of luck, do you?" He's laughing at me.

I take both of his stretched-out hands, and he pulls me up with ease.

We both start to bend again to pick up my stuff. This time, he stops and holds his hands up. "You go. I don't want to hurt you again."

I bend to fetch them, and just as I stand up straight, he's being passed a shopping basket for me to put my stuff in.

"Thank you, Mark."

God, that smile on his face is doing things to me, and I feel myself getting angry because of it. I know I'm red in the face. I could put it down to the bump of heads, but he'll know it's not.

I notice the lady who gave him the shopping basket is still hovering about. "Thank you, for the basket," I say to her directly. She just stands there, watching us.

I place all my things in the basket, turn to find a checkout, and walk away without saying a word to Mark. I don't know why; he's done nothing wrong. It's me and my conflicting feelings.

"Heather, wait up. What's wrong? Why are you leaving?"

I shouldn't take it out on him, but I just can't help myself. I'm usually the last person to be confrontational.

"First off, you didn't even thank that lady for passing you the shopping basket, and that's just plain rudeness. Then you knocked me flying, bumped my head, and laughed at me. I don't like being laughed at Mark."

I'm making such a fool of myself. I have no idea if he thanked her or not, I just threw that in. I need to leave now; I'm mortified. People are watching me rant, and it's busy in here.

I turn quickly and head for the checkouts before he has a chance to say anything. I'm on pins as I pay for my stuff. I expect him to come up behind me at any minute. I turn slowly, but he's not there. I guess I must have scared him off.

I rush to the doors, and I regret it as soon as I step outside. The cold hits me like I just stepped into a freezer. I rummage for my gloves and scarf, putting them on fast, then pull my hood over my head and start to walk. The cold makes my eyes water, and I can't see where I'm going.

I'm trying to gauge the direction I'm headed when, all of a sudden, a horn blares at me and I'm being dragged backwards. *What the hell is happening?*

"You just nearly got yourself killed."

That voice of his. I swear, it's like an elixir.

I don't turn to look at Mark. Instead, I continue to let him hold me to his firm body. I watch as the driver of the car that almost killed me makes rude gestures at me. I didn't even know I was crossing a road.

It suddenly hits me; I was nearly killed. Toby flashes in my head. His stern look when he didn't agree with me. How could I have been so stupid? My body goes limp thinking about it. My knees try to give way under me, and Mark's grip tightens slightly as he feels me weaken,

"Are you okay, Heather? If you hadn't left in such a hurry, I wouldn't have had to save you."

He's right. I'm embarrassed at the way I've acted. It's like I can't function in his company. He turns me slowly to look at him. I'm hiding under my hood; I don't want to see disappointment in those beautiful eyes.

"I was calling for my car so I could take you home, then I turned around and you had vanished. The assistant told me which door you had left out of, so I ran to catch up to you. It's freezing out here." I slowly trace my eyes up his body to his face. He's only got his suit on; he must be freezing. Oh, God. What have I done?

"I'm sorry you had to save me. You must be freezing. You need to get back inside."

Just then, a big black car pulls up. I watch as he moves to the back door and opens it.

"Please. Get in so I can take you home." I hesitate and look up at him. He raises his eyebrow. "Humour me. Please, Heather."

I scowl at him and walk to the car with my bags and climb into the back, only because I don't want him to freeze. He gets in beside me. I pull down my hood and take off my gloves and scarf; it's hot in here.

"I had my driver put the heat on full blast for us." I buckle myself in and stare ahead, not looking at him. "Are we going to talk?"

I turn to him. "What would you like to talk about?"

"Us."

"What us, Mark? I met you on a plane. That's it. I don't know you, Mark. We talked for a couple of hours. I enjoyed talking to you, but that's where it ended." I watch the downturn of his mouth as the smile dissipates and sadness fills his eyes. I notice the slight retreat into his seat.

"Mark, look, we talked, and it was good. But we don't know each other. You're acting like I've wronged you in some way."

He plays with the gold diamond ring on his pinkie finger. I didn't notice any rings on the plane. This strong, confident man that oozes power seems to be weakening. Maybe it's all a front and this is the real man.

As if he read my mind, he pulls his shoulders back to sit tall and slightly puffs out his chest, transforming back to the man I met on the plane. "I'm sorry, Heather. I thought we clicked on the plane. I really like you. When you didn't reply to my text messages, I thought you didn't like me and I'd read it all wrong. I'm good at getting it wrong." He laughs to himself and looks at his fingers, twirling his pinkie ring round. He looks back at me. "I shouldn't have texted you on Christmas Day. I was having a bad day and I remembered you said you didn't like Christmas. I thought If you had texted me back, we could have talked for a bit." He shrugs. "I read it all wrong. Let me take you home."

I remember now he said he didn't like Christmas. Maybe he wanted a bit of company on the phone. "Mark, I do like you, it's just, well..." Now it's my turn to look at my hands in my lap.

He suddenly moves closer to me and places his finger under my chin, turning my head to look at him. He looks me in the eyes. "Can we start again? I feel it's gone a little sideways. Hi, I'm Mark. Nice to meet you." He smiles his captivating smile at me. I'm already tingling from his touch, never mind throwing the smile in too.

I smile back and nod. "Hi, Mark. I'm Heather. It's nice to meet you too." We both laugh.

"Will you have dinner with me tonight, Heather?"

Toby pops straight into my head, but for the first time, I don't feel guilty. I think doing what we did on Christmas Day and making it a Toby Day has somehow made it easier for me. Before I know what I'm doing, I nod. "Yes."

The smile on his face is to die for. He leans in and kisses my cheek. "Thank you," he whispers. "Do you want to go now for a late lunch?" He looks at his watch. "Or do you want to go home and get changed and I can pick you up later?"

I look at the time. It's only three-thirty. "Can you drop me home and pick me up later? Around seven-thirty. Is that okay?" The smile hasn't left his face.

At seven-thirty on the dot, he pulls up outside. I had to tell Sylvia and Charlie I'm going out with him, that I met him on the plane, and it's just dinner. They didn't ask me any questions. I think they needed to come to terms with it, but I wanted to be open with them. I've picked up my phone so many times to tell him not to come, yet I didn't go through with it. I've had knots in my tummy since he dropped me off earlier.

I'm at the door, waiting for him. I didn't want him to come and knock for me. That would just be weird.

I didn't want to be too dressed up, and with the weather being so cold, I just went for a trouser suit. I didn't bring many going-out clothes with me as I didn't plan on going on any dates. I'm wrapped up in my big Canada Goose coat. It's long to my knees and I have on my thick woolly scarf and thermal gloves. It's Toronto at Christmas, after all.

"I would say you look lovely, but I have no idea what's under there." He laughs, and I join him.

"Hey, it's freezing. I should be by a log fire with a hot chocolate, not going out for dinner." He smiles, but it's a mischievous, knowing smile. I raise my eyebrow at him. "What's that look for?"

He taps his nose secretively, then opens his car door for me. It's the same car we were in today. I climb into the back, and he follows. We drive for about fifteen minutes, then turn down a long, winding road.

"Don't worry. I can see panic on your face. I was going to take you to a restaurant, then I thought this would be far better." I look out of the window just as we pull up outside a massive house that looks like a log cabin. "My chef is inside rustling up a meal as we speak."

I think he's letting me know we will not be alone. I must look worried. He gets out and opens my door for me. Taking my hand, he leads me up the steps, where the door is opened by an older lady as we approach.

"Welcome, Master Mark," she says, then smiles at me.

"Hello, Judy. Sorry I haven't been around lately. You know what it's like at this time of year and all the travelling. How are you doing? How's Cyril?"

"We're both good, Mark. Nice to see you. I have everything prepared as you requested. Marco is in the kitchen. If there is anything else you need before I leave, please let me know."

"You get off now, Judy. You know I don't like you out in this weather. It's dark. Let me just get Heather settled and I will walk you to your house."

He leads me inside to a big living room, which has the most amazing huge, roaring log fire. Next to the fire is a table with a pot and a bowl of marshmallows on. I turn and smile at him.

"Hot chocolate and a roaring log fire, just as you said. I will be back in about ten minutes. Judy lives on the grounds in her own house, but I like to make sure she gets home safe." He smiles, bends down, and very gently kisses me on the lips.

He turns and leaves, and I'm shocked. But, oh my God, the feelings I got from that gentle kiss have me tingling all over.

I pour myself a hot chocolate and add marshmallows, then curl up on the couch in front of the fire. I place the hot chocolate on the table at the side of me and lean right into the cushions. I feel so at home here and I'm glad I didn't dress up too much.

The next thing I feel is a featherlight kiss on my forehead.

"Leave me to sleep, Toby." I bat with my hand, but then I realise it can't be Toby.

I slowly open my eyes and Mark is crouching in front of me. I see the confusion on his face as his eyes narrow and his brow furrows. Oh, shit. I sit up quickly and look around, remembering where I am. "I'm sorry, Mark."

He stands up without saying a word. His shoulders are tense as he stands in front of the fire with his back to me. "Is Toby your boyfriend? Are you seeing someone, Heather? Is that why you weren't answering my text messages?" He slowly turns to me. I'm watching his face as he looks at my hands on my knees. I think he's looking for a ring. I wear both my rings on a chain around my neck. I pull out the chain and hold up the rings.

"Toby was my husband." I turn my head so he can't see the tear slip from my eye.

"Was?" I nod. "You're divorced?"

"No. He died. It was a few years ago now. That's why I haven't been back for so long. My in-laws are here."

He's kneeling in front of me in seconds. He takes my hands and stares into my eyes before looking at the rings on my chain. "I'm so sorry, Heather. You're far too young to be a widow."

He hangs his head, and I don't know why, but I stroke his hair. He takes my palm and kisses it before pressing it to his cheek. He smiles, giving me a knowing look. Of course. He lost his grandad not so long ago as well.

"Do you want to eat now, or would you prefer I take you home?"

I look at the sadness on his face. Does he want me to go home now he knows I have baggage?

"No, I don't want you to leave. I can see the question on your face. I just want to make sure you're ready for this. If Toby's death is still too raw, then I completely understand. I know it's not the same, but I'm still grieving for my grandfather. He meant the world to me. I don't suppose the feelings will ever go, but I know we have to get on with our lives and just remember them and cherish the time we had with our loved ones."

He's right. It's what I've been telling myself since getting here. I know it's time. I will always love Toby, no matter what, but I have to get on with my life.

"Food would be good right now." Just as I say this, my tummy rumbles. I look down at it and then at him, and we both laugh. He has the sweetest face when he laughs. He's such a nice guy. *I wonder why he isn't taken.*

He takes my hand and helps me up off the big, comfy couch. He doesn't let it go once I'm up. Instead, he leads me to the kitchen where the table is set up for us to eat. There is a chef still cooking.

"Hey, Marco. How are we doing buddy?"

"Practically ready for you, sir. Please sit and I will serve it up. I've put the drinks you requested in the ice bucket."

Mark walks me to a chair, and just like a gentleman, he pulls it out for me to sit. We don't speak as Marco busies himself plating up our food and serving it. He then pours our drinks. I laugh as he pours a Coke for me and a Dr. Pepper for Mark. He tells Marco that will be all and for him to head home while the weather is playing nice. He thanks him and tells him he will see him soon.

We eat in silence at first, stealing glances at each other. The food is to die for. We make small talk in between bites. He's easy to talk to. "Do you live here on your own, Mark?" I curse myself for asking that when his brow furrows.

"Yes, I do. My mama and sisters don't live far from here. I wanted to stay close to them. I have two sisters. Tammy is twenty-six, and Hetty is twenty-three. Tammy has just moved in with her girlfriend in town, while Hetty still lives with mama."

I feel myself getting giddy knowing he lives alone, meaning there is no-one else… hopefully.

"How old are you?"

The corner of his mouth turns up slightly. "I'm thirty-one. What about you?"

"Twenty-six."

"Nice." He smiles as he puts a forkful of food in his mouth. I take a sip of my Coke, smiling back at him. "Do you mind talking about Toby? I understand if that seems awkward."

I place my drink on the table, not looking at him. I can do this. Toby was the biggest part of my life, and If I'm going to get on with it, then I have to be able to open up about him. I look at Mark and see pity and sadness in his eyes.

"We were young. Childhood sweethearts. I loved him and still do. Toby and his family moved here when we were in high school. It was hard being so far apart, but we made it work." I tell him about Gran and then moving here. Mark listens and occasionally asks me questions. He's genuinely interested.

After our meal, we sit back in the living room beside the roaring fire. It's such an amazing, cosy house. So homely. Even though we're alone, I've not felt unsafe at all, and he's a real gentleman. We're comfortable with each other. Being in his company feels the same as with Toby, if that's at all possible. I feel safe. I know I've only just met him, but this connection is special. I'm drawn to him. Not just his looks, even though he's gorgeous, but it's like I have this thin cord pulling me in further and further. I sometimes get the feeling we've met before, but that's not possible.

We're so at ease with each other, I lie back with my feet up on the couch.

"Mark, this couch just swallows me up. I could fall asleep right here," I say as I yawn for the third time.

He laughs and starts to mimic me yawning. I grab a cushion and throw it at him. We laugh again until he starts to tickle my feet that I hadn't realised he had placed on his lap. I wriggle and squeal. It makes him laugh more. He then starts to massage my feet. Pure bliss.

I feel a slight movement and open my eyes, wondering where I am. I remember feeling relaxed after my amazing meal, then talking to Mark...

Crap.

I bolt upright. The fire is out, there's a blanket wrapped around me, and Mark is standing by the couch, looking down at me with one hand in his pocket and the other with his thumb at the corner of his mouth. I give him a timid smile.

"I'm so sorry I fell asleep again. It's just so relaxing in here. What time is it?"

He's dressed in slacks, a shirt, and a tie loose around his neck. He wasn't dressed like that when I went to sleep. It's then I realise it's light; the curtains are open. Oh, crap. Did I stay out all night? Sylvia will be frantic.

I rummage around for my bag, and finding it, I pull out my phone. I have missed calls and lots of text messages from them all. Oh, no. *Why didn't I have my phone on loud instead of silent?* Panic starts to rise in me.

"Hey, hey. Calm down. It's okay." Mark is holding both my forearms, bending to look me in the eyes.

"No, Mark. It's not okay. What will they think of me? I told Sylvia and Charlie I was going for a meal with a friend."

I told them about Mark. I'm so ashamed. I don't want them thinking badly of me, especially since we have all only just come to terms with accepting Toby has gone. Tears start to run down my cheeks, and Mark pulls me to him and strokes my hair, telling me it's okay.

It's not okay.

"Can you please drop me home, Mark?"

He pulls away and bends to my face, gently kissing the tip of my nose. "Phone them and let them know you're safe so they don't worry anymore. It was a simple case of you falling asleep. You haven't done anything wrong. Now, calm down. Breathe with me in and out. Slowly, in and out."

I follow him, and I can feel myself calming down. I know he's right. I'm a grown woman and I don't have to answer to anyone, but I should have texted them to let them know I was okay.

"Now, I have coffee ready and some toast in the kitchen. Call them, and then have a coffee and something to eat. I'll drop you off on my way to work. Is that okay?" I nod.

He smiles, kisses my forehead, and heads to the kitchen.

I'm gripping the phone to my chest as I watch him leave. I take a few more deep breaths, then, with shaking hands, I open my screen and press Sylvia's number. I don't know why I'm shaking so much.

"Sylvia, I'm sorry I didn't ring you. I fell asleep and I've only just woken up. Please forgive me. I'm mortified. My phone was on silent. I had no intention of staying out." I ramble on, but she tells me to shush and that as long as I'm safe and everything is okay, I never have to explain anything to her. I tell her I'm just about to have a coffee and will be straight home.

I walk into the kitchen as I'm saying goodbye, and my eyes connect with Mark's immediately.

"Mark, I'm sorry for my meltdown. I panicked; I didn't want them to think badly of me." Now, I'm also afraid I may have scared him off with my panic attack. It's been a long time since I last had one. I watch as he picks a coffee cup up and walks towards me. He stands in front of me and hands me the cup. I take it and timidly smile up at him. He bends slightly and smiles back. He holds the tops of my forearms and gently rubs them

"Never apologise, Heather. You have nothing to apologise for. I understand this is all new for you after losing Toby. Now drink your coffee, grab some toast, and I'll get you home." He kisses the top of my head and turns to leave the kitchen. I stand there, thinking how this man who doesn't know me has seen me get a bit testy with him and go into a meltdown, and he doesn't seem fazed by it.

I walk into Sylvia's with my head low. I feel as though I'm doing the walk of shame. Thea is sitting on the couch. Great, that's all I need.

"So, who was the hot guy who just dropped you off? Give me the deets! Come on, don't keep me waiting. What's his name? How did you meet? Did you really just fall asleep?" she asks, showing me quotation marks with her fingers. She's laughing as she's grilling me. I want the floor to swallow me up.

"Stop it, Thea. Don't you have work to get to? Leave Heather alone. She doesn't have to tell you anything." Sylvia steps in, trying to get rid of Thea so I don't have to be any more embarrassed than I already am. Charlie has already left for work, thankfully, and once Thea leaves, I sit and talk to Sylvia.

"I was so tired, and I was sitting on the most comfortable couch, and I just fell asleep. I woke up this morning with a blanket thrown over me. I couldn't believe I had fallen asleep, and he didn't wake me. I think I like him, Sylvia, but I have all these doubts in my head because of Toby. I feel like I'm cheating on him or betraying him. It doesn't feel right that I like someone else. I don't know what to do or how to get over it." I look at the mug of coffee in my hand. I don't want to see hurt on her face.

"Heather, look at me, love. You're going to be in a conflict with yourself no matter if it's now or in ten years. You love Toby, I know that, but you do have to take the steps to move on. Whether it's with this Mark or someone else, it will happen, and you have nothing to feel ashamed about. You're a beautiful young woman. You have your whole life ahead of you. Just take it easy, see what happens, and go with your instincts. Don't hold back. Toby would never have wanted that. He would want you to find someone who loves you as much as he loved you. Someone who can give you the full, happy life you should have had with him. You can't grieve forever, love." Tears flowing down my cheeks. Sylvia grabs me to her side, and we sit with her hugging me for a while. I know she's right.

I've just spent my last week in Toronto. Mark took me out each night and some days, and it's been great being myself again. I've been lost since Toby died, and I felt like I had died with him. Mark has brought me out of myself and found the me that loves life and loves to laugh. I never thought I could ever be or feel like this again. After Toby died, there were dark days when I didn't want to be here and live without him. I could never see this happening in my future, or ever thought I had one without Toby

It's New Year's Eve, and I'm going out with Mark. Sylvia and Charlie are out at a friend's party. Thea is out with her friends, and Fiona went back to New York yesterday. I was very tearful saying goodbye to her, JT, and Thomas. I promised I would come visit them soon.

I'm just finishing putting my hair up when I hear a car pull up. I quickly finish, grab my bag and shoes, and run down the stairs. I open the door just as Mark gets to it.

"Hey, Heather. Wow, you look absolutely beautiful. You take my breath away." I smile but watch as his eyes become hooded, and he moves closer to me. I have to look up as he moves into my space. He's come close a few times before, but we have never actually kissed properly. He cups my face with his hands

"Heather, I've wanted to do this since the day I met you, but I need your permission. This is a big step. May I kiss you?"

I'm floored by the beauty of this man and the gentleman he is. He's thinking about my feelings in all this and not just of what he wants. I've wanted this too; I was just so conflicted about Toby, but I want this more than anything. He's looking deep into my eyes, and I smile and nod. He slowly bends and very gently kisses me on the lips. Tingles run through my body as I kiss him back. He still has a hold of my face, and I open my mouth just as his tongue starts to edge in. I feel a little strange kissing another man, but boy, does he know how to kiss. I hold his waist and pull him into me, and the kiss starts to get a little heated. My tummy is doing flip-flops with all the butterflies inside. It's partly nerves, but mostly desire. I start to struggle a little as Toby comes to mind, and I pull away.

"Are you okay? Was that too much? I'm sorry. I didn't mean for it to get heated like that."

"No, it was perfect, Mark. Don't apologise." I smile and kiss him gently on the lips to show it's okay. "Now, let me re-do my lipstick and let's get going."

I step back into the house and quickly do just that. I notice how flushed I look, but I like the look on me. I start to analyse my feelings after the kiss, and I feel just like I did all those years ago with Toby. The tingles, the tummy turns, and the heat coursing through my body.

I turn to leave and see him leaning against the door jamb with his arms folded and one leg crossed over the other, watching me. I still can't fathom how this god of a man is single. Although we talk constantly, I still don't know a lot about him. He knows more about me. Maybe we need to rectify that. My tummy suddenly flops again, but not in a good way. A thought just entered my head about what happens next. I go back home the day after tomorrow. What will happen then? Is this just some kind of holiday fling? How have I not thought about that until now?

"Hey, what's the matter? You went from smiling to sad." He stands behind me and wraps his arms around my waist, with his chin resting on my head. He's looking at me in the mirror.

"I just had a thought about something. I don't want to discuss it now. Let's go and enjoy tonight. It's been a long time since I celebrated New Year's Eve." I turn and take his hand, leading him out towards the car.

We arrive at the CN Tower. I've been up here before for dinner, but when I walk into the revolving restaurant, it's all elegantly decorated. Most of the tables have been removed, and they've made a section of the restaurant into a dance area with a DJ. It looks so different.

We spend the night talking with different people. Everyone seems to know Mark. We eat, drink, and then we dance. I thought it would be a disaster, drinking and dancing on a revolving structure, but we manage it. It's not like we're drunk or anything. At midnight, we are all handed a glass of champagne. The clock strikes and we all cheer.

I look at Mark.

"Happy New Year," We both say at the same time. In unison, we put our glasses down, then we slam into each other and kiss. Everything around me doesn't exist as he takes my mouth hard. This is better than the first one; there's no thinking, or hesitation. It starts to get heated as my hands find their way to the back of his head, and I rake my fingers through his hair. His hands are on my waist, pulling me into him. The cheering brings me to my senses, and I pull away, breathless. We smile, then move to the windows to watch the fireworks. Mark is standing behind me with his arms wrapped around my waist and his chin on my head. I can see his reflection in the window, and he has the biggest smile on his face that mirrors my own.

We head back to Mark's house after the party. I want to spend time with him. I only have this last day before I fly home tomorrow.

Inside the house, he makes me a hot chocolate with marshmallows. We sit on the couch by the fire; I take off my shoes and put my feet up, leaning into him. He puts his arm around me and pulls me in, and I rest my head on his chest.

"Heather, what did you want to say before we went out tonight?"

"Can we talk about it later? I just want to enjoy my time with you. This is my last day here. I want it to be a happy one." I lean up and kiss his lips, and he smiles as he kisses me back.

I turn so I'm on my back, looking up to him, and he slumps down so he can be comfortable kissing me. I feel the tingles all over my body and the heat rising as his hands start to wander, first up my thigh to my tummy, then to my breasts. He's so gentle as he squeezes and pinches my nipples, which sends funny tingling sensations right down to my core. It makes me want him and I'm ready to take this further. I have feelings for Mark. I never thought I'd feel again. Yes, I'm still conflicted because of Toby, but if I take Toby out of the equation, I think I'm falling in love with Mark. I know I hardly know him, and he's the first person I've kissed since Toby, but I really believe there's something between us.

I stand up, and his hooded eyes watch every move I make. He licks his lips provocatively, and he shuffles to the edge of the couch,

"Come here, baby." He pulls me by the waist to stand in between his legs. I place my hands on his shoulders as he places his on my backside. We look intently into each other's eyes, and he leans his face into my tummy. I instinctively start to stroke his hair, running my fingers through the blonde curls.

"Heather, I've never met anyone like you. You're funny, intelligent, beautiful, caring, and passionate. I love your long brown hair, and your eyes are like the ocean. I get lost in them." He looks up at me, then frowns. I have tears flowing down my cheeks at his words.

"Ditto," I tell him, leaning down to take his mouth.

As we kiss, his hands move up my legs under my dress. I breathe in at his touch on my inner thighs that send pulsing shockwaves through my entire body. His hand moves slowly until I feel him brush against my panties. I edge my legs open slightly to give him access. He rewards me with a smile before ploughing his tongue into my mouth and duelling with mine. He moves my panties aside with one hand, then, with the other, he starts to stroke me. I gasp, screwing my eyes shut, but holding his head so he can't move from kissing me. His fingers stroke inside my folds. Gently, he inserts a finger and starts to move it in and out. I crouch slightly, widening my stance again to let him have more access. We stare at each other, blue eyes to blue eyes. The intensity in that stare makes me want to lose all inhibitions. He inserts another finger and moves around inside me. His thumb finds my nub and rubs at it. I move to his rhythm, panting, still looking into his eyes, smiling at the beauty I see in them. I throw my head back as the feelings intensify, arching my back. I pant harder; I'm getting close to orgasm. It's been so long.

He suddenly stops before I reach my climax. I look down at his smiling face. He moves his hands from under my dress, turns me around, and slowly pulls the zipper down. Once it's fully down, the dress falls to my feet. I stand in front of him in just a strapless bra, panties, suspenders, and stockings. He turns me back to face him.

"You're stunning. You take my breath away. I need to make sure you're fine with this, my beautiful girl. If you need me to stop, just say the word. I understand completely."

"I want this, Mark. There's no need to stop. I'm ready."

His smile melts my heart. He pulls me into him and starts to kiss my tummy. His hand finds my panties again, only this time, he rips the sides and pulls the material away from me. He inserts his fingers once again. I gasp, and he kisses down my tummy towards my core. I open my legs wider, and he pulls me to his mouth and starts to lap at my juices. He inserts his tongue and, oh my God. I grab his head, pulling it into my pelvic bone. It hurts, but I don't care. He's licking and sucking. He plays with my nub with his thumb. His other hand moves around, and he starts to stroke up and down my lower back and over my ass. I'm pulling him into me harder, trying to get his tongue deeper. I must be nearly breaking his nose. *Oh, God, I'm going to kill him at this rate. He's going to suffocate in there.*

I want this. I need this. I explode right in his face. With my release, I scream out with my face to the ceiling, digging my nails and fingers into his scalp as I gyrate, wanting him to get his head in there. Shocks and shivers course through my body; even my scalp is tingling. I want to push him away from me, to give me a breather, but I also want him to carry on with the onslaught of his tongue inside me. Tears stream down my face as I bite my lip.

No, that's it. I'm done. I push his head away and fall onto him, knocking him back on the couch. He laughs at me as I lay on his chest, trying to catch my breath. Holy cow. I don't think I've ever felt anything like it. With Toby, it was mostly just missionary sex. He never went down on me. I did him, a lot. It was his favourite.

I want to taste Mark. I lift myself up and look at him. His nose is squashed, red, and wet, and his lips are swollen. His face goes from smiling to one of confusion and concern as he notices my tears.

"Oh, Heather. I knew it would be too much. Are you okay?"

I laugh. "More than okay. It's my turn." I slither down his lap until I'm sitting on the floor in front of him. I proceed to pleasure him with my mouth and tongue, just as he did to me.

When he's come down from his high, I sit on his lap, kissing him, tasting each other. I want to feel him inside me. It's time. I raise up and line up with his cock. He has lines on his brow, and I can see the worry.

"Are you sure you want this, baby? We can stop if you're unsure."

"I want this more than anything, Mark." He grins from ear to ear, grabs my hips, and I slam down on him. Fast and hard is how I want this. It's been so long. We go at it until we both climax at the same time, both screaming out our release. He's fucking amazing. How the hell am I going to walk away from this now?

I fall forward, burying my face in his chest. His cock is still inside me, but I don't have any intention of moving. He wraps his arms around me and holds me tight as I let the tears pour out of me. I'm the happiest I've been in so long, yet along with the ecstasy, euphoria, and the love I feel for Mark, I have such sadness, loss, and guilt inside of me.

We both fell asleep. It's the cold that wakes me. I'm still on Mark's chest, but I can't hear the fire and there is a bitter chill in the air. I slowly move, but I disturb him.

"Hey, are you okay?"

I smile, nodding. "Yes, just cold."

"Oh, God. The fire's gone out." He holds out his hand. "Come to bed with me. I'll keep you warm." He has a knowing smile on his face.

❄

I wake to the smell of strong coffee. I open my eyes slowly. I don't even have the duvet on me as it's so warm in here. I stretch out with my hands above my head.

"Wow, now that's a sight I could get used to. Good morning, beautiful. How are you feeling?" I smile as he leans over, giving me a kiss.

"Are you asking if I'm ready for round four? If you are, then the answer is hell yes."

He laughs, and this time, he lifts me and turns me over so I'm on all fours. He plays with his cock on my core before entering me with force, almost knocking me flying into the headboard. I reach under me and play with his balls as he slams into me with everything he has, gripping my waist hard. He then moves a hand around the front to play with my nub, and I explode in no time. He follows me shortly after, and we roll over and laugh.

"Well, Happy New Year to you too, Mr..." It just strikes me; I don't even know his last name. I know very little about him. We've spent almost a week in each other's pockets, and I hardly know him. I sit up and look at him.

"I don't know your surname. I don't know what you do for a living. You know almost everyone in Toronto." I laugh at the craziness of that. "I don't know what you like or anything."

He looks at me like I've gone mad. "I like you," he says, leaning over and kissing my tummy with a smile.

I push him away and scoot up. "We never talk about you, Mark. I don't know if you're with someone, or why someone who looks like you doesn't have women knocking their door down. Why do you want to be with me? I've been broken. I have baggage, and I'm boring. What is it you see in me? Is this just a fling? I don't know why I'm here."

I pull my knees up, placing my arms around them, and lean my head on them. I don't know where all this has suddenly come from. I think I'm in love with him, yet I don't know him. Have I betrayed Toby for this... whatever this is? *No*, I did this for *me*. But I do love him. I know I do. I wanted to talk to him later about where we go from here, but I just blurted it out.

He sits up and pulls me to him, sitting me on his knee so I can look at him.

"I never thought about all that stuff, Heather. It's just been so easy with you. You've not questioned me about anything. You asked about my family, but that's about it. No, I'm not seeing anyone but you because you're beautiful inside and out, and I can't get enough of you."

I turn and look around his room, seeing if it's a man's room or if there are any signs of women. I don't know why I'm feeling insecure. I've had the best night of my life, and I know that's terrible on Toby, but it has been. I'm in love with this man, I know I am. The feelings I have say I am.

I notice some photographs on the tall set of draws. There are no photos downstairs. There is a picture of Mark with his mum and sisters and an older man. Then there's a picture of him and the older man again, both dressed in suits, and the older man has his arm around Mark's shoulders. From here, the older man looks nice with his white beard, but he also looks familiar. I don't know where from.

"Is that your grandad?" I nod towards the picture.

"Yes, the old fool. I loved him. He owned an exceptionally large department store here in Toronto and one in London. The store is Randolf Department store. The one you were in last week when we bumped into each other. I inherited them and I now run them." I gasp. Oh my God.

He owns Randolf?

"So, you're Mark Randolf?"

He nods.

OH, SANTA!

Why does it ring a bell? I look back at the picture, squinting at it. Oh my God. I know him.

"How did he die? You said he died a few years ago."

"It was five years ago now. He was a good age. Too old to drive if you ask me. He was eighty-six when he died in a car wreck. He had a couple of drinks. He forgot to bring the Christmas presents to our house and insisted on driving back home to get them. It was Christmas Day. He should never have gone out, but we never saw him again."

I close my eyes; I can't believe what I'm hearing. How? It must be a coincidence. There's no other explanation for it. I suddenly feel dizzy and sick.

"It's why I don't celebrate Christmas anymore. I still miss him the old coot." I climb off him slowly and move over to the picture to get a close look.

"Simon Randolf," I whisper as I drop the picture and it smashes.

Mark rushes over and lifts me up to place me on the bed so I don't cut my feet. I can't look at him. I turn into the pillow, and I cry. I cry so hard. How can I be in love with the man whose grandfather killed my husband? How can this be happening? It must all be a horrible mistake.

"Heather, what is it? You're scaring me. What's wrong? Please talk to me." It takes me a little while to calm down. He's trying to give me space. I slowly turn and see his face is screwed up as if in pain.

"Did you know?"

He looks at me quizzically.

"DID YOU KNOW?" I scream at him. I'm starting to get hysterical. I sit up and push his chest. "Did you fucking know all this time? Have you been playing me? Was this all out of sympathy? Oh my God, you paid for my seat on the plane, didn't you? You knew who I was! You had to know. You felt sorry for me. You wanted to help, out of sympathy." He tries to grab my wrists to stop me from hurting myself as I start to pull at my hair. "You knew it was me. You had to. You know what he did."

"Heather, please stop. What are you talking about? Yes, I paid for your seat on the plane. Only because I heard you talking to the air steward, and I couldn't have you getting off when I knew it was the last plane out. I was just being nice because I could. But I don't know what else you're talking about. Please tell me."

I watch him closely. Is he telling me the truth? I don't know anymore. I'm so angry with myself for letting this go as far as it did. How did I not know it was the owner of Randolf's who killed Toby? It never even crossed my mind about the name. I know I was in a state of shock when it all happened, and I didn't take any notice of anything going on around me. I was just in a daze all the time, barely surviving. Even making the decision to go back home wasn't the right one, and Sylvia did try to talk me out of it. I had no-one back in the UK, but in the frame of mind I was in, I just couldn't be around Toby's family or be where the accident happened. I was oblivious to everything and everyone around me, even at the funeral. I could just about function.

Does Sylvia and everyone else know? They haven't met Mark, and maybe if they had, they would have known who he was.

"Heather. Tell me what it is. What do you think I know?"

"DID. YOU. KNOW. HE. KILLED. MY. HUSBAND?" I scream at him, emphasising every word. He falls back onto his arse on the floor.

"No, it can't be. No, you have it wrong, Heather. He couldn't have killed Toby. No wa..." He hangs his head, and I see his shoulders moving up and down.

The penny just dropped. He pulls his knees up to his chest and buries his head in them. I get off the bed and walk to what I think is his closet to grab a sweatshirt. This will have to do for me getting home. I need to leave. His grandfather ruined my life.

I run down the stairs and take his keys from the hall table as I fight to put my coat on. Thank goodness it's a long coat. I head out front, trying not to fall on the ice and snow, and I unlock his car and drive off. It's a straight route to Sylvia's house, and I've driven in Toronto before, just not in a very expensive sports car. It's New Year's Day, and the roads are quiet, but I drive slowly, trying to concentrate with everything going around inside my head. I wipe away at the tears streaming down my face. I just can't wrap my head around all this. As I turn the corner, I see something out of the corner of my eye. Whatever it is hits the car. I automatically slam on the breaks. The roads are icy, and it sends me careening off the road.

OH, SANTA!

❄

"Heather, can you hear me, baby? Please open your eyes. Please, Heather. I don't want to lose you. You're going to be okay; you just need to wake up. I love you, Heather. I love you so much."

At first, I thought it was Toby talking to me. I thought it was all a dream and he was alive, and it was me that was dead, but Toby's already been to see me. I saw him as clear as day, standing in the light. He was telling me everything was going to be okay.

"Heather, my sweet Heather. It's not your time yet. You have everything to live for. You know we always said everything happens for a reason. I believe this is it for you. You were meant to be with Mark. I know it's hard to say, but I see the love you have for each other. I will always love you, but you need to move on now, baby. You will never forget me, I know this, but just know this is meant to be. Mark isn't responsible for his grandfather's actions. Try not to blame him for what someone else did. He's suffered enough, as have you. It's time to go back. I love you, Heather." I tried to reach out as he started to disappear into the light, but he vanished.

"I love you. Please wake up. I spoke to Sylvia and Charlie. They knew it was my grandfather, but I honestly didn't know. I mean, I did know back then, but I didn't put it all together when I met you. Please give me a chance."

"I love you too, Mark," I try to croak. I don't know if he looks at me; I haven't opened my eyes. I don't even know if he heard me.

"Heather, baby. Can you open your eyes? Can you look at me?"

I try to open my eyes. Slowly, the light starts to penetrate my sight. I blink. It hurts, and they start to water. I have to close them again

"Can I have some water, please?" I feel a straw at my mouth, and I suck carefully. I'm so thirsty. "What happened, Mark? Where am I?" I slowly open my eyes to slits to look at him.

"You were in an accident. Luckily, the snow slowed you down, but you hit your head pretty bad, and you broke your leg and shoulder. You're in the hospital, baby, but you're going to be okay. The doctors were worried about your head. They had to operate to relieve the pressure from a bleed. It was all successful. We've just been waiting for you to wake up. Do you remember anything?"

I sip more water, and then he wets my lips with a sponge. I try to think.

"I remember something hit the car. Oh, no. Your car. I'm sorry. I slammed the brakes on and I guess with it being icy, I lost control. Oh, God, Mark. What if I had died just like my parents and Toby?" I pause for a moment. "I remember your grandad. I heard you talking to me just now. I just need time to process it." He looks down at his hand holding mine and lets go. When he looks back at my face, I see the downturn of his mouth, and his eyes look vacant and lost. He rises from his seat.

"I need to get the nurse and doctor to let them know you're awake." He's sullen as he speaks, and he bends to kiss my forehead, lingering for a few moments, before turning to leave. I hate that he's hurting as he takes a back glance before leaving.

I've just found out I've been in the hospital for a week. I should have left for home the day after New Year's Day. It's a good job I don't have any pets or anyone to get home to. I do, however, have clients waiting for orders. Now I have a broken shoulder that's going to take time to heal. I'm going to have to cancel the orders I have. I hate letting people down.

❅

Apart from when I woke up in the hospital after my accident, I haven't seen Mark at all. I'm at Sylvia's to recuperate until I'm able to fly back home. She's more than happy for me to stay with them. I'm hurt and angry that Mark hasn't been to see me or even called me. It's me who lost my husband at the hands of his grandfather, not the other way around. Surely it's me who should be having a hard time with this. Why should I be the one to call him? Sylvia says he probably needs time to process it all. Apparently, he never left my side from finding me until I woke up. When I ran from his place, he immediately followed me. He saw the skid marks, then the smoke. He stopped to check it out and couldn't get to me quick enough when he saw it was his car that had run off the road. She said he had a tough time with it because of his grandfather, but he wouldn't leave me. She told me Mark isn't responsible for his grandfather's actions and neither of us should let it come between us.

※

I'm heading home to London today after being given the all clear to travel. I can't believe he never came to see me or even text me to see how I was doing. I love him, but I feel stupid for doing so. I'm so angry with him. How could he not even want to find out how I am? I've come to terms with him not being responsible for Toby's death. I know he suffered losing his grandfather. I just wanted to see him to explain. I feel so despondent about leaving without seeing him.

In the airport, I search for Mark everywhere, just in case he turns up like they do in the movies. I just want to see him one last time. I'm going to text him. It's the least I can do, even if it's just to give myself closure.

Mark, I'm on my way back to London. I just want to say thank you for the most amazing time spent with you whilst I was here. You helped make Christmas memorable again. I know you're not responsible for what your grandfather did. I realise that, and I shouldn't have said I needed time. I'm sorry you lost him too. Thank you, Mark. Look after yourself. I love you. Xx

I hit send before I can delete it.

I'm sitting on the plane, looking out of the window as people board. I was on first because I still have my leg in a cast. It was sad leaving Sylvia, Charlie, and Thea. I even cried leaving Dusky. I promised I would come back and see them very soon.

"Excuse me, Ms Borbon. I'm sorry, but we have to move you from this seat. I've just been told the life jacket under the seat is missing and so we're not able to utilise it."

"Wait, what? Not again. How unlucky can one person get."

"There is only one seat available. Let me grab your bags. Do you think you can follow me to your new seat?" I don't want to, but what choice do I have? I nod for her to lead the way.

I follow her as we walk towards the front of the plane. I'm being watched by everyone again. I pass lots of empty seats in economy, so why did she say there was only one seat available? We enter first class.

"I'm not paying an upgrade to sit in here. This is not my fault."

"There is no charge."

What the hell? Why couldn't they have been like this on my way to Canada? I get settled in my seat.

The take-off was a bit ropey, probably with all the snow. We level out and the air stewards set about getting our meals ready. I'm in the middle row again, in the exact seat I came in. There is no Mark in 10K opposite me this time, though. It makes me sad. I eat my meal, then the stewards come round with drinks.

"Excuse me, Ms. Borbon, would you care to join me at the bar for a drink?"

Oh my God. I would know that voice anywhere. I turn behind me, and Mark is standing there, smiling down at me. I try to undo my seatbelt, but I fumble with the clip. My broken shoulder is still not right. He suddenly appears in front of me and kneels to help me. He doesn't move, he just stares at me with the biggest smile on his face. As usual, my tummy flips. I should be angry as hell with him, and I am, but for him to be here in front of me is far outweighing any anger I have. I'm searching his face. I want to make sure he wants to be here for me.

"Hey," I whisper.

"Hey yourself."

I lean forward just as he does

"I've missed you, Mark. I'm sorry you had to put up with me and my baggage. I'm sorry I messed up your life. I'm sorr..." He leans in and shuts me up by kissing me. I wrap my arms around his neck and kiss him back.

"I've missed you more than I thought possible. I've been outside your house every day, just wanting to see you, to get a glimpse. I've walked up to the front door so many times I'm surprised the neighbours didn't report me. I can't miss you anymore. I tried with everything I had to stay away because I didn't want you to blame me for what my grandfather did. I didn't want to be a reminder to you of what he did. The pain I saw on your face when you found out it was my grandfather who killed Toby tore me apart inside. I just wanted to grab you and comfort you and tell you it wasn't true. I honestly didn't know. Charlie kept me up to date on your recovery. He told me when you were leaving. I couldn't let you go. Not without telling you again that I love you. I don't know how it happened so fast or why it happened, but it did. I love you."

Tears slip from my eyes as I hug him to me.

"I love you with everything I am, Mark."

❋

I'm back in Toronto. I've been here for three months. This is now my second Christmas in Toronto, only this year, I now live with my husband. I'm now Mrs Randolf-Borbon. It was Mark's idea to keep Toby's surname as well. I love that man. He's so caring and considerate. I've moved into his log cabin, and I have my own workshop where I make all my bespoke jewellery. I even sell it in Randolf Department Stores. My business has taken off. I'm still designing my pieces, but I'm hiring a small team that I will train to help me make them. I couldn't be happier, especially as we just found out we're having a baby. Sylvia and Charlie are over the moon for us, and they can't wait to be our baby's grandparents.

I will always love and miss Toby. I believe things happen for a reason. I believe all the grief and coincidences that have happened were to bring me to Mark and this point in my life. I never dreamed I would ever get over Toby. Life throws us some devastating curveballs at times. I am learning to embrace Christmas once again with my new family and promise to never lose one again.

The End

ALSO BY LYNDA THROSBY

Standalones
A Christmas Wish

Catfish

Chef

The Best Day of My Life

The Pain Series
The Pain They Feel

Poppy's Revenge

His Rightful Queen

You Broke me First

Cabin Fever

by

C.L Stewart

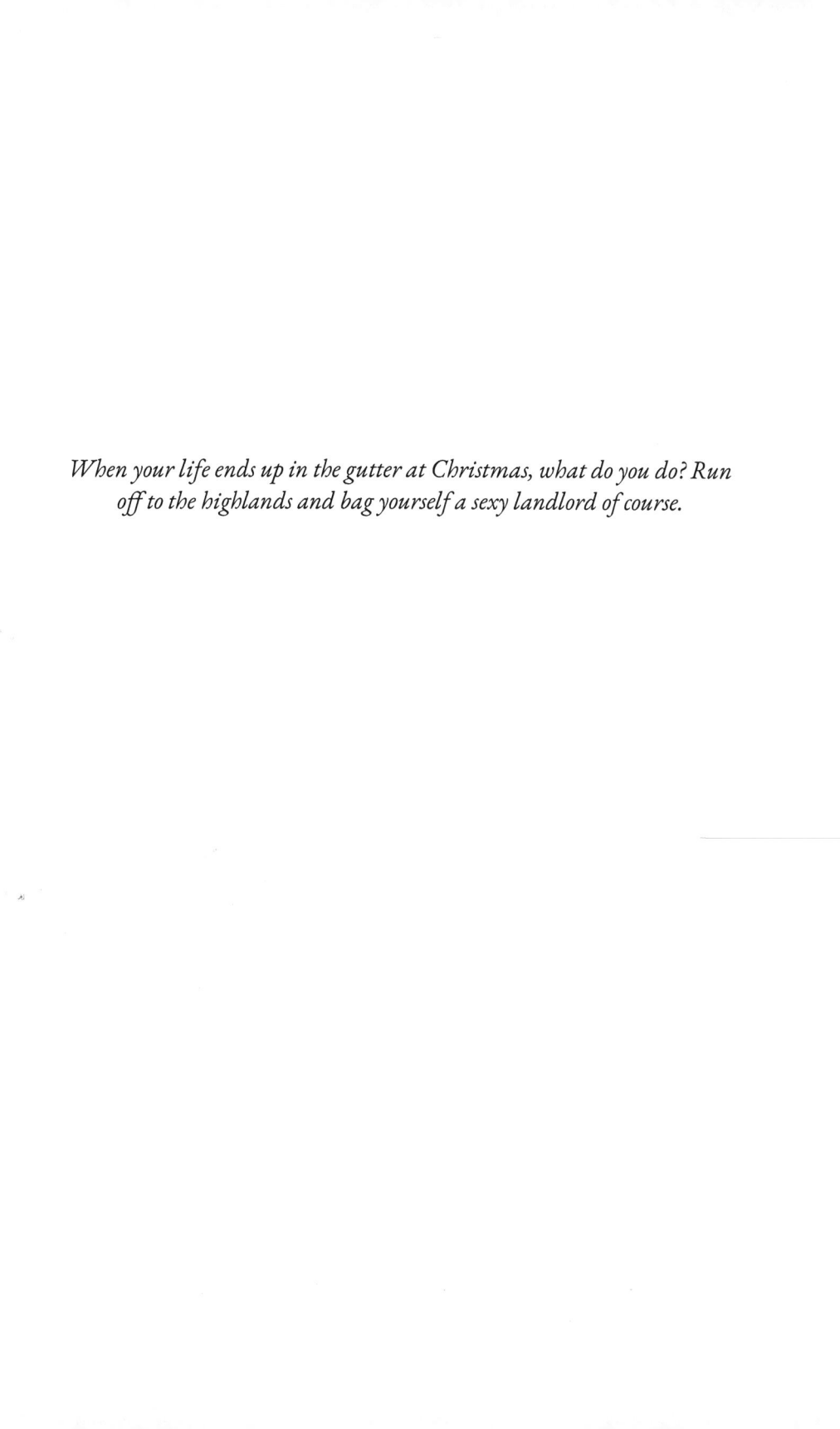

When your life ends up in the gutter at Christmas, what do you do? Run off to the highlands and bag yourself a sexy landlord of course.

Chapter One

Georgie

What did I ever do to deserve this? My mind whirs as I stand in the doorway of my boyfriend's bedroom. The scene unfolding in front of me makes me question if I even woke up this morning. In a day that is slowly but surely bearing a strong resemblance to something you would watch in a cheesy rom com; this is the icing on the goddamn cake.

Working for a local plumbing company couldn't have been a better fit for me. The owner and his wife were the loveliest employers I could ever have asked for, and my job was so easy; it was stress-free, easy money. I adored my lovely little flat in the centre of Edinburgh. My boyfriend was a nice guy. He was charming, confident, and always treated me well. I saw myself spending the rest of my life with him…until this morning.

"Fuck, Georgie. Uh, what are you doing here?" His scrambling on the bed to pull the covers over himself would have been comical if it weren't happening to me.

A giggle from the bleached blonde sitting in his bed with him roils my stomach. I stare at her smug, smiling face, and have a strong urge to knock her out.

I close my eyes, count to ten, and take a cleansing breath. "Don't stop on my account, please."

"Fuck." His reply is clipped.

The giggles coming from the blonde are starting to make my blood boil, and I shoot her a scathing look. "Something funny, skank?" I ask in a tone I've never had to use in my entire life. And I know I didn't mean the words coming from my mouth, but it seems to shut her up nonetheless.

She closes her mouth and has the grace to look apologetic. Ian, on the other hand, has a strange look of relief on his face.

Cocking my head to the side, I give him a smile as I take in how the two of them look together sitting in the bed. They resemble a couple. I mean obviously they do; there are two of them. But they look good together. Better suited than we seem to be. At three inches taller than Ian, we always garner stares from strangers. The petite frame of his bed buddy complements him better than I ever could.

"Can we talk? Alone?"

"Um, sure." He glances at the woman who gives him a reassuring nod.

I roll my eyes and make my way out to the living room, taking a seat on the sofa and sighing. Ah, the sofa. The very one I bought him as a housewarming gift. We've had many a fun time on this sofa. If nothing else, at least we'll have the memories.

"Georgie, I'm so sorry." Ian appears in the doorway in a pair of grey joggers and a white T-shirt. In his haste to dress, he's put his shirt on inside out.

"Hmm. Let's not get all sentimental here, Ian. We both know you're not sorry because you'd never have done it if you were. To be honest, after the day I've had, this is the least of my worries."

"Georgie…"

"Shh." I cut him off. "Listen, I'll tell you about my day, then I'll gather my stuff and leave. I know this isn't the first time you've done this, and I know there's a relationship happening between you two. Did she know about me?"

"Yeah." He shuffles his feet, bowing his head the way a scolded child would.

"Why didn't you just end it with me. How long has this been going on?"

"Six months."

"Jesus, Ian, I could have found myself someone else by now. How fucking selfish of you."

"I know and I really am sorry. I just didn't know what to do. I do love you, Georgie, but..."

"Just as friends?"

"Yeah, I think so."

"Well, today has been just wonderful. I arrived at work this morning to find the place locked up and a sign on the gates reading 'Business in liquidation'. The fuckers bankrupted the business and disappeared. Then I went home to a notice to vacate from my landlord. He's selling the property with immediate effect and wants me gone in two weeks. So what did I do? I came to see my wonderful boyfriend."

"I hate what happened to you. I've made it worse."

"Well, that's where you're wrong. What you've done today is make me realise that there's nothing keeping me in Edinburgh anymore. Unemployed, homeless, and single. A triple whammy if you will. So like I said, I'll gather up all my stuff and be gone."

"Is that it? Are we just going to leave it like that?"

"What do you want me to do? Make you both a post shag meal or something?"

"There's no need to be like that, Georgie."

"Really?" My head is aching from all the information I've had to process today, and this tool here is asking me to leave on better terms.

"Okay, I get it you hate me."

"Pity party for one here," I shout as I stride past him and back into his bedroom where the blonde bombshell is sitting on the end of the bed, dressed in a fucking Christmas jumper and a pair of shorts. I want to punch her in the face and remind her that it's still November.

I set about gathering up all my stuff out of his drawers, making sure to accidentally drop some of his clothing on the floor. Ever the neat freak, even my stuff is all lined up Marie Kondo-style. *Let that spark joy, you arsehole.*

I leave the room with my clothes and walk to the kitchen where I know Ian keeps his car keys. Lifting them from the hook, I saunter out swinging them on my finger.

"What the fuck, Georgie? You can't leave me without a car."

"Can't I? Who owns the car?"

"Well, you do, but…"

"But nothing. I own the car, Ian. Your name is nowhere on the keeper's details. Why should I leave the car with you? You cheated on me. You've made a fool out of me. I was ready to settle down with you and you broke my heart. You don't get the car because you don't want me. Have a nice life and don't darken my door again. If you find anything else of mine here, just bin it. I don't want to see you again."

"You vindictive bitch." His sneer is unbecoming of him, his anger palpable. And it makes my heart sing with glee. I knew taking the car would get to him.

"Have a nice life. Hope she gets everything you never managed to give me."

"That was low."

Yes, it's low. But when your boyfriend never manages to last long enough to give you an orgasm and fucks off to clean himself up right after, you kind of lose some compassion for him.

Smiling at him, I leave his flat and walk out into the cold November afternoon. A stuttering breath leaves my body. Fuck! My life is in the gutter, and to top it all off, I'll be homeless for Christmas.

Chapter Two

Georgie

The problem with being homeless, jobless, and single so close to Christmas means that almost everyone already has their holiday plans in place. And they don't include me. I should have been spending Christmas with Ian and his parents, but instead, I'm googling places I can crash temporarily. I'll never find a place as cheap as the one I already have; that's for sure.

My parents are heading to London to spend Christmas and New Year with my grandparents, so I really can't bring myself to tell them about my predicament. I know as soon as I do, I'll get the third degree from them about my life choices. My dad has never liked Ian, but he could never pinpoint the actual reason. I love my parents to bits, but I'm not them. I didn't get their ambitious genes and never stayed in college long enough to get a qualification, much less go to university and get a degree like they did. Dad's saying of always having something to fall back on rings in my ears, and I roll my eyes and take a large swig of my wine.

The light is fading fast at night now and as I sit on my sofa and stare into the darkness outside my window, a sense of failure weighs on my shoulders. It's taken losing the little of what I had to make me realise how miserable my existence really is. I'm almost in my mid-twenties, and in the blink of an eye, I have nothing left to show of my adult life.

"Cheers, you fucking dick," I say to thin air, lifting my glass and toasting Ian. I down what's left and fill the glass again from the cheap bottle of wine on the side table next to me. I can feel myself getting tipsy. However, I couldn't care less. I'm already in the gutter so why not go down in a blaze of glory.

I pull up a new Google page and type in 'homes for rent Scotland'. Do I really want to trawl through all this and go through the rigmarole of trying to find a place at such short notice before Christmas? An idea pops into my head that I know is mostly fuelled by my semi-drunken state, but it seems like a good plan.

Clicking on the bookmark I saved years ago for holiday rentals in Scotland, I check out what's on offer as some kind of short-term fix to my current predicament. I know before I even look there will be no availability for anything around the Edinburgh area. With Christmas markets in Princes Street Gardens to all the festivities going on at the Castle and the huge Hogmanay party in the city, it isn't surprising that everything within a twenty-mile radius is booked up for the next month or so. The tab for the available properties catches my eye, and I click on it to see what might be lurking there. As the image pops up, I chuckle. The place is described as a 'Charming Log Cabin in the Idyllic Highlands of Scotland'. Now, I don't disagree that the highlands are idyllic. It's the word *charming* that's made me laugh. There's only a picture of the outside, and while it looks charming enough, I have to wonder why there are no photos of the inside. The one thing that really catches my eye though is that I can have this place for four weeks over Christmas and New Year for less than one week's rent on my flat. Having been taught from a young age how to save money well, I have a year's worth of rent in my savings account so this will never break the bank. It's only for four weeks anyway and I suppose there are worse places to spend Christmas alone. I'm so pathetic.

I drink the rest of my wine in one go and hit the Rent button. Fuck my life to hell and back.

2 WEEKS LATER

Standing on the street that has been my home for the last two years, I look up at the windows of my former flat. For some reason, I don't feel as sad about leaving this place as I thought I'd be. I'm meeting the landlord here to hand over the keys and get my deposit back from him. I got the good news about getting my deposit back after his inspection a few days ago. I've been a great tenant so I knew there wouldn't be a problem with it.

I see Graham, the landlord, across the street as he waves animatedly. He's obviously excited to be getting the flat back to sell and be moving on with his life. Must be nice. While I have to start all over again.

"Georgie, sorry I'm a wee bit late," he shouts as he runs across the road, narrowly missing being run over by a white workies van.

"It's okay. I've just put the last of my stuff in the car." I point to my new Volkswagen SUV, purchased by selling mine and Ian's cars. Selling that Mercedes was cathartic and brought me a bit of closure in what was an otherwise shitty time of my life.

"Nice wheels."

"Well, I'm off to the Highlands for a few weeks so I thought since it's the middle of winter, I should do the right thing and get a vehicle that can handle snow."

"Listen, I'm really sorry about the short notice on the let."

"Graham, I was pissed when I got the notice out of the blue, but you did me a huge favour. I can leave everything behind now and start afresh. I think it's the boot up the arse I've needed for a long time."

I hold up the keys and watch them dangle back and forth off my finger.

"Well, good luck with the rest of your life, and thanks for being such a great tenant." He takes the keys, hands me my deposit refund receipt, and tips his head to me. "Safe travels."

"Thanks. You too."

He turns in the direction he came from. I take one last look up at the flat and smile. I do need this, and a little time away from the bustle of the city might give me some clarity about where exactly I want my life to go from here.

Chapter Three

Finn

I knew it was too good to be true that someone would actually want to come and stay for Christmas in my piece-of-crap cabin. I was excited at the thought of making extra money over the holidays since it's our slowest time of the year. In all honesty, I only listed the place on a whim. In my heart, I never expected anyone to take up the offer.

Auchengarry is a remote little village in the west highlands of Scotland near Glencoe, but it's always busy in the summer at the height of the tourist season. I bought the cabin at the end of the summer season this year. The owner is one of my regulars in the pub I run, and he sold it to me for a steal. What the old bugger failed to tell me was how much work it required. I've done my best to weatherproof it, but beyond that, it isn't exactly a five-star accommodation. I was shocked when I got the email to tell me someone had booked the place for Christmas and New Year. The failure in the design of my plans was that I didn't take a deposit for the booking. The site I listed it on gave the option to have a deposit or none. In my mind, there was no way anyone was going to take the place anyway, so it never occurred to me to add it. Needless to say my customer never showed last night. I'm not out any money; it just would have been nice to have a little extra income over the holidays.

As I make my way up the snow-covered single track towards the cabin, I'm surprised to see a car sitting outside it. He must have made it after all, and well before it started to snow last night. I bring my pickup truck to a stop behind the car and pull on my gloves and woolly hat. My feet crunch on the white powdery snow as I jump down from the truck. I head over to the car and wipe the window of the driver's door, cupping my hand against the glass to see if there's anyone in there.

The figure in the reclined seat lies under what looks like a tartan picnic blanket. When I knock, they stir and turn to face me. The woman gives a loud shriek and jumps into the back seat, pulling her blanket tight around her.

"Sorry, sorry," I say, stepping back from the car, holding up my hands.

The car moves a little from side to side as the woman climbs back into the driver's seat, and the door opens before I can say or do anything to help. She squeals as a huge lump of snow falls off the top of the car and hits her right in the face. Unfortunately, I'm the sort of person who can get a fit of the giggles at a funeral, so this is hilarious to me. I burst out laughing and don't stop even when I see her thunderous scowl. Her blue eyes are striking against the wintry backdrop of the snow-covered cabin, and her icy stare makes the air seem colder.

"Oh yeah, this is very funny. As if I wasn't cold enough." She stands up straight and brushes the snow off her clothing.

"I'm sorry but that was funny."

She lets out a long, exasperated sigh and shakes her head, her long blonde hair swishing around her shoulders. "Well, since you're the only person I've seen since I got here last night, maybe you can help me. Do you know who owns this" —she turns to the house and air quotes— "cabin?"

"I do know," I reply, not giving myself away until I can be sure she doesn't want to murder me.

"Could you kindly point me in his direction, then? I was supposed to be meeting him here last night, but I ended up getting lost. By the time I got here, it was late, and my phone has no signal up here in the middle of nowhere. And to top it all off, it started snowing. You couldn't have made it up."

"You're Georgie?" I frown at her. "Sorry for my surprise; I was expecting a man. You didn't add a prefix in your email."

"Oh, bloody hell. That makes you Mr McAllister, then."

"Finn," I say, holding out my gloved hand.

She doesn't reciprocate, and I'm left standing looking like a spare tool.

"Do you realise how cold it is to sleep in a car, especially when it's snowing? I couldn't keep my engine running in case I ran out of fuel through the night. I'll be surprised if I don't die from hypothermia." She stomps her foot and wraps her blanket tightly around herself.

"Woah." I take a step back from her and hold my hands up. "I was here for almost two hours last night waiting for you. I did try to call you, but it went straight to your voicemail. I even stuck a note to the door with my phone number and address."

"There was no note on that door when I got here. Believe me if there was, I'd have been knocking down your door." Somehow, I don't doubt she's serious.

"I apologise that you didn't get it, but you couldn't have expected me to wait here all night for you."

"Ugh, whatever. I hope to hell you have the keys. I swear I've lost all feeling in my toes."

"I have. I'll show you inside and let you get settled. Again, sorry for the confusion last night."

She rolls her eyes at me as I walk past her. Approaching the door of the cabin, I smile. This is going to be an interesting few weeks with this woman as my tenant. I pull my keys out of my jacket pocket and hand her the spare set. I open the door and flick on the light to combat the gloom inside. Georgie follows me in and tuts. I turn to look at her and find her shaking her head and muttering to herself as she looks around. Okay, so it's not hotel standard, but it is habitable. I don't know what on earth she was expecting. It's clearly stated in the description I put online that the place is remote, and the building requires upgrading. I'm only charging enough to cover the utility bills and make a small profit.

It's an absolute steal for a cabin in the highlands, especially at this time of year.

"Fuck my life," Georgie mutters under her breath.

"Sorry?" I ask, knowing what I heard but wanting her to elaborate.

"Ugh, nothing. Is there wood for that?" She points to the wood burning stove.

"There's fresh wood in the bunker outside. I stocked it up when you made your booking so it would be here for you when you got here."

"At least you got something right."

She's pissing me off now. "Look, no one is forcing you to stay here. You booked the place. It's not my fault if you didn't read the description properly." I pull a card with my details on it out of my pocket and hand it to her. "There are two numbers. And my home address. If you need anything else, give me a ring. I'll leave you to it since it's obvious you don't appreciate me being here."

"Aren't you going to help me light that fire or show me around?"

I head for the door and look back around at her before I leave. I smile at her sullen face, knowing by now it will piss her off, and shake my head. "Nope," I say and pull the door closed behind me.

"Arsehole," she shouts after me.

I shake my head as I reach my truck. Yup, this is going to be an eventful Christmas.

Chapter Four

Georgie

I've been looking at the flames licking the inside of the wood burning stove for the last two hours, wallowing in my own self-pity this morning. I've flip-flopped between outrage at Finn and feeling bad for talking to him the way I did. Every time I feel bad, I look around at this shithole of a cabin and realise he deserved it. I honestly don't know what I was expecting, though. I've seen plenty of Instagram-worthy photos of log cabins in the highlands, and I think I set myself up for disappointment right then.

My day yesterday consisted of trying to light this goddamn fire. The wood was damp, and it wouldn't take a light. I used some bunched up kitchen towel as a fire starter and almost set myself on fire. I managed to get it lit, but I had to bring a load of wood inside to dry out a little. I'm pleased to say my fire making endeavour this morning went without a hitch. I also scrubbed the kitchen and bathroom, which both looked as though they'd been preserved from the fifties. The one thing I'm grateful to Finn for is that he had at least put milk in the fridge. I ended up so jacked up on coffee yesterday throughout the day that I crashed hard last night and slept like a log.

Yesterday's snow has cleared in the overnight rain. I need to pick up some stuff from the nearby village to make the place look more like a home. A sim card is essential too. I'm all for being off the grid a little, but I do need my phone.

I dress in the warmest clothes I can find in my bag and head out into the cold and overcast December morning. The drive to the village only takes me ten minutes, and it's so quiet that I find a parking space easily. It's a novelty, considering you need a permit to park in Edinburgh. My first port of call is the post office where I buy a new sim card and get my own number diverted to it. It's like I've grown an arm back when I'm able to get a signal again.

The next stop I make is to a little hardware store that looks like it has more than just DIY stuff. They have decorated the place like Lapland, and I think there must be over a hundred Santa ornaments all over the shop in different sizes. The decorations range from old-fashioned foil, dangly ones that I'm sure date from the seventies, to modern ones in different pastel and muted colours. In the back of the shop, I find the Christmas section that has the loveliest twinkly lights and decorations. I pick up a few packs of lights and a miniature desk-sized Christmas tree. I'm not overly fussed about Christmas this year. It only serves to remind me how alone I am. But it might be nice to make the cabin look a little cosier than it does now.

Placing all the stuff on the counter, I ring the service bell and wait patiently.

"Oh hello, dear, sorry to have kept you waiting."

I take in the older woman as she appears at the counter from behind a beaded curtain. She has a Mrs Claus look about her with her red blouse and Christmas-themed knitted sleeveless cardigan. Her friendly smile puts me right at ease.

"No worries. I wasn't here long."

"Are you here on a wee trip?"

"Yes, I am. I'm staying in Finn McAllister's cabin."

Her smile perks up at the mention of Finn's name, and I do an inward eye roll. Okay, the man is a hottie, and I imagine in a place like this, if he isn't attached, he's bound to be the most eligible bachelor. There can't be many young single men away up here in the highlands.

"Hmm. Has he had time to do the place up yet? I know he only bought it from Jock Henderson a couple of months ago."

I've watched countless movies about small villages where everyone knows everyone and their business, but I've never been to one as remote as this.

"Did Jock decorate it last in the fifties?"

"More than likely. It's been in his family for a very long time."

"Then no. He hasn't decorated it yet. It looks as though it's stuck in a time warp."

"Ouch, that's a shame. It really needs a little TLC. The place is solid though."

A little TLC is an understatement. "Yeah, it does," I say, smiling at her. "I'm just going to make it look a little more festive."

"Well, I'll tell you what, I'll give you a wee Christmas discount. Are you here on your own?"

Ugh, the dreaded question. "Yeah. I've had a bit of a rough month already, so I decided I needed to get away from the city and do some thinking."

"Edinburgh? I can tell from your accent. I'm good with accents. I knew Finn was from Glasgow when he first moved here."

So he's a Glaswegian! Interesting.

"Well done." I smile at her obviously well-trained ear. "Yes, that's where I hail from."

"My name's Moira by the way. I run the coffee shop next door too, so if you're looking for a coffee and a quick bite, just pop in."

"Georgie," I say, holding out my hand.

Moira gives me a firm handshake and then proceeds to ring up my goods on the most antiquated till I've ever seen. It's like one from a sweet shop in a period drama.

"That'll be twenty-five pounds, please."

I hold up my phone. "Do you take contactless?"

"Sure do," she says, pulling a phone with a little box attached to the top of it out from under the counter. "Only for the out of towners. Locals seem to prefer to pay in cash. This poor wee thing hasn't been used since the end of the summer season."

OH, SANTA!

I tap my phone on the box. "Thanks for your help today. You've been very kind."

"Enjoy your holiday and don't be a stranger. We're very friendly here."

"I won't, thanks."

I lift my bag from the counter and make my way out the door. The little mini market catches my eye and I head over to see what's on offer for dinner tonight. My little oven tv dinner last night left me feeling hungry.

The shop is quiet except for a young blonde girl staring at the feminine hygiene products. Christmas carols are playing from some tinny sounding speakers. It's quite nice to hear something traditional instead of Christmas pop music that blares from every shop in Edinburgh at this time of year.

As I walk past the young girl, I hear her curse under her breath and then she lets out a long sigh.

"Are you okay, sweetheart?" I ask, frowning at her perplexed look.

She looks at me sheepishly and chews on her lip. "Um, I, um, need some of these, but I don't have any money for them. My dad is at work in the pub, but I'm too embarrassed to go and ask him. I usually have money in my purse for them, but I forgot it."

"Show me what you want, and I'll get them for you. But only if you help me find something nice for my dinner tonight."

She smiles at me, obviously feeling a little more at ease. "Thank you."

"I'm Georgie. What's your name?"

She tilts her head and I see the hint of a smile form on her mouth. "Iris," she says.

"Lovely to meet you Iris, and that's a beautiful name."

"They were my mum's favourite flowers."

"How lovely."

"My dad told me about it. She died when I was young, and I don't really remember her."

Poor little girl. Going through puberty would've been bad enough. She hands me a pack of sanitary towels, and I stick them in my basket. We walk in silence to the bank of freezers, and I turn to her.

"Okay, what should I eat?"

"Got an oven?"

"Yup, and it's all sparkly clean too."

"Pizza, then. And potato wedges with cayenne pepper mayo. And some Coke to wash it down."

"You're a little genius. I could murder an absolute carb-fest right now."

"Pizza is the best food ever. My dad often takes me on a day trip to Inverness and we get a pizza there."

"I completely agree," I say, smiling at her enthusiasm for pizza, and put the frozen stuff in my basket. Iris sources mayo and cayenne pepper for me and drops them into the basket.

We head to the till and the cashier rings all the goods up. I hand Iris the towels and she stuffs them into her tiny bag hanging over her shoulder. After paying, we walk out the shop.

"Thanks for this, Georgie," Iris says, patting her bag.

Movement on the other side of the street catches my eye, and I look up to see Finn waving at us. I will admit he's a good-looking guy and dressed in jeans and a plaid shirt he looks every inch the highland villager. But I'm still mad at him and no amount of charm from his deep brown eyes will change that.

"Oh great, *him*," I mutter under my breath.

"What do you mean by that?" Iris asks.

"You know him?"

"Yes, he's my dad."

Oh, shit!

Chapter Five

Finn

I don't know why my thirteen-year-old daughter is walking out of the shop with Georgie, but the look on the poor woman's face is a picture. I cross the road to greet them and watch Georgie's face change through a spectrum of emotions. I've never been one to take pleasure in other people's suffering, but this is giving me a toasty feeling.

"Hey, sweetheart," I say, pulling my beautiful girl in close to me.

"Hey, Dad." She wraps her arms around my waist and hugs me tight.

"Georgie." I tip my head to her and smile. "So you've met Iris, then."

"Uh huh." It's all she says, and I can tell that there had been a nice interaction between them until the moment she realised I'm her dad.

Georgie narrows her eyes and smiles at Iris. "You knew who I was, didn't you?"

"Yup. When you told me your name. Dad came home in a huff yesterday morning and he said you were a bit of a handful. What did you do to him?" She laughs, and I want the ground to open up and swallow me.

Georgie raises her eyebrows at me, a small smile playing on her lips. "Oh, he did? Hmm."

"Well, we didn't exactly hit it off, did we? What were you two getting friendly about anyway."

She clears her throat and is about to speak but is cut off by Iris who pipes up to answer for her.

"She was looking for some dinner inspiration."

I take in the outline of a pizza box in her plastic bag. I laugh and shake my head, eyeing Iris who gives me that smile that always puts a lump in my throat. She looks so much like her mother it hurts sometimes.

"Pizza? I'll give you a word to the wise about Iris McAllister. Never ask her for food advice or you'll eat nothing but pizza and potato wedges."

"Dad!" she says, obviously embarrassed in front of her new friend.

"It's true, though. You're a wee pizza fiend."

"I make a mean homemade pizza dough. I might make one for you if you want."

My daughter's eyes light up, and I look at the two of them, noticing a definite spark between them. I'm sensing that the show Georgie put on yesterday was one of exasperation and not because she is a horrible person. Iris is a bit of a loner but it's hard to make many friends when there are only twenty-two schoolchildren in the whole village. The local school encompasses children from age five to eighteen, and Iris is the only child in her year at the school. She doesn't have many friends, but the kids in this village are all so lovely and they band together when they need to.

"Dad, would that be okay with you? Can Georgie come and make dinner for us?"

She's so excited and I really don't have the heart to turn her down, but I don't want to rope this poor woman into being our chef for the night.

"Honestly, please don't mind her. You're here on a holiday. We don't want to intrude on your peace and quiet."

"Please. I'd be happy to cook in a properly functioning kitchen, and I think I'd enjoy the company. Well, some of it," she says, winking at Iris.

"Yay. I'll make sure he behaves himself, Georgie." Iris pats my shoulder. "I'm going home, Dad. Will you be late tonight?"

"I don't know, sweetheart. I'll let you know."

"Okay. Bye, Georgie. It was nice to meet you."

"And you."

Iris heads off, and we both stand in silence for a few seconds.

"So, um, I think I should apologise for yesterday."

"It's okay. I know you were probably freezing and frustrated, and I wasn't exactly being chivalrous to you."

"I'm not a horrible person, you know. I've had the worst few weeks of my life lately, and I just wanted to get away from it all."

"It's okay. Want to come in and get a coffee? Breakfast is still on. I'm sure the chef can knock you up a wee bacon sandwich."

She contemplates my offer for a second and then nods. "Sure."

"Great. In you come."

I head in through the door of the pub and she follows. My phone vibrates in my back pocket, and I pull it out to see a text from Iris.

She's very pretty. I like her. X

I roll my eyes.

Don't even go there, young lady. x

Iris doesn't have a good track record with matchmaking when it comes to dear old dad. She tried to set me up with her teacher once in a very elaborate scheme she concocted that wouldn't have been out of place in a Disney movie. Unfortunately, as lovely as she was, her teacher wasn't into men, and we ended up having a very funny and friendly 'date'. Iris was gutted, and I think she's made it her personal mission to find me a new wife. I do think it would be good for her to have a mother figure in her life, but I'm not about to marry the first woman I find. I haven't found her yet, but I haven't given up hope.

"Take a seat," I say, motioning towards a barstool.

"Thanks."

She hops up on the stool and takes off her jacket and hat, letting her blonde hair fall down to her shoulders. Her cheeks have a rosy glow as the heat of the pub warms us up. I set about making us some coffees.

"What would you like?"

"A mocha if you have it on your menu."

"Certainly do. Do you want any food?"

"No, I'm fine. Have to save myself for my gourmet dinner tonight. Do you own this place?" she asks, looking around as I prepare the frothy milk and coffee.

"No. I just run it. The owners are an older local couple and they spent years running it but had to eventually call it a day. I'd only been doing menial labouring jobs to keep a roof over mine and Iris' heads when I found out they were looking for someone. I jumped at the chance, and I've been here ever since. Six years in January in fact."

"What brought you away up here then? Moira says you're from Glasgow."

"My wife was from this village. We met in Glasgow, but she had to come back up to look after her mum. She had a stroke and was in a bad shape. So I upped sticks and followed her here. Her mum passed away shortly after we moved, but we never went back to Glasgow. I don't think I could go back to living in the city again." I put the mugs down on the bar and head round to the other side, taking the barstool next to her.

"What happened to your wife?" She looks down at the bar. "I'm sorry, you don't have to answer that. You don't even know me."

"No, it's okay. I assume Iris told you she died."

"Yeah, she did. She's a lovely kid."

"She's my reason for getting up in the morning. She was only two when Kate died. She was in a car accident in the middle of a particularly bad winter. Iris was in the car with her and luckily she was in the back on the opposite side to Kate, so she didn't have any injuries. Her car was taken out by a lorry that jack-knifed on the A9. She died at the scene, and the fatal accident inquiry concluded that there was nothing either of them could have done to prevent it. It was just a horrible accident."

"I'm so sorry. That must have been tough to lose her when Iris was so young." She places her hand on mine, and although they're cold, it's strangely comforting. Obviously remembering herself, she moves her hand back quickly and picks up her mug, blowing on the warm liquid.

"It was tough, and I can say for certain if it hadn't been for that little girl, I wouldn't be here."

"Well, I can say for certain that you've brought up a lovely young lady. But there's something I must advise you on and you can tell me to mind my own business if you want, but I do think it's worth thinking about."

"Don't know if I like where this is going."

"It's not a huge deal, but I guarantee your daughter will silently thank you for it. Obviously having a mum or a female presence is good for a young girl of Iris's age. Did you know she buys her own period products?"

She seriously could knock me down with a feather right now. Never in my life have I felt so small and useless.

"Oh, fuck. I didn't even know she had started." I let out a long sigh and hang my head in shame. "Now I know the reason she started doing her own washing. I honestly thought she just wanted to help around the house. Fuck sake," I say louder than I had intended and wince at the fact that everyone has stopped what they're doing to look at me.

"I'm sorry, Finn. I didn't mean to pry. I met her in the shop, and she didn't have any money with her. Please don't be hard on yourself. It wasn't my intention to make you feel bad."

"Well, it certainly did that. Sorry, I'm going to have to get back to work." I stand and walk away from her, through to the back of the bar.

How could I have been so blind? Iris is a fucking teenager; of course this was going to happen sooner or later. And having a complete stranger point it out just makes it a million times worse.

I peer out from my hidden place and see Georgie gathering all her stuff up, forcing her hat on her head and frowning deeply. I don't have it in me to go out and apologise for my petulant behaviour.

I head into the bathroom and look at myself in the mirror. "Here's your fall from grace, you idiot," I say to my reflection. I have some major making up to do with my daughter. And with Georgie.

Chapter Six

Georgie

Ugh! I take a bite of my now cold pizza and wince as I chew on the hardened cheese. Sighing, I put the plate down on the coffee table in front of me. I've been mulling over the argument Finn started with me in the pub over something that really shouldn't have caused an argument in the first place. He didn't have to treat me like that.

Lifting the plate, I head for the kitchen and dump what's left of the pizza in the bin. I'm about to wash the plate when I hear a vehicle outside. Narrowing my eyes, I head for the cabin door and put the security chain on. I've watched enough horror films about women being murdered in remote log cabins. I refuse to go down like that. Finn's truck come into the view as I peek out the blinds. He heads for the door, and I feel all the anger that's been stewing in me since I left the pub bubbling up to a bit of a rage.

I pull open the door with force and almost rip my fingers off as it snaps back into the frame. I've forgotten to take the security chain off and now I look like a right twat. Loosening the chain, I open the door to find him standing there with a smile on his face. That same smile he had the day we met. It takes all my will power to not knock him on his arse.

"Peace offering," he says, holding up what looks like a takeaway and a box of glass coke bottles.

A sigh escapes me.

"Come in," I say, defeat heavy in my voice.

He tips his head to me, and I move to let him past the door. The waft of the food smells as he goes has my mouth watering. It's fish and chips, after all.

"Have you eaten?" he asks, placing the bag down on the counter and looking at my plate in the sink.

"I made the pizza but ended up not eating it on time before it went cold. I wasn't really feeling it anyway."

"Look, Georgie, I'm really sorry about earlier. I should never have spoken to you like that or acted so childish."

"Pfftt. Damn right you shouldn't have. I was only trying to help. And it wasn't you I was trying to help by the way. It was Iris. You're a man. You don't know what it's like to grow up as a teenage girl."

He holds his hands up. "I know that. That's why I'm here. I know what you were trying to do, and I was out of line. I've been her only parent since she was two years old, and I have no female relatives to help me with her. I thought I was doing well until you pointed out a glaring fact of life that I completely missed. It's not an excuse, but my god, did that make me feel like a failure." His head hangs low, and he starts playing with the handles of the plastic bag on the counter.

"You're not a failure, Finn. You've both been through so much in your lives, and like I said earlier, you should feel very proud of the young woman you've raised. I forgive you. I know your reaction was self-preservation. You're not the only one who feels like a failure."

He furrows his brows. "You? You don't strike me as someone failing at life."

"Looks can be deceiving, you know. Let's plate up this food and I'll tell you why I'm really here."

"Okay," he says and sets about tipping the food onto two clean plates and opening two cokes. He sticks a fork in each of the fish and hands me my plate and a bottle.

"Thanks."

We take a seat on either end of the small sofa. Spearing a fat, golden chip with my fork and shovelling it in my mouth, I groan as the flavours burst in my mouth.

"Best chippy in the highlands," Finn says, smiling at my obvious pleasure.

"It's nice."

"So, spill. What happened to you?"

"Ugh. I'll keep this as short as possible. One day at the end of November, I arrived at work to find out my bosses had put their business into liquidation and done a runner."

"Ooh, that's low."

"Ha. Oh, I'm not done yet. So I stood around at the gates of the yard and chatted to the rest of the workers who were turning up. After an hour of collective outrage, we decided to call it a day and go home. In Edinburgh, as you probably know, the rents are expensive, but mine was very reasonable and my landlord was great. Well, when I got back home after being made unemployed, I found a hand delivered letter through my door giving me two weeks to vacate the property because the landlord was selling up."

"Fuck, that sounds like the day from hell." He takes a huge piece of fish into his mouth and stops mid-chew. "What? That's not all?" His muffled words make me laugh.

"Nope. I've saved the best for last. My boyfriend, Ian, also had a flat in Edinburgh and we'd been together for almost two years, so naturally I assumed I could probably move in with him. After I'd had a bit of a cry at my shitty life, I headed over to see him. You know, as a girlfriend would do to be comforted by her boyfriend. Well, no prizes for guessing what I walked in on."

"No way. Did you catch him cheating?" He puts his fork down and focuses on me, looking at me as if he's watching a juicy drama on tv.

"In one morning, I became unemployed, homeless, and single. Now you see you're not the only one who feels like a failure. I ran away from all my shit. I haven't even told my parents. I'm their only child and I'm a failure at life."

"That's some story. But you're not a failure. All those things that happened to you were beyond your control. Just like Kate's accident was beyond ours. I came here tonight to apologise but also to thank you. I sorted out a cupboard in the bathroom with as many sanitary products as I could find. I had no idea what I was looking for and Shug in the mini market looked at me like I had horns on my head as he stood there ringing it all up."

Ha, that paints a funny picture in my head. "Oh dear. Were you both red faced?"

"Oh yeah, we were. I don't think there's been a time I've been in Shug's store where I have spent less than half an hour chatting to him, but today I was in and out in minutes. I left a wee note on the door to tell her it was her cupboard and that I was sorry I was so blind to her needs. She came out of the bathroom and just hugged me tight. We didn't say anything to each other, but I could tell how much she appreciated it. So thank you. You helped me be a better parent to her."

"You're welcome. Now how much easier would things have been if you just said that earlier?"

He shakes his head and eats the last of his food. "Yeah, I know." He takes a swig of his coke and puts the bottle back down on the table. "I need to go. Iris is going to a sleepover movie night at the school tonight. Elf, I believe it is. Since there aren't many children in the village, they do this now and again as a way of giving them something to do. It breaks up the monotony of the week for them. She loves it because she gets to look after the young ones. I think she has her mother's maternal instincts." His sweet smile is accompanied by a sadness in his eyes.

"Thanks for coming here tonight. I appreciate it."

We both stand, and he takes our plates to the kitchen.

"Just leave them on the side. Go and sort Iris out and tell her I'm holding her to that pizza dinner at some point."

"She'll love that."

I walk him to the door and we both reach for the handle at the same time. Our hands brush momentarily. He looks at me, and I see the fire from the wood burner flicker in his eyes. My breath hitches, and I'm taken by surprise when he leans in and kisses me. I wasn't expecting this, but somehow, deep down, I think I've wanted it since the moment I met him. I get the feeling it's loneliness that's keeping me from breaking away from him, and so I'm glad when he does it first.

"Sorry," he says, looking a little sheepish.

"Don't be."

"Hmm. I'm sorry I really have to go. I don't want to, but Iris needs me."

"Go. I'm here until after New Year. I don't have anywhere to go, remember?"

He leans in and kisses my cheek, lingering long enough for me to take in his woody scent. "I'll see you later."

"You better."

I stay at the door until he's out of sight up the driveway and let out a heavy sigh, my breath misting in front of me in the cold air. I don't know what I'm thinking letting this happen, but right now, my heart is about to burst out of my chest, and I don't want to think about the consequences. No matter how much of a disaster my head knows it will be.

Chapter Seven

Finn

I've spent the last hour since I dropped Iris off at the school pacing my living room. I don't know what possessed me earlier kissing Georgie like that. We met not so long ago, and I don't even know her. I think it was how she was with Iris that got my attention. Yes, that's stupid, and I can't base my feelings on solely that. But I don't allow myself the luxury of relationships for that very reason. There is no one on this earth that I've ever been willing to trust around my daughter. I would never put my own feelings before Iris's happiness, ever. She's my entire world. Then why am I so torn over Georgie?

I pick up my phone and open a text to her. Staring at the phone, I'm unsure of what to say to her. Do I ask her to come over? Then what? And where would this go if anything were to happen between us? She leaves after New Year, and we probably won't see her again. But I can't stop thinking about her.

I'm about to type something into the phone when my doorbell rings. I stow the phone in my pocket and answer the door to Georgie standing on my doorstep.

"Oh. Hi. What are you doing here?" *What an idiotic question to ask.*

"I couldn't settle. You've invaded my mind."

"Come in."

I move to let her in, and she turns to face me as I close the door. We stand in silence for the longest time, and I feel a little out of my depth. It's as though I've forgotten how to act around a woman. After Kate, I've only been with three other women and even then, I felt nothing for them.

Georgie takes off her jacket and folds it over her arm, pulling it in close to her with the other.

"So, what do we do now?" she asks.

"I honestly have no idea. This is so complicated. If it were just me I had to think about, I'd bed you right now. But it's not just me. I can't let Iris get hurt because of me."

"Didn't you think about that when you kissed me? What am I supposed to make of this? Should we just forget it ever happened?"

I drag my hand down my face. "No, that's not what I meant. If anything happens between us, it has to stay under wraps. Iris can never know."

Georgie walks toward me and stops when she's millimetres from touching me. She's so close I can feel the heat radiating off her body. She drops her jacket to the side of us and steps into me so that our hips are touching. I swallow hard and take a steadying breath. Unable to resist the temptation, I smash my lips against hers, and she reciprocates with a surge of pure adrenaline.

Georgie groans against my mouth and reaches down, grabbing my hands and pulling them round her waist. I envelop her and pull her in as close as I can, never breaking contact with her mouth. As our kiss becomes fevered, she turns her body and pushes herself right against my rock-hard dick. I want her so bad, and I can tell from her kiss that she feels the same. Lifting her into my arms, I press us against the wall, and she squeals at the suddenness of the move, making me smile.

"Sorry," I whisper against her mouth.

"Don't apologise," she answers and deepens the kiss.

My body is about to go off like a rocket, and I have to concentrate on not letting myself get too carried away before I can get her naked. I move us back from the wall and let her stand.

"I want you to tell me you're sure about where this is going and that you understand it can't be anything more."

"I do. I can't let this be anything more either. You know that. I'm in no position to. I'm homeless, for fuck's sake."

Taking her hand, I lead her up the stairs to my bedroom. Unfortunately, I wasn't expecting company, so the place is in a bit of a riot.

"Sorry, I dumped these clothes here with the intention of putting them away tonight," I explain, stuffing the wrinkled clothes into a laundry bag and throwing it down to the bottom of the bed.

"Nice fairy lights," says Georgie, pointing at the tiny twinkling lights wrapped around the head of my bed.

"Oh, how embarrassing. Iris thought I needed to be more festive. She decorated my room last week. I've got all sorts of little trees and snowmen everywhere. She loves Christmas."

"So do I. That's why I was trying to make the cabin look more festive."

She looks around at all the tiny ornaments my daughter has left around, and I can see her pain. It must be awful to be adrift like that, especially at this time of year. She catches me watching her and proceeds to strip out of her clothes right in front of me. Her mismatched underwear makes me smile. I love a woman who doesn't give a shit about appearances. She has a beautiful body, and I'm mesmerised by her.

"Come here," she says, beckoning me with her finger.

I oblige and walk closer to her. I'm nervous as hell around her, but I'm trying to appear as confident as possible. I've already been emasculated once today. It would not do to have it happen twice.

"You're perfect, Georgie."

"This body takes a lot of work, believe me," she says as she pulls the hem of my T-shirt, hoisting it up and off. "Mmm. And so does this by the look of it." She runs her hand across my abs, and my dick pulses in my jeans.

"You're going to kill me, woman."

She gets up on her tiptoes and whispers in my ear, "Well, get naked and fuck me already, then."

I close my eyes and try to compose myself as sparks fly all over my body. I have no idea how I haven't passed out. I strip out of the rest of my clothes, and she does too until we're standing in front of each other naked. I'm surprised when she puts her arms around my neck and jumps up on me, planting her lips on mine and kissing me with a sense of urgency. She flexes her body against me, rubbing herself against my dick and getting herself off on the friction. Her heat feels so good on my skin and her enthusiasm spurs me on. I turn us and lay her down on the bed.

"Georgie, I don't have any condoms. I'm sorry. This isn't something I do much."

She smiles up at me, and I take in the sight of her lying on my bed, her blonde hair splayed out like a halo behind her.

"I have some in my jeans pocket. I didn't bring the condoms with the intention of doing this, I promise. I've always had it drummed into me by my mum that the prevention is better than the cure. I'm on the pill anyway. Although given that Ian was having an affair for six months, I can't say wholeheartedly that I'm clean. Sorry." She shrugs, and her cheeks redden with obvious embarrassment.

"That wasn't your fault. You don't need to apologise." I hop off the bed and grab her jeans, holding them up, and she nods. I grab one of the few condoms she has stuffed in there. Opening it, I roll it on and get back on the bed, kissing her as I settle in between her legs.

She puts her hand between us and grabs my pulsing hard dick, rubbing it up and down her pussy and getting herself off on it. I can do nothing else but watch her face as she comes on a groan, her eyes closing and her back arching off the bed. Her glorious tits are pushed towards me, and I take one in my hand, rolling her nipple between my fingers. I press the head of my cock against her, pushing in a tiny amount, and as she nods her agreement, I go the whole way, hitting her deep inside and eliciting a sexy as fuck moan from her.

"I can feel that. So deep. So nice," she moans, snapping whatever control I have left. I buck my hips into her and grab her ankle, pulling her leg up to rest on my shoulder. The change in angle has us both groaning and it only serves to make me harder.

"I'm sorry, Georgie. It's been so long, I can' hold it."

"S'ok, hard and fast. Do it."

I ram into her and pick up the pace. She meets me thrust for thrust, and before long, I'm shooting my load like I'm a fucking teenage boy. The hot spurts don't let up and I'm still hard, so I keep going, and Georgie comes on my dick, her inner muscles clamping down on me in waves.

"Fuck," she moans as we both finish, our heavy panting ringing in my ears.

"You okay?" I ask, looking down into her beautiful ice-blue eyes, the fairy lights twinkling in her irises.

"Better than okay. If you haven't done that in a while, you certainly haven't lost any form."

I laugh and feel my now softening cock slide out of her. Grabbing a cloth from my bathroom cupboard, I throw it in the sink, wetting it under the warm water while I take off the condom and discard it. I return to her with the cloth wrung out and place it between her legs.

"Thank you," she says with a sweet smile and takes the cloth from me, giving herself a pat.

"Will you stay here with me tonight? Iris won't be back until morning, and I really don't want you to go."

She stops what she's doing and looks at me for a few seconds before answering. "I don't want to go either."

I take the cloth from her, and she scrambles under the covers, cosying in and pulling the duvet back, inviting me in beside her. Throwing the cloth in the laundry basket, I get into the bed and turn to face her, pulling her into my arms. She lays her head on my chest and snuggles in beside me.

"You're a good man, Finn McAllister. Don't ever forget that."

We lie in silence, and I reach over and turn off the bedside lamp. A sense of dread consumes me because I've fallen for her, and I know it has to end someday soon. Knowing someone you care for is going to leave your life is just as bad as the shock of losing someone suddenly. I know I could change that, but there are too many hearts at stake and mine certainly can't take another kicking.

Chapter Eight

Georgie

It's Christmas day tomorrow and I've been walking back and forth in this cabin since I got up this morning. Finn has invited me to spend the day with him and Iris, but I'm having a crisis of conscience.

Ever since we spent the night together, we've met up every day since. We've managed to keep our tryst hidden from Iris, but I think she's becoming too attached to me being around. If I'm not having dinner with them both, I'm in the pub. I know people are talking about us now too. This is a tiny village and news travels fast, but gossip and half-truths travel even faster.

I told Finn I'd see him at the pub today, all the while second-guessing my decision. I'm falling in love with him, and I've become too close to Iris. She called me her new best friend yesterday and it freaked me out. I know I'm being irrational, but I fear that if I stay here any longer, I'll hurt them both when I have to leave.

My phone rings from the kitchen, and I hesitate to answer it, thinking it might be Finn. I stand on my tiptoes and peer at the screen from as far back as I can. It's as though I don't want whoever is calling to see me. I'm relieved when I see it's only my mum.

"Hi, Mum." I try to sound my usual chirpy self.

"Hi, my wee darling. How are you?" Mum grew up in South Africa but has been in Scotland since she was eighteen. While her accent is more Scottish now, some South African still comes through sometimes, especially when she's mad or scared. I used to wind her up on purpose just so I could hear it.

"I'm good, Mum."

"I haven't heard from you in a while. I just wanted to let you know we've arrived safely at gran's place. Are you and Ian looking forward to tomorrow?"

Ah yes, the one thing I haven't done is tell my parents about my fucked-up life. They don't even know I'm in the highlands.

"Yeah, looking forward to it. Mum, can I ask you something?"

"Sure, sweetie. Are you okay?"

"Yeah, I am. You and Dad got together pretty quickly. How did you know he was the one for you? I mean, did you know you loved him before you found out you were pregnant with me?"

"I think I always loved him even when we were just friends at work. Are you sure you're okay, honey? Are you and Ian having problems?"

I sigh heavily.

"Spill the beans now. I know there's something wrong with you."

Busted.

"Ian cheated on me. We broke up at the end of November."

"Oh darling, why didn't you tell us?"

"Because the day I found out he was cheating, I also lost my job and my flat. I'm so sorry, Mum." I fill her in on my *woe is me* life.

"Oh my god, what on earth were you thinking not telling us. Where are you right now?"

"Um, I rented a cabin in the highlands. Auchengarry. It's a lovely wee village and the guy that owns the cabin is..." I trail off, not sure what to say about Finn. He's lovely, sweet natured, is a wonderful father. And I'm in love with him.

"You like him, don't you? How long have you known him?"

"About a week. Do you think that's too soon to be falling for someone?"

"Not at all. Look at your Auntie Gina and Uncle Steven. They were head over heels about each other almost instantly. The heart wants what it wants."

"I don't know what to do. He's asked me to spend Christmas day with him and his daughter, but I don't feel as though I can. I have to leave in a week or so, and I don't want to get so close that I hurt them when I go."

I hear her suck in a breath through her teeth. "A child certainly complicates things. Listen, if you're not sure about this, you have to tell him. Don't lead him on because it won't end well for either of you."

"You're right, Mum. Thanks."

"So, does this mean you'll be moving back home until you find somewhere else to stay?"

"Would that be okay with you both?"

"Ugh, I'm not even going to answer that stupid question. Are you okay for money?"

"Yeah, I have a lot of savings. You and Dad taught me well."

"Do you want me to tell Dad what's happened? I mean, it's just as well we're in London, because when he finds out about what Ian has done to his little girl, he'll throttle him."

"You can tell him, but please tell him I'm glad I broke up with Ian. It wasn't going anywhere, and I think we were only running on familiarity. He did me a favour."

"Okay, sweetheart. Take care up there. I hear the weather is going to be a bit awful later today. We'll call you tomorrow."

"Okay, Mum. Love you."

"Love you too, sweetheart."

We hang up, and I hold my phone close to me. It's painful, but I know the decision forming in my head is the best one to make. It'll hurt for a while, but it's the only way I can save us all a complete heartache in the long run.

I tear a sheet of paper out of my small diary and write a note to Finn.

Dear Finn,

I want to thank you and Iris for your hospitality while I've been here. You have been very gracious hosts, and I'll always cherish your kindness. Unfortunately, I must leave early. I hope you will understand that this is not because of anything you've done. I simply can't bear to hurt you both when the time comes for me to leave. It's better for everyone this way. Please believe me when I say I never meant to hurt you.

Georgie x

I lay the note on the coffee table and head into the bedroom to pack up my stuff. Tears fog my vision, and I have to keep stopping to swipe them away. As soon as my bags are full, I load all my things into the back of my car. The rain that started earlier in the morning has turned to sleet and there's a gloominess in the atmosphere. Fat flakes of snow and pelting rain coat the outside of the car in a slushy mix, and I know I have to get away soon before it gets worse.

I make sure I've left nothing behind and stop at the door before I leave and lock up. I hope Finn and Iris can forgive me. They have each other. I'm sure they'll forget about me soon enough. I head out and lock the door behind me, leaving the key on the hook on the mailbox by the door so that Finn sees it when he comes looking for me. I run to my car, avoiding getting too soaked. I head down the driveway, and when I get to the end, I stop at the junction. To my right is the village. Finn and Iris will both be there at the pub getting the place ready for a Christmas Eve party they apparently hold every year. To my left is my road home. Home. What home?

I close my eyes and the tears that have been perched on my lower lids fall onto my jacket, mixing with the melting snow. I flick on my indicator and turn out of the junction. Left and away from any more heartbreak.

Chapter Nine

Finn

I've been calling Georgie since before lunchtime and can't seem to get a hold of her. She was supposed to be here at the pub with me and Iris to help set up for tonight's Christmas Eve party. It's always a great laugh, and I can't wait to include Georgie in the village festivities.

"Sweetheart, I can't get Georgie on the phone. I'll have to go to the cabin and make sure she's all right."

"Can I come too?" my bright-eyed girl asks, jumping down from the bar stool she's been perched on and putting on her jacket.

"Okay. But put your hat and gloves on too. The weather's turned quickly out there."

I grab my own jacket and let the others know we're heading out. The sense of community spirit in this village makes me glad to call it home. Everyone is always willing to help out no matter what.

We head out into the snow and get into the pickup truck as quickly as we can. We make the short drive to the cabin, and as we pull up outside, I see that her car is gone.

"Stay here," I tell Iris.

OH, SANTA!

I get out and go to the door of the cabin and see Georgie's key hanging on the mailbox. A cold sense of dread prickles my skin as I lift the key and unlock the door. The place is gloomy in the fading mid-afternoon light, but the eerie quiet tells me once and for all that she's gone. All her stuff is missing, and the place is just as it was when she arrived here, albeit a bit cleaner.

The piece of paper sitting on the coffee table catches my eye and I lift it and read it out loud to thin air. When I'm done, I crumple it in my hand.

"She left without saying goodbye?" Iris's question startles me.

"I told you to stay in the truck. Yes, sweetheart, she's gone."

"Why? What did we do wrong?"

"Nothing, honey," I say, trying to sound as reassuring as possible. "I think she just felt homesick, that's all. But I'm a little worried that she left in this awful weather. You know how bad it gets."

She nods at me. "We should go and look for her."

"I don't know. I don't think it's wise to go out too far in that snow. The snow gates are closed at Glencoe, and I would imagine the ones further south will be closed soon too."

"Dad, we have to. What if she's had an accident? Please, Dad."

My poor girl. She knows all about the accident that killed her mother, and I can hear the panic in her voice that it could have happened again to someone she has come to care about. I've come to care for her too. Very much. I only wish I'd been man enough to tell her.

"Okay. We'll go as far as we can. But if we don't find her by Glencoe, we come back. I can't justify putting you at risk."

"Thank you, Dad. I love you."

"I love you too, Iris," I say, pulling her into a hug. "Right, let's go and see if we can find that crazy woman."

We head out of the driveway and onto the main road. I call the pub and let them know where we're going. It's an unwritten rule that you never venture out in the snow like this without letting others know where you're going, and if possible, your route.

The thick snow crunches under the truck's huge off-road tyres as we make our way slowly along the road. Not even a mile into our journey, the snow becomes so thick that I fear the truck might veer off the road into a ditch, and I worry that this might be exactly what has become of Georgie.

Another few miles of driving has us almost at Glencoe.

"Dad, look," Iris says, pointing to the side of the road in the distance.

I follow where she's pointing and see the outline of a snow-covered car. If it hadn't been for Iris's eagle eyes, we might have missed it completely.

"Well spotted."

"Do you think it's her?"

In my heart, I want it to be her, but the angle the car is sitting at looks as though it's left the road involuntarily.

"Let's go and see."

I bring the truck to a halt as close to the side of the car as possible and get out, taking Iris with me this time. It would not do to leave her in the cab in case another car struck us. We trudge through the snow and get to the car. Wiping the driver's window with a gloved hand, I find Georgie sitting there, staring blankly at her windscreen. I knock on the window, and she turns her head and looks at me. As soon she realises it's me, she bursts into tears. I swipe as much of the snow off the door of the car as I can and open it. She all but leaps from the car and into my arms.

"I'm so sorry, Finn. I'm so sorry. I should never have left." She talks between sobs and my heart aches for her.

"You're coming back with us, and I'll get Tommy at the garage to get your car collected. His tow truck is like a monster truck. Is that okay?"

She nods and looks sheepishly at Iris. "I'm sorry, sweetheart," she says, and Iris moves forward and hugs her tight.

"Come on, let's get back before it gets any worse out here."

We all head back to the truck and Iris jumps in the back, letting Georgie take the front seat. I ramp up the heat to full and she puts her hands on the air vents.

"I'm so sorry, guys. I never meant for this to happen."

"What were you thinking going out in this?"

"When I left, it was sleeting. The snow hadn't started as bad yet. But it turned so quickly, and I'm just not used to driving in weather this bad."

"Did we do something wrong?" Iris asks from the back seat.

Georgie looks at me as tears fall from her cheeks. "No, you did nothing wrong, sweetheart."

"Iris, let Georgie heat up a bit before you bombard her with questions."

I turn the truck and we start to head back to the village, slowly and with extra care since the snow is still falling.

"No, she deserves answers. You both do. I honestly don't know what I was thinking. I've... well, I've got close to you both over the last week or so and I got freaked out that things were moving too fast. I have to leave for real in just over a week, and I couldn't bear the thought of hurting you both. I guess, I was trying to save all our hearts from hurt. But I didn't think about what not saying a proper goodbye would do. When my car skidded and I came to a stop there on the side of the road, I was terrified and instantly thought about you two. Knowing what you've both been through made me feel incredibly selfish."

"Do you love him?" Iris asks, and I glare at her in the rear-view mirror, silently begging her to shut up.

"Sorry?" Georgie asks.

Iris laughs. "Do you two think I'm stupid? I'm thirteen. I'm not blind. I know there's been something going on between you. I've seen how you've been looking at each other."

"My ever-observant child," I say, smiling at her in the mirror.

"I think I do. It's strange because we haven't known each other long, but I feel a connection to both of you. I just don't know where it can go from here because I have to leave. Edinburgh is too far away from here."

"What's keeping you in Edinburgh?" I ask her.

She contemplates my question for a moment, then smiles. "Nothing. I have nothing there anymore. I mean, my parents live and work there, but that's not enough to stay."

"You can stay with us," Iris chimes in with a huge smile on her face. I know she needs a female influence in her life, and I know she has taken a shine to Georgie. I just don't want her to stay out of guilt.

"You can have the cabin for as long as you need it. We won't expect anything from you that you're not ready to give."

I glance at Georgie, and she smiles, her tears making her eyes glisten in the dusky light. I'm shocked when she takes my hand and squeezes it.

"Thank you," she says. "I'll take you up on that offer and we'll see how things go. Is that okay with you, Iris?" She twists in her seat so that she can see better.

"Yup," Iris says, nodding and smiling wide.

We drive the rest of the way back in an easy silence; Georgie holding my hand the whole time and Iris humming along to songs on the radio. My heart is full of love for both of them, but my head is telling me loud and clear not to take anything for granted. It's going to be a tentative time, and I have to make sure Iris is protected no matter what happens between us.

❄

Georgie

The Christmas Eve party in the pub has been a huge success and I now see why Finn and Iris love this village. I've met almost everyone that lives here, and they've all been so welcoming. It came as no surprise to me that everyone already knew there was something between me and Finn. It was the hot topic of the night, and to be honest, I haven't felt as uncomfortable as I thought I would.

I'm helping Finn clear up the bar as the last of the partygoers say their goodbyes, each one wishing us a 'Merry Christmas' as they go.

"You okay?" Finn asks, breaking into my daydream as I clean the same bit of the bar over and over.

"Yeah, I'm fine. Just thinking about what a strange few months I've had. You know, I thought my life was great. It never occurred to me how quickly things can change, and when they did for me, those changes were catastrophic. Much like how your life changed when Kate died. You know when I realised that I was making a mistake?"

"When?"

"The moment I flicked on that left indicator to leave the village. I knew I was being irrational, but in my stupid head, I was doing us all a favour. I have no home and no job. What on earth was I thinking going back to Edinburgh to nothing. I got spooked because I only just met you and the feelings I have for you scared me to death. It just felt so quick and like a knee-jerk reaction to becoming single. I was with Ian for two years and it was over in the blink of an eye."

"I understand more than you know. After Kate, I never gave my heart to anyone else. Iris is my entire life, and I didn't think it was fair to bring anyone else into our lives and risk losing someone else. But then you turned up. And things changed. I changed. It probably had more to do with Iris than me, to be completely honest. The way you instantly connected with her made me look at you through different eyes. Her eyes. I thought I was protecting her all these years, but it turns out it was me I was protecting. I have no idea if we can make a relationship work or if you'll get sick of living up here and will want to go back to the city, but I'd sure like to give it a go."

I put down my cloth and round the bar to where he's standing. Reaching up, I cup his face in my hand and press a soft kiss on his lips. He pulls me in close and holds me tight against him.

"I'm in," I whisper against his mouth.

"It's Christmas, guys," Iris says, startling us both, and we look at the huge iron clock above the roaring fire in the pub. The minute hand has just ticked past midnight.

"So it is," says Finn, smiling. "Merry Christmas."

"Merry Christmas," Iris and I say in unison.

Finn beckons her to join us, and she puts her arms around us both and hugs us tight. No matter what happens between me and her dad, she'll always be my friend. I may just have found my forever home.

Epilogue

Finn

1 YEAR LATER – CHRISTMAS DAY

The sound of Georgie and Iris singing cheesy Christmas songs as they make breakfast reverberates through the house. I never thought I'd have this life after Kate died. I had resigned myself to the fact that it would just be me and my girl against the world. That world has been changed beyond what either of us ever dreamed. Georgie has been a beacon of light to us. She saved us when we were both lost, and she's given us a much brighter future.

I sit down on the edge of the bed and stare through the white bars of the crib that we took so much time choosing a month ago. Our tiny daughter, Holly, was born three weeks early and I haven't been able to take my eyes off her since. It's Christmas and this should have been her due date, but I get the feeling she just wanted to share in this moment as much as we did.

The baby stirs and lets out a piercing squeal. I lift her gently into my arms and head downstairs with her. As soon as Iris sees us, she makes grabby hands and takes her little sister into her arms. Iris is an absolute natural with her and has showered the beautiful little bundle with so much love since we brought her home.

"Let's go and see the lights, shall we?" Iris coos to her, walking out of the kitchen and through to the living room where we have the most beautiful Christmas tree.

"Hey you," Georgie says, planting a kiss on my cheek as I join her at the cooker.

"Hey, beautiful. I'm having a hard time concentrating on anything right now. I can't wait to give Iris her presents."

"I know. Me too. I've been so close to blurting it out all morning. Do you think she's going to be okay with a present like this?"

"I know my daughter well. She's going to freak out. You know how much love she has in her heart. This is going to be the best present she'll ever get."

She smiles, her blue eyes shining bright. "I love you, Finn. Both of you. Thank you for making me part of your family."

"Thank you for adding to our family. You've made me happier than I ever dreamed I could be. You're our angel in disguise. And I love you too." I pull her in close to me and kiss the top of her head. She lets out a long sigh and pushes me back.

"Right, breakfast is ready. Let's get this eaten before I burst and give the game away."

We take the plates filled with pancakes and bacon through to the dining table. Iris has expertly set it with Santa napkins and a tablecloth filled with snowmen. We settle Holly into her swinging chair and the three of us eat our breakfast and chatter about nothing in particular. Georgie and I glance at each other every now and then and exchange smiles, and as soon as Iris pops the last piece of her pancake in her mouth, Georgie jumps up from the table.

"Present time."

"Yay," Iris shouts, and Holly screams with fright. "Oops, sorry. I forget she's still so tiny."

"It's okay, sweetheart, go into the living room and I'll get her," I say, nodding in the direction of the open door.

I lift Holly from her chair and join them next to the tree, my heart about to burst at the smile on Georgie and Iris's faces. They each know something about their presents that the other doesn't and they look so eager to get started. This is going to be a fun day.

❄

Georgie

"Dad, you go first," Iris says, handing Finn a long box and giggling so hard that I think she might pee herself. "I bought this for you with my own money."

I have no idea what's in the present, but as Finn unwraps it, I see a huge smile form on his face.

"You little toerag. What is this supposed to mean? Are you saying I have an excess hair problem?" He holds up the ear and nose hair trimmer, and Iris rolls back on the floor in fits of laughter.

"Sorry, Dad. I couldn't help it. It's just too funny."

"Mhm. I'm thinking I might just be cancelling Christmas for you, young lady." He smiles at her and pulls her in for a hug. "I love you, sweetheart."

"Love you too, Dad. Okay, it's Georgie's turn," she says, bouncing up and down excitedly.

"Okay, okay. Here you go, love of my life," Finn says, handing me a parcel wrapped in beautiful silver paper. The little reindeer pictures on it shimmer on holographic foil and I don't want to open it and ruin the paper.

"Open it," Iris squeals, and I laugh as Finn grabs her and ruffles her hair.

"I don't know who's more excited here. Leave Georgie alone and let her open her present in peace." He looks at me and grins. "But seriously, woman, just open the present already."

"Okay."

I rip the paper open and find an inconspicuous brown box inside. It has a small burgundy velvet ring box. I look at Finn and suck in a breath. His smile tells me all I need to know, and Iris's excitement proves she's been in on this too. I open the box and nestled in the white cushion is the most beautiful white gold ring with a cluster of diamonds in a square and a princess cut diamond in the middle. The lights from the tree hit it in all the right places and it sparkles like the sun on water.

"This is so beautiful." I look up at Finn and tears form in my eyes.

"Georgie, you came bounding into our lives a year ago and gave us back our smiles. Both of us love you dearly and we thank you from the bottom of our hearts for giving us Holly. I want to make this official, and with Iris's blessing, I would like to ask you to be my wife."

I nod at him because I can't speak. He takes the ring from the box, and I give him my hand. The cool metal slides on and fits perfectly.

"Thank you. Both of you." I pull them both into a hug. Poor Iris is in tears.

"You okay, sweetheart?" Finn asks her.

"I'm fine, Dad. I'm just happy because now we can be a proper family." She swipes the tears from her eyes, and we smile at each other.

"Well, I think it's time for your presents, Iris. I think you need to open this one first."

Finn stands and leaves the room to collect the big box we have hidden in our bedroom. He carries it in and places it down in front of her and she looks at him with big wondrous eyes.

"What is it?"

"Open it and find out," I say, finding it hard to hide the glee in my voice.

She opens the box tentatively as though something is going to spring out of it and hit her. She furrows her brows and looks up at me, then looks back down at the open box.

"What is it, Iris?" I ask.

"A piece of paper," she says, smiling.

"What does it say?" her dad asks.

She takes a stuttering breath and lifts the piece of paper out of the huge box.

"Dear Iris. I love you with all my heart and I want to thank you for welcoming me into your family. You are the best big sister Holly could ever have asked for and I'm so proud to have you in my life. I would be grateful if you would do me the honour of allowing me to legally adopt you and call you my daughter. All my love, Georgie."

She looks up at me with her bottom lip trembling and, just as I did a few moments ago, all she can do is nod as tears stream down her cheeks.

"Come here, sweetheart," I say, pulling her into a tight hug. "I love you to the moon and back."

"I love you too, Mum," she says against my shoulder, and my heart feels as though it's about to flutter out of my chest.

So here we all are on Christmas day, sitting around the tree. Finn with his hair clipper, me with a fiancé, and Iris with a new mum. What more could a happy little family want?

ABOUT THE AUTHOR

For as long as she can remember, Claire has been a hopeless romantic. She can always be found dreaming up HEA's for her characters. Claire lives with her husband and three children in Lanarkshire, Scotland (bet you're thinking of rolling hills, castles and men in kilts, Outlander style). Her love of her home city of Glasgow is more than apparent in her books so far.

If you loved Cabin Fever and want to keep in touch, Claire would love to hear from you. She can regularly be found on Instagram and Facebook, and if you like to get your hands on exclusive material you can join her Facebook reader group, Claire's Glasgow Kiss, and sign up to her newsletter.

ALSO BY C.L STEWART

Standalones

My Summer at The Pink Flamingo

The Soul Series

Shattered Soul

Saviour of The Soul

Heart and Soul

The Game Series

The Intimidation Game

War Games

Game Changer

Wicked Game (Coming Feb 23)

Second Class Santa

by

Danielle Jacks

SECOND CLASS SANTA SYNOPSIS

Stacey

All I want for Christmas is a special visit to see Santa with my son, Zain.

Life has been hard since I became a single mum as a teen, but I've always tried to stay positive. When we visit a local garden centre a few days before Christmas, I'm hoping to get a magical experience. Unfortunately, the Santa we see is second rate, and our experience is ruined.

Can the guy pretending to be Mr Claus restore the festivities, or will Christmas shine a little less bright?

Sonny

All I want is to return to my regular job and forget I messed up Christmas.

After losing a bet, I step into Santa's boots for the day. The suit is stuffy, and the kids are mischievous. When a young boy visits the grotto, I ruin his festive experience. His mum wants me to apologise for being a disaster, but I'm not forthcoming. I've had a rubbish day and I just want to forget the whole experience rather than correct my bad behaviour.

Can I redeem myself and save Christmas, or will I be known as bad Santa from now on?

Chapter One

Stacey

It's the last few days in the run-up to Christmas. My fake tree and budget baubles are on display, and there's a trim of tinsel on the living room window. Standing back to admire my work, I'm pleased with how it looks. I grab a few presents from the top of my wardrobe and put them under the tree.

"Which one is for me, Mummy?" Zain, my four-year-old says while jumping up and down.

"They're all for you baby." I bring him into my arms and squeeze him tightly.

"Will your present come from Santa?"

"If I'm lucky, he might have something for me, but I already have the best gift right here." I kiss his forehead and he rubs it off with his arm.

"Hey!"

I tickle him and we both roll around on the floor, laughing.

"Stop, it tickles!" Zain giggles.

"That's the point," I say, smiling.

Seeing him happy melts my heart. Zain means everything to me, and even though I can't give him a lot, I aim to make Christmas as magical as I can. "Why don't we go see Santa at Strawberry Fields Garden Centre?"

"Now?" He turns his head to look at me.

"Yes, now." I arch my brow up and pull my mouth to one side, hoping to impress him with my plan.

He cheers loudly, and a wave of love washes over me. Every child deserves to see Santa at Christmas, and my budget will stretch to a local shop. I'm a single mum with a part-time job, which makes money tight, but I want to spoil my boy.

Once Zain starts full-time school in September, I'll hopefully be able to up my hours at Dazzling Clean. I work as a domestic cleaner in the nearby area. With more money coming in, we'll be able to have more luxuries, but for now, we're struggling through.

We put on our coats and shoes before locking the door. I got my two-bedroom council house in Northampton when my parents kicked me out. It isn't paradise, but it's my haven, and seeing the wooden *Santa Stop* sign on the grass makes me smile. With what little we have, I try to make sure Zain doesn't miss out on anything. Having him at seventeen was both difficult and a blessing. Even though my family didn't approve, I wouldn't change my life.

❄

I get off the bus with Zain still in his almost-too-small-for-him pushchair. A shiver runs down my back and I pull the zip on Zain's coat up to the top. It's a short walk to the garden centre. I hurry along the path, fighting against the salted grit. The cold air is making my nose feel like it's freezing off. I wrap my scarf tighter around my neck and snuggle down into the soft material. It is December so I shouldn't complain, and I'm glad there's no slippery ice.

Once inside Strawberry Fields Garden Centre, the magic of Christmas makes the low temperature worthwhile. The festive scenes are beautiful, and Zain's big blue eyes light up with amazement.

"Look, Mummy! A polar bear."

The life-size glittery bear dances around a mirror ice rink track.

"It's beautiful."

OH, SANTA!

We look at the modern and traditional decorations. There are sparkly sausage dogs, furry snowflakes, and brightly coloured drummer boys. Our walk-around leads into aquariums, and we watch the fish. Zain likes the clownfish, and his little eyes light up when one moves into the pirate ship ornament. "Do you think he'll find treasure?" he asks, pointing in the fish's direction.

"Or maybe a gift from Santa." I smile.

"That would be so cool." He claps.

"Yes, it would."

After purchasing a ticket from the till, we join the long queue to see the big man himself. The wait is long, but Zain doesn't complain once.

"Can we get a hot chocolate after seeing Santa?" he asks, eyeing up the café sign he's seen many times before. He must recognise it as the place for sugary snacks.

"No, baby. I'll make one when we get home." I ruffle his hair.

"Okay." He doesn't seem upset. I wish I could get him a luxury drink, but I can make the same thing at home for a fraction of the price.

An elf comes down the line, handing out sweets, and I let Zain take one. Almost an hour later, we arrive at the front of the queue. Zain's excited as I get him out of his pushchair. We move up to the red ribbon inches away from the grotto.

"I'm sorry, little man. Santa needs a few minutes break and then he'll see you," a friendly lady in an elf costume says.

We wait patiently as a guy in a red t-shirt and tight red trousers disappears from the back of the makeshift building. I can't see his face, but his muscular physique and black hair aren't anything like the Santa I was expecting. Another fifteen minutes pass until he finally reappears with a coffee in his hand. He snaps a picture of himself next to the grotto before going back inside. The elf peers around the door, and he must give the signal he's ready to go.

We finally gain access to the ribboned area. The elf takes our ticket, and we walk inside. "Well, hello," Santa says. His black hair is covered by a fake white wig with a matching curly beard. The jacket of the costume is better than when I saw him outside, but he's way too young. Zain seems happy with him, though. Thank goodness he has a good imagination.

"Merry Christmas, Santa," Zain says.

"Have you been a good boy?" Santa crosses his muddy boots. The untied laces dangle, ready to be tripped over.

"Yes. My mummy says I've been the best." He jumps around excitedly.

"That's great, kid. I will try and bring you something special on Christmas Day." He hands him a gift from a box labelled *under-fives*.

"Aren't you going to ask him what he wants?" I ask. We paid £20 for less than five minutes with a Santa that doesn't seem so great. I hope the present is good.

He points to a scroll on the wall. "I already have the letters, and my elves are filling the orders."

Zain cocks his head to the side, and his lip starts to wobble. "We didn't do a list." His hands scrunch up tight as his eyes well up.

"That's why we came to see Santa today, isn't it, Zain? So you can tell him what you want." I scowl at the guy in the suit. *He'd better fix this.*

"Okay, tell me what you'd like." He waves his arms wide, reminding me of a genie about to grant a wish.

We've discussed what he wants. Tractors and dinosaurs are already wrapped ready for the big day.

"I'd like a train that goes around the Christmas tree," Zain says with confidence.

"I thought you said tractors and dinosaurs." I hope he'll change his mind. There is no train waiting for him, and I'm not sure if I can stretch my budget to get one.

Santa clicks his fingers, pointing right at him. "No problem, kid. It's already in the bag."

"Yes," Zain says as he bounces on the balls of his feet, accidentally knocking over the takeout coffee Santa left on the floor. The lid pops off, and the hot liquid seeps into the carpet.

"That's going to stain, and I've only got one suit. Get an elf in here!" he shouts. The drink barely touched his shoes, never mind his suit.

"Sorry," Zain says with his eyes cast down to the floor.

Santa pulls off his beard and jacket. He bends over the chair arm to pick up the cup while an elf helps to mop up the mess. "The stupid kid knocked it over."

"Mummy, he's not the real Santa." Zain's hands cover his cheeks as he stares in horror.

"He's one of Santa's helpers," I say. The costume did nothing for his gorgeous face. Even hot and sweaty, his dark features are striking.

"It's too damn hot in this suit and having to put up with this crap is too much," the guy says, getting to his feet. "This was the last straw. I'm going to get another coffee and I'm not coming back." He leaves in a huff.

"Great. What am I going to do now?" the elf says to herself before turning to me. "I'm so sorry. Please take any present you want."

"We have a present. What we wanted was to have a nice experience with Santa." I fold my arms. There should be training for these guys. They shouldn't just allow anyone to get the job.

"I'm really sorry. I'll give you your voucher back and you can come back tomorrow to see Santa. We elves need to get back to the workshop and Santa will return tomorrow to make up for today's disappointment." The elf smiles, although her watery eyes show her frustration.

She hands over our receipt from the till, and we leave. We make our way towards the area where we left the pushchair.

"Did I do something wrong?" Zain asks, scratching his arm. I come to a halt so I can look at him.

"No, baby." I hug him and try to reassure him that he didn't do anything bad.

I put him back in the pushchair once his smile has returned. As we exit the area, I hear the crowd of angry people demanding their money back. We swiftly make our way to the till.

"What's happened now?" one of the cashiers asks.

"Your Santa vacated the building."

The cashier slaps her head. "Not again. I'm really sorry. I'll give you your money back and you can return tomorrow."

"How many Santas have you had? I mean... how many elves have played Santa in place of the big guy?" I knit my eyebrows together in a frown. When I picture Santa in my head, a guy old enough to be my grandfather comes to mind. They must've been desperate to hire that guy. He'd be perfect for a mistletoe kiss, but not for playing the big man.

"Too many. Santa's very busy in his workshop preparing for the big day, but if we explain the situation to him, I'm sure he'll make tomorrow's visits extra special." She takes my ticket and refunds my money without me asking.

"Thank you," I say quickly, exiting the garden centre. The trip to see Santa was a disaster, and now I need to buy a toy train. The only silver lining is that I got my money back. Merry freaking Christmas.

❄

"You're being dramatic," Ellie, my best friend, says when I rehash what happened earlier at the garden centre.

"Honestly, he took off his clothes right in front of us," I say, waving my arms in the air.

"He said he was hot," Zain says.

"How hot are we talking?" Ellie asks with a grin. The guy was a looker, but that's not the point.

"I had to come up with a reason why he took off his coat." My eyes are wide, hoping she'll drop the subject. Hot Santa was a mess.

"He was just one of Santa's helpers." Zain shrugs like that explains it before going to play with his toys.

Ellie pouts. "Do I have to repeat myself? Come on, Stacey. How hot was bad Santa?"

"Fine. He was good-looking, okay? Are you happy now?" I roll my eyes. The guy who was playing Santa was drop-dead gorgeous. He was also a disaster with children.

"I knew it. You can't hide a crush from me. Spill the details. Give me a number on a scale of one to ten." Her perfectly manicured fingers wiggle for me to pick a number.

I take a deep breath. She's not going to stop until I give her what she wants. "Ten. He was smoking."

"Maybe I need to visit Santa." She winks at me, and I shake my head.

"Guys like him are what got me into this mess. I love my son, but if

I'd been head smart, I'd be at university rather than scraping by." My bleach blonde hair needs a cut, and my nails could use some love. My eyebrows are my best feature right now, and that's only because I watched a tutorial about styling them to suit my face shape on social media.

She stands and pulls me to my feet. "Let me ask my brother to babysit and we'll go out for a drink. You need cheering up, and I'm buying."

I give her a hug. "You don't have to do that."

"Yes, I do. I'm not taking no for an answer. Go get ready and we'll go to the Black Swan."

It'll be nice to take a night off. "Thanks, Ellie."

Dean, Ellie's brother, looks after Zain whenever we go to the pub. He's older and responsible. Zain likes him, although he says he reads boring books.

I change into a red jumper and black jeans. I've just put on a little make-up when Dean arrives. He scoops Zain up and takes him to play dinosaurs in the living room. We say goodbye before we head out for the night.

Chapter Two

Sonny

"That's the last time I'm taking you on for a bet." I poke my friend, Ferris, as I approach him in the local pub, the Black Swan.

"That bad, huh?" He laughs wickedly.

"The grotto they put me in was smaller than my car, the Santa suit was sweltering, and the screaming kids were little shits."

"The mums were hot, though, right?" He winks at me.

I shake my head. I'm not a player like Ferris, and I'm not looking for a woman either. Women and sex are on his mind way too much. His idea is flawed though. If he got a regular girlfriend, he wouldn't have to try so hard to get some action.

"And you can't handle your liquor or you wouldn't have agreed to race me around the cricket ground when you could hardly stand up." He gets to his feet and pats me on the back. "Let me get you a beer," he says as he walks away.

He goes to the bar, where he flirts with the barmaid. I take a seat at his table, resting my work boots against a nearby stool. Being at Strawberry Fields meant I missed a day's work at my usual place. I enjoy the job I'm trained to do. I'm a plumber by trade. Fixing and working with my hands is the sort of work I should be doing, not making small talk with young children.

When he returns, he's got himself a fresh pint of beer and me half a lager. "Very funny," I say sarcastically. Usually, I drink out of a bigger glass; he's making out I can't handle my alcohol.

"If I want you back with me in the yard tomorrow, you should take it easy."

I've never missed a day of work due to a hangover. "I probably made the last kid cry before I quit. I need something stronger than this." I scrub my head over my face. It's been an awful day, but it doesn't excuse my bad behaviour. I was an animal in that grotto. It was like I was caged in and I was going to suffocate if I didn't get out. I blew up over something that was an accident, but I'd had enough. Usually, at work, I'd take off some layers if I was getting too hot, but that wasn't an option. Everything just got too much. My mouth feels dry, and I quench my thirst by downing half the lager in the glass.

He covers his face, laughing. "You're a badass Santa."

"His mother probably thinks I'm just an ass." A vision of her shocked face when I shouted at her son for spilling my coffee flashes through my mind. Inwardly, I cringe, taking another big gulp of my lager, hoping to wash away some of the guilt.

"Bad Santa might work for you in here." He reaches into his bag and pulls out a hat.

I push it away. "My jolly days are over."

Two women enter the pub, and the blonde looks familiar. They go to the bar and greet some friends. One of them orders a round before they sit at a nearby table. Ferris is already eyeing them up, and I shake my head.

"Blonde or brunette? Which do you prefer?" He bites his lip.

"Tonight, I want a drink and to relax. Can't you forget about getting laid for once?"

"No way." He gets out of his seat and walks over to the women. I finish the contents of my glass and go to order another drink. Once I've paid and collected my drink, I can hear loud talking behind me.

"You!" I glance over my shoulder to see a petite blonde storming towards me. She's the familiar woman I saw entering the pub. I turn around, coming face to face with the stern-looking beauty. I try to side-step her, but she's headed straight for me. She pokes me in the chest before I make it back to my seat.

It's usually Ferris that gets women riled up. When I look into her big blue eyes, I realise who she is. "Oh, crap."

"You've got that right. You ruined my little boy's Christmas." She jabs me with her finger again.

"That's a bit extreme." I move past her and take a seat. Unfortunately, she isn't done yet. She follows me. "What are you doing?"

"Men like you shouldn't be trusted to be Santa's helper. I'm holding you accountable for ruining my son's visit to see Father Christmas." She towers over me, folding her arms. Her tone makes me think of my high school headmaster. I'm getting a telling off, and there's no way to get out of it. Unlike my old teacher, this woman is having a different effect on me. She's feisty, and it's kind of a turn-on.

I've never been so passionate and vexed about making someone angry before. I'd like to kiss her and hurt her with my words all in one. "Your kid will get over it."

"He shouldn't have to. All you had to do was ask him what he wanted for Christmas and tell him he had been a good boy. Instead, you stripped off and proved you weren't the real deal."

Laughter from the other table turns my head, and Ferris winks at me. Something inside me switches. My friend is usually the one to play games, but tonight, I'm curious about how far I can let this go. She's making it sound like I took *all* my clothes off. It's not like I told her son Santa is just a fantasy. I don't like the way she's eyeing me with distaste. I want her to find me attractive. Yes, I did a bad thing, but I'm not a bad guy. Usually, I'd let something like this go, but my ego won't let me. "Oh, I'm the real deal. You just need to give me a chance." I wink at her before grinning. Winning her over won't be easy, but I'm ready to have a little fun with trying.

She rolls her eyes. "I don't think so. It was a guy like you that got me pregnant. All I want is an apology. Maybe a drink, and I'll be on my merry way."

Should I feel bad for her or be insulted? "I'll buy you a drink."

"Great. That's a good start."

"If you sit with me while you finish it."

Her enthusiasm dwindles. "Why would you want me to sit with you?"

"My man Ferris over there is trying to get lucky with your friends. If you leave me here, one of two things is going to happen. Everyone will come and sit with me, or one of your friends will take your place. I want to enjoy my pint and then I'm leaving." I open my wallet and throw down a twenty-pound note. "Go get yourself a drink."

"Who says chivalry is dead?" She looks at the money but doesn't take it.

"I'm sorry. What part of my actions made you think I'm a gentleman?"

She hesitates like she wants to say something more but decides against it. She slaps her hand onto the table and swipes the money. I get a few minutes of peace while she's at the bar.

The women Ferris is entertaining are hanging onto his every word. They howl with laughter, and I'm officially ready to get out of here.

When my new friend joins me, she places the change and a small glass on the table.

"What are you drinking?" I ask.

"It's just lemonade, but I want my friends to think it's Peach Schnapps with lemonade."

I furrow my eyebrows. "Why?"

"Have you ever tried to look after a small child with a hangover? No, of course you haven't. It's not something I want to do."

"Has anyone told you that you have a bit of an attitude problem? You shouldn't judge a book by its cover."

"What, so I'm wrong? Are you a nanny or something?"

There's no way she thinks I'm a childminder. "See there's that attitude again."

"If you spent one day in my shoes, you'd understand what my problem is."

The original bet with Ferris is what got me into this mess, but how hard can looking after one boy be? "Okay, you're on."

She coughs. "Excuse me?"

"I'm working tomorrow, but how about you show me how hard your life is on Saturday?" I'm calling her bluff.

"That's Christmas Eve."

"So?" I shrug.

"Haven't you got somewhere better to be?"

I pretend to think about it. "Nope. But if you're scared, I'll back off."

"The only thing I'm scared of is you ruining Christmas."

I take a drink. "If that's how you want to be."

"I'm not going to invite you to my house." She shakes her head and crosses her arms.

"Your loss."

"Why? Do you have a train that goes on a track around the Christmas tree like the one my son asked you for?" She raises an eyebrow.

"Nope. It's just me." She mentioned having dinosaurs and tractors rather than railway presents, but I'm not Santa Claus. I'm offering my time, not a second run at being Santa.

She sighs. "I don't even know your name."

"Sonny. I'd say it's a pleasure, but the jury is still out on that one."

"Is this how you usually treat a woman?" She leans forward, invading my space like it will intimidate me, but I don't bite. Instead, I take the cool response.

"I don't know what you mean." I relax back into the chair.

"Hostile." The word comes out bitter.

I laugh, ignoring her distaste. "I shared my name. Now it's your turn."

She taps her hand on the table while she decides if she's going to tell me what I've asked. "I'm Stacey."

"That explains it. Your name means fruitful, which makes sense. I can't imagine you giving up on anything you want."

"How do you know what Stacey means?" She pouts, and it's kind of cute.

I'm not an expert in defining people's names. My sister's friend has the same name and they used to annoy me with facts from their girlie magazines. I don't tell her that, though. I'd rather remain mysterious.

"You underestimated me. I know a lot of things you wouldn't expect me to."

I finish my drink and buy another round. Stacey is fun once she starts to relax. By the end of the night, we've made no promises to meet up. I'm disappointed when she leaves and I can't text her goodnight.

Chapter Three

Stacey

"What do you want to do today? Should we go see if we can find another Santa?" I ask.

Zain finishes his breakfast before he answers. "He won't be the real Santa. I don't think we should do that again." He screws up his face.

Sonny made a mess of our Santa experience, and I want to erase the damage. Seeing another guy in a suit might not be the answer. "Shall we watch Christmas movies and eat chocolate?"

"I thought we didn't have treats before dinner?" He folds his arms like he's offended I'd suggest something so crazy. I bite my lip to muffle a laugh.

"It's Christmas. This one time it won't hurt." I hug him, hoping he'll ignore my double standards.

We settle in front of the TV with our drinks.

"Can I have my blanket? I'm cold." Zain shivers.

The temperature has dropped. I hand him what he's asked for before I touch the radiator. The cold metal cools my skin. I go to the boiler where I see the flame has gone out. After trying to get it to reignite, I call the council.

"Hello. You're through to Northampton Council. How may I help?"

"My heating isn't working. The light on my boiler has gone out."

"Okay. I'll take your details and an engineer will be with you as soon as he can."

"I have a four-year-old. Is there any chance you can give me a rough time? He's cold." Zain's wrapped the blanket around himself, pulling it up to his chin.

"I'm sorry. I'll try my best to make it a priority." Her voice sounds kind, and I believe she'll try to help.

"Thanks." It's lucky I have the housing company to fix the problem as it might be expensive.

The temperature drops further during the day, and we put on more layers. Zain and I snuggle up on the sofa while we wait.

A few hours pass before there's a knock on the door. I answer it to find Sonny on my doorstep. He's wearing overalls and a plain white vest, looking totally gorgeous. Why is he at my house and what is he wearing? My heart rate speeds up. Not because I'm scared he's a stalker. I'm shocked to see him and secretly a little happy. I didn't want the other night to be our last meeting.

"What are you doing here?" I ask.

His eyes widen with surprise at the sight of me. "It seems you need my help."

"You're a regular superhero." I place my hands on my hips. Just because I'm glad he's here doesn't mean I have to let him know that.

"I'm an ordinary plumber. Do you have a boiler that needs fixing?" He picks up his bag of tools from the ground.

"I hope you're a better plumber than you are a Santa. Come in." I lead him into the kitchen. It's strange seeing him in my space. He looks bigger and more muscular. The Santa suit was hiding a lot and, in the pub, I wasn't looking at him like this. I'm seeing him as more than an annoyance now. Anger is no longer clouding my thoughts and he is an attractive guy.

Zain comes over, scratching his head. "Aren't you the bad Santa?"

Sonny leans down to his level. "Sorry, little man. I wanted to play a joke and pretend to be Mr Claus."

"It wasn't very funny." He shakes his head.

"Can you forgive me?" He holds his hands up in a plea.

Zain studies him for a few seconds as if trying to work something out. "So, if we went to see Santa again, would it be the real one or an elf helper?"

Sonny looks at me before he speaks. "Sure. It would be the real Santa."

"Mummy says sometimes it's an elf. He's a very busy man." He rubs his forearm while twisting on the spot.

"Your mum is very wise." Listening to him compliment me makes my stomach flutter. I like hearing him praise me and saying the right things to my boy.

Zain seems to accept his answer and apology. Sonny and I smile at each other. I'm grateful he's tried to fix his mistake. "Come on, Zain. Let's get out of Sonny's way."

We go into the living room and Sonny gets to work. We put on some cartoons and snuggle up together. It doesn't take long for the boiler and radiators to start making noises.

"You need some new parts, which I've ordered. I've temporarily mended the problem, but I'll have to come back after Christmas." Sonny leans against the door frame.

"What if something goes wrong again?" I get to my feet.

"Hopefully, it won't. The piece I've fitted should hold. If it doesn't, you can ring the emergency line and someone will come out."

I'm not ready for him to leave yet. I'd like to know more about him because he seems different now he's not pretending to be something he's not. He's relaxed and not so prickly. "Are you staying for a coffee?"

He clears his throat. "Sure. Coffee would be great."

We go into the kitchen, and I make the drinks. "Thank you for your help."

"It's no problem." We sit at the small dining table. The clock on the wall ticks by for a couple of seconds and I fidget nervously. The silence is too much and I try to think of something to say.

"Did Ferris go home with Ellie? She hasn't called me yet."

He unzips his overalls and gets comfortable. He doesn't seem to notice I'm nervous. "Ferris was late to work so I didn't see him this morning, but he did text me. He went home with one of your friends. It could've been Ellie."

"Is your friend a player?"

"He's a good guy, but he likes the chase so he's not ready to settle down." Reading between the lines, he means *yes*.

"What about you?" I cringe. That wasn't a smooth way to suss him out.

"I'm not like Ferris if that's what you're asking. Right now, I'm busy with work, and talking to women isn't my strong point. I'm not looking to date anyone."

"Dating's overrated." I shrug, and he nods in agreement.

"Exactly. Especially at this time of year where everyone has Christmas obligations."

"What are you hoping Santa will bring you?"

"From Santa, I'd like an expensive car. That would be a nice gift for Christmas. What about you?"

I laugh. He just wants a boy's toy. "I'd like Zain to have the perfect, magical day."

He frowns but recovers quickly. "What about for yourself?"

I shrug. "My happiness comes from my son. If I had all the money in the world, I'd take him to Lapland to meet the most authentic Santa."

He rubs his hand down his neck, unintentionally showing off his toned arms. "I hope you don't mind me asking, but where's Zain's dad?"

"I was still in high school when I got pregnant. He couldn't handle everything when Zain was born."

"Does he see him now?" He tilts his head to the side and makes strong eye contact.

"No. He went off to university and never looked back." Good riddance. We don't need him. He dropped me when I needed him most and didn't look back. He never wanted to see Zain and it hurt like hell for the first year. I'm stronger for his rejection.

"I'm sorry." He touches my hand and offers a weak smile. This is a softer side of Sonny I've not seen before.

"Zain is my everything. I wouldn't change that." I look at the baby photo I have of him on the wall and smile.

"Good for you."

Our chat turns more superficial after that, and I enjoy his company. We finish our drinks before he helps me wash the cups.

"I'd best get back to work." He pulls out a business card. "If you have any problems or want to talk, this is my mobile number."

"Thanks." My smile is beaming, and I wish I was better at hiding my feelings. I like Sonny, even after his screw-up at the garden centre.

Chapter Four

Sonny

It's Christmas Eve, and Stacey is all I can think about. She doesn't seem to have anyone but that little boy, yet she doesn't seem to want to find happiness for herself.

After picking up some gifts for my family members in town, I find myself in the jewellery store, looking at necklaces. Would a small box of gold brighten her Christmas?

"Are you looking for something in particular?" the jeweller asks.

"Yes. I have a new friend, and I'd like to get her something that isn't too over the top." It's hard to define what Stacey is to me, but I cringe at the way I explained myself.

"Do you know what she likes?" She smiles. Maybe she thinks I'll be able to narrow it down. Unfortunately, I don't know enough about Stacey yet.

I shake my head. "No."

She looks around the store before clicking her fingers. "Then I'd go for something simple. We have a range of necklaces with gemstones. They're pretty and elegant but not heart-shaped. Unless you want something a little more affectionate."

I hadn't considered she might take the gift as meaning more than it does. I'm not sure what my intention with Stacey is, but I don't want her to think I'm coming on too strong. I'm not trying to make her fall for me. We've only just met, and I want to know her with no expectations for the future. "That sounds great."

The jeweller shows me to the collection, and I pick a blue gemstone, avoiding the romantic colours. As I'm walking past the toy store on my way out, I remember her joking about a train and Zain asking for one from Santa. When I was at the house yesterday, I only saw dinosaurs and tractors. Going into the shop, I pick a bright green motorised train that goes on a track, hoping it isn't one he has.

Once I've wrapped gifts, I drive to Stacey's house to drop off the presents. I didn't add a card or a gift tag. When I realise she isn't home, I leave them on the doorstep, making a swift exit. I don't need credit, although it's a shame I won't see her reaction to what I bought her.

Later that night, I get a message from an unknown number.

Merry Christmas. I hope Santa brings you that car.

I smile. This has to be Stacey.

Have you opened your surprise gift?

I will at midnight. Thank you.

Had she already guessed it was from me?

Why are you waiting? I may not be the best Santa you've ever seen, but I promise not to tell anyone you opened your gift early.

You're the rule breaker, not me.

I wish I could see her reaction to our messages. It can be hard to read the mood in a text sometimes.

Are you going to wait up?

Yeah.

Do you want some company?

I have a strong urge to see her.

It's late.

I frown. She shut me down, and it's understandable because it is late, but I wish things were different.

We can text or talk on the phone. It doesn't have to be in person.

Disappointment washes over me. I'd like to see her open the gift. I'm also aware I'm giving mixed messages. I shouldn't have told her I wasn't looking for a girlfriend because it wasn't true. I'm looking for someone special. I like her and want to spend some time getting to know her. If that leads to more, I'd be totally okay with that.

My phone rings, and I answer. "Hello."

"Hi. Thank you for my and Zain's gifts, but you didn't have to."

"I know I didn't, but I wanted to." I can't believe she called. She could have said she was tired and ignored me.

I can hear paper scrunching in the background. "It was nice of you."

"Are you wrapping presents?" It's almost midnight and she's running out of time to sleep. Maybe that's why she turned down my offer to come over.

"Yes. I have a few more to go. I'm sorry, but I didn't get you anything." The tape makes a noise again and it sounds like she's breaking it off with her teeth.

"I didn't expect you to." It wasn't a pity present. Stacey stirs something inside me. She makes me want to be kinder than normal. It might just be Christmas spirit, but I don't think it is.

"You're sweet."

I frown. *Do I want to be called sweet?* "I'm just making amends for messing up your Santa visit."

"You're forgiven." She pauses. "What are your plans for tomorrow?"

"I'm seeing my parents and sister. How about you?"

"It's just me and Zain. I'm making dinner and we're going to watch cartoons all day."

Her Christmas sounds fun. Since my sister and I grew up, the magic has faded away. "I'm jealous. I love cartoons."

She laughs. "Of course you do."

"What?" I ask innocently.

"You're such a kid." I can imagine her rolling her eyes.

"Are you trying to tell me you don't enjoy watching *Thomas the Tank Engine*?"

"Fine. Maybe you're right." We stay on the phone until midnight, when she finally opens her gift. I can hear the paper delicately breaking apart. I hope she likes what I've chosen. *What if she hates it?*

"Sonny. Wow. It's beautiful." Her words sound sincere, and I can breathe easy again.

"You like it." I can't stop smiling.

"Yes. If you were here right now, I'd kiss you."

"Well, now I have to come over." I'm half joking. It's doubtful she wants me there at this time, though.

"You can't. I need to go to bed. Zain might wake up early."

"You play unfair," I say in a sulky voice. She's kept her feelings towards me close to her chest and it makes me curious. *What does she think of me?*

"Listen, Sonny... Zain and I come as a package. I'm not looking for a fling. I'm thankful for your kindness, but that doesn't mean I'm going to sleep with you."

"Duly noted." I know she comes with extra responsibility, and I need to figure out if I can handle it before I say too much more.

"I need to get some sleep. Goodnight, Sonny."

"Goodnight, Stacey."

We hang up. I wanted to say more, but making promises I'm unsure I can keep isn't a good idea. I don't have a clue about children. If I give myself time, I'll know how badly I want to see her again. I finish getting ready for tomorrow before climbing into bed.

Chapter Five

Stacey

Seeing how happy Zain was on Christmas Day made all my effort worthwhile, and we're still watching festive movies a few days later.

I touch the gem around my neck on the necklace Sonny gave me, Zain drew me some great pictures, but this is the gift that makes my heart flutter. Sonny and I haven't texted or spoken since I opened my gift, though.

I stare at the phone. *Should I text him?*

Opening our messages, I fixate on the box to type in. My phone starts to ring, and I drop it like it's too hot. I scramble to pick it up. A picture of Ellie and me in the park is on the screen. "Hello," I say.

"Hello, beautiful," she sings down the phone.

"Where have you been?"

"I'm sorry. I should've called on Christmas Day."

"It's okay. We did text. Are you going to tell me what's going on with you?" I get up from the sofa, leaving Zain to watch the film.

"Nothing too bad." Her voice is high-pitched, giving away her lie.

"You forget I know you better than anyone." I go into the kitchen and shut the door.

"Fine. I had an argument with my brother and I've been trying to make amends." Ellie and Dean are close. It's unlike them to fall out.

"What? How did that happen?"

Ellie doesn't always think about the consequences of her actions and can be reckless at times. I don't know if this is Ellie's fault, but I doubt she's the innocent party. We've been friends for a long time, and before Zain, we were more alike. Now I have responsibilities.

"I borrowed his drone that he got from our parents for Christmas and kind of lost it. We've been searching the neighbours' gardens but haven't had any luck finding it."

"Are you for real? How did you do that?" Dean likes his gadgets, and Ellie should've left them alone.

"I don't know. I just wanted to try it out. Did you know they cost about a thousand pounds for a good one? I'm working overtime to try and save up for a new one." At least she seems to have a plan.

"Do you need anything from me?" She knows I can't loan her the money, but I still ask.

"No. I've got it covered."

"Okay."

"Anyway, I don't want to dwell. I want to catch up with my bestie."

"Did you go home with Ferris that night we went out?" I ask.

"Yes. What happened with you and Sonny?" Since I went home from the pub, I haven't spoken about Sonny, so I'm guessing she's spoken to Ferris and maybe Sonny mentioned me or something.

"He apologised with a gift." I try to keep my voice even, like it's no big deal.

"Ooh, what did he buy you?" She squeals down the phone, sounding way too excited.

"A necklace." I touch the gem again as I lean against the sink.

"That's so sweet."

"Yes. I guess it was."

"When are you seeing him again?"

"I'm not sure if that's a good idea." I shake my head, even though she can't see me.

"You can't be afraid of getting into another relationship just because Zain's dad was an asshole." Her words turn bitter.

"Sonny told me he isn't looking for a girlfriend, and he hasn't texted me in a few days."

"If you're coming across as standoffish, he might give up before anything happens." Ellie knows me better than anyone, and I usually shut down male advances. It makes sense that she jumps to this conclusion.

Sonny's different, and I didn't tell him I wasn't interested. I've also not told him that I am. Ellie probably has a point. If I don't show how I feel, I'll never know if he was being kind or considering dating me. "Thanks for the advice; I probably needed to hear it. I do like Sonny, and I don't want him to think I'm not into him. He's a great guy and I could turn up the flirting."

"Make sure you do."

My phone buzzes, and a message from Sonny comes through.

Are you free for me to fix the boiler this afternoon?

Yes.

"Sonny works for the council and is coming to my house to fix something this afternoon. He just texted me." I try not to sound as excited as I feel.

"Do use both a favour. Put on a nice top and flirt hard with him."

"Okay." I smile. I'd like Sonny to see me as more than a potential friend, and I'm willing to try Ellie's plan. She's right. I'm scared of letting someone in, but if I don't, I'll always be alone.

"Okay. I'll phone you tomorrow."

"Be good. See ya later."

"Text me updates on Sonny."

❄

Sonny arrives after lunch, and I let him inside. He's wearing his overalls again and looking as sexy as he did the first time I saw him in them.

"Afternoon." I don't miss him checking me out.

"Can I make you a drink or something?"

"I'll get the job done, and then a cuppa sounds great."

I smile. "Okay, I'll leave you to it." I'm slow to move out of the kitchen. Once I'm settled on the sofa next to Zain, I listen to Sonny working. Before I was actively interested in Sonny, it was so much easier. Now my palms are sweating, and I can't sit still.

Sonny's here.

Go flirt with him.

I don't know how.

Stop texting me and just go talk to him.

I kiss Zain on the head, hesitating for a while longer before returning to Sonny's side.

"How's it going?" I ask.

"It'll take time. Can you pass me the 17mm spanner?"

"Sure." It takes me a few seconds to understand which one it is, and I hand it over.

"Thanks."

"Did you have a nice Christmas?"

"Yeah. My mum made dinner and I got a year's supply of socks."

I laugh. "Everyone needs socks."

"Did you get any good gifts apart from the love of a small person?" Pride fills me. I'm glad Sonny listened to what I said about Zain.

"Some cute guy bought me a beautiful necklace." It's easier to pretend I'm talking about someone else.

"He must be really sweet, which is gross," Sonny says, keeping up the pretence.

"I think you mean a good guy. It might've just been a *sorry* present." I bite my lip, hoping he'll correct my misconception.

"If he didn't like you, he would've just bought you a candle or something. Seeing you in his gift is probably giving him the feels."

He's better at flirting than me. It's probably because I'm out of practice. "Maybe he should buy her dinner or something."

"Stacey." He gets up, moving away from his work.

"Yes?"

"Do you think you could get a babysitter for New Year's Eve? I'd like to cook a meal for you."

I frown. My best friend and her brother are usually my childcare options, but with their current situation, I can't ask Dean. Ellie will be partying the night away, so that rules her out too. "I'm sorry. I don't have the money to get someone to watch Zain on New Year's Eve."

"Okay. We'll make it work. How about a dinner for three?"

Our eyes meet. His offer means the world to me. "That would be nice."

He shows me his dirty hands. "I'm going to finish up fixing your boiler, and then, when I'm cleaned up, I'm going to kiss you. If you don't want me to, you have about thirty minutes to tell me you're not interested."

Butterflies flutter in my stomach. I'm hopefully giving all the right signals that I do want this to happen. Sonny isn't like other men that have been interested in me. He might not have made a good Santa, but he's a good man. He seems to have taken his time to think about what it would mean for us to have dinner, Zain included. "I look forward to it."

I check on Zain and make sure he has everything he needs. His juice is filled up and he has a snack. The movie is going to be on for at least thirty minutes more, and he's happy sitting in front of it. When I hear Sonny running his hands under the tap, I leave Zain in the living room.

Sonny is by the sink with my tea towel in hand when I walk into the kitchen. "The problem's fixed."

"Thank you."

He puts down the towel and we step towards each other. Our faces are inches apart, and I can smell his minty breath mixed with engine oil. My heart begins to race as we stare into each other's eyes. "Can I kiss you now?"

"Do you think we should talk about what that would mean first?" It will be easier if we both understand the expectations of each other before we take the next step. It might be just one kiss, but it has the potential to change everything. Zain hasn't seen me with a boyfriend, and I've never had to think about anyone more than the two of us.

He unzips his overalls and folds them down to his waist. Somehow, his white vest is still clean, and his chest muscles are barely covered. Quickly, I look up, hoping he didn't see me staring. "I understand you have a child and it makes you cautious about letting someone in. I can't promise you we are going to last forever, but if you don't give me a chance, we'll never know."

He's completely right, and my best friend gave me the same advice.

I put my hands on his chest, moving closer. His lips hover over mine hesitantly. "I want you to kiss me," I say.

He doesn't have to be told twice. He captures my chin in his hand, pulling me towards him, and I allow my body to nestle into his. Our lips connect. It's like magic, and I swear I feel a spark. His lips are soft, and he tastes of mint. His kisses are filled with passion, making it the best first kiss ever. If I'd allowed myself this on Christmas Eve, the necklace wouldn't have been my favourite gift. Sonny is a pleasant surprise all on his own. We kiss until we're eventually interrupted by Zain.

Our first moment of passion isn't in the perfect setting, but it's real. I'm hoping Sonny and I have a chance to be more than a Christmas story.

Chapter Six

Sonny

I'm picking Stacey and Zain up soon for our date. I never thought I'd be going on a first date with a woman and her kid, but I'm drawn to them. It's not just Stacey. I like Zain too.

Once my table is set for my guests, I get in my car to pick them up. As I get closer, I realise my palms are sweaty. I'm excited to see where this could go, and I want to make a good impression on them both.

The curtains twitch when I make my way to the door, and I knock. It takes a few minutes for Zain to open the door.

"Hi," he says.

"Hello."

"Mum says I can only bring one toy. Do you have something to play with at your house?" He crosses his arms.

"Maybe you should pack two." My house isn't really child-friendly since I have none of my own.

"Yes." He fist pumps the air. He disappears into the house like he's on a mission to scoop up his toys.

I'm left in the doorway as he disappears. Although I've been in the house before, it feels wrong to invite myself in. Stacey eventually materialises, with Zain following close behind.

"Sorry for taking so long to get ready," Stacey says. This is the most beautiful I've seen her. Her sleek blonde hair flows down her back, and her pink lips look edible. She's wearing a sexy, black, sparkly dress. If I could describe love at first sight, Stacey in this moment would be it. She's breathtaking.

"It was worth the wait. You look gorgeous."

She smiles. "Thanks. You look nice too."

Zain pushes past his mum and gives me a twirl. "What about me?"

I hadn't realised Stacey and I were so focused on each other until we break eye contact to take him in.

"You're handsome, my favourite little man," Stacey says, picking him up and kissing his forehead.

"A shirt with dinosaurs on is so much better than a plain blue one. You're the better dressed out of the two of us," I say.

"Are we going now? I'm hungry." Zain pouts, making us both smile.

"Sure thing. Let's go," I say.

Stacey lets Zain down and he collects a bag of toys.

"I said one toy," Stacey says.

"Sonny said he doesn't have anything fun to play with at his house. He said I can take more."

Stacey glares at me. Maybe I'm in trouble. "I'm sorry if I overstepped. I don't have any toys. Only a TV."

"It's fine. But be careful. First, it's an extra toy... next thing you know, you'll be out looking for the real Spiderman scaling New York City."

"I've always wanted to go to the Big Apple." I smile.

She laughs before ushering Zain outside. "Let's get through tonight first, then we'll see."

I take his bag of toys while she locks the door. "That sounds like a plan."

The drive back to my house is a little awkward at first until Zain starts singing nursery rhymes. We all join in, and I don't care I'm not the best singer.

When we get to my home, I show them around before leaving them settled on the carpet in front of the TV. They set up the trains, and I feel a sense of pride when Zain chooses to play with the one I bought him.

My apartment's open plan, so I can see them from the kitchen area. I fry my lemon and herb chicken while the fresh pasta shimmers.

Once everything is ready, I serve it up. We sit at my small table. Zain stares at his food, then at me.

"Thank you. This is lovely," Stacey says.

I pour them both a glass of the expensive soft drink I bought.

"This looks gross," Zain finally says.

"Zain! Sonny was nice enough to make you a special meal," Stacey whisper-shouts. Her eyes are wide, trying to communicate how serious she is.

He curls up his lip. "Don't you have any beans or Thomas pasta?"

"Zain," Stacey scolds again.

I laugh. "It's my fault. At his age, maybe I'd have turned my nose up at this too. Let me check what I have."

"I'm so sorry. I should've told you to get something kid friendly. You don't have to find him something else." Stacey shakes her head.

"I want to." I get up, abandoning my meal, and search the cupboards. "I have bagels and a tin of ravioli."

The tin drops onto the worksurface with a bang.

"It's alive," Zain says in response to my clumsiness.

"This is the food of the dragon realm. Only the brave can eat it." I'm improvising because I don't have anything else to offer.

His eyes widen with amazement. "Really?"

My attempts at persuasion actually impress him. Kids are easy to please. "Do you want to become as courageous as a knight?"

"Yes. I do."

"Bagel and ravioli?"

He nods. "I accept your mission."

It's hard not to laugh, and when Stacey does, I don't hold back.

Less than ten minutes later, we're all back at the table, enjoying the food.

"Thank you," Stacey says, watching Zain gobble up his meal.

"No problem. What do you think of my cooking? I hope I impressed at least one of you."

She bites her bottom lip before she speaks. "The ravioli looks good." She fights back a smile. "I'm messing with you. You've done a great job. I'm impressed."

"Enough to consider a second date?"

"When I speak to Ellie, I'll arrange a sitter."

"I'm looking forward to being alone with you."

She looks unsure of herself, avoiding eye contact. I put my hand on hers. "We can take it slow. We could go to the cinema or a restaurant next time."

Her fingers entangle with mine. "I'd like that."

We finish our food and settle in front of the TV to watch *The Grinch*. Zain falls asleep on his mum's lap, and she strokes his hair lovingly.

"Do you want me to take you both home?" I whisper.

"Soon." She looks at the kitchen area and then gives me a puzzled expression. Her bottom lip is almost pouting. "I hope you haven't hated our date."

"What made you think that?" I frown, not understanding where this is coming from.

"You put a lot of effort into making a fancy meal and it didn't quite go to plan. I'm sorry for that."

I take her hand in mine once more. "Hey. Don't think I haven't enjoyed myself. I didn't mind making the extra food and I've liked having you both here. Granted, I want alone time with you, but it's only so I can get to know you better."

"Do you question *The Grinch* being my favourite movie?" she asks, trying to lighten the mood.

"I bet you're a rom-com lover."

"It's been a long time since I chose a film for myself." Her lips tighten at the realisation.

"Well, that's going to change."

"I'd like that." She leans towards me, trying not to disturb Zain, and kisses my cheek.

"What was that for?"

"Because I wanted to."

I kiss her cheek before getting a pillow for Zain's head. Once he's laid on the sofa, we stand facing each other in the centre of the living room floor. I lean in and kiss my girl. It's soft and romantic. Kissing Stacey is unlike anything I've felt before. I'll never get enough of her lips.

The date wasn't perfect, but it's the best one I've ever had. I'm disappointed when it's time to take them home, but I'm excited for what might come next.

Chapter Seven

Stacey

"Sonny and I have been texting non-stop since New Year," I say.

Ellie brushes my hair with my paddle brush as I sit at my dressing table mirror. She's helping me get ready for my date with Sonny.

"I'm really happy for you," she says.

"Who would've known a visit to Santa would get me a date?" I'm hoping it might turn into a relationship, but we don't have to rush to label it.

"Next year, I'm taking Zain to see him. I need a hunky man gift wrapped under my tree." She gives me a satisfied smile, like she's pleased with her plan.

"I thought you were untameable, like a wild horse." I pretend my hands are a butterfly and make it float away.

"Just because I've not found the right guy doesn't mean I'm not looking for love."

"What kind of man is going to keep your interest for more than five minutes?" I laugh. I can't imagine Ellie settling down with anyone.

OH, SANTA!

"That's why I need Santa's help. The guy has to be as crazy as me to keep up." She laughs.

"When Sonny picks me up, you can ask him if he has any more single friends. Although, if things go well between Sonny and me, you might not be able to escape your one-night stands."

"If you don't get your dress on, Sonny might want to skip straight to dessert." She stops messing with my hair. She slaps my butt as I stand. "Get some clothes on, and before you say it, underwear doesn't count." Ellie helped me pick every part of my outfit, including my matching bra and thong set. She helps me fasten my lacy red dress in place.

There's a loud knock at the door and Zain shouts upstairs, "I'll get it."

I grab my shoes, and we all make our way to the door.

"Wow, you look stunning," Sonny says as I come into sight.

"Thank you," Ellie says.

I roll my eyes, laughing. "I think he means me."

"I know. I'm still taking the credit." She smiles smugly. If she hadn't helped choose my outfit, I might've picked something less sexy.

"Ellie's going to let me watch the real Spiderman movie," Zain says, bouncing around.

"Yeah, and we're going to stay up late eating chocolate until we're sick," Ellie adds.

"Are you sure you want to leave Zain with her?" Sonny asks. The amused smile on his face lets us know he's at least half joking.

It's cute that he's worried about Zain, but I know my best friend can handle it. Ellie enjoys getting a rise out of people, but she'd never do anything to harm anybody.

"If he's sick, Ellie will have to clean it up. She won't want that. Okay, we'd better go." I move closer to the door, kissing Zain on the head as I pass.

"Goodnight," Sonny says, and repeats the sentiment. We leave Zain and Ellie to their movie night.

We go out to the car, and like a gentleman, Sonny helps me inside.

"Where are you taking me?" I ask.

"I've booked a local restaurant."

"Great."

It's a short drive to our destination at the lakeside complex. Sonny is the perfect date, holding doors, pulling out my chair, and pouring me a glass of wine from the bottle he ordered. I glance at the menu when the waiter leaves us to browse.

"What do you fancy?" he asks.

"Apart from you?" I eye him over the menu, glad I can be open about my feelings while taking Ellie's advice to flirt hard. I like Sonny and I'm willing to give him a real shot. I'm done holding back.

"Hey, that was my line."

"It would've been cheesy if you'd said it."

He laughs. "Maybe you're right." We both turn our attention back to the food choices. "I'm going to get surf and turf."

"I don't even remember the last time I went out for an adult meal. I want to pick the most grown-up meal there is."

"Gammon and egg?" He chuckles.

"I'm going to have the steak."

"Good choice. Are you sure you don't want scampi with it?"

"No, thanks. I'm good with just the beef."

The waiter comes back and takes our order.

"After the food, I have a surprise for you."

"Oh, yeah. What kind of surprise?" I'm curious about what else he has to offer. This is the first date I've been on in this kind of setting. I can't imagine what else he could give me to make it better.

"I'm not giving away spoilers." He shakes his head.

"Now I wish I'd only ordered a dessert."

"Your patience will hopefully be worth it."

Sonny hasn't rushed me into anything, and I like that he lets me set the pace. I think back to that first day at the garden centre. Under stress, he lost his cool, but he's more than made it up to me. He must've been *really* stressed because he's handled everything after that so much more calmly. He made Zain a different meal on our date, and not once has he tried for more than I'm offering. "When we met, I thought you were an overrated Santa imposter. Every meeting after that, you've proven you're a good guy. Whatever you have planned, I'm sure it will be great."

He looks down at the table, avoiding eye contact. A look of pain crosses his face as he looks back at me. "I was at the garden centre

OH, SANTA!

because I lost a stupid bet with Ferris. But if I hadn't gone, I wouldn't have met you."

"That's nice of you to say."

He leans over and kisses me gently on the lips. "I'm glad we met."

"Me too."

The waiter brings our food. "Thank you," we both say to him.

"This looks delicious," I say once we're alone.

"Better than my ravioli?"

"Don't you mean your lemon and herb chicken?" I start to cut into my steak. "I liked it."

He smiles. "Okay. Maybe I'll cook it again next time I have you over to my apartment."

"Sounds great. I make awesome tacos. Maybe I can return the favour one day."

"I wouldn't say no to that."

Looking up at him, I say, "I have a good feeling about us."

"So you should. I'm awesome."

I laugh. "And you ruined it."

Making future plans, even if it's to enjoy food, already has me picturing Sonny as my official boyfriend. He's sweet and fun. Not just for Christmas.

"One day you'll tell me I'm awesome."

"Maybe." I wink at him, earning me a laugh.

We eat our food while enjoying some light-hearted conversation. Sonny pays for the meal, and we take a walk around the lake next to the restaurant. He holds my hand, and I snuggle into his shoulder.

"I've had a great time."

"The night isn't over yet."

"When's this big surprise happening?"

"Soon."

"It's a good job I'm not too impatient." I start to walk fast towards the car, and he strides to keep up. I'm almost running when I slip on some ice and begin to slide. Luckily, Sonny has a hold of me. He steadies my steps.

"Careful." He pulls me close, and I meet his lips with a soft kiss.

"Thank you for saving me."

"Come on. Let's head to mine." We begin walking again, and I take it slowly so I stay on my feet.

When we get back to the car, he drives me to his apartment. "Don't look so worried. We can keep it as fun and easy as you like."

"I trust you." I smile. It's been a while since I've been with a guy. I meant what I said, though. I have faith Sonny will make all our experiences together pleasurable.

He opens the door to his apartment and turns on a light. The living room area is decked out like a Christmas grotto. "I want a do-over." He puts on a Santa hat that was hanging on a peg near the entrance.

"You want to be Santa again?" My eyebrows furrow.

"Only for you." We move into the makeshift grotto, and he kisses my lips. Unlike the gentle one he gave me in the restaurant, this one is filled with passion. His tongue dances over mine. His soft lips send a warm, fuzzy feeling over my body. It's magical in a way I didn't expect.

"I thought we were going to do grown-up things?" I ask, flicking the pompom on his hat.

"We are. I brought the film *Happy New Year* to watch." He holds the DVD box up.

"You've thought of everything."

"I want this to go well."

"It already is."

Epilogue

Stacey

ONE YEAR LATER

It's a few days before Christmas, and my fake tree is almost present-free as I pack up our suitcases. I make sure the fairy lights are switched off before standing back to admire my tidy living room.

Sonny and Zain have gone to the shop to buy some sweets for the trip to the airport, leaving me to finish off at home. This Christmas is going to be so much better than the last. I'm working more hours, and Zain is in full-time school. Sonny has been a big help, and our adventure to Lapland is a gift from him. I'm so excited to see Santa that I couldn't sleep.

I move our bags to the doorway and put on my coat. Once my shoes are on, I move everything outside so I can lock the door. My timing is perfect. I can hear Zain's laughter as Sonny chases him up the garden path.

"Careful. I don't want anyone getting injured," I shout. There's no snow, but there could be ice.

"Lighten up, Mum. It's almost Christmas," Zain says. He looks like he's about to burst into hysterical laughter at his comment.

"Hey. I can be fun," I say in protest. He's a cheeky little man and needs tickling. I run after him and pick him up so I can spin him around. I'm careful with my footing, but there doesn't seem to be any frost on the ground. When I have a firm hold on him, I start to tickle under his arms.

Sonny wraps his arms around us. "You're both entertaining to me."

I give them both a kiss. A warm feeling fills my chest. These two men mean everything to me. We hug for a few minutes, and I love it. I could stay here all day, but if we don't make a move, we will be late. "We should go. We don't want to miss our flight."

Zain and I hold hands as we walk to the car, while Sonny brings our bags.

We make our way to Gatwick Airport while eating cola bottle sweets. After parking the car and checking in, we wait for our flight number to come up.

"Thank you for bringing us," I say to Sonny.

"It's the least I could do after last year." Sonny squeezes my hand.

"I'm sure there were cheaper ways to make it up to us." I wrap my fingers around his hand.

"But they wouldn't be as magical."

"We're going to see the real Santa, right?" Zain asks for confirmation. We've already talked about this, but after last year, he needs reassurance.

"We're going to his house. We'll see the real toy workshop, reindeers, and elves. We're going to see everything for real. Santa might be busy making presents, but he will make time for you," I say.

"I'm going to ask him for a creeper," Zain says.

My jaw drops to the floor. I'm not even sure what that is, and I certainly haven't got it in the suitcase.

"Don't worry. Santa has it covered," Sonny says, winking at me.

I relax my shoulders back. The tension I'd been holding slips away. I didn't realise I was on edge. It's good to have someone to share the responsibility of getting everything right with. Since Sonny and I got together, things have been easier.

Zain and Sonny work their way through a magazine while I sit with a romance novel. I'm pretending to read it, but in reality, I'm watching them.

Zain is giddy as he finds the clues to the puzzle they're working on, and Sonny is in his element. He's like a big kid. When he catches me looking, he smiles, and I grin back. I love these guys more than life itself.

❄

Finland is cold. I mean, bitterly cold. A shiver runs down my spine as I help Zain into his snowsuit. Sonny wriggles into his thick coat, and then I put on mine. We've checked into our lodge and are due to be picked up by a sled to see Santa.

Once we're ready, we hear the ringing of bells.

"He's here!" Zain shouts, jumping up and down.

"Let's go see the big man himself," Sonny says, rubbing his gloved hands together.

When we're ready, I lock up the lodge and we walk through the snow to the sled. An elf greets us and helps us onto the wooden seat. The bells are on the reindeer's coat, and the jingle sound gives me chills.

Zain sits in the middle, and we hold onto each other as the sled sets off.

We take the scenic route, past the candy canes and Christmas trees. The red ribbons and twinkling lights look magical. The elf sings to the reindeer, and Zain is mesmerised. His face is full of cheer as he takes in the sights.

Once we arrive at a large log cabin, the elf slows the sled until we stop. Sonny helps us get off and we go inside. Mechanical toys line the walls. They move, sing, and sparkle. Zain's mouth forms an o.

"Wow," he says, and it melts my heart. I don't know who is enjoying this the most.

We move through the area until we arrive at a big velvet curtain. It's beautiful, with no cost spared. Everything is rich with colour.

An elf greets us. "Welcome. You must be Zain. Is this your mum, Stacey? And Sonny? I'm Holly." She shakes our hands. Her movements are full of joy, and it's energizing.

"How do you know my name?" Zain asks.

"I know all the boys' and girls' names that are on the good list." She covers her mouth and giggles. "Shh, don't tell Santa I confirmed you're on the right list."

"I won't," Zain says, shaking his head.

A bell rings, and the elf leads us through the curtain. Santa is sitting in an armchair next to a fireplace, reading a book. The sound of burning wood is relaxing, and the smell of cinnamon orange fills the air, making my mouth water.

"Zain, is that you?" Santa asks, looking up.

"Yes, Santa. I've been a good boy. The elf told me I was." He points at the elf, and she covers her mouth, smiling.

Everyone laughs. *I know not to trust him with a secret.*

Santa is brilliant. He looks perfect with his oversized trousers and soot in his beard. His jacket looks soft enough to sleep on. "What do you want for Christmas?" he asks in a kind voice.

"A creeper," Zain says looking at Sonny.

"Fantastic," Santa says. "I want one of those too."

"You like Minecraft?" Zain's little mouth falls open. Santa is doing better at understanding his request than I did. Sonny and Zain have been playing computer games together, and it's great to see them bonding well.

"I do. The elves and I play it all the time." He gives a belly chuckle like he's thinking of a fond memory.

"I'm a gamer with Sonny." He points at him with pride, and I smile again. He's so cute, and I'm happy he's accepted Sonny into our lives.

"Excellent," Santa says.

We have our picture taken, and Santa tells us a story about the elf workshop. Zain gets a present, and we share a tray of mince pies. I bite into it, savouring the rich taste. This might be the best mince pie I've ever had.

We have an amazing time, and Zain is even giddier when we leave. We make our way back to the sled, and the elf takes us back to the lodge. We have a week full of activities, and this is just the start of our holiday, but for now, we can relax.

Once I've made us cups of hot chocolate, we sit down to watch a movie. Sonny kisses my cheek as we snuggle up. I have a feeling Christmas this year is going to be absolutely perfect.

The End

ABOUT THE AUTHOR

Danielle lives in Yorkshire, England, with her husband, daughter, and tortoise. She enjoys reading, watching the rain, and listening to old music. Her dreams include writing stories, visiting magical places, and staying young at heart. The people who know her describe her as someone who has her head in the clouds and her mind in a book.

ACKNOWLEDGMENTS

Thank you to Melanie, Jackie and my amazing editor Karen. I couldn't do this without you.

Connect with Danielle Jacks

ALSO BY DANIELLE JACKS

Standalones

The Heart of Baker Bay

Kickflip Summer

Dirty Kisses and Conflicting Wishes

Burned by Fire: A Firehouse 13 Novella

Confessions of a Sophomore Prankster: A FratHouse Confessions Novella

Romance Under Aquarius: A Stargazing Novel

Santa's Baby

by

R.T. Fritz

Prologue

Christmas is a time for family. Or at least that's what I've been told.

I grew up in foster care, and most of my Christmas involved getting cheap dollar store presents and slightly better food than usual.

I'm almost twenty-six; my first quarter century is closing as the new one forms. And all my life has been focused on something other than me. I never let myself take care of *me*.

Then came last Christmas, Santa gave me a present that changed my whole world.

But instead of a new bike or the latest tech gadget. He gave me a baby.

His baby.

No, this is not some cheesy Hallmark movie where Santa's son searches for love. Just a night of passion, one that left me with a stick and those two lines that tell you that your world is about to change. One day, I'll have to tell this child about their father. And considering I don't know his name, who knows how I will explain it.

Chapter One

Meadow

I feel like the biggest Christmas cliché.

I'm sitting on this stool in some dive bar on Christmas eve. I sip slowly on this whiskey made of fire as the clock ticks closer and closer to that dreaded day. I'll be alone as always, nothing but paperwork and teddy bear designs for me.

Owning a store where you can make your own bears is not a common job. Most people just assume I mean Build-a-Bear, but no. I'm the idiot that thought, you know what, I'll just make my own store.

Bear's Meadow has been my pride and joy for all these years. I opened the store because, as a kid, I loved to draw animals and make them my playmates. Foster homes made it hard to keep stuffed animals. All the moving meant things got lost a lot. But my pictures were always there. After college, I found myself searching for something more. And then one trip to the mall, I sat in the cafeteria and watched the kids leave Build-a-Bear, showing off their animal's clothes and accessories. Soon my idea took form, and I knew I had to make it.

So I sketched away at bears, wandering toy stores for all the inspiration. I made my first design, called Candy Cotton. A pink bunny with white accents. I designed a pink lavender tutu dress. I sold out of them in a week. I made each design a standard outfit, but kids had the option of picking another if they preferred. I would be on my sewing machine for hours at a time, making new clothes of all kinds for the bears. Before I knew it, I had bought space in a local mall and owned a thriving business.

But slowly, over the last year, this shift has been coming over me. I feel like I'm missing something.

So here I am, hating my drink and surrounded by the smell of stale cigarettes and cheap beer. I'm still in my uniform, brown dress pants with a green and red sweatshirt, all topped off with my Christmas apron with the store's name emblazoned on the front. Plus, I still have my elf hat on.

"You are definitely in the wrong place." My body tightens at the words of a man with a thick slur in his voice. He isn't wrong, I shouldn't be here, but it was the first open bar I could find.

"Hey man," I hear a different voice say. "Even Santa needs a drink."

Santa?

I turn on my stool to find... well, Santa.

Dressed in a cheap red and white suit, made out of what I can only assume is the itchiest material known to man. He has on a matching hat, and his fake beard is pulled under his chin, showing off his angular jaw, which has a five o'clock shadow of brown hair. His heavy black boots stomp towards me. His eyes scan mine.

"What? Never seen Santa before?" he asks, moving to a stool on the far side of the bar.

"No, I... um..." I stutter, realizing I have been staring at him for longer than is polite. "I'm sorry."

He grumbles something under his breath before flagging down the bartender. "Give me a scotch, three fingers and leave the bottle."

The bartender nods, pouring his drink into a highball. "Got to pay ahead if I'm leaving the bottle."

"Can't give Santa a discount?" he asks sarcastically, pulling out a few twenties.

"I'll give you the first free. The rest you pay, asshole."

He nods, handing over the cash, then downing his first drink.

"Rough day?" I ask him, unable to stop myself.

"What gave you that idea, little elf?"

He isn't wrong. I'm tiny. Even on the stool, you can tell I had a hard time getting up. Calling me five feet is a gross overestimation. I make up for my lack of height in my curves and tits. My hair is brown, trimmed in a bob, and slightly curled. And I have these large brown eyes that make people think of Emma Stone.

"I mean, the downing a whole glass of scotch is a start," I say, turning to face him fully. "Then there's the fact you walked in here wearing a Santa suit, which I am sure means you just came from the mall and want to live up to the mall Santa stereotype. Am I doing good so far?"

He glares at me, his green eyes shooting knives straight through me. Maybe it's the whiskey giving me this sudden confidence, or maybe I just want to forget my own problems. I mean, that's the only reason I'd push this guy, right?

"Don't pretend you know me," he says.

"I only run on what I see of you." I hop off my stool, collect my drink and swallow it with one gulp. The burning fire down my throat makes my heart clench. I move closer to him, leaving only one stool between us. I grab the bottle of scotch and pour myself a glass.

"I didn't invite you for a drink," he exclaims, taking the bottle from me. "Why can't you leave me alone?"

I shrug, not really knowing the answer myself. "Hey Keith, put the scotch on my tab."

The bartender nods, returning the money to Santa.

"I can buy my own liquor," he says, the agitation climbing in his voice.

"I am aware, but I stole some. And to be honest, if you wanted to be alone, you would have bought a bottle and gone back to your house. So my guess is you want company. I am giving it to you."

He ignores me, swallowing another scotch and pouring the next. We sit in silence for a moment. I nurse my drink slowly, the world starting to spin. Mixing drink is a bad idea.

"Why are you here?" he asks me quietly, his eyes locked on the wall of drinks ahead of him.

"Same as everyone here. Alone on Christmas, and this is better than sitting at home wallowing in depression and loneliness."

"You lonely?" he scoffs, turning towards me. His eyes soften as he looks at me quizzically. "You seem like the type of kid who's the apple of their parent's eye."

"Don't have those," I say, swirling my drink around the cup.

"Oh fuck," he replies, looking remorseful. "I'm sorry. I can be a dick."

"Hey, it's cool," I explain, giving him a forced smile. "I'm a foster kid. I'm used to not having family."

"I know the feeling," he responds, topping off my drink. "Mine just pretends I don't exist."

"I'm sorry."

"Don't really care. Besides, if they found me like this, they'd have a stroke."

"You know you can take off the wig and beard. Or the whole outfit."

He looks at me as I suddenly realize I just essentially told him to get naked.

"I just mean the outfit must be hot."

He chuckles, his first real smile since he got here. "If you want me naked, all you have to do is ask."

Before I can further dig my grave, he takes off his hat and wig. Revealing thick auburn hair, full of unkempt curls. It's the first time I've seen his full face. His eyes are small, but the bright green color shines through. The stubble on his face seems more like he hasn't bothered to shave in a while rather than a style choice. Under his eyes, beneath the purple hue, is a light dusting of freckles.

Once he takes the coat off, I see his lean frame. He's surprisingly fit, not how you would imagine a mall Santa looking.

"You can take a picture if you want." He flashes his teeth, a small dimple forms on his cheek. At least he seems happy.

"I'll pass." I giggle. "Having a half-dressed Santa picture on my phone may raise some questions."

OH, SANTA!

"Probably," he sits back down. "Cheers."
Our glasses clink together.
Well, getting drunk with Santa will be a fun story.

Chapter Two

Meadow

The ringing. Shrill and painful, cutting through my ear drums. I bury my face further into the warmth below me. My body is lulled by the rhythmic thumping of a heart.

Wait, whose heart is that?

I open my eyes. The sun has started to rise, filling the room with light. And then I realize what the warmth is.

The guy dressed as Santa, his naked chest where I have nestled my head. And I am naked. I look down and see he's fully naked too.

What the fuck did I do?

I sit up quickly, scanning the room, trying to figure out where I am. The small room is filled with the air mattress I'm lying on. Oh God, this guy doesn't even have a real bed. The door is at most a foot away from his mattress. The door itself has white paint chips coming off it. The floor is covered in clothes, more than just the clothes from last night.

Then I remember the ringing. My phone.

I move quickly through the clothes littering the searching for my phone, finally finding it in my apron.

"Hello, is this Meadow Park?"

"Yes, that's me," I whisper, collecting my clothes and searching for a bathroom. I pray he doesn't have a roommate who might catch me with all my bits on show. I find it quickly down the hall from his room.

"This is Garrison's towing," the man says. "I am waiting at your car. Can you confirm it's a 2006 Toyota Corolla?"

"Yes, that's my car," I respond cautiously. Did they tow my car?

"Are you nearby?" he asks me, irritation filling his voice.

I hold my phone between my ear and shoulder, pulling my pants on. I lost my underwear at some point, and there's no way I'm going to look for them now.

"Yes, is something wrong?"

He huffs loudly. "You called about locking your keys in your car."

I search my brain for the memory, but I come up with nothing. I don't even know where I am. I know my car is parked outside the bar.

"Right, of course," I say before pulling my sweater over my body. "I will be there in five."

He hangs up without another word. Can't say I blame him. I'm sure he'd rather be anywhere but my car, helping open it cause I was an idiot who locked her keys in the car.

My phone tells me it's almost six, and the battery is at six percent to top it all off. I pull up Google Maps, typing in the bar's address, thanking God I'm only a block away.

The room is spinning hard. The bottle of scotch is down to its last drop, the clock ticking closer and closer to midnight. Santa and I are the only two left, except for the bartender who has occasionally been chuckling at us. I mean, we are an elf and Santa getting absolutely wasted on Christmas eve. Any kid who saw us would probably burst into tears on sight.

"Okay, so you own a store that makes teddy bears. But you aren't Build-A-Bear."

I take a shot of the scotch, the burning sensation having dulled significantly. "Yeah. I am fighting big Teddy Bear. It's an important fight."

"Big Teddy Bear is definitely a dangerous monopoly."

"Why are you a Santa?" I ask him, resting my head on the bar for a moment.

"Pays the bills," he responds curtly.

"I can't imagine it keeps you rich the whole year."

"Seasonal gig, obviously." He rolls his eyes. "Sort of been out of work, and bills need to be paid."

"No particular career path?"

He shakes his head, taking a long sip of his drink. "It's complicated."

"It's probably not," I say, trying to meet his eyes. "People just say that 'cause they don't want to talk about it."

"I don't want to talk about it then."

"See," I say a little too loudly. "So much easier."

"With you," he replies, "nothing is easy. I mean, you won't leave me the fuck alone, so I'm sure you want to pry into my life."

"I just saw you needed someone," I shrug. "And to be honest, I did too."

He studies me for a moment. "Well, I guess we both ended up in the right bar."

"Wait." I jump straight up, making my head pound at the sudden move. "You actually admitting you needed someone to talk to?"

He rolls his eyes, shaking his head. "I tolerate a little elf harassing me."

"I'm a cute elf," I tell him confidently.

"Yo, I'm closing in five," Keith says, wiping the counter. "I want to be home for Christmas."

I look up at the clock. Eleven fifty-five.

"Fuck, I need to go," I say, nearly falling over once my feet hit the ground.

"You've got time, little elf."

"No, I won't be any more of a cliché."

He catches me as I try to stumble over. "What do you mean?"

"I'm not gonna be that lonely barfly who spends Christmas alone with a drink."

"Trust me, little elf, you are nothing like a barfly," he says softly, catching my gaze. His hands rest on my cheek, gently brushing the suddenly warm flesh.

"Yet here I am," I respond with a sigh.

"Don't worry about the Christmas clichés," he tells me. "Christmas is one big cliché."

"Thank you for the drinks," I say, moving away from his hands.

"You paid for them," he reminds me, collecting his Santa apparel. "I'll walk you out."

I don't argue with him, I'm pretty drunk and having a hard time standing. Having help out is probably a good thing.

I feel the blast of cold air as we hit the snow-covered streets of downtown Chicago. Thick snow falls from the skies, blanketing the streets and cars. Already, the snow is at least two inches.

I reach for the keys to my car so I can get my jacket out of there before I call an Uber. But going through my purse, I can't find them.

"Oh fuck," I say, frantically looking through every pocket for them.

"What's wrong?" he asks.

I finally give up, realizing my mistake. "My keys are locked in the car."

"How did you manage that?"

"I wasn't exactly in a good mood when I came here."

"Don't you have an extra set?"

"In my apartment, which I don't have a key to. And I doubt my landlord will be around to let me in."

"Oh, shit," he replies, looking around the streets.

I take out my phone to call a tow truck company, praying they aren't busy.

"Sorry, ma'am, it'll probably be four hours before we can get anyone to you."

"You've got to be kidding," I groan, throwing my head back in frustration. "What am I supposed to do until then?"

"I can't help you, ma'am," the woman replies in a bored tone. "Do you want the truck to come or not?"

"Yes, send the truck. Merry fucking Christmas to you." I hang up without another word.

"You have a friend to stay with?" he asks me, reminding me he's even there.

"Tanya is out of town," I sigh, reminding myself of my only friend. She's also one of my employees. I gave her the week off so she could go visit her family in Indiana. "I'll have to find an all-night diner or something."

He shifts nervously, avoiding eye contact. "My place is just down the block. You can hang out there until the tow truck driver gets here."

I freeze a moment. Am I actually considering going to this guy's apartment? A guy I just met who's dressed as a mall Santa?

"I... I don't know..." I trail off, studying him closely. He really isn't a bad guy, from what I have seen.

"I promise I'm not a murderer," he offers. "And I realize that's not much."

I look at him. The shyness on his face makes him even less scary. Not that he was before, he just seemed grumpy.

"You got coffee?" I ask. Going to his place is better than freezing outside or sitting alone in a greasy diner.

"I have been told I make the best coffee." He chuckles. He gestures me down the street.

Well, that explains why I am here, just not why we were naked on an air mattress.

I take in a deep breath, close my eyes and go to a happy place. I have no time to process what happened last night. The minute my clothes are on, I'm out the door. I zoom down the five flights of stairs, praying I didn't wake up... Santa?

I never got his name. I'm officially a slut.

My thoughts are stopped by the surge of wind and snow trying to knock me over. Five inches of snow cover the streets as plows begin their arduous task of clearing the thick white snow. My boots are buried in the snow as I fight the wind to my car.

Once I arrive, the driver is in his truck mid-cigarette, his hands look covered in dirt and oil. He looks extremely unimpressed.

"Hi, I'm Meadow," I say, crossing my arms over my chest as the cold wind rushes past me.

"Fucking hippies," I hear him grumble under his breath. "Can I get an ID?"

I pull out my wallet to show him my ID, then gets to work opening the car up. I stand there jumping up and down as my teeth start to chatter.

I try to focus on remembering last night. What made me decide to sleep with a nameless guy in an apartment that looked like a college students.

My sweater is over my head, leaving me in my dress pants and my Christmas-themed bra. Each cup is red and has an emerald green ribbon with white embroidery around them.

"Your tits are wrapped just for me." He smiles wickedly at me. His mouth trails kisses from my shoulder, nipping at my collarbone. I feel a shiver cross over me, but my body feels like it's on fire.

His fingers skillfully unhook my bra with one twist, letting the cups fall to the floor.

"These are the prettiest nipples known to man," he tells me. "God, I don't even know your name."

I pause; nerves hit me hard. "You can call me little elf."

"Does that mean you'll call me Santa?"

"Depends how hard you make me come," I reply, staring down at him. My breast nestled close to his face.

"That won't be a problem." His hands tighten in my ass, carrying me down the hall.

"I can walk, you know," I remind him as he readjusts me in his arms.

"I like you close, little elf."

I tangle my fingers in his soft curls, pushing my breast into his face. I can't believe I'm going to have a one-night stand.

With him, it just feels hotter; the danger and frantic heat between us, I just can't stop. I want every part of him.

"Yo, lady," the gruff voice breaks me from my thoughts. "You can get your keys. That's eighty-five dollars."

"Sorry," I say, pulling out my wallet. "You take credit?"

He grumbles again, going to his truck to pull out the machine. I pay him quickly before pulling out all the cash I have and handing it to him. "For your troubles. Merry Christmas."

I see a crack in his stern face, the corner of his mouth lifted. "You too."

Once he's gone, I pull out my coat with my keys inside. I wrap the coat tightly around me, feeling the first bit of warmth I've had since I woke up.

I crank the heat to full blast as I pull out. My car shakes as it pushes over the snow around me.

Once I turn off this street, yesterday will be forgotten. And this morning. I will never think of Santa again. Except in my dreams.

Chapter Three

Silas

I wake with the familiar headache of another bender. I force my eyes open, only to regret it as the sun blinds me. My head pounding in rhythm with my heart. I sit up on the shit air mattress I bought, air half deflated, so my tailbone digs into the ground.

The air in the apartment is absolutely freezing. I hunt through the piles of dirty clothing to find a warm sweater and some sweatpants. After a trip to the bathroom to relieve my painful bladder, I'm headed to the kitchen to see what food I have. The fridge is bare, as I expected, except for some leftover pizza and a bottle of soda.

This has never been my life plan, living in a shit apartment, taking whatever job I can get to pay the many bills I have. When I came back from England, I thought I was making good strides. I moved there with my parents when I was twelve, and being near them wasn't something I could handle anymore. Their attempt to run away from their problems became the reason I was tormented.

I packed my bags and came back to where I was born and lived the best years of my life. I got accepted to university with a scholarship, and I worked on a double major in software programming and linguistics.

After I finished, I began work on designing an app to help children with speech delays. It combines electronic communication with learning to speak. My idea was to not only have them learn, but the app would track the patterns in their communication. This would allow parents to see where they struggle most in speech. I have been working on it since I graduated, every spare moment I had.

Finally, after years of pedaling my app, a company offered to help me with development and testing. I thought I was finally going to get where I needed to be.

Before I could finish, however, the company I worked for went bankrupt. My former boss was arrested for embezzlement, fraud, and tax evasion. It left me back at square one.

So here I am, thirty, and living like a kid out of college.

I take a bite of the days-old pizza, trying to ignore the smell of stale cheese and tough crust. Some color catches my eye. I look at my pants and see a pair of red lace underwear.

Fuck, did I pick up someone at the bar? I search my brain for a memory of last night, but I come up empty.

Well, whoever it was is long gone, but I can still smell the faint scent of jasmine and citrus.

My phone goes off, singing Sweet Caroline to me. It's my favorite song, and I figure I could have one good thing happen when the phone rings.

"Hello?"

"My man!" the voice on the other end shouts. "Merry Christmas, you filthy animal."

"Hello, Marcus," I sigh, taking a seat on the couch. Marcus and I met in university what feels like a lifetime ago. We both worked in the same office before the fallout. But luckily for him, he decided to move on before everything went down. I was so lost in my work; the red flags weren't even on my radar.

"Now, is that any way to talk to your best friend?" he asks me cheekily. "One who is about to be your Christmas savior."

"What are you talking about?" I ask him, sipping from the scotch bottle on the table.

"My boss is looking for a new developer, and I managed to sweet talk him into getting you an interview. He already knows about Harris Corp. So, you busy Monday?"

"No fucking way," I reply in disbelief. "You have to be joking."

"On Christmas? Never." He chuckles. "You want the interview or not?"

"Of course I do, you son of a bitch."

"Great, I'll let my boss know. He'll call you after the holidays."

I hang up the phone and jump. My whole body is full of adrenaline, vibrating with excitement.

Once I manage to calm down, I realize the red lace is in my hand. It's a strange feeling not remembering her. Yet, I feel like I should. Everything in me wants to know what happened last night, but I just can't find it.

Chapter Four

Meadow

I'm the biggest fucking idiot.

I look down at those evil double blue lines. The shame of my drunken Christmas hookup courses through me. I can't decide if I am angry or about to fall apart.

It's been almost three months since Christmas. Today is Valentine's day, to be exact.

I haven't had any signs that I was pregnant. Except for my boobs throbbing when I hear a child cry, which happens a lot in my line of work. That, and I've started putting pickle juice in my coffee. I have no clue why. I hate pickles.

The minute Tanya realized what was wrong, she was gone and back with three pregnancy tests and a massive bottle of water.

"Babe," she whispers softly outside the door. I'm locked in the employees' bathroom, staring at the test like it will change if I look hard enough.

"Yeah, give me a minute," I say, wiping the tears from my eyes. I clean myself quick, washing the smudge mascara and eyeliner.

The minute I leave this bathroom, my future is set. I will be a single mother, and I'll have to explain to my child that their father was a mall Santa. Shame punches me hard in the gut, and the tears threaten to fall again.

"No," I whisper to myself, glaring at my broken reflection. "You are strong, be brave."

I square my shoulders, ready to face the world outside.

I open the door to find Tanya on the other side. Her soft green eyes comfort me.

Tanya is thirty-five, but she looks twenty. Her long blonde hair falls passed her waist in soft waves. She has very feline features that match her slim form. She towers over me with her five-foot-four stature and four-inch heels; she could be a model on a runway in France. Instead, she works happily here, with a boss almost a decade younger than her. She's my only real friend, but I don't get much choice in the matter. She saw me stumbling into her interview, and from that moment on, I was her best friend. An extrovert adopted an introvert.

"You got knocked up," she says more as a statement rather than a question.

"Seems like it," I sigh, walking over to the break room. I start to pour a cup of coffee, but Tanya is there to snatch it out of my hands.

"Can't have that if you're... got a bun," she rephrases as one of the part-timers walks in to grab a water.

"Look, not here," I insist, searching the fridge for the Gatorade I put in there yesterday. But the minute I open the lid, the smell of green apple fills my nose and hits my stomach like a rock. I barely manage to put the bottle down before I'm racing to a trash can. My leftover pickle coffee and scone come violently back out of me. It feels like it will never end.

"Sweetie," Tanya sighs, rubbing my back until the retching stops. She offers me some water and guides me back to a chair.

"What are you going to do?"

I turn to her abruptly. "What do you mean?"

"Well... Are you gonna..."

"No," I say a little too loudly, causing Tanya to flinch. "I won't get rid of this baby."

"I just wanted to make sure you know your options," she assures me, taking a seat next to me. "What about the dad?"

"Tanya," I sigh. "Until about five minutes ago, I was just the weirdo who put pickle juice in her coffee. I haven't even absorbed that I am, you know."

"He deserves to know," she tells me, putting her arm around me. "Go home, get some rest. I can close up tonight. I'll bring some pickles and pizza once I'm done."

I nod, taking another gulp of water. "I'm dead on my feet."

I go to my office, which is just a closet-sized room with a desk, two chairs, and my laptop. I save the new designs for Easter bears and grab my coat and keys before locking up to go home.

The store is busy as ever, with couples going through the bear-making process, kids running around with different animals, and others showing off their custom designs. I have two workers who sew up the pieces of outfits that the children create from the different materials floating around.

"Meadow!" I turn to the sound of my name. Connie, one of my most valued customers, walks in, a huge grin covering her face.

"Hey," I say back, moving to hug her. "How's Alex?"

"Good," she responds. "I tried calling the store, but the line was constantly busy. I came to ask if you are still having quiet hours tonight."

My store has a low sensory hour every other Tuesday starting at five. It's for children like Alex, who have autism or sensory issues. The lights of the store are turned down, the music is turned off, and the kids get to explore and relax. Connie is the reason I started it. She brought her daughter to make a bear one day, but the noise got to Alex, and she started to panic. When I asked Connie if I could help, she asked for a quiet room. I gave them my office and watched Alex play her games in silence.

"I'm so sorry," I reply, hating myself for forgetting. "I should have called you guys. Valentine's day means no slowing down."

"That's what I figured," Connie responds with a kind smile. "I'll get in touch with the other parents to let them know. Are you ok? You look unwell."

"Yeah, just a little nauseous," I say, keeping things vague.

Connie studies me a moment, looking around her before whispering. "I remember with Alex, the smell of oranges made me paint the floor like a Picasso."

"Am I that easy to read?" I ask her, chuckling lightly.

"Just a mother's sense," she explains. "Let me walk you out."

"You don't have to," I start.

"Nonsense, I don't want you getting sick alone. Plus, I have to head home to Alex, so I'm going your way."

I nod, falling in step with her. My mind races as I picture what's to come with the pregnancy.

"How did you do it?" I ask Connie as we enter the parking garage. "I mean, how did you get ready to be a mom?"

"Oh, there's no getting ready. You just take it one day at a time. Nothing is ever going to follow the linear path everyone thinks it will."

"I just don't know where to start."

"I'm going to assume you found out recently?"

I nod, my eyes turn downward in shame.

"Have you told the father?"

"No," I sigh. A cold gust of wind blows through the garage. I tighten my coat around me, and my arms instinctively protect my belly. I now notice the little bump that's started to form. "He was a drunk hookup. I don't even know his name."

"Oh, hon," she says, pulling me into a hug again. The tears fall again. "I'm so sorry. I shouldn't have asked."

"It's okay," I choke out, trying to hold back the sobs. "You couldn't have known how much of an idiot I am."

"If you're an idiot, then so am I."

I look up at her, confusion crossing my face. She's probably in her forties; she doesn't seem like the type.

"I was twenty-three when I got pregnant with Alex," she explains. "Barely an adult in attitude. My parents kicked me out, and I tried to find the father the whole pregnancy. I was terrified, sure I wasn't going to keep the baby. But then that first ultrasound, that tiny little bean that was my baby, it changed everything. You won't know what to do most of the time, and it's scary as hell, but in the end, my little bean was all that mattered."

She's right, I hope. I know this will be a rough road, but I have to believe in myself.

"Thank you." I pull her into a tight hug. She squeezes me just as tight; her warmth covers me and fills me with a power that pushes back the fear and shame.

"Now," she says, letting me go. "I want you to come to me if you need anything, alright."

"I will," I promise her. "Thank you for everything."

As I pull my car out, I give one final wave to Connie, then descend to the floor-level exit.

I know it's not much right now, but this little life means everything to me. And I will do anything to protect it.

Chapter Five

Silas

"How's work going?" my boss Grant asks me, poking his head into my office.

It's been four months since my interview, and everything has been going unbelievably well. I have gotten so much progress done on my app, which I am getting ready to start beta trials on. So far, I've only tested the app on people without speech delays, trying to perfect the algorithm.

"Great," I say with a massive grin, turning away from my computer full of stats. "Beta trials start in May, hopefully. I'm trying to find a few subjects still."

"That's good to hear." He enters my office and sits in the chair across from me. Grant is in his fifties, though he never acts like it. He's not the expected button-up suit with slicked-back hair and a stern demeanor.

He's tall with grey hair, styled like a character out of *Grease*. He wears jeans most of the time with casual button-ups. I remember coming into my interview, I wore the only suit I owned that I ironed meticulously. I was surprised that he was the man interviewing me.

Grant is one of the nicest guys around. He never has a problem when it comes to talking with others. There's never an awkward moment of silence around him.

"I have a friend whose daughter could benefit from your app," he tells me. "if that is okay with you, of course."

"I need people to test it out, and that saves me finding one more."

"I'll have Lina send you her contact information." He is about to rise from the chair.

"Thank you," I say, rising from my chair and offering him my hand. "You giving me this chance. It means so much to me. I never thought I would make it to this point."

"You did this all on your own," he assures me. "I just gave you the job you deserved. People doubt others on such little things. You didn't deserve that doubt."

"Thank you," I repeat, flinching slightly.

Grant walks out, almost running into Marcus in the process. "Slow down there, boy. You wouldn't want to hurt your boss after all." He jokes, dancing around him.

Once Grant has left, Marcus turns to me with a mischievous grin. "Cancel whatever plans you got tonight. I got us VIP passes to Luxe tonight."

Luxe is a very exclusive bar in the downtown area. Unless you have a lot of money or you are a hot supermodel, getting in is impossible.

"I've got work to do," I tell him, moving back to my algorithm checks.

"Nope," he says, pushing down my laptop screen, leaving it open a fraction so it doesn't fully shut off. "You have been locked in either this office or your apartment since you got this job. You need a night out."

"Marcus," I sigh, rubbing my temples to fight the headache coming on. "I'm exhausted. Why would I want to go?"

"Easy," he says with a cocky grin. "Hot pussy and unlimited drinks."

"There's always a limit to drinks," I remind him. "Fine, one hour, that's it."

Marcus shakes his head. "Sure, one hour. Be there by seven." He drops the pass on my desk, a black onyx card with gold detailing on the X.

What have I gotten myself into?

After changing into dark jeans and a burgundy button-up, I throw on my leather jacket to head to the club. My Uber waits for me as I exit. Once there, I flash the pass to the bouncer, who opens the rope to let me in.

The music pumps blast at an ear-shattering level. The floor is full of people grinding away to the beat. The dark corner of the club is filled with couples who are probably doing more than just making out.

I find the VIP area and follow the staircase up. The room has a glass wall staring down at the dancers. A private bar sits on the far end as lights flash colors around us.

This place is what I imagine it would look like in real life.

In my twenties, clubs like this were fun, drunken hookups, grinding on hot girls who were clawing for my cock.

But that was then, and this is now.

"What can I get you," the waitress purrs at me. She's wearing a dark black dress with gold trim. The dress pushes her ample cleavage up to the point you think they'd fall out. She's pushing herself closer to me, invading my space.

"Scotch," I say, moving away from her quickly. I scan the room, finding Marcus with some other guys I don't know and a girl who's grinding on his lap.

"Hey man," he says, offering his hand. "Sorry, I can't exactly get up."

He winks creepily as the girl brushes her hair back. She looks at me, licking her lips as she scans my body. She's attractive; crystal blue eyes with dark brown hair. A slim figure but with actual curves. She's not a stick.

"Angela, meet Silas," Marcus says, his mouth next to her ear.

"Pleasure," she says, rolling the 'r.'

"Here you go, handsome." The waitress comes back, rubbing her tits on my shoulder.

"Thanks," I reply curtly.

"Name is Marnie," she says. "If you need anything."

"Thanks," I say again, waiting for her to leave.

"Come on, man," Marcus says. "Loosen up a little. You need to have some fun."

He's not wrong. I spend all my time working, but in a way I prefer it. Knowing I get to do what I love again. That's what matters to me. This stuff, it's just something people assume is fun. Then once they get here and realize it's not, they overcompensate for it by pretending.

"Look, man, it's just not my scene." I take a sip of my drink.

"Dude," he says, pushing Angela off his lap gently. "Just have a drink, dance a little."

I roll my eyes, downing the last of my scotch. "Fine. Angela." I stand and offer her my hand, which she takes enthusiastically. Marcus smiles gleefully, turning to talk to the guys he was with.

About an hour passes, Angela and I switching between dancing and drinking. The others are pretty chill but clearly more into the girls around them than our conversations.

"Let's get out of here," Angela whispers in my ear.

Suddenly my brain unlocks itself.

"Let's go," I tell little elf, guiding her to my place. I wrap her in the Santa jacket the mall loaned me. I was supposed to give it back at the end of the night, but the guy who takes the costumes had already left by the time I was done.

She seems to warm up, but I tuck her into my side anyway. She doesn't have much to cover her with her keys and jacket locked in her car. I offered her to come by my place to wait for the tow truck.

The truth is, I didn't want her to go. I would have locked her keys in that car if it meant another hour with her. Her smile is infectious. She's funny and hot as sin. Her body's curves make my mouth water. It took a lot of effort to not look at her tits hidden behind the sweater and apron, but even under those layers, I could still see how perfect they are.

I try to control my cock as I hold her close, but it's a losing battle. I angle my body so she can't feel it. But it's looking for her. Luckily these pants are baggy on me.

"I'm sorry," I tell her as we make it to my building. "Elevator has been busted since I got here, and my place is five floors up."

She just shrugs. "I need the cardio."

I chuckle, pulling out my key. Once it's unlocked, I hold the door open for her to get in.

We make our way up the stairs. I keep behind her in case she passes out or stumbles. I take a second to regain control of my balance.

After a few missteps, we make it to my floor. My apartment is only two doors down from the stairwell.

I feel the shame build, knowing the disaster she's about to see. "I didn't realize I would have company, or I would have cleaned up."

She shrugs again; her eyes seem to be a mile away.

I reach for the handle when I feel a tug on my shirt. I look over to see her attempt to pull me down. Confused, I lower myself to her level. Before I can react, her lips are on mine.

"Hello?" I hear Angela's shrill voice calling to me in annoyance.

"I...um..." I say, trying to collect myself after the memory exploded out of me. Suddenly shifting back to the present, the hard bass hits my head hard. The lights are blinding me.

"Dude, you okay?" Marcus asks, looking extremely concerned. "I'm going to get you some water, man. You look white as a ghost."

I barely notice him move, nor the feeling of Angela's hands on my arm.

What is happening to me?

I've had drunken hookups before. They all meant nothing to me, even in my younger years when I forgot who the girl even was. But this one. It's different. I want to know more. From that memory, I can now feel her lips on mine. The softness of her lips, the taste of scotch on her tongue. The way her hands tangled in my hair.

"Hey, Silas," Marcus says loudly over the music. I again am brought to the present. He offers me a glass of water, but I don't take it. I can't.

"I have to go," I say quickly, grabbing my coat. "I just need out of here. I'll see you tomorrow."

I don't wait for a response; I just make a break for the door. Once out in the late spring air, I feel less suffocated by the memories. They still haunt me, even if I can't remember them fully.

I pick a direction and just start walking. I don't know how long I walk, but by the time I am able to calm down, my shins are on fire, and my breath comes out in gasps.

OH, SANTA!

I flag down a cab driving past me. He breaks quickly and pulls over. "Can you take me to a bar on Jackson?" I ask him.

"Dude." He looks at me like I'm an idiot. "I'm gonna need you to be more specific."

I think for a moment, remembering my old apartment there. I rattle off the address to him. He shakes his head before turning on the meter.

I'm given more time to think while we drive. I can't understand why this matters to me. I'm not impulsive. I have plans, and they are followed. Deviations are expected, but always a backup is ready. Now here I am, going to some dive bar because of a little elf I met there. I don't know this girl, her name, why she matters to me right now. I didn't remember her when I woke up, so why now?

The cab driver rolls up and tells me about my total in a bored tone. I throw him a fifty before heading out. I don't wait for change. I just want to get out of there.

My old building stands before me; historic but dilapidated. One of those places the historical societies don't want to tear down but don't want to pay for the upkeep either. The guy who owned it when I was around gave us cheap rent, but with cheap rent comes cheap shit.

I walk down the street, trying to find the bar I was at with her. Each shop leads me further and further from my place, making me convinced it was only a dream.

But then I find it. Belgrave Pub. I recognize it immediately.

The door chimes over my head. Looking around the bar, it's mostly empty. Two guys are throwing darts on the one end, and a man and woman, both in their late forties, I would guess, are nestled next to each other.

"Yo, Santa," a man behind the bar calls. "That's got to be you. I never forget a face."

"Do I know you?" I ask, moving slowly towards the bar. I bury my sweaty hands in my jacket pockets.

"Name's Keith," he says, offering his hand.

"Silas," I reply, shaking his hand.

"So let me guess, you're looking for the elf?"

I look up at him, confused. "How did you..."

"Ain't my first rodeo," he chuckles, picking up a glass and bottle of scotch. "Hookups happen. Every once in a while, people come back looking for that girl or guy."

"How did you..." I ask again, stupidly. I down the scotch he poured me, which he fills up again.

"Bartenders intuition. Now I'll tell you what I tell most people who come here. I don't know her name, and if I did, I'd tell you."

"I had a feeling you wouldn't." I shrug, slowly spinning my glass. "I just had to come back, though."

"No worries, my man. You got a card?" he asks me.

I reach in my wallet, pull out the brand new stationary, and hand it to him.

"If she comes back, I'll give you a call." He pulls out a drawer under the bar with a collection of business cards.

"You ever find anyone?" I ask him.

"Happened three times for sure," he explains. "The first time, I got invited to their wedding. They are happily married and living in the burbs with two kids."

"Wow," I respond, leaving the second scotch untouched. I pull out my wallet to pay, but Keith shakes his head.

"Nah, man, this is on me. Hope you find your girl."

I nod, not sure how to answer. This last hour has been a whirlwind, and I can't really think of what I want. I just want to see her, know she's real and not some bullshit Christmas movie.

Chapter Six

Meadow

"I feel like I'm carrying a beluga whale in this dress," I tell Tanya as I lay back down on the couch.

It's the end of August, but the summer heat still going strong. I'm about to be eight months pregnant, and this baby feels like a bowling ball parked on my bladder.

"You look great, girl," Tanya assures me. "Besides beluga is the new fall look. You're ahead of your time."

I roll my eyes before holding my arms out. "Help me up, please?"

With a great loud grunt, we manage to get me upright again. I look at myself in the mirror. I'm wearing a light blue maternity dress. I'm using it to announce the gender of the baby. I had been holding off telling people, and now I only am doing it because Alex wants to know.

Between Connie and Tanya, I am well taken care of. Both have been by my side this entire time. Taking me to appointments, doing Lamaze with me, and just holding me when I feel like I'm falling apart.

The first few months were rough. All I could eat were pickles and toast. I was on some pretty heavy anti-nausea medication for a while. But once I hit the twenty-fourth week of pregnancy, that went away.

Today, Connie and Alex are holding a baby shower for me. Alex, who just turned sixteen, is over the moon about it. After the day I talked with Connie, we've become fast friends. She and Tanya get along great, too, and now the four of us are best friends.

"Come on, Miss Beluga," Tanya says, taking my arm and guiding us downstairs.

The other new thing is the house. It's a two-bed one-bath condo. Once I knew the baby was real, I had to get a better place for us than my studio apartment in the middle of downtown. I wanted my baby to have space to play. The backyard of this place is gorgeous, with lush green grass and a small porch. Connie gave me Alex's old play equipment since she has outgrown most of it.

Once downstairs, I see the decorations Connie and Alex put up. My entire first floor is covered in streamers and balloons.

Alex is excited about my arrival. "Baby."

Alex has speech delays. She's mostly nonverbal except for a few words and phrases.

"Want to feel the baby?" I ask her, watching the light fill her eyes. She moves forward quickly, carefully placing her hands on my belly. She stares as the little guy kicks me left and right. At least he's giving my bladder a break.

She moves her hands away, moving back over to her tablet without another word.

"She's been so excited today," Connie chuckles, watching Alex curl up in a ball as she normally does, a slight rocking motion starting. "She's just got into this trial for a new speech app, and she's been talking up a storm with it."

"Oh wow," I say, my hands cupping my stomach as a small twinge hits my back. "What trial?"

"This app called Jules Words," she explains. "I got an invite for it back in May. They were looking for kids with all types of speech delays. The app is supposed to come out in December."

"Is it helping at all?" I ask her, and another cramp hits me again. I sit down on the couch opposite Alex, who is looking over at us cautiously. She seems to be studying me hard.

"Oh, it's been great for her," Connie says. "She can now say mango.

You should have seen my face when I heard her say that. I was in the kitchen—"

A pain crosses my stomach hard, worse than the last. "Oh, God."

I breathe through it, taking deep breaths and trying to relax my body.

"Baby okay?" Alex asks, moving closer to me. Her hand moves hesitantly to my belly.

"Yeah, don't worry," I assure her. "Baby's just running out of room."

She takes her hand off my belly but stays close to me. Bringing her tablet with her.

"You sure?" Connie asks me softly. "That seemed pretty rough."

"It's just Braxton-Hicks, I'm sure."

The pain hits again, but it feels weaker this time. "People are gonna be here soon. You finish setting up. Alex can keep an eye on me."

Connie looks at me once more before heading off to the kitchen.

"You know I've been trying to think up baby names," I tell Alex, and I lean back into the couch, sticking my feet on my coffee table. "You got any ideas?"

She doesn't respond or look from her tablet, so I assume she isn't interested.

"Alex," a feminine robotic noise says to me. I turn towards Alex, who makes eye contact with me for a brief moment. This must be the app Connie was talking about.

"You think I should name the baby after you?" I laugh. She giggles, rocking herself forward a little and then back. "You know I got pregnant around Christmas, and I wanted to find a Christmassy name."

She sits still for a moment, hitting some buttons on her app.

"Reindeer." It says.

"That could be fun." I smile at her. "How about Rudolph?"

She gets a look of disinterest, shaking her head.

"I'll have to look up the other reindeer, I guess."

She pops open Google, searching up the reindeer, when suddenly I feel a trickle come down my leg. At first, I thought I had peed myself. But it's not pee. It feels almost like mucous. Then a rush of liquid follows.

"Shit," I gasp as the labor pains start. "Connie, Tanya."

"Baby," Alex says, tears forming in her eyes. I can see her start to panic.

"It's okay, Alex," I tell her as calmly as I can. "It seems the baby is ready to come out and meet us."

"Honey?" Connie says as she enters the room, Tanya flanking her.

"Baby is coming now," I tell them, another contraction ripping through me.

"I'll get your bag." Tanya runs upstairs in a flash. Connie sits beside me and helps me breathe.

"Let's get you in the car," Connie says, taking Tanya's keys from the table. "Alex, can you see if Tanya needs help?"

Alex nods, moving quickly to where she went up.

"It's too early," I choke out as Connie helps me down off the couch and out the door.

"It's okay," she assures me, holding me up by my arm. "You'll be at the hospital before you know it. Alex and I will be right behind."

I nod as she unlocks the door, settling into the front seat as Tanya comes running out with the bags.

"Drive safe. You're okay."

The ride starts off fine enough, except for the shooting pain as my body contracts. We get stuck in traffic about ten minutes from the hospital, and I feel myself start to panic.

"Fuck, come on, assholes," Tanya shouts out her open window.

"Tanya," I say, trying to remain calm. "This baby is coming."

"I know we'll be there…"

She looks at me as I pull up my dress. The baby's head is right there.

"Mother—"

I quickly rip the panties I'm wearing, my hands resting around where the head is coming out. The only way to phrase it is instinct took over. I breathe through the contractions, pushing the tiny head out of me.

After a couple pushes and a lot of screaming later, he's here. His loud wails fill the car. I just hold him, unable to contain my pure joy as I sob on him.

"Meadow," Tanya says, pulling her phone from her ear. "You need to clear the mucus from his face."

With shaky hands, I do, resting him on my forearm, keeping his face down, letting gravity do the rest.

"They have EMTs on the way," Tanya assures me. The rest of what she says isn't absorbed. All I can think about is that I have a son. He's got his father's auburn hair too. I wonder what color his eyes will be.

"Hey, little guy," I whisper to him, rubbing his back gently. I watch as his body begins to shake, his skin cool to the touch.

"I need a blanket," I tell Tanya, moving my little man to my chest. She reaches behind me, pulling the bag up front. She searches until she finds a soft blanket. I pull the straps of my dress down, laying him on my bare chest before covering him with the blanket.

His wails slow the minute his skin touches mine. His body relaxes into me as if he knows he's safe.

"Look at those eyes," Tanya coos at him. You got your momma's eyes."

I feel a wave of disappointment hit me. I wanted him to have his father's eyes. I wanted him to be a little copy of him, so I could remember the man who gave me my world.

I wanted to find him, but I didn't want him to feel rejected. My son didn't deserve to be hurt by my choices. And yet, I feel I have hurt him. I've deprived him of the chance to meet his father, someone who should be a big part of his life.

"EMTs are here," Tanya says, leaving the car to flag them down.

I hold my bundle tightly to me. "I'm gonna do right by you. I'll be the best mom I can be. And I will try to find your daddy."

He lets out a yawn, curling himself closer to me. Today is the start of my new life, just like him.

Chapter Seven

Meadow

"Hey there, Blitzen," I cringe as he chomps on my nipple. "You may not have teeth, but that still hurts."

After a short stay in the NCIU, Blitzen Alex Park was ready to come home now he's four months old. His eyes are exactly like mine, large and brown. He's got a tiny little nose and very chubby cheeks. He's grown so much in the last little while. It's hard to remember that he was so small when he was born.

"Bitzen," Alex says as she barrels into the room, her face full of joy. When I told her his name, I thought she'd scream the hospital down with joy.

I named him Blitzen after his quick arrival into the world and after the reindeer as Alex suggested. Bitzen is her nickname for him.

"Alex," Connie says sternly. "I told you that you needed to wait for him to finish eating."

Alex cries out in frustration, clearly not impressed with the idea.

"It's okay," I say as I put Blitzen over my shoulder. "He's finished up. Just needs to be burped. Alex, why don't you go set up his toys in the living room."

OH, SANTA!

She nods, leaving the nursery. I pat his back gently, trying to push out the gas he seems to have an abundance of. He's a good eater, almost too good. He'd eat all day if I let him.

"Everything going well?" she asks me.

"As good as it can be," I say with a weak smile.

The truth is I'm exhausted. I'm up half the night with him, feeding, changing, or just holding him with no clue what's wrong.

"He still isn't sleeping," she states as Blitzen lets out a loud burp. She moves to him, taking him from my arms. "You have to let your mama sleep."

He coos at her, curling up in her arms.

"Have you had any luck?" she asks me. I let out a long sigh, reminding me of my search.

"Sorry, lady," the man says gruffly, scratching a place not appropriate in front of a stranger. "I've lived here since February and ain't no young guy living with me."

"Thank you," I reply turning to leave.

"Come on by if you, don't find him," he says crudely. I can almost hear the sleazy smile in his voice.

It's been a month since Blitzen was born. I finally built the courage to come find him. It seems that I'm too late, though.

My next stop is the bar where we first met. My hope is that someone will remember him. The walk is slow as I try to examine everything between his former place and the bar we met at. The first snow is falling softly, blanketing the wet pavement. And I'm on a hunt for Santa Claus.

I pull my coat tightly around me as I enter the bar. It's just like it was the day I came in last year, though things look a bit better. The floors look to be brand new, and the tables have all changed too.

"It's the little elf," I hear the familiar bartender call out. "It's been a while, come here."

I walk to the bar cautiously. The place is completely empty except for him. I sit down on a stool as he brings over a bottle of whiskey, the same drink I was having that night.

"Thanks," I say before he can pour the drink, "I can't drink."

"Oh, no worries," he says, putting the bottle away and filling the glass with water instead. "So, you came looking for Santa?"

"How do you remember me?"

He gives me a crooked smile. "I always remember the customers that need me to be their memory."

"Must be a superpower." I take a sip of water.

"You know," he says, leaning on the bar. "I was like you once. I met a girl and got beyond wasted. When I woke up, all I got was a note telling me she had fun. I looked for her for years, but I never found her. So when I opened this place, I wanted to make sure others didn't end up like I did. Sometimes, it works out, Other times, I never find them. But I always do what I can."

He walks over to a drawer, one filled with small business cards. He searches through them before pulling out the one he wants.

"Our place flooded last month," he starts to explain, handing me the water-stained card. "But this one still survived. He came looking for you."

There in black print is his name. It's not Santa or something cheesy like Nicholas.

Silas Farris.

I told myself I'd call him when I got home, then I chickened out and said I'd do it the next day. Eventually, the next day turned to next week, and here I am. December and no closer to calling him.

The stained card blurred out where he worked, only a number and his name seeming to survive. I tried looking up the number, but it was unlisted and likely just a cell phone. I googled his name, but all I could find were a couple pictures of men who weren't him.

"I..." I start to say to Connie. "I know his name."

She looks up at me, shocked, followed by a happy smile. "That's great!"

"I found out last month."

"Why didn't you say anything?" She sits on the ottoman across from me, rocking Blitzen gently.

"I got scared," I explain, readjusting my nursing bra. "All I have is his card, and it got water damaged. I can't tell him over the phone."

"Let me see," she says firmly, like a mother talking to her disobedient child.

I get up and walk to my room, opening the jewelry box where it's sat since I got it.

OH, SANTA!

I hand it to Connie, avoiding her eyes as I take Blitzen back from her. She studies the card closely, and I watch as her eyes widen.

"I know him," she says, looking up at me excitedly. "This is the guy with the app."

"What?"

She nods excitedly. "Grant Harris, he's the guy who got me into the trial for the speech app. Grant is funding the guy's app. I met Silas."

"Oh," I say, my stomach dropping to my feet. It feels like all the blood is rushing out of my head.

"I know this is scary," she tells me, squeezing my knee. I look up into her eyes, mine filling with tears. "But he needs to know. You need him to know. And so does Blitzen."

I nod, tears falling like a waterfall. Blitzen, who had fallen asleep at some point, jerks a little as one of my tears hits him.

"Bitzen," Alex shouts up from the living room.

"We kept her waiting long enough," I chuckle, rising from my chair. "Will you go with me?"

"Of course," she says, offering me her hand. "You're doing the right thing."

"I know," I sigh, turning towards the stairs. "That's what makes this so hard."

Chapter Eight

Silas

Running on more cups of coffee than any doctor would allow and sheer determination, I prepare for the official launch of Jules Words. It's been hectic all around the office with final checks and tests. But now, it's time for the launch party.

I never thought this day would come, but here I am. My dream is becoming a reality.

I'm dressed in a black suit with a white-button up and red tie. I try to keep my curls under control, but with the wet weather, it just seems to do its own thing.

"Look at you, all spiffy," Marcus says, leaning against my office door. He's wearing a navy blue suit with a white-button up and a charcoal grey tie.

After what happened at Luxe, I told Marcus about what happened. He's been really understanding about it. Besides, he got to take home Angela, so he didn't care in the end.

"One of us has to look good."

He adjusts his lapels, standing up straight. "I look hotter than you, man."

"Keep telling yourself that," I laugh. "Let's get down to the party."

We walk out my door, starting to chat about his latest app idea, when I am stopped dead in my tracks.

"Hey Santa," my little elf says, wearing a long black dress.

We stumble onto my air mattress, mouths tangled and hands roaming each others' bodies.

Left in only her pants and panties, I quickly pull them off as I set her on the floor. Her hands already gripping the bottom of my t-shirt.

"Lay down, little elf," I tell her, planting one last kiss on her lips. She lays down as asked, moving further back on the mattress. She crosses her legs, her fingers tracing her lip as I pull down the suspenders holding my pants up. They fall off of me almost immediately.

I drop down in front of her, grabbing each of her ankles to spread her legs. Her swollen folds are almost dripping wet.

Her body is perfect.

"Nobody should be this perfect," I tell her, kissing my way up her leg. Her back arches high as I inch closer and closer to her pussy. "I'm going to own all of you tonight."

I let my tongue graze her folds, listening to her sweet whimpers. "You are trembling for me, my little elf."

"Please," she begs, lifting her hips towards my mouth.

Without another word, I dive into her. And I eat her like she's the sweetest dessert ever.

I listen to her as she cries out, begging, demanding more. I suck on her clit, sending her over the edge. She rides my face through her orgasm.

"You are so pretty when you come," I tell her, kissing my way up to her. "The way your lip twitches makes my cock ache for you."

"Fuck me," she says as I suck in one of her nipples.

"I intend to," I assure her, capturing her lips with mine. "In so many ways."

"It's you," I whisper like I'm in a dream picturing her in front of me. Her brown hair brushed to one side, longer than I remember it being, falling past her shoulders. Her eyes are large and brown, framed by thick lashes. Her lips are plump and a beautiful shade of pink. I remember wanting to bite that lip. "My little elf."

"Meadow," she says shyly, looking anywhere but at me.

"This is her?" Marcus asks, reminding me he's even here. "No way, this guy hasn't shut up about you in months."

I watch her face flush pink as she takes a peek over at me. "Marcus, get lost."

He nods, his usual smug grin covering his face. He takes Meadow's hand and kisses it. "Wonderful to meet you."

"Get out of here, you little weasel," I say through gritted teeth.

He runs off, leaving both of us in stunned and awkward silence.

"I'm Silas," I offer her my hand, which she takes. "Silas Farris."

"Meadow Park. It's a been a while."

I let out an uncomfortable laugh. "Yeah, been a year, huh."

"You seem to be doing a lot better than the last time I saw you."

"Yeah, got my life together," I explain. "Do you want to come into my office and sit?"

She nods, allowing me to lead her there. She sits in the chair on the far side of the office. I pull up my chair to sit across from her. "Do you want a drink?"

"You got scotch?"

I laugh, taking the bottle out of my desk drawer. "I was going to celebrate with this later, but now seems a good time."

I pour us both a glass. She takes a big gulp, the nervousness in her eyes gets deeper.

"What made you come find me?" It seems like a good start. "Not that I didn't want you to. I mean."

She laughs at my awkwardness. "I wanted to find you too. It's a bit of a long story."

My curiosity peeks, and I settle back in my chair. "I got time."

"I don't want to ruin your night," she insists. "But I knew if I didn't come here now, I never would."

"Hey," I say, moving to grab her hand. Tears threaten to fall as she tries to fight them. "It's okay, tell me."

"After our night," she says, releasing my hand. "I just wanted to move on, you know. I didn't expect anything to come of my hookup with a stranger. But I... I got pregnant. You have a son."

I drop my glass in shock. Blood seems to leave my body. "I... I have a son?"

OH, SANTA!

Meadow nods, taking in the rest of her drink. She grabs some Kleenex from my desk and moves to clean the floor. I can't move. I can't breathe right. Everything is numb.

"I swear he's yours," she insists, though she doesn't need to. I believe her. In my heart, I know this child I've never seen is mine.

"What's he like?" I ask her, my breath finally calming down.

"He has your hair," she smiles, pulling out her phone. The chubby little guy has my auburn hair. He's got my nose too. Any small bit of doubt is gone.

"What's his name?"

She looks a little apprehensive. "Blitzen."

I laugh, my smile threatening to break out of my cheeks. "Got to have one of my reindeer?"

"I figure he was conceived on Christmas and by Santa. It seemed appropriate."

"I want to meet him," I tell her. My body shakes with excitement.

She stiffens slightly, fear filling her face. "You want to be in his life. You don't have to; this wasn't planned."

"He's my son," I assure her. "I want every part of his life."

She nods. "He's here."

"Really? Where?"

"My friend Connie," she explains, "her daughter was in your beta trial for her app. She and her daughter are at the party with him."

"Let's go." I stand, taking her hand and practically sprinting out of the room. She giggles as I drag her along.

Chapter Nine

Meadow

I watch as Silas meets his son. His face is full of joy, and tears build up in his eyes. We are just outside the room where the party is going on. Connie took Alex back in after putting Blitzen in Silas' arms.

He holds Blitzen in front of him, his hand holding his neck as he examines him closely.

"He's perfect," Silas whispers in sheer awe as he curls Blitzen in his arms. "How could something be so perfect?"

I watch him count his toes and fingers, something you hear fathers and mothers do when the baby is born. Something he missed.

"I regret that I didn't find you sooner," I admit to him. "You missed so much."

"I did," he says quietly. "But I won't miss another moment."

After Silas found out about Blitzen, we fell into a sort of rhythm. Every morning, he comes by with coffee and muffins, saying good morning to Blitzen and helping with whatever needs to be done. Then he leaves for work, but not before giving Blitzen a kiss, then kissing my cheek. Then at the end of the day, he comes back to spend the evening with us.

"I think he's hungry," Silas tells me, walking into the kitchen where I am cooking us dinner. Blitzen starts to cry, but Silas is there soothing him. He's wearing his usual work attire. A white button-up, his tie is gone, and the top few buttons are undone, showing off his collarbone. He's also wearing a pair of dark dress pants. I try to tell him to bring more comfortable clothing, but he never wants to. I am waiting for the day Blitzen pukes all over his nice clothes, and he regrets his decision.

"I'll get the casserole in first," I tell him, opening the oven. I set the timer for thirty minutes.

"Come here, munchkin," I coo at him. One brush of Silas' skin sends my heart racing. The tension between us has been thick the last week. My body can't help but react to him. He's the man who got me pregnant. Even if I can't remember the exact details, I know he did.

"I'll just go upstairs," I say quickly, avoiding his gaze. "Can you keep an eye on dinner?"

"Sure thing, little elf. Call if you need anything."

Something about the way he calls me little elf makes my core clench. My whole body reacts to his words.

Once in the nursery, I go about feeding Blitzen, pulling down my top, releasing the clasp on my shoulder. Once he latches, I try to relax, but this silence, it leaves me far too much time to think.

Being near Silas so much is reminding me of the reason I slept with him, even though I can't remember. My body does, though. I don't want to complicate an already unconventional situation, but I can't help my desire. I don't think he sees me that way in any case, so it just leaves me thinking about him. Dreaming of what we could be.

"Meadow," I hear a whisper. My eyes open, not realizing I had fallen asleep. Silas is there, brushing a finger across my cheek. My boob is still hanging out, but Blitzen is in his crib, making those little snorting noises.

"Oh, sorry," I say, putting my bra back in place.

"Don't apologize," he tells me, crouching down in front of me. "Is Blitz sleeping ok?"

"He's had a few rough nights," I lie to him. Blitzen's been allergic to sleep since Silas came into his life. It's like he knows that Dad isn't around. I try to calm him, but it's not the same for him.

"How about I stay tonight?" Silas offers. "I'll stay on the couch or something. That way, you can get some sleep."

"You don't have to. I'm sure you have things you want to do tonight."

"I'd rather be here with my family," he says, setting loose a million butterflies in my stomach. The way he says my family, it seems too real.

"Ok," I agree, barely able to get the words out.

"Great." He smiles brightly. "I just took dinner out of the oven."

We settle in with dinner, making polite conversation along the way as he tells me about his latest app idea.

"So what inspired Jules Words?"

He pauses for a moment, his eyes looking far off into his mind. "My sister, Julianna, she's the reason."

"I didn't know you had a sister."

He nods, picking at what's left of his casserole. "She was younger than me. I was five when she was born. She was my best friend growing up. My parents, they are very cold people. My sister and I were raised by nannies. When she was three, her speech started to regress. She wouldn't look you in the eye, and she seemed to want to play with me less. My parents didn't like the idea of a disabled child. Not in their perfect world.

"She was kept away from me a lot after that. She was sent to every therapist you could think of, my parents looking for a cure as if there was anything wrong with her. By the time she was five, my parents had given up on her. They sent her to school and pretended she wasn't around."

"Where is she now?"

"She died," he says with a thick voice. "She had a heart condition no one noticed until it was too late."

"I'm so sorry." I take his hand and give it a squeeze. "She would be proud of you."

"I hope so," he says, holding my hand tightly.

"Your parents missed out on two amazing children."

He nods, holding back the anger I'm sure he's buried deep within him. "I told them the day I left that they had no children anymore. Haven't heard a word since."

"Sounds like a good thing." I collect the plates, taking them to rinse off in the sink.

"Can I ask you something?" He rises from his chair, turning to face me.

"Of course, Silas."

He takes in a deep breath. "Do you ever wonder what would have happened if you hadn't snuck away that morning?"

"Sometimes," I tell him honestly. I lean back on the counter. "I regret that you missed out on so much of his life. I hate that I walked out on you."

"I hated it too," he says. "Not you, just that you felt you had to. I was in a terrible place when that happened. I would have expected any sane person to run from me that night."

"You don't deserve to be judged by your worst moments."

"I think so much about that night," he tells me, moving closer to me. "When I saw you, I swear it was like nothing I ever felt. And the way you just talked to me. No intentions of anything else, you just were there for me. A complete stranger in a disgusting costume."

"You looked like you needed it," I say to him. "And so did I."

"Ever since that first memory of you hit me, I haven't been able to get you out of my head. You just pushed your way in and set up shop. I never wanted to let that go."

I am silent, too stunned to speak as he moves within a breath of me. I feel the heat that radiates off him. His earthy smell fills my nose.

"Please tell me you feel this too." He leans his head down, resting his forehead on mine. One small move and our lips would be touching. "Please tell me you want this as much as I do."

"Yes," I manage to squeak out. "I want you."

"Thank God."

He lifts me effortlessly onto the counter, his mouth on mine before my ass even hits the granite. My legs wrap around his waist, pulling him tighter to me. Our lips are frantic, starved for each other.

My fingers move to unhook the buttons of his dress shirt. His hands slip under my shirt, pulling at the material. Once all the buttons of his shirt are free, I lift my arms so he can take off mine.

Blitzen has other ideas as I hear him whimper through the monitor.

"Fuck," Silas whispers, his face buried in my neck. "I'll get him."

"I can do it," I tell him, hopping off the counter.

"No," he says, brushing his lips over mine. "You are going to go to your room. I want you to lay in the middle of the bed, naked. And you don't touch yourself. I want you hot and needy when I come to you."

One more kiss, then he's gone up the stairs. I take a deep breath; his words have exactly the effect he wants.

I take the monitor with me, taking the steps two at a time in my excitement.

My bedroom is small but big enough for the dresser and my queen-size bed, a treat for myself when I moved in. The dark purple comforter and the dark grey sheets are neatly made. I place the baby monitor on my dresser, taking a deep breath as I set about his commands.

Chapter Ten

Silas

"There you go, little man," I say as I wrap him in his swaddle, a fresh diaper on him has made him much happier. He's already dozing off as I lift him from the changing table.

As I lay him in his crib, I am reminded of the fact I am a father. His father. My life has changed so much. He has changed me.

"I know I missed things," I whisper to him. "But I will give you the world. You and your momma."

Once I hear those soft snores, I know he's out. I take one last look at him, watching his shoulders rise and fall with each breath.

I close the door gently before I think of what is waiting for me in the room across the hall. She wants me just as much as I want her. Maybe this complicates things, but I want this. Us.

I open the door and just about explode on sight. She lays there so perfectly, her legs spread wide as she leans on the pillows. She plays with her lip, sending painful jolts to my already aching cock.

"You are so perfect," I say, unbuckling my belt. She gets up on her knees, crawling toward me. Once she reaches me, she rips off my belt, moves to the button on my pants, and pulls down the fly painfully slow.

"I don't remember much," she says seductively, her eyes full of lust. "But I do remember I was deprived of this."

She yanks off my pants, my boxer going with them. My cock stands proud, her hand wrapping around the shaft. She moves slowly, her hands exploring me and teasing me. A pearly drop leaks out, and before I can comprehend what she's doing, her hot mouth wraps around the head of my dick.

"Fuck," I grunt out as her tongue swirls around. Her eyes stare at me as she slowly descends further down me. I have to hold back on my urge to thrust into her.

Before I lose it, I pull her off my dick. "Lie back."

She does, spreading her legs. "You wet for me, little elf?"

"So wet," she pants. "I need you inside me, please."

"After I get my taste." I bury my face in her, sucking the sweet nectar from her slit.

I bring my fingers to her entrance, teasing her as I circle her. She's panting hard, her body desperate for me.

"Silas, please," she begs me, her voice in pain.

"Anything for you, little elf."

I push in two fingers, curling them at just the right spot. I move to her lips, swallowing her moans. I feel her contracting around me. My thumb circles her clit, pushing her further and further over the edge.

"That's it ,squeeze my fingers, come for me."

"Silas!"

Watching her fall apart is perfection, the way her eyes sparkle, the pink filling her cheeks. And that smile, one of pure euphoria.

I get up off the bed, moving to find my wallet and praying the condom in there hasn't expired.

"Fuck," I curse, looking at the date. "You have any condoms?" I dread the idea of leaving her to go get some

"You don't need that," she pants, sitting up to look at me. "I got the implant after he was born."

"You sure?"

"I haven't been with anyone else since you," she says shyly. "Have you..."

"No," I reply honestly. "Been pretty busy this year, didn't even think about. Well, other than you."

"Then come here." She grabs the back of my neck, pulling me to her. I settle between her legs, my cock sliding between her folds.

"This is a dangerous game," I tell her, rubbing the head of my cock over her. "But I want to play so bad."

I slide into her in one thrust, fully seated in her hot pussy. "Fuck, it's like you were made for me. Perfect."

"Fuck me," she demands, clenching down on my cock.

I smile down at her wickedly, pulling out of her slowly, watching the frustration fill her face. Then just as she's about to cry out, I slam back into her.

The whimpers she makes as I thrust in and out of her are so perfect. I keep a fast pace, watching her come undone.

"Fuck I need you," I pant hard, the familiar build coming fast. "I need you to come with me. Play with yourself."

Her hands move to her clit, and I can feel her orgasm coming, her walls trembling around me.

"I'm gonna come," she cries out, biting her lip tightly.

"You don't bite that lip," I tell her, kissing her deeply, my tongue running over her now swollen lips.

I swallow her cries as she explodes around me. This pushes me over the edge, erupting inside her. The idea of my cum inside her, like I could get her pregnant again, does something to me I can't understand. Like I own her.

Pulling out, watching my cum drip from her, it amplifies that feeling. She is mine, and that will never change.

Chapter Eleven

Meadow

ONE YEAR LATER

Time has flown past us. Blitzen is just over a year old and happy as ever. His hair has grown in as curly as Silas'. And he's developed an attitude he probably got from me. He's in charge of the house in his mind.

He's got Silas wrapped around his finger. He is a daddy's boy through at through.

With Tanya's help running the store, I'm still able to be home with him a lot, and Silas has made his hours work so he can spend the rest of it with him.

"How is it only noon?" I ask, collapsing on the chair in my office. Tanya sits across from me, sipping on her third coffee.

"Hey, at least we can close early."

I pull off one of my shoes and rub my foot. "Yeah, but that means the next three hours are going to be a nightmare."

"Hey guys," Connie says, walking into the office with Alex. She smiles widely, walking over to hug me. "Rough day?"

"Don't even get me started."

She chuckles. "Does it mean it's a bad time to tell you there's a visitor outside and that he brought a reindeer with him?"

I look at her, confused, but put my shoes back on.

Outside, the store is filling quickly with kids all screaming about Santa being there.

There, in a fake beard, red coat, and all, is Silas. He's holding little Blitzen who is dressed in a reindeer onesie, looking happy about all the attention he seems to be getting.

"Mrs. Claus," Silas says in a jolly tone, keeping up the Santa impression.

Silas and I have been dating this last year, trying to learn more about each other and be something other than Blitzen's parents. And it's been amazing. I've fallen head over heels for him. He's one of the most genuine men on the planet and a perfect gentleman. The fact he makes me come harder than I ever have is also a plus.

"Santa," I smile, placing a chaste kiss on his lips. "I can't wait to take this off you later."

"Behave," he growls back. "These kids don't need to see what I'm gonna do to you."

"Can't wait."

I take Blitzen from Silas, kissing his face. "How's my little munchkin?"

"Dada," he smiles, clapping his hands.

I sigh. "You know I was the one who gave birth to you. Can't you say Mama once?"

"Sorry, little elf," Silas says with a wink. "I'm his favorite."

I roll my eyes, bouncing Blitzen on my hips. "So what brings you by today?"

"Blitzen wanted to make a special bear for you."

"Oh really," I coo at my little boy, who is giggling like crazy. Silas pulls out the box, one we give every kid when they make their bear.

I take the box from him. "What's in here, Blitzen?"

Inside is a reindeer, wearing a green sweater and a red nose. But then I realize that's not his nose. It's a ring. A gorgeous ruby ring with green gemstones on either side with a white gold band. And the shirt—it says, 'Will you marry Daddy?'

I look up to see Silas on one knee, my eyes welling with tears. Parents and kids surround us as the parents try to keep the kids away from Silas.

"We did things a little out of order," he starts. "But this last year, you have given me two of the most amazing gifts. You gave me that little boy, and most importantly, you gave me your heart. Now I want to give you something to show you how much you both mean to me. I want to give you my last name. Meadow Elizabeth Park, will make me the happiest man on earth and marry me."

Tears fall hard as I try to hold back sobs. Blitzen hugs me tightly, babbling as if he's trying to soothe me.

"Yes," I say without any doubt.

The parents all clap as Silas pulls us into a hug. Our sweet little family. Our Christmas story.

ALSO BY R.T. FRITZ

The Story of Who I Am

Santa, My Enemy

by

SJ Ransom

Chapter One

Justice

"Caroline, let's just have fun tonight, all right?" I begged my girlfriend of four years. She was a wild child, and everyone knew it. Even though she was dating me, she got caught with the football coach. I still loved her and stood beside her. But her crazy ways were driving me nuts.

"We are not too drunk to leave. Let's go, Justice," she whined for the hundredth time.

"No, Caroline." I turned to my best friend, Griffin Jefferson, and started talking to him. I ignored Caroline, and she walked away.

It was graduation night, and I wanted to have some fun. I wanted to relax, but I didn't count on Caroline doing something stupid. I could hear screams from the crowd, but in my drunken haze, I couldn't make out exactly what she was saying.

"She's going to crash," someone said as I looked for Caroline. I wouldn't put it past her to do something crazy, like jump into the swimming pool from the second-floor balcony. Griffin came running back in, pointing toward the door.

OH, SANTA!

"Bro, your car just took a turn on Sycamore Street. Who the fuck's driving it?" Griffin looked at me and I closed my baby blue eyes.

"Fuck. Fuck. Fuck," I muttered to myself as I grabbed Griffin.

"We have to go after her," I told him as we walked out the front door.

"Dude, we are both wasted. There's no—"

The booming sound of a car wreck cut him off before he could finish.

"No!"

I wake with a jolt. The same nightmare filters through me, even after twelve years. I've forgiven myself, but the memory still haunts me. I wipe the sweat off my forehead with a tissue I grab from the bedside table. Looking at the clock, I groan with irritation.

It's not even four in the morning. "Fuck it. I can go get some work done at the pub."

As I drive downtown, I think about the luck that fell into my lap. My lawyer came to the prison not even five months ago to tell me my father had passed away. The old man left me everything he owned. That included this farm right outside of Timberland, Texas. His bank account held a little over ten million dollars, and suddenly, I was rich.

Shock doesn't begin to explain how I felt—how I still feel. It's taken me this long to realize what I want to do with myself. I'm free from prison. I shouldn't have even been in there to begin with, but alas. I have a home to call my own and a business about to bloom into a gold mine.

I'm one lucky son of a bitch.

Chapter Two

Suzie

Sitting at Miss Fussington's bakery across the street from my bookstore, I look out the window from my booth. The blaring neon light cheapens the scenery.

"O'Malley's Pub," I mutter, the bitterness eating at me. I bite my lip at the idea of an *O'Malley* being near me. It's taken me years to get over that sorry-no-good Justice O'Malley. Now, here he is, strutting that perfectly shaped backside of his from his truck to the front door of his pub.

Why did he have to put his pub right next door to my bookstore? I mean, come on, I sell books that are erotic in nature. You would think a pub would be good for business, but no. It certainly isn't.

I think back to what my sister told me all those years ago. *"Justice is the cool kid, Suzie. But never trust a man in a leather jacket, with a ring in his ear, and a wolf tattoo on his chest."* It didn't matter, though. My twelve-year-old heart was sweet on him at the time. I only ever saw him at school. He never came to our house. I think it was because our grandmother would have shot him.

"Hey, Suzie." Miss Fussington interrupts my thoughts. I smile as she sits down.

"I see you saw the new pub." She lays a flier for the grand opening on the table.

"Yup." I entertain her but I can't muster much of a reaction, at least...not an appropriate reaction.

She *tsks*. At seventy-years-old, she's still spry and a bit of a hellcat.

"Stop that right now, Suzie Gellam. The pub opens two hours after you close shop." Miss Fussington laughs at me. "You'll be in bed and asleep by the time it's in full swing."

If only Miss Fussington knew that Justice killed my sister. She would pitch a fit. A small smile quirks my lips upward as I think about her picketing and boycotting on my behalf. I school my face and look at her—unamused—as she cackles. I'm not in the mood to laugh. I slide out of the booth and lay a five-dollar bill down.

"I must get back to work, Miss Fussington. See you tomorrow for book club."

"Chin up, sweet cheeks. That man is fine."

The last thing I hear before stepping out the door is Miss Fussington chuckling again. I grunt and make my way across the street as a plan formulates in my mind. That pub will not open.

Not on my watch.

Chapter Three

Justice

"Son of a mother fucking bitch," I mutter as the lights go out. A crackling sound hisses in the air as the light bulbs and glass scatter to the ground. My bartenders scream and start running around, missing the glass as it falls from the ground by mere seconds. The power didn't just blink out like a rolling blackout. No, this is completely out because the generators didn't kick on. Why didn't they kick on?

Why did it have to happen on opening day? I throw the tablet I'm holding. It hits the wall in front of me and shatters. The device falls to the ground with a sickening thud, and I realize I've just thrown a thousand-dollar device.

"Fuck." I cringe as I pick up the broken pieces. The girls find a booth and sit down as the bouncer opens the front door. I sigh, anger boiling in my blood.

"What caused this, Spade?"

He grunts. "I'm not sure. One minute I'm getting ready to open the doors and let the crowd in. The next minute, I hear a sizzling sound and

OH, SANTA!

the girls screaming. Everything okay?" he asks. "Aside from the obvious..."

I nod. "Yeah, turn the crowd away for tonight," I tell Spade as I head to the back door. *What the hell happened?* The night air hits my nose and I take a refreshing breath in.

Deep breaths calm me—until I see that the other stores still have power. *What the fuck?*

I walk around the building, passing the row of breaker boxes. I see the one for the pub wide open with the wires cut. My box is the only one that was tampered with and my generator nowhere in sight. This was a blatant attack on my pub. What is going on? I rack my brain, trying to figure out if I have any enemies, anyone who would purposely do this. I can't think of one.

I walk around to the front of the pub, trying to get a handle on my anger. The most stunning woman is messing with a box of flowers on the sidewalk. My knees go weak and my breath halts. I walk over to her and she stands; she's taller than I expected. She has to be at least five-foot-eight. My God, those ample curves practically make me drool. I resist the urge to readjust myself. My resistance does not stop my brain from conjuring an image of her on her knees, her mouth stretched wide around my cock, and those honey-colored eyes peering up at me.

When she looks at me square in the eye and huffs I almost cum in my pants.

"What do you want?" She glares at me.

That just makes me want her even more.

What do I want? Fuck, I want her underneath me, screaming my name. I gulp, pretty sure me saying that to her would not go well.

"I've lost power. Can I use your phone to call the electric company?"

She rolls her eyes at me, and I laugh. She's feisty and I want more of it.

"Go away," she says as she turns to walk into the shop behind her.

"Damn, Angel. Who pissed in your wind?"

That ass sashays as she steps toward the door. She looks back at me over her shoulder and snarls. "You did, bucko. Isn't that obvious?"

I'm stunned from her abrasive tone. She opens the door, shuts it, and locks it before I can move. My friend Spade comes out and asks me if I'm all right. I nod to him, but I'm not sure that I am. That woman has me in a whirlwind of emotions.

Emotions I've tried to tamp down over the years.

Shit. I'm in trouble.

Chapter Four

Suzie

Sleep mocked me last night. The encounter with Justice had my mind going crazy. That's why I'm sitting in my favorite chair in the shop, reading the news article about the pub. I think I'm trying to assuage my guilt. Even with the inkling of guilt coming over me, a smirk creeps onto my face as I read about the vandalized breaker box. What has me in a fit of giggles is that Justice probably thinks the worst is over; unfortunately for him, he hasn't seen anything yet. As soon as his electric is fixed he'll need a plumber. I laugh. I wonder if the paper will write about *that*.

The grandfather clock in the corner chimes, letting me know that it's time to get ready for book club. Every Tuesday at two in the afternoon, my three best friends and I meet to discuss the book of the week. Miss Fussington is already here with her famous sweet tea. Marlene will be here any moment with her sandwiches; she owns the deli shop one block down the road. Dakota is always the last to show up. She owns the tailor shop right next door to Marlene's deli. She brings nothing because she can't cook. I always supply the pie.

I honestly don't think Dakota would show up if there wasn't pie. Dakota comes rushing through the door, looking frazzled.

"Sorry. Sorry. I know I'm late."

Everyone laughs. It's a normal occurrence, so we are used to it. Right as I am going to tell her it's no big deal, Justice walks in. My body clenches with the anticipation of sparring with him again. Miss Fussington and the girls stare at him. I huff as I move to stand in front of them. There's no need for them to be gawking. *Shit, is that jealousy I'm feeling?*

"What do you want?" I ask, knowing that, as a business owner, I'm being rude. I don't care.

He stands toe-to-toe with me, forcing me to look up at him. Good gravy, he's tall. I didn't realize his height when I spoke to him yesterday, probably because our interaction was clouded by my anger. He's at least six-foot-four with muscles for miles. I think about what he looks like under the shirt he's wearing. Embarrassment and anger flood my body and I take a step back.

"I saw you outside by the water line today," he says to me with a hint of speculation in his tone.

"And?" I raise an eyebrow at him.

"Did you tamper with my water pipes?"

I laugh and cross my arms under my breasts. "And why would I do that?"

"Suzie, don't play dumb with me."

I almost can't school my face, but I do. This man is my enemy, and he deserves everything I'm doing. His short black hair looks tousled, like he's been running his fingers through, it and I have to put myself in check yet again. Who gives a shit what his hair looks like?

"How do you know my name?" I change the subject.

His eyes pierce me with a look that makes me quiver.

"I make it my business to know who is around me. Now, don't play dumb. You've messed with the pipes."

He clearly thinks his tough guy act should intimidate me. It doesn't. I stand my ground and square my shoulders.

"I know nothing about pipes." This is a complete lie. My father was a plumber, and I used to work for him. He steps closer to me, and I feel the heat radiating off him. He smells so good. I bite my lip to keep myself from fidgeting. I don't want him to know he affects me.

"The water company can't figure out how the pipe lost an integral part, one that connects the pipe to the main water line. Are you having any issues?"

His tone seems softer, but it doesn't matter. A soft chuckle escapes my lips. "With my pipes?" He nods, and I bat my eyes at him. "No, I have no issues with my pipes being clean and running smoothly."

What the hell am I doing? Did I just bat my eyes at him and make a sexual innuendo about pipes?

Chapter Five

Justice

Hot damn. Suzie blushes and I grin like a damn fool. This woman is something else.

"You need to go now. You aren't welcome here," she mutters, but her words lack conviction.

I grab her hair, pushing my hands in roughly until I can squeeze. I hear the others gasp in shock.

"Don't test me." As my anger mixes with my desire for her, I growl. I'm scaring her. I can see the fear underneath all that bravado.

She scrunches her eyes at me. "Or what?"

Fuck me, she's salty. I yank her head back hard, and she lets out a short, deep moan and I grin. Yeah, she likes it rough.

"Keep up this attitude and find out, Angel." I bend down so that we are eye-to-eye. "Believe me, I'll enjoy every minute of making you bend to my will." I kiss her lips, taking my time to plunge my tongue into her mouth.

She stumbles backward as I release her. I hear Miss Fussington talking, but I don't stay. I've got work to do if I'm going to dig up some dirt on Suzie.

OH, SANTA!

❄

Did I sneak into the apartment above the bookstore? Yes, I did. Do I regret it? No, I don't. But I'm going to have to talk to Suzie about the back door being unlocked. It's a way thieves could muster a quick getaway, even during business hours.

I rummage through her belongings, trying to find something I can use against her. After an hour, I've still not found anything. She's the definition of squeaky clean. This makes me want to sink my dick into her and dirty her up. I want to hear that pouty, sultry voice scream my name in pleasure.

As I round the corner of the kitchen, I see a picture that gives me pause. What the hell? I cut my thoughts and actions off as I hear the keys rattling into the lock of the front door. *Shit*. I walk with quiet, hurried steps to the bedroom—my heart in my throat.

I stand still for a moment, and my eyes land on a photo in a frame. *Caroline*? My eyes must be playing tricks on me. This can't be reality. I've got to get out of here, but there's no window in the bedroom.

"He-hello?" There's a slight quiver in Suzie's voice. No doubt she heard me close the bedroom door as she entered the house, despite trying my best to be quiet. I rush to the wall behind the door. I'm surprised the door covers me as she opens it. My heart is pounding with adrenaline. I've realized my mistake as I watch Suzie looking in the closet. I forgot to wear a mask.

She's mumbling to herself as she comes out of the bathroom and sets the umbrella in her hand down on the bed. I'm overcome with need for her as she laughs at herself for being paranoid. I've never felt the urge for someone like this. Even her laugh turns me on.

My lips curve into an evil smile as I slam the door shut. Suzie jumps and yelps as she sees me. "Hello, Suzie Q." I wink at her and walk right up to her. Her hands ball into fists and she snarls at me.

"Get out of my house."

Chapter Six

Suzie

I'm mad, but I don't move an inch as he comes closer. All I can think about is how I shouldn't have closed shop. But I was tired and wanted to rest after the book club meeting. Looking up, I see something dangerous in Justice's eyes. I should stand down. Instead, I straighten my spine as he reaches out and grabs my neck. He is squeezing quite hard as he moves us until my back hits the wall. I push at him as the air leaves my lungs.

Justice crowds my space and laughs at my attempts to push him off me.

"I already told you that your attitude would get you into trouble. Now, shut up and listen to me."

His demand enrages me. "No!" I spit at him, bringing a knee up to slam him in the crotch. He laughs again and swats my thigh. I gasp in shock. That should have hurt, not sent tingling sensations down my spine.

Justice kisses me. When his lips touch mine, sparks fly between us. The fight in me waivers as he pushes both hands into my hair, guiding my head to tilt to the right. He's devouring my mouth, causing me to clutch at his waist to ground myself.

My mind flashes to Caroline and the guilt churns in my stomach. I bite Justice's tongue and he jerks backward.

"You're a bitch. You know that, right?" He yanks my hair, causing me to whimper. Not that he hasn't been rough with me before, but this time it hurts. Tears well in my eyes.

That doesn't stop me from glaring at him. "So?" I've challenged him once again. There should be some survival instinct to stay alive, but I can't help but provoke the bear.

He lets go of my hair only to bring both hands to my face and force me to look up at him. "So?" he says with an eye roll. "I'm going to show you exactly what happens to brats that don't know their place."

His lips come down on mine again. They are supple and demanding. I kiss him back. My mind hovers between my anger and want for him. I'm not sure I hate the way he makes me feel. My hips thrust toward his and he moans. Those oversized hands of his travel down my face to my neck and then my shoulders. I huff as my senses come back to me as he touches my right breast.

I push him enough that he releases me. He's left me enough room to scoot past him, but he blocks me. "You need to leave." There's no gumption in my words. I'm too exhausted to think about my pure disdain for Justice. He growls when I shove at his right arm. I slap him with my left hand, causing him to become feral. He wrestles me to the ground. The fear of him trying to do something more than I'm willing to let him do hits me and I fight him. He laughs at my feeble attempts to escape from hold.

"Angel, stop fighting me. I won't hurt you."

I stare at him, angry, fearful, confused, and full of lust. I wiggle against him. The feeling of him between my thighs is uncomfortable, even if only because I don't want to admit how good he feels.

"Never!" I scream at him. The way he is pushing against me makes me quiver. I roll beneath him, trying to hide my want. Justice kisses me and lays flat on top of me.

"You'd be still if you knew how hard you make me by fighting this."

Chapter Seven

Justice

I kiss her, stopping her from talking. I hear a small moan slip out from her. The feeling of her soft body under me, still wiggling, makes me stop.

"You're so crude." She looks at me, wide-eyed, and those lips look bruised from my kisses. I want to roar with satisfaction. Instead, I kiss down her throat. Her pulse is beneath my lips as I linger, feeling her body shift underneath me. I turn her on. There is a desire to delve into her, but I smile against her pulse. I lick the vein before sucking on it.

She stills beneath me. Her nipples are hard, I can feel them through her clothing. I chuckle. "If you'd stop for five seconds, maybe we could have a pleasant conversation."

"You have some nerve. No. Now get off me." She kicks at me, trying to shake me.

"You only struggle because you're turned on." I loosen my grip on her only to bite her neck. She groans and stops fighting. Her breathing quickens and she turns her head, pushing her neck into my mouth. My cock throbs with the need to sink into her.

"I won't hurt you, Suzie." I kiss her forehead and stare into those warm eyes of hers. I could get lost within their depths for hours if she would let me. There's lust in them, but I also see so much more. Why does she still feel fear? Does she really think I'm a psycho?

"Says the man who broke into my apartment." She rolls those pretty little eyes at me, and I grin.

"Only because I want to know more about you." Fuck, I shouldn't have told her that. She blushes and looks away. Oh, so she's not as angry at me as I thought. I smirk and take her chin in my hand, pulling her face back toward me.

There are tears in her eyes, and that causes my heart to stop beating for a moment. Fuck, I don't enjoy seeing that.

"Please, just leave," she whispers. Even though I know she wants me to go, I just can't help myself. I thrust my hips against her and feel her tremble.

"Oh, Angel." I kiss her cheek and hold her. "I'm a good man, if you'd just give me a chance."

She goes limp in my arms, and I know I could push for more. Instead, I get up and help her to her feet. "I'll leave, but we aren't through here. The next time I get you alone, I'm going to show you just how good I can make you feel."

I leave before she can protest too much.

❄

The next morning, I send Suzie a dozen black roses. I did it to piss her off, and she didn't disappoint me with her reaction. I can tell roses aren't her favorite flower just from the peonies that are everywhere around her shop. The delivery man got the roses shoved back at him. I laugh at my angel. She's made my day. I must laugh too loud, because her head pops up as the delivery man runs to his delivery truck.

She yells at me. "You pig!"

Her gumption makes me smile. Suzie flips me off and goes back into her store. I notice she is decorating for Christmas. My phone lights up as I press the power button and look at the date once it boots up. Shit,

Christmas is around the corner. I know what I want. I sure hope she's ready to be my gift wrapped under the tree.

Better yet, unwrapped.

Chapter Eight

Suzie

I'm still thinking about my sister, even after a restless night of sleep. Having these strange and opposing feelings for Justice is killing me. I'm losing the battle between what's right and wrong. I know I should keep him at an arm's length, but it seems the old crush I had on him is in full swing.

The idea of his lips and hips against me still plays in my mind as I turn away the roses he sent me. I try to conjure up an image of Caroline and Justice together; anything to keep me from wanting him. The image I have of Justice and Caroline blurs, fading into one of Justice and me instead. I close my eyes. This is wrong. So very wrong.

※

It's been one week since my run-in with Justice. His grand opening is happening tonight, and I hope he doesn't succeed. In another way, I feel defeated. I wanted to stop him from getting his pub opened, but it felt like an empty vendetta. How long could I really keep him from opening?

A loud bang gets my attention and I turn toward the front door. I closed shop a few hours ago; there should be no one around. I walk around the counter of my food display, making my way to the front. A sharp intake of air comes without thought, the sight in front of me unsettling. My entire display and flower arrangement are crushed. It took me hours to fix that display and I was so proud of it.

It's as if my world has fallen down around me; it may seem dramatic, but I had hoped that the line outside would have been cordial and mindful. Obviously, that was a stupid thought because this is the complete opposite of cordial and mindful. I march over to the pub's doors and cut in front of everyone. I don't care if they like it or not.

The bouncer refuses to let me in, and I raise my voice in a feeble attempt to get my point across. "Your disgusting thugs stepped on my peonies!"

I hear his voice before I see him. "Peonies? Why is someone yelling about peonies?" Justice rounds the corner and my anger spills over.

I point my finger directly at him. "You!" I growl in frustration. "Your neanderthal, club-going thugs have ruined my entire display! Do you even understand how long that took me?"

He laughs and tells the bouncer to let me through. He widens his eyes at me as if he's thinking I've totally lost my marbles, but I don't give a damn what he thinks. I shake with anger and anxiety at being in such a noisy place, especially after what's just happened with my display. Justice winks at me, and I flip my hair at the bouncer, sticking my head up high. *Screw them all.*

As I step out of the crowd, Justice pulls me to him. He bends down and kisses me without warning. I gasp into his mouth and shove at him.

He chuckles. "Little Angel, don't you ever just stop? You are driving me crazy."

I snort and look him dead in the eyes. "Please keep your stupid people out of my walkway. They ruined almost two hundred dollars' worth of flowers and countless hours of work."

He shrugs at me and shakes his head. His left hand runs through my hair and settles at the nape of my neck. "Nah, this is a free country. They can do whatever they want."

My eyes go wide, and I plant my fists on my hips. My right foot taps on the floor and I feel my nostrils flare. "Oh, really? No?" I tug his hand from my hair, and I smile an overly sweet smile right before I storm off toward the bar.

Chapter Nine

Justice

I watch as she angrily hurries toward the bar. That plump ass of hers is swaying in those yoga pants she's wearing. Her shirt has ridden up to her waistline. Fuck, that's hot. What is she going to do? That's the only thing I can ask myself as I see her smirking at me.

"This is war, Justice."

"Oh, shit!" I exclaim as she grabs a pitcher full of beer and chucks it to the ground. Liquid and glass scatter across the floor. People scramble out of the way, trying like hell to avoid the beer splatter. I watch in fascination as she turns to my bartender, Ruby.

Fuck. Ruby isn't someone you want to mess with. She's done a stint in the pen and won't think twice about gutting someone. I walk over and grab Suzie from behind. I graze the back of her head with my lips. She shivers in my arms, and I smile.

"You are asking for it, aren't you?" I ask as I pull her toward the dance floor, holding her against my chest. As her hips brush against my cock, I groan loudly. I look up at my bartender as she swears, cleaning up the mess my feisty little angel just made. Ruby looks at me and I nod at her. She knows I'll pay her for dealing with the pissed off customers that Suzie just made for us.

The DJ turns on a slower-paced song, and I nod his way in thanks. I keep a firm hand on Suzie's stomach as I sway our hips together. Her body is stiff, but I hear the hitch in her breath. She's moving her hips into me, and I know she's as turned on as I am. She isn't ready to give up yet.

"Just relax, Angel." I try to calm her, but I don't think I'm doing a great job of it.

"I'm not your *Angel*." Her voice is barely a whisper, yet I hear it, even over the noise. The shakiness in her voice and the pitch of her need lace together within her words.

I chuckle as I move my hands along her stomach. With each circular motion, I inch closer to the top of her yoga pants.

"Hush now." I bite her earlobe. "Just relax and let me make you feel good." She trembles in my arms as I wiggle my fingers between her skin and the pants.

"You're right though, you aren't my angel. You're my *naughty* angel." I lick her ear and continue to move my hands down the front of her pants. I feel her bare pussy against my palm and my cock rages.

She jolts in my arms and tries to step away from me. "I... I..."

I cut her words off as I pull her back to me. "I think you came over to see me under the guise of being pissed, but what you really want is for me to drag you to my office and fuck you.

Suzie shakes her head in denial. "No. I..."

I turn her to face me, and that's my mistake. She backs away from me with a wild look in her eyes. "I can't do this." She flees from me.

I've scared her away again. My angel is a skittish little thing. I know I can't do anything now, but fuck, my cock needs her.

Chapter Ten

Suzie

My entire body is on fire as I run to my store. I unlock the door, run inside, and relock it. The lights are off, but I know my shop. I make it to the stairs and up to my apartment in record time. I have never been touched like Justice just touched me. My mind is swimming into the deep end of betrayal, and I can't do it. I need to stay focused on keeping Justice far away from me.

With determination, I take a shower and then put on a pair of sleep shorts and a tank top. I get into bed and look at the clock. It's only ten in the evening on a Friday night. I don't care; I need to sleep this feeling off. Tomorrow will be better. *It must be!*

I jolt upright when a loud banging rattles my door. I must've fallen asleep, but I'm not sure how long I've been out. A haze settles over me from being woken up out of a dead sleep. I drag myself out of bed and yell, "Coming!" My hair is a mess and the robe I grab barely covers my butt. I open the door and look at who is disturbing me. Justice stands in front of me, seemingly agitated. He cracks his knuckles and glares at me. The moment I open the door a fraction more, he dominates the area in an instant, including me.

OH, SANTA!

"What do you want?" He is a persistent bugger; I'll give him that.

"We are going to have a chat." He moves me to the side and slams the door shut behind him. I step back, my heart racing as he locks the door. Anticipation and distrust run through me. The glare I send him doesn't dissuade him from crowding my space.

I look over at the mantle and see it's only two o'clock.

"It's two in the morning. Whatever you want to talk about, you can wait until the sun comes up. Please leave."

He doesn't hesitate to draw me to him. I fight the feeling of *home* that I have as he pulls me somehow closer. My home is not with this man. I know this. But for some reason...my body thinks otherwise. I smell his cypress scent, and I want to cave into my need.

"Why do you hate me so much? What have I done to you to earn such hostility and distrust?"

How does he not know? How can he not know who my sister was? If I'm being honest, he hasn't technically done anything directly to me. Well, nothing that I haven't craved from him, anyway. I've been a total bitch to him, but in my mind, it's called for. The want for him recedes, and I frown at him.

"You should already know what you've done." The words come out brutal and cold. The silence wraps around us. He looks like I've run over his cat as his hands fall away from my body. Justice stumbles back and looks at me.

"What the fuck, Suzie?"

My mind reels in shock. He really doesn't know. I gulp, trying to hold back tears. My body shakes, and I stumble toward the counter. I pick up the only picture I have of my sister, and I thrust it toward him.

He takes the picture from me, and he stares at it for a long time. All I can think is, *how can he not know that Caroline was my sister?*

Chapter Eleven

Justice

"Caroline," I choke out. I stand here, confused as hell. Is... Is this Caroline's little sister? The photo...It wasn't my mind playing an evil trick on me.

"You killed her twelve years ago."

Holy fuck. I close my eyes and count to ten to get a grip on myself. I set the picture down on the counter and look at her. She steps back and runs into the couch. Without thinking, I reach for her and keep her from falling to the ground.

"Don't run from me. Let me explain."

"How can you explain anything? You took the only sister I had. It killed my grandmother. More than my sister's crazy ways ever did." Her words cut me to the core. She chokes on a sob as I wrap my arms around her waist. Suzie is bawling into my chest, and I am glad she isn't trying to kick me out of her house. She needs me right now. I have to tell her the truth.

I'm in shock, though, at how much of a mess my angel is. The gut-wrenching sorrow in her sobs is killing me. Suzie believes I killed her sister, and maybe it's partially true, but it isn't the full truth. The truth is more sordid. It haunts me every night, but I've done my time, and Suzie shouldn't hate me.

With a gentle nudge and some guidance, I sit us down on the couch. She growls and pounds her fists against my chest in frustration. I hold her fiery stare and push the hair out of her face. It breaks me to see her like this, so devastated.

"Please, just give me five minutes. If you want me to leave after that, I'm gone." She tries to say something, but I put a finger against her lips. "Give me a chance to explain, Angel." She rubs her nose on the sleeve of her robe as I stroke her hair. This seems to calm her down.

"Your sister and I went to Griffin Jefferson's graduation party. We were both drinking, and I shouldn't have let her take my car."

Suzie stops me from talking and pulls away from me. She's shaking her head in denial. "No, you are lying. You... you killed her because you caught her with the football coach."

I pull her back into my arms, forcing her into my lap so I can keep her still. "Be quiet, Suzie. Listen. Please, hear me out," I plead, hoping she will hush, and let me finish."

Suzie takes a deep breath and nods. *Finally.* "We got into a bit of an argument, and she wanted to leave. I told her no, and she grabbed my keys when I turned away. I didn't even realize she took them because I was so engrossed in my conversation with Griffin. She left the house, and I never noticed her absence. By the time Griffin noticed my car being driven off, it was too late. Your sister drove my car straight into a tree."

Suzie screams at me because it's not what she wants to hear, but I kiss her and continue.

"The love of my teenage years was dead. She was a broken mess, bleeding everywhere. I couldn't think. It felt like I was floating outside my body. Nothing made sense."

I stop talking to catch my breath as the memory assaults my mind. "We were fighting because she told me she was pregnant, and the baby wasn't mine. She didn't want to keep it, but I did. It didn't matter if it was the coach's baby. I would have helped her and made myself a family. That's how much I loved her."

I don't tell Suzie I couldn't forgive myself for letting Caroline drive while she was drunk. And it took almost ten years of jail time and counseling to get my head on straight. I look at Suzie and see her teary eyes. She looks back at me with something I've never seen before. It almost looks like gratitude.

Chapter Twelve

Justice

I look at him, shocked and confused. I knew Caroline was a wild child. She did whatever she wanted, whenever she wanted. That's what caused our grandmother to have a heart attack. But I didn't know she was pregnant.

He doesn't give me time to process before he continues. "I knew her name had already been through the wringer because of what happened. What I didn't want to happen was for her to be known as a murderer. If they found out she was pregnant, it would sink your entire family into the mud."

I take a deep breath as he shifts and settles me closer to him.

"I made myself the driver. I couldn't let anything else tarnish her name, so, I had Griffin beat the shit out of me and make it look like I was the one driving. We pulled her out of the wreckage, and I held her as Griffin called the police. I went to jail for drunk driving and vehicular manslaughter to keep further bad press about your sister out of the papers."

The years of sorrow and hate I've endured for nothing... Dear God, was it really this easy to lose sight of good people? I can't speak. My words feel like they've evaporated in my throat and I'm coming up with nothing. For the last twelve years I've held this grudge against an innocent man. I should apologize, but I don't. Instead, I pull back and look at him.

"I... I don't know what to say, Justice. I want to believe you, but I..." He cuts me off with a shocking kiss, and our mouths mingle. We both moan, playing with each other's tongues. He pulls away from me and holds my face in his hands. I struggle to get back to his mouth; to lose myself in something that doesn't seem so complicated.

"Not right now, Suzie. You're too emotional, and we would regret doing this tonight." He kisses along my neck, groaning. "Although, you being in my lap tempts me."

I squirm in his lap, and he lets me go. "No, you're right. I need time to understand what's going on here. Thank you for your side of the events, Justice, but I need to find out if that's the truth."

He stands up and nods. "You do. Here's Griffin's phone number. He moved a few years ago, but he can confirm it." He hands me Griffin's business card from his wallet and wraps his arms around me and hugs me tight. "I'll give you twenty-four hours. Then I'm coming for you, Angel."

He leaves my house, and I feel like my life has been turned upside down. I don't even understand my feelings for him, let alone how it might feel to *not* hate him with such vehemence. I take a while to lock the front door and get back to bed, meandering around through my place like I'm lost. And maybe I am.

❄

I'm dragging my feet today. I tossed and turned all night with thoughts of what happened to my sister. Miss Fussington woke me up with her phone call about me not being open on time. I stand here now, trying to get her coffee to her, and I can't seem to find my motivation.

"Christmas is just around the corner, Suzie. Are you going to fix that display?"

I shrug and hand her the hot coffee. "It's two weeks away. I may fix it if I can find a vendor for the flowers."

"Do you have any plans this year?"

"No. I'm going to visit my grandmother's and sister's graves like always."

Miss Fussington gives me a small smile. It's a smile I've come to know quite well over the years, one I'm on the receiving end of anytime someone finds out about the deaths of my loved ones. "Well, maybe this year something new will come about. My offer still stands. You can come with me to visit my daughter."

I smile at her and shake my head no. "Thank you, Miss Fussington. I'll be just fine."

Chapter Thirteen

Justice

Trying to stay away from Suzie for twenty-four hours is killing me. I've cleaned my house, mowed the lawn, and now I'm on my way to fix her damn display. Griffin called me and told me he scheduled a meeting with Suzie. I told him to just tell her the truth. He was basically asking me if he should lie for me, and that speaks volumes about our continued friendship. However, the truth is always the best option.

As I watch Suzie pull away from the store, I pull into my parking spot. Miss Fussington is outside, fixing her special of the day sign. I wave to her and she waves back, giving me a thumbs up. I had called her early this morning to find out where Suzie got her flowers and decorations. While I was no expert at Christmas displays, I could fix something up in a jam.

❄

Sweat poured down my back as I put the last piece of the display together. Suzie pulls into her parking space and looks at me through her windshield. I smile at her, and that beautiful blush creeps up on her cheeks.

"What are you doing, Justice?" Suzie asks as she climbs out of the car and locks her doors.

I stand up from my kneeling position and spread my arms out. "Do you like it?"

Her approval of what I've done means something to me. She looks at everything I've done and surprises me. She hugs me and I blink for a moment, trying to calm myself down. Shit, she has me in knots.

"It's wonderful. Thank you." She looks up at me with a smile and I bend down and kiss her.

"You're welcome, Angel."

I let her go as she steps back. "Why don't you come in so we can talk?"

This is an offer I won't refuse. She unlocks her shop, and I step in with her.

Suzie asks me to lock the door and steps over to the food counter. She turns on the coffee pot and tells me to sit anywhere I like. Her being nice to me almost has me in a fit. My damn cock doesn't know what to do with itself and neither do I. Apparently it doesn't matter how she acts to me, I want her all the same.

With coffee in hand, she sits down and passes me a cup. "I talked to Griffin today," she says, and the silence between us is amicable for once. I don't say a word, waiting for her to continue.

"Griffin confirmed what you said. I have to say, I wasn't sure if it was true, and I called the detective over my sister's case; they directed me to the records department. I can get a copy of the cause of death. Griffin confirmed she was pregnant. I believe you're telling me the truth."

She didn't tell me if she still hated me. No, she sat there looking at me over her cup of coffee, peering into my soul. I felt sick to my stomach that Suzie had to go through all the trouble, but I knew she needed this.

My phone rings, and I excuse myself from the area. "What's going on, Spade?"

"We have a problem. There's a bunch of money missing from the safe, and the beer cooler is missing a shit ton of beer."

"Fuck me. I'll be right there." I turn toward Suzie. "I have to go, but

I'll be back."

I don't wait for her to say anything as I rush out. Just what I needed. An interruption while the two of us are finally ironing things out. *Fuck.*

Chapter Fourteen

Suzie

I haven't seen Justice since Saturday afternoon. It's Tuesday, and our book club is in full swing. Marlene, Dakota, Miss Fussington, and I are discussing the Christmas party that Miss Fussington is holding tomorrow night when Justice comes into the store wearing a Santa suit.

He winks at me and hugs Miss Fussington, which makes her blush. "Hello, ladies."

Miss Fussington opens her mouth before I can say a word. "You keep getting better looking each time I see you, young man." She gropes him and then proceeds to spank his ass.

I gasp as he laughs and walks over to me. I hug him, happy to see him. This gives me pause because I'm truly happy. Sure, things in the past have given me enjoyment, but this is true happiness. I don't know what to do with myself.

"What are you doing dressed like that?" I ask him, staring at him as he winks at me.

"I'm going to the children's hospital to play Santa for the day. The hospital will shut down outside visitation after this week for the holidays. They limit visitors to family only, and they need some cheer in their lives because some kids are from shelters."

Miss Fussington, Dakota, and Marlene all sit swooning over him. I must admit, I've been wrong about him. I bite my lip and he growls at me, pulling me into him.

"You tempt me so much, Angel. Tonight, I want to take you somewhere. Are you willing to trust me enough to be alone with me?"

Wow, he asked instead of demanded. I'm in shock. A laugh bursts from within me. *Do I trust him?* The idea of being alone with Justice excites me, but I'm still stuck on the guilty feeling. My need for him tries to overtake my brain.

"I don't know, Justice. I need to..." He cuts me off with a kiss. My brain short circuits and the girls gasp behind me. I tremble in his arms as he grabs my butt, pulling me closer.

"Give me a chance, Suzie. I promise I won't do anything to cause you any harm."

It's stupid. I shouldn't trust him. After all, I don't even know if he's over my sister. I need to talk to Caroline. I wish that was a possibility. Maybe if I could speak to her I wouldn't feel like I was betraying her.

"All right. I'll go with you tonight."

He smiles and tells me to be ready at five. I walk him to the door and give him one last kiss.

Miss Fussington chortles loudly. "Suzie's getting some tonight." I glare at my dear friend. She's so inappropriate.

Chapter Fifteen

Justice

I love children, and seeing their faces light up like a Christmas tree never gets old. There is sadness associated with this type of volunteer work. Some of these children are homeless, and this is the only hope they have. I do this so they will have some happy memories.

The hospital staff on the fourth-floor smile and waves goodbye to me as I head to the elevators. My phone goes off as I step inside and take off my Santa hat.

"What's up, Spade?"

"Got a problem at the pub. You need to get over here."

My eyes close in frustration. Why can't I have one day of peace?

"What kind of problem?"

"You remember the beer cooler being broken into? Well, boss, someone broke the windows out and a pipe burst. There's water everywhere. Also, now the wine and vodka are gone."

"What the fuck?"

"Yeah, um, I called the police. They're headed this way. That girl from the store next door was in the back of the club earlier, too. But she's nowhere to be seen now."

"What was she doing?"

"I'm not sure. We don't have cameras out in the back. The cameras in the front of the pub are shot out. We gotta replace those. All I can tell you is the girl has been gone for about half an hour."

Thank God Suzie is safe. The second thought in my mind tells me she doesn't have a gun, but she could have done this. But why would she? Rage fills me, and I sink into dark thoughts. Maybe Suzie didn't want to go out with me. No. Suzie did *not* do this.

I debate what's going on during the ride to the pub. Who could have done this? Why was Suzie in the back of the pub? I've talked myself into a frenzy about the whole situation. I need to know what is going on and who is behind this. My anger is boiling over and I'm going crazy. If she did this, it would be the end of me.

I pull into the parking lot to see a detective and two patrol officers talking to Spade. Getting out of the truck, I shake with uncertainty. I walk into the pub and the water damage is so bad the bar is buckling. *Fuck.*

Shit, I'm going to have to start from scratch with this place. The only thing that keeps me going and not sitting down in despair is that this doesn't seem like something Suzie would do. Unfortunately, doubt has crept in.

Chapter Sixteen

Suzie

Today's customer volume has been low. The urge to see my sister drives me to close the store early. Before I do, I leave a small little basket by the back door of Justice's pub. He usually comes out here every day before he opens the pub. I wanted him to have one of my pies. I'm pretty sure no one will get into it, but I could be wrong. Oh well, it's the thought that counts, right?

The guilty feeling is eating me alive as I drive to my sister's grave. To tune it out, I turn on my favorite Christmas album, *A Very She & He Christmas*. I sing along to get into the mood for my date with Justice. The drive goes quickly, and I park my car on the gravel next to my grandmother's and sister's graves. This is the only thing I don't like about this place; it feels wrong to park so close to them.

I visit my grandmother first; it's customary and I'm one for tradition. I move on to my sister after a bit. "Hello, Caroline," I say, my voice shaking. It happens every time I come here. The memory of the day I buried her floods into my mind. Tears roll down my face, the images from the day I lost her still ingrained in my mind. Even after all this time, I still can't even begin to process the magnitude of everything.

I place the flowers on her grave, and I touch her headstone with my trembling hands. My bottom lip quivers as I remind myself to breathe.

"Sissy, I don't know where to begin," I say but think better of it. "Well, that's not quite true. I love you and I think you'd like me to be happy. But I feel guilty for being happy and wanting Justice. The need I feel for him is so strong."

I stop talking and clear the lump in my throat. "Justice didn't kill you. I spent all these years thinking otherwise. I know you went wild after our father took his life—after our mother ran away with the mailman. I know the actual story now, but I still feel like I'm betraying you. He's a good man, Sissy. If he took the fall for you and was willing to take the baby as his own, it means he cared for you, and he was looking out for our family."

The longer I talk to my sister the better I feel. It's like a weight has lifted from my chest, and I can breathe easier. Everything that has gone on in the last few weeks comes out, and the sun shines down on my sister's grave. I know that's a sign that everything will be all right. I smile, happy that I came to visit my sister.

❆

I have about forty minutes until I'm supposed to meet with Justice. I put my vehicle in park and realize there's police everywhere. The red and blue flashing lights seem to go on for a mile. Justice is standing outside and talking to a detective. *Oh no.* What happened? I unbuckle myself and step out of the car.

"Justice?"

I walk over to him, and he stares at me, pissed. I shudder under his scrutiny and my mind fires on all cylinders trying to figure out what is going on.

"And this is the woman that was in the club talking about how you've got yourself a war?" the detective asks Justice and all Justice does in return is nod.

What? What did he just say?

"Miss."

"Miss?"

I blink, realizing that I am standing here, mute, with my mouth wide open. The detective looks at me, and I blink again, trying to clear my mind.

"Yes, Detective?"

"We need to speak to you privately."

"Right," I whisper, still unsure of what's happening here. "Let me just open my shop, and we can talk there."

My hands shake as I try to open the door. I step in and so does the detective. *What is going on?*

Chapter Seventeen

Justice

I feel like an asshole, but I couldn't lie to the police after my employees told them that Suzie had made the threat. The look of betrayal and confusion on Suzie's face makes a pit form in my stomach. This could easily fuck up my chances with her.

"Get to work, guys. We have a lot to do if we want to get this place opened back up in a week."

"Don't you think we should wait for insurance?" Ruby asks. I hang my head; she's right.

"Yeah, of course. You're right. Take the night off. I've got to call the insurance company." At this point, I'm livid. I know now that Suzie didn't do this. One look at the confusion on her face—the hurt—tells me that she didn't do this. But the question remains, who the hell did?

I know I'm supposed to give the police time to talk to her, but I stand out on the sidewalk and look in her shop, playing with my phone. She's in the chair facing the door with her arms crossed under her breasts. Her eyes are downcast as the police officer comes out of her shop holding her phone and keys.

"Don't ask. I won't tell you what I'm doing. You need to go back over to your pub, Mr. O'Malley," he tells me as he steps over to her car. I sigh with shame, knowing that Suzie is a suspect in this.

I don't want to cause waves, so I go to my truck and get in. With a few taps on my phone, I'm connected with my insurance agent. They tell me they can get to me tomorrow evening and not to expect an estimate right away. I close my eyes in frustration. *How much shit can one day hold?*

Instead of sticking around, I drive off. I need to clear my head, and standing around waiting to talk to Suzie will not help me. It's a fact; I can already tell that any headway I've made with her is gone. I push the pedal down to the floor and speed down the main drag toward home.

❄

The blaring of my phone is driving me nuts. I turn over to see it's one o'clock. I pick up my phone and see it's the police department. Fuck, what happened now?

"Hello?" My voice is groggy from sleep, but there's not much I can do about it.

"Justice, this is Officer Montgomery. I'm calling to let you know that there was a break-in at your pub."

"Fuck me. Are you serious right now?"

"Yes. I'm going to need you to come down to the pub and identify if anything is missing. The perpetrator got away before we got on scene."

"The alarm company is sleeping on the job again. Shit." I am so mad a black and red haze covers my eyesight.

"Um, Justice. Ms. Gellam called it in. They tried to get into her shop and the blaring of the alarm for the bookstore woke her up."

Fuck. No. No. No. "Is she all right?" My panic is rising, and the old familiar feeling of drowning—of suffocating—sinks in.

"Yes, she's safe. I'm here along with two other officers."

"I'll be there in ten minutes."

Chapter Eighteen

Suzie

The past couple hours have been intense.

The police officer and detective questioned me for an hour about where I had been. They focused on the threat I made at the pub. I told them everything they wanted to know. There was no reason to lie. I even gave them my phone and my car keys because I have nothing to hide.

Those two items alone could confirm where I had been: Lakewood Cemetery. A twenty-minute drive south. I had been there for about three hours. I assumed they could add up the facts and figure out for themselves that there's no way I'm the culprit they're searching for. I know they're just doing their job, but having that knowledge does nothing to stop the ache in my heart.

When the officer finally confirmed my story by my car's GPS and my phone's map system, they told me they wouldn't take me into the station; instead, they'd get a warrant from my phone carrier to confirm there had been no tampering of the evidence.

I told them that was fine, and I'd provide anything they should need going forward. Once they left, my will to keep up was gone. I closed my store completely after seeing Justice's truck was gone. I armed the security system and went upstairs, dejected.

I can't blame Justice for telling them about the threat I made in the pub. What more could I expect?

Cooking myself something to eat, I try to reason with myself that this isn't personal; no amount of self-therapy helps me feel better about this situation, though. I finish eating and go to bed. Tears run down my face until I close my eyes and let the dreamworld take me.

❄

A blaring siren wakes me up and I jolt out of bed. *That's an alarm*, I realize, and I immediately call the police. I'm not brave enough to go downstairs to find out who's trying to sneak into someone's store. My own store has an alarm attached to the front door. If someone jiggles the front door hard enough, it'll go off.

To say my heart's racing is an understatement. I pull on a robe and sneak downstairs after ten minutes. The police are here, and I suddenly breathe easier. Seeing that my books are safe makes me feel better as well.

"Suzie?"

I turn to see Justice standing by the door, looking at me. My anger at his accusation comes back in full force. I squint my eyes at him.

"What do you want, Justice?"

He pulls me into his arms and holds me tight. "Thank God you are all right."

"Put me down," I demand. But if I'm honest, his arms feel really good around me.

"No. Now let's make sure the police clear out of here, and then I'll take you home. We can discuss this somewhere more private."

I arch my right eyebrow. "Home? You think I'm going anywhere with you?"

"Come now, you can't possibly stay here. It's not safe."

"No. Go away, Justice. Let the police do their job."

"The fuck I will. You listen to me, Suzie. You are coming home with me."

The police officer closest to us laughs. "Suzie here is a hellcat. I'll be surprised if she doesn't kick your ass for being a douchebag."

I look at the officer and see that it's Dakota's brother, Percy. "Yeah, yeah. Is it safe to stay here? Nothing was taken, and the person didn't get into my store."

"No. I think it best if you stay somewhere else for at least tonight."

I nod. Great, there goes my defense. "Fine. I'll call Dakota and let her know I'm on my way."

"Sorry, but Dakota is out of town with our sister, Mercy."

Shit. I forgot about that. "Oh, all right. Thank you, Percy."

"No problem, Suzie. Have a good night."

Chapter Nineteen

Justice

The police officers leave after another twenty minutes of questions and promises to do an hourly sweep around the block. We have to figure out what is going on; I can't have Suzie in danger.

"I'm going to go back upstairs. You can leave," Suzie says with a flip of her hair and a snarl.

I catch her as she walks past me. "Like hell I am. You are going home with me."

She looks down at my hand on her upper arm and looks back at my face. "You told the police I was a threat. You had me questioned like a criminal. I will not go home with you."

"Suzie, so help me God, I will spank your ass if you don't fucking shut your mouth, grab a change of clothing from upstairs, and come back down here to let me take you home."

She stares at me, and I have a feeling she is going to challenge me. Suzie's stubborn as hell, and while it turns me on, her safety is my number one priority right now. I pull her toward me so our bodies align, and I can get a better hold on her. Our lips touch, and I force my tongue into her mouth. She opens for me, and I have a feeling I can win her over.

"Be a good girl and do this for me. Let me get you to safety until we can figure out what's going on here."

Suzie huffs and stares into my eyes. "Fine. I will go with you, but we are talking about this whole criminal thing."

I chuckle and swat her behind. "Good. Now go upstairs and get some clothes. I'll be right here waiting for you."

For once, Suzie doesn't sass me, and she goes upstairs. She takes ten minutes to come back down. I catch the bag as she throws it at me. She smirks at me, and I shake my head.

"Feisty one, aren't you?" I nip at her neck as she locks the store behind us. We walk next to each other on the way to my truck. She makes a beeline for her car, but I grab her. "Oh, no you don't. You are riding with me."

She growls at me in frustration. "They did not tamper with my car, Justice."

"You don't know that, *Suzie*. Now get in the truck, dammit."

I watch her sashay that hot ass of hers over to my truck, and she yanks open the door. She steps in, looks me square in the eyes, and slams the door shut as hard as she can. I laugh hard at her attitude. Fuck, she keeps me on my toes.

The ride home is not in silence like I thought it would be. No, she tells me off from the second I get into the vehicle until the moment I put it in park at my house. I smirk the entire time, because while I am happy that Suzie agreed to go home with me, I'm also aware I fucked up today.

"Are you done, little girl?"

She gets out of the truck and shuts the door before coming around to the front. "I'm not your little girl."

I pull her to me, kissing her to shut her up. "Yeah, Angel, you are."

Chapter Twenty

Suzie

My anger dissipates as he kisses me. I want to stay mad at him, but his lips turn me into a mess. His hands run through my hair, pulling me onto my tiptoes as he forces me to enjoy every inch of his tongue in my mouth. Justice pulls me hard into his body and lifts me up, so I wrap my legs around his waist. He makes me feel things I shouldn't feel, but I don't want him to stop. No, I kiss him back. As he bites my bottom lip, I lose myself in him.

"Put me down; you'll hurt yourself." I blush, hiding my face in his neck as he walks toward the house.

"Shut your mouth. You aren't heavy at all, Angel." He walks up the three steps like I weigh nothing. I'm in awe of him being able to carry me, enjoying it as he pushes me against the side of the house to help support me as he plays with his keys.

He gets us in the house, and after he shuts the door, he turns around and places me against it.

"Damn. That's it. Don't fight me. Let me make you feel better," he whispers in my ear as he lifts the dress that I changed into off my body. My nerves tingle as his fingertips touch me, teasing me. My body is humming, and all I want is for his hands to touch my wetness—to touch what he's created, what he's done to me.

"Please, Justice."

He nips at my peaked nipples through my bra as he hooks his fingers into the straps to take it off me. The rush of cold air against my skin makes me arch into him as that wicked tongue of his causes me to whimper and beg him for more. I open my eyes to stare at him, too embarrassed to tell him I want more. I can't hold his gaze because I'm almost naked in front of him. He pulls my legs down from his waist and flings my bra to the ground.

"Hey. Eyes on me, little girl. None of this shy shit."

I giggle at his words, and he smacks my bottom.

"Angel, I mean it, eyes on me." He hooks his thumbs in my panties and moves them down my legs.

Dear goodness, no one has ever been this close to me. "Step out of them," he demands, so I do. He takes off my ballerina flats, and picks me back up, lifting me over his shoulder.

"Hey!" I exclaim as the world tilts, and I bounce against his muscles. Damn, he's strong.

"You are gorgeous, curvy, and amazing. None of that stupid, shy shit, you hear me?"

I land on the bed with a yelp as he tosses me off his shoulder. I bounce a little and laugh as he gets on the bed with me. My answer to him is to pull him down and kiss him. My body trembles as he grabs my hips and pushes my legs apart to settle himself between them. I gasp against his lips as he sucks my tongue into his mouth. His skillful hands send shivers down my spine as he runs them along my thighs.

Justice pulls back long enough to take his shirt off and unzip his pants. He doesn't even pull them down. He takes out his cock and I get my first sight of his penis. I've never seen one up close before. I bite my lip as he runs his hands through my hair, making sure that we are making eye contact as he smiles down at me.

"Shh. Just relax. I've got you."

Chapter Twenty-One

Justice

I'm the luckiest man in the world. Suzie's chosen me, and there's nothing better than having her in my arms. I feel the tightness in her body as I move a hand down to stroke my cock against her wetness. She is sopping wet. I push the tip into her body and freeze. Fuck, she's tight.

I must stop too long for her because she wiggles and looks at me with worry in her eyes. "Don't... don't stop, Justice."

Her quivering whisper tells me she needs me as much as I need her. I lose all control and thrust my dick straight into her. I cannot describe the tightness of her pussy and how it feels around my dick. As she screams, I blink at her.

Fuck me. She's a virgin. Holy mother of God. My pride swells inside of me as I devour her lips with mine, taking her scream into my mouth. I feel like a king who has just won his ultimate battle to claim the land. On the flip side of it, I feel like a jerk for taking her so roughly.

I kiss her tears away, stroking her hair, trying to soothe her. "Shh, sweet Angel. I've got you, baby." She looks at me, a pained expression on her beautiful face, and I want to beat the shit out of myself. I also want to climb a mountain and crow like a damn rooster in honor of being her first.

"You're mine now, Suzie. Only mine." I growl into her lips. I can't stand the idea of her not knowing she's mine. The idea of causing her pain crushes me as she whimpers and wiggles against me. I kiss around her face, taking each tear she sheds.

"Are you all right, little girl?"

She sniffles as she looks at me and nods. I need her words like I need my next breath.

"Use your words."

"Yes." She looks at me and I see it. The want is back. Her eyes are no longer clouded with pain. "Please move."

That's all the encouragement I need. I rock inside of her, giving her every inch of my cock. She trembles and that tight little pussy of hers clamps down on me. My eyes roll to the back of my head as she clenches, trapping me inside of her.

"You feel so good. So tight and such a good girl for taking my cock."

She grins at me, and I feel it, her body is relaxing and letting us both enjoy the movements of us coming together. I stare at those luscious lips of hers, open in the shape of an O, telling me on their own that she is close to her orgasm. My need to hear her beg for her orgasm is running through me. I stop moving by a damn miracle.

"Do you want to cum, Suzie?"

That decadent blush is back, and her moans tell me the story I need. I thrust one time into her, balls deep, and then I move back to just pushing my tip inside of her. Smirking down at her, I push back in an inch and her hips push upward, wanting more.

"Please."

"That's not good enough, love. You need to convince me to give you that orgasm."

Her nostrils flare out, and I almost cum. Fuck, I love when she gets riled up. It's the single most wonderful thing she can do to turn me on. I pump into her hard and fast. It's too hard for a virgin, but I can't stop. Hell, she's into it. Those sexy noises she's making send shivers down my spine.

"Make me cum, Justice."

That high and mighty demand makes me chuckle. I stop moving and she groans out in rage. I grip her hair and force her to be still.

"Try again, little girl."

She cusses at me, and I laugh. "Justice, damn you. Please, I need you. I need to feel you deep inside of me so I can come for you."

Well, fuck, that says it all, doesn't it?

Chapter Twenty-Two

Suzie

Justice made me cum twice before he came inside of me, and we fell asleep in each other's arms. I couldn't sleep for the longest time, but when I did, I dreamed about him. I moan and stretch as my thoughts turn naughty. Justice is licking me, making me beg for another orgasm.

"Justice," I whimper, arching my body into his skilled tongue.

His mouth is full of my pussy, but he talks against my clit. "Good morning, my sweet little Angel."

My eyes fly open, and I could cum from the sight of him peering up at me. His mouth is on my body, licking me, making me tremble. *This is definitely not a dream*. Thank God. He winks at me and thrusts two fingers into my sore body. I orgasm for him. The rush of bliss flowing through me is overwhelming.

"Justice!"

He licks me until I come back down to reality. I'm panting as he kisses me, sucking my tongue into his mouth to twirl around with his. I mewl for him, and he laughs.

"That's my good girl." He touches my breasts, pulling on my

nipples. I giggle with embarrassment and hide my face in the crook of his neck.

"No more of that shy shit, remember?" He pulls me to face him, but I can't. I kiss him to keep from having to look at him. Justice spanks my right thigh and flips us over. "I'm glad you enjoyed your wake-up call."

"I did. Very much so. Thank you."

"Sweet girl, you're welcome. Now I need to get up so I can get to the police station." His words damper the air between us.

"Do you want me to call the glass company I use?" I offer. I know that someone trashed some of his windows.

"My very own personal assistant. I could get used to that."

I swat his chest and roll my eyes at him. He holds my hands down by my sides and bites my neck.

"Be good, Suzie."

I whimper as he bites along the curve of my collarbone.

"If you know a good security firm, that would be good," he says.

With a stretch, I push my body into him, but I roll out of bed. "I do. Get a shower. I'll get my phone and start making calls."

"Look at you trying to take control."

I stick my tongue out at him, and he winks at me. "Get used to it, Bucko."

He shakes his head and goes to the bathroom while I make phone calls.

❄

Justice left me at my bookstore an hour ago. I'll be honest, I miss his cocky ass. A commotion comes from next door as I sip on my latte. I rush outside to see what's going on, afraid someone is doing something worse to Justice's pub.

I smile when I see the insurance adjuster is over there, and the glass crew is trying to clean the mess. Justice pulls up just as I am about to call him.

"Nope, you stay over there. There's too much glass for those precious feet to be walking over here in those ballet slippers."

I roll my eyes at him. "Okay, Dad."

His eyes dilate, and he growls out a warning. "I'll show you *daddy* if that's what you want." He grabs me and bites my ear. "I have no problem being your daddy, little girl."

"Stop that." My feeble words come out in a whisper. Justice referring to himself as *daddy* makes my body shake with need.

"I know you creamed in your panties. I can smell you." Heat floods my body. I want him right here, right now. He bends down and nibbles on my neck, making me cling to him.

Chapter Twenty-Three

Justice

I have to let Suzie go, but not without a warning first. "Behave, little one. The security crew you called will be here shortly. Now, go back to the bookshop, and I'll be there later." He kisses me and pats my butt as he pushes me toward my shop. God, he drives me wild.

This wasn't the only reason I sent Suzie back to her stop. The police have no leads, and I'm getting angrier. Money I earned from selling some of the cattle I owned went into this pub. I don't want to touch the money my father left me—that's why only my own money went into this place. I try not to think about it as the security crew puts in the new cameras and a failsafe to keep hackers out.

"Justice, does the shop next door have cameras in the alley or in the building's front?"

It's a light-bulb moment for me. I jump up and punch the air in what seems like the first victory of the day.

"Yes, they do. I'll go ask Suzie for access."

Marcus from Timberland Security laughs as I hightail it out of my office. I rush into Suzie's store to find her helping a customer. A man? In an erotic bookstore? Why? My hackles rise with indignation, and I storm over toward them. I stand one aisle over and to the right so I can snoop.

"Well, if you get this book, Josie will learn how you like to do things in bed." Suzie is quiet in the way she talks to her customers. She doesn't make them feel stupid or get impatient. It's fascinating to watch her work, but I don't like how close he is to her. I walk up behind Suzie and the man's head snaps up.

"Justice." She chuckles. "I'll be right with you." She turns toward me and hugs me, standing on her tiptoes to kiss my frown. I watch as she takes the man to the counter and rings him up.

"See you next time, Mr. Davidson."

When the man is gone, I pull Suzie into my arms and kiss her, staking my claim. She giggles as I nibble on her bottom lip.

"What was that for?"

I brush her hair out of her face. "To make sure you remember who you belong to, Angel."

She looks amused at my statement, but I wink at her, and she laughs.

"Got a question for you. Do you have access to the cameras in the front of your store, or maybe the alley behind us?"

She nods and takes my hand, leading me to her office. "Everything from the last forty-eight hours is on the server. I use the cloud to back up the footage."

"You're a lifesaver." I sigh and sit down as she pulls up the footage.

It takes me an hour to comb through it, but I find what I'm looking for.

"Son of a bitch." I startle myself by how loud I scream and pound my fist onto the desk.

Suzie walks in and hands me a coffee. "You've been in here for a while and you were yelling. What's going on?"

I point to the screen where I've frozen the frame. She gasps and sits down next to me.

"That's your bouncer."

I nod at her, numb. "Yeah."

She hands me a USB drive to download the footage.

"I can't fucking believe it. The man knew me in prison." I'm livid. I can't see straight and all I want to do is punch someone. Instead, I kiss Suzie and tell her I will be back.

She stops me before I can make it too far. "Justice, let the police do their job. Give them the evidence and then let them work."

I don't want to do that. I want to go find the no-good bastard and tear him limb from limb. But I look at Suzie, pleading with me to calm down and deflate a little. She wraps me in a hug and I instantly calm.

"I mean it, Justice. No more violence for you. No more jail. Please."

"Promise." I kiss the top of her head, hugging her tight. "I'll be back."

Chapter Twenty-Four

Suzie

While I wait for Justice to get back, I finish the last of the decorating I wanted to get up for Christmas. I smile and turn out the lights. Justice should be here any moment and I want him to feel happiness. At least for tonight, I want him to stop thinking about his pub. I'm worried he will do something stupid, but I will not accuse him of anything. In my heart, I know he'll do the right thing. Or at least, I hope he will.

It's six o'clock in the evening and Justice still isn't here. It's been hours since he walked out the door. *Where is he?* I call him and it goes straight to voicemail. My hands shake at the idea of something bad happening to him.

Worry gnaws at me as another three hours pass. I sigh, lock up the store, and head upstairs. I'm heartbroken. Maybe I put too much faith in Justice. We were going to spend the evening together. Or is this his way of trying to be nice? Did he get what he wanted and now no longer wants me? I sniffle as scenarios fly through my mind.

A loud ruckus makes me jump. I look out my window to see Justice

OH, SANTA!

in the alley. He stumbles and crashes into the trash can. I get a good look at him; he's bloody and bruised.

"Dammit, you promised," I grumble to myself as I make my way downstairs. Once I reach him, I realize he's muttering to himself and trying to sit up. He falls back over, and I move toward him.

"Is he alive, Justice?" I ask, looking at him with shock. If the bouncer looks even half this bad I'd venture to say he's not doing so well either. Justice looks like a dump truck ran him over.

Black locks of his hair cover his eyes as he nods his head. "Yeah, but he's in the hospital under police custody. If he goes back to jail, the gang he owes will kill him. I did him a favor by making him look like hell."

I don't understand any of that and I realize I don't care. I'm glad he's here. Bending down, I push his hair out of his face. The skin under his left eye is bulging, already swelling up over the bottom of his eye.

"Come on, love, let's get you upstairs."

He groans and cusses as I try to get him to my place, allowing him to lean on me for support. It's a slow process; Justice has to stop every few feet to catch his breath. I can tell by looking at him—and by the way he's wincing—that he has at least a couple broken ribs. I hold on to him with a gentle hand and guide him into my apartment.

"I had to do it, Suzie. He betrayed me, and once you betray a prison friend you make an enemy for life."

"Hush now, let's get you settled. It doesn't matter why you did it."

"Thank you, Suzie."

"Don't thank me yet. You should be at the hospital."

"Nope. I'll be fine in the morning."

I doubt that, but I don't tell him as much. I strip the blood-stained clothes off him, and he sits down on the toilet in my small bathroom. Gentle and patient as I can, I clean his wounds. I stay silent because I'm afraid I might tell him off.

"You're mad at me."

"Yes. You broke your promise and missed our evening together." I sound like a whiny teenager.

He chuckles, and he pays for it. He holds on to his ribs and stares at me, with pain in his eyes. "You were worried."

"No," I lie, but he shakes his head, calling my bluff.

"Tell me, little girl, why are you pouting that lower lip of yours?"

"You're important to me, Justice. I thought you had taken my virginity and then decided you didn't want me." I put two ace bandages around his ribs, and he sucks in a painful breath. His hiss tells me his wounds are far worse than he's letting on.

Chapter Twenty-Five

Justice

If I could feel shame for what I did, it would eat me alive right now. I take in the way my salty angel takes care of me and how she is sniffling. She isn't tearing up. No, she is trying so hard not to be angry at me. My ribs hurt like hell. Although I won in the end, I took a hell of a beating. I'm feeling even worse because she's here helping me, and she thinks I don't want her. Fuck me.

Suzie steps back and runs a washcloth under the water. "You should go to the hospital," she repeats herself as she cleans the rest of my face. She isn't wrong, but I won't go. Both of us know that if I go, I'll end up in jail. That can't happen ever again. I pull her to me. The idea of leaving her makes me nauseous.

"What? And miss Christmas Eve and Christmas? Not a chance, sweet girl. You've fixed me up as good as any doctor could."

I can see her wheels turning.

"Don't argue with me, Angel. Let's go to bed." She laughs at my gruffness. "I will never leave you or treat you like that, Suzie."

She washes my face and neck, trying to get the blood off me. "All right, Justice. But…"

I kiss her to keep her quiet. My busted top lip screams at me to stop. There's no way in hell I'm stopping. I'm too busy getting caught in the taste of her lips to break free from her. She trembles against me.

"Damn. You make me forget everything."

Her smile is bright and honest. It hurts me; I don't deserve her. We walk into the bedroom, and I slump onto the bed as I watch her undress.

"You are the most beautiful woman I've ever seen."

She watches me for a moment, shaking her head. "Not even close but thank you."

"Why do you say that?"

"Have you looked at me? I'm not exactly thin."

Anger consumes me. I pull her down on the bed, despite the agonizing pain in my ribs. "Don't say that. I don't want to hear another word like that coming from you. I will take you over my knee and spank you. You have the body of a goddess."

I ignore all the pain shooting through me. This is more important. How dare Suzie think poorly of herself? Her giggle gets me, and I smile at her.

"Are you serious?" She looks at me with hope my words are true.

"Yes, as serious as I am that I love you."

Her eyes pop wide and she almost collides with my broken nose as she moves.

"What... what did you say?"

"I..." I place a kiss on her neck.

"Love..." She shudders as I kiss along her right shoulder.

"You..." She moans as I kiss each of her nipples.

"Forever..." I kiss her gently on the lips and look her in the eyes. She is uncertain, but there is a need in her eyes. It pains me to think she doesn't believe me.

"Do I need to show you?" I grind my erection against her pussy. She climbs on top of me. My ribs choose to remind me that I'm not at full strength.

"Fuck," I gasp out.

Suzie scrambles off me. "Did I hurt you?"

"No, my love. I can't take you tonight, but you didn't hurt me."

Her mouth pops open and she blushes. "We can wait."

"The fuck we can. Tomorrow I'm going to bend you over a desk or table and make you cream for me."

She giggles and lays down beside me. "I love you, Justice." She curls around me. As we fall asleep, I think about how lucky I am.

I have my girl. I don't know what else I could want for Christmas.

Epilogue

Suzie

Justice brings the coffee to me as I watch the lights flicker through the night out on my balcony. I love this time of year. It's amazing how much better Christmas feels with Justice sitting beside me. What's even crazier is that I get to stop feeling guilty over my sister.

My life has changed within a short month. I've had the pleasure of getting to know the *real* Justice. I take a deep breath as he gets on his knees in front of me.

"We've had a rough start, but I want you." He smirks at me as he spreads my legs. "For now, I want you to relax and enjoy."

I don't know what he is doing until he moves my shorts to the side and licks my clit. I gasp at the way pleasure runs through my body. He teases me as he darts his tongue inside of me. It's a magnificent feeling as his fingers tease my body, making me whine for him.

"That's it, Angel, take it." He shoves three fingers in me, filling me to the brim. I scream as he spreads his fingers inside of me. I whimper with need, but he pulls back.

"Oh, no you don't. Not letting you get off yet." He stands up and tells me to bend over the railing of the balcony. I blush at the idea of being outside and someone seeing us.

"Shh. No talking, just allow yourself to feel. Be in this moment with me." He pulls my shorts the rest of the way down and grasps my hair in his fist. He takes me with one smooth thrust of his hips, filling me completely. Justice keeps my hair in his fist, and he bends over just enough to whisper in my ear.

"Fuck, Angel, you are mine forever." He forces my head to the side so I can see the ring in his hand. I blink in awe.

"You are going to marry me."

I laugh and then sigh as he forces his cock deeper inside of me. "I love you, Justice." My words fuel the speed of his thrusts as he puts the ring on my finger. I moan his name. I can't believe he just proposed to me. Well, it wasn't exactly a proposal. It was more of a demand, and I love it because it was just like Justice to demand something.

"I love you too, Suzie."

I whisper his name as he grabs my hips and fucks me. My future is with the person I thought would be my enemy forever. I cum for him, my body giving way to the bliss that only he seems to pull out of me. This year, I can say that Justice is my personal Santa. He's brought me the greatest gifts of all: the truth about my sister's death, pure happiness, and himself.

The End

ALSO BY SJ RANSOM

Psychos in Love Series
Psychos in Love

Psychos Take Love

Psychos Love Forever

Standalones
She's a Mad Hatter

Printed in Great Britain
by Amazon